# The New Neighbours

DINEY COSTELOE is the author
of twenty-three novels, several
short stories, and many articles
and poems. She has three children
and seven grandchildren, so when
she isn't writing, she's busy with
family. She and her husband divide
their time between Somerset and
West Cork.

Also by Diney Costeloe

*The Throwaway Children*
*The Lost Soldier*
*The Runaway Family*
*The Girl With No Name*
*The Sisters of St Croix*
*The Married Girls*

# DINEY COSTELOE

# *The New Neighbours*

HEAD
*of* ZEUS

First published in the UK as *Dartmouth Circle* in 2001
by Castlehaven books
First published as *The New Neighbours* in 2017 by Head of Zeus Ltd
This paperback edition first published in 2017 by Head of Zeus Ltd

9 7 5 3 1 2 4 6 8

A catalogue record for this book is available from
the British Library.

ISBN (PB): 9781784972677
ISBN (E): 9781784972653

Typeset by Adrian McLaughlin

Printed and bound in Germany by CPI Books GmbH, Leck

Head of Zeus Ltd
First Floor East
5–8 Hardwick Street
London EC1R 4RG
WWW.HEADOFZEUS.COM

# The New Neighbours

*April*

*Chapter One*

Mary Jarvis sighed as she looked out of her sitting-room window. She could see her neighbour, Sheila Colby, bearing down on her door like a galleon in full sail. Her face was glowing with indignation and she was obviously bursting with news. Knowing that the quiet hour she'd promised herself before going to St Joseph's was now doomed, Mary set aside the *Telegraph* crossword and went to open the door.

"Mary, you'll never believe it, it's dreadful," Sheila exploded even as she crossed the threshold. Her curled grey hair bounced round her ears and her powdered jowls quivered with consternation. "It's dreadful," she repeated.

"Come in, Sheila," Mary said mildly as Sheila hurried past her into the hall. "Come upstairs and have a coffee, I'm just having one."

She led her friend upstairs to the sitting room and waved her into a chair. "I'll just get your coffee," she said, going into the kitchen. She poured a coffee from the percolator and carried it through into the living room. Handing it to Sheila, she resumed her own seat by the window.

"Now then, tell me, what on earth has happened?"

"Ned Short's sold his house at last," Sheila announced dramatically.

"Well, I'm pleased for him," remarked Mary, sipping her own coffee. "Since Jane left him it's been a millstone round his neck – far too big for him. And I'd have thought," she continued, "that

3

you'd be delighted. You've never liked either of them. I'd have thought you'd be thrilled he was going."

"But Mary," Sheila was extracting every ounce from the dread news she'd come to impart, "it's been sold...", she put her cup and saucer down with a clatter, "...to students. What are we going to *do*?"

"Do?" Mary looked surprised. "What can we do? There's nothing we can do. Ned's entitled to sell his house to whomever he chooses and whoever wants to can buy it. Not that he's had much choice, he must have leapt at this chance, I should think."

"Gerald says there'll be rowdy parties and noise all the time," wailed Sheila. "It's all right for you – you don't live next door. The noise won't be coming through your walls!"

The houses in Dartmouth Circle were in three terraces of four, set at right angles to each other round a communal garden; 'sixties' town houses on three floors with an integral garage beside the front door. Mary Jarvis occupied number five, the end house in the centre block. The Colbys were her immediate neighbours, sandwiched between her and the Shorts. On the other side of the Shorts lived Shirley and David Redwood, another retired couple.

Mary could see Sheila had a point, and she said, "No, I suppose not, but having students in number seven will probably affect the whole Circle."

The residents of Dartmouth Circle always referred to their cul-de-sac as "The Circle". Somehow, having a private name for their road made for a feeling of community, of belonging.

"Gerald says..." Sheila very often prefaced her remarks with "Gerald says" and it irritated Mary, particularly as she was fairly certain that Gerald, who was mild-mannered and inoffensive, seldom made any of the remarks attributed to him, and his name was used to cloak Sheila's own less charitable thoughts and ideas. "Gerald says that the value of our properties will go down when they move in. The whole Circle will suffer."

"I don't see why it should," replied Mary, even as she wondered if, in this case Gerald, or more probably Sheila, might be right. "There's a student house on the corner of Dartmouth Avenue, and Mrs Old's house, two doors away from that, sold very well last month, I'm told. It didn't seem to affect the price she got." Mary didn't actually know what Mrs Old's house had sold for, but she felt the need to disagree with Sheila who was always so dogmatic about things.

However, as she was on rather shaky ground, she went on almost without a pause, "How did you hear?"

"Ned told me himself," answered Sheila. She drank some more of her coffee and replaced her cup carefully on the table before going on. "I met him at Molly's when I went for the paper this morning. He was full of it. 'Contracts actually exchanged this time, Mrs C,' he said. 'Oh Mr Short, I am pleased for you,' I said. 'I do hope it's a nice family moving in, or perhaps a young couple, the quiet professional sort, you know.' And he laughed at me, Mary, laughed that dreadful, common laugh of his and said, 'Doubt if it'll be quiet, Mrs C, it's been bought as a student house. I heard them say they're hoping to put nine or ten into it.' Nine or ten, Mary! In a terraced house like ours! Can you imagine? Next door?"

Mary had to admit a certain sympathy at the thought. "Do the Redwoods know yet?" she asked.

Sheila shook her head. "No, I don't think so. I think they're still away. I came straight home to tell Gerald of course," she went on, "and then I did give their doorbell a ring, but there was no reply, so I assume they aren't back yet. I know Melanie had the baby last week, I told you it was a girl, didn't I? Anyway I think they were going to stay for a while to help with little Todd."

Well, thought Mary wryly, if anyone knows their plans it'll be you.

"Anyway, Shirley didn't know how long they'd stay."

"Not all that long if I know David," laughed Mary. "He hates to leave his garden at this time of year."

"Well, they'll be devastated when they do hear," asserted Sheila. "They like their peace and quiet and they'll have the same problems as we will – all the noise and the comings and goings with ten of them!"

"I really doubt if there'll be ten living in a house that size," soothed Mary. "They wouldn't fit in."

"Of course they would, they don't care how they live, people like that. Gerald says they'll probably smoke pot or worse. What *are* we going to do?"

"I agree it's not what any of us would have chosen to happen," Mary said briskly, "but as there isn't anything we *can* do about it, we'll just have to wait and see and make the best of it. Now, I'm sorry to have to turn you out, Sheila, but I'm due to help with the lunches at St Joe's today and I've got to go."

Sheila drained her coffee cup. She considered her neighbour was taking the whole thing far too calmly, and wanted to jerk her into awareness of the dreadful reality that was about to overtake them. "Gerald says we should call a meeting of the Residents' Association," she began, "and form a committee."

"A committee?" repeated Mary incredulously. "*Gerald* said that?"

"Yes," replied Sheila firmly, "well, a sub-committee…within the Residents' Association, so that things aren't allowed to get out of hand."

It seems to me that it's *you* who's getting out of hand, thought Mary. "And just what will this sub-committee do?" she enquired dryly.

"Keep a strict eye on number seven," Sheila said. "Warn them about being a nuisance and call the police when they are."

"Call the police?" Mary was exasperated with such an attitude. "Sheila, you don't know anything about these young people yet. You've no idea if they're going to cause a nuisance, make a noise, give rowdy parties, take drugs – they may be perfectly normal youngsters."

"Yes," agreed Sheila ominously. "That's what I'm afraid of! Anyway, I shall go and see Anthony Hammond this evening. As chairman of the Residents' Association he must be told."

When Sheila had departed to her long-suffering Gerald once more, Mary stood at her third-floor bedroom window and looked down into the gardens spread out below her – her own, paved, with tubs of shrubs about to bloom; the Colbys' next door with neat lawn and daffodils and hyacinth glowing in the weeded beds. Beyond the Colbys' was Ned Short's garden, an overgrown wasteland complete with rusted bicycle, discarded fridge and a roll of rotting carpet. Beyond this again was the Redwoods' garden, loved and tended, already a profusion of colour.

How would David and Shirley Redwood like living next door to a student house she wondered? It really couldn't be much worse than living next door to Ned Short, could it? The rows from his house had been heard all over the Circle. Mary smiled to herself. Ned must have known Sheila was thinking that any neighbours would be an improvement on him, that's why he'd taken such delight in telling her it was going to be a crowd of students. Surely he must have been exaggerating when he said nine or ten? Just winding Sheila up to watch her spin. A piece of quiet revenge for all the implied insults and unpleasant barbs that he'd had to endure over the past months, little things which Sheila was so good at slipping into an apparently innocuous conversation. Mary couldn't help smiling as she recalled the horror on Sheila's face, but even so, the idea of a house full of students next door but one to her own did bring on a mood of foreboding.

Still there was really nothing to be done about it, she told herself, so I'm not going to let it worry me yet. And giving herself a mental shake she set off to do her stint at St Joseph's, the local church's day centre for the elderly.

As she was getting into her car, she saw Ned Short coming into the Circle. She smiled and waved. "I hear you've sold at last, Mr Short," she called. "You must be very pleased."

"Told you already, has she?" said Ned with a jerk of his head towards number six. "Knew telling her would be the best way of spreading the news."

"Yes, I did hear it from Sheila," said Mary with a smile.

"Tell you it was students, did she?" enquired Ned innocently.

"Yes," said Mary, matching his innocent expression, "it'll be lovely to have some young people around. The Circle has become positively geriatric, don't you think?" She got into her car and spoke through the open window. "When will you be on the move then? Some time soon? We shall miss you."

"Soon as the sale goes through," answered Ned. "This place only has bad memories for me. Don't worry, I'll soon be gone – then you'll have the students."

He watched her drive away and then turned towards his own front door. He was, indeed, relieved to have sold at last. The house had been on the market ever since Jane had finally walked out; the divorce was through and Jane was pestering him for her share of the money. He hadn't got the asking price of course, there was no way anyone in their right mind would have paid that with the house in the state it was. He grimaced at the front door as he opened it, its pitted paintwork blistered and peeling. The four small panes of its window were cracked and dirty and the entry phone, standard equipment in all the Dartmouth Circle townhouses, hung out from the door-frame, broken. Many prospective buyers had turned back at that door, hadn't even bothered to view, turning away from the unprepossessing frontage without knocking. Others, attracted by the Dartmouth Circle address, had ventured inside, but had been unable to visualise what the dirty, battle-scarred house might become, or had balked at the cost of the transformation. When Nicholas Richmond had made an offer at the bottom end of the price range that Ned had privately considered acceptable, Ned had leapt at it, delighted to be shot of the place at last.

He went inside and looked round at the gloomy place that was his home. The light bulb in the hall was broken and there was a pervasive smell of garbage, cats and stale air. Then he gave a bitter laugh. Whatever Mr Nicholas Richmond did with the house, Ned would lay money on it that the students who inhabited it would reduce it to its former pig-sty status in no time flat.

Well, serve the old cow next door right, he thought viciously. Stuck-up bitch with her net curtains and trailing geraniums. He laughed aloud at the recollection of Sheila Colby's face when he'd broken the news about the students. She was the worst in the Circle by far. Probably old Mary Jarvis would be equally glad to see the back of him, but at least she had not made it so obvious. Not that he was sorry to be leaving Dartmouth Circle. He and Jane had never really fitted in to the little community of retired couples and rising stars. They had been one of the few families with teenage children living at home. Robin and Karen were the only children in the Circle who went to Crosshills Comprehensive. The few other children in the close had attended Beechlands Preparatory School, Belcaster High or were away at boarding school. When Robin and Karen had left home, Jane had gone too, moving in with Joe Briggs, the landlord of the pub where she had worked part-time as a barmaid.

Ned had been left to fend for himself and had made a poor fist of it. The house was far too big and he camped out in the living room with only his cats for company. When he was made redundant, he lowered the asking price for the house; it was time to sell and move on.

Well, at least I've got somewhere lined up to go to, he thought, picturing with some pleasure the one-bedroomed flat he'd agreed to rent in Brighton. I've always liked the sea.

He put the kettle on the stove and dropping a teabag into a chipped mug, began to make a list of what he would take from the house. There was too much for the flat, he'd leave the rest for Jane and the kids to fight over.

As Ned Short drank his tea and made his list, Sheila Colby, never one to let the grass grow, was discussing with Gerald how to mobilise the Dartmouth Circle troops in the face of the student invasion; or rather she was outlining her plans to a largely acquiescent Gerald, who with a long-developed skill appeared to be all attention while actually finishing his crossword.

After forty-three years of marriage to Sheila, it was an art he had perfected.

"I shall go and visit everyone in the Circle," she was saying, "a united front is what we need, a strong representation so that things don't get out of hand. With the Redwoods still away it's up to us to take the lead, don't you think? I'll go and see Anthony Hammond, that will alert the Residents' Association."

Aware of a pause in the barrage of words, Gerald said, "I don't think there's any rush you know, if they've only just exchanged contracts."

"But we have to be ready. If everyone's aware of the problem, we can consider some strategy. They may move in straightaway. We *must* be prepared."

"I doubt very much if they'll move in before the beginning of the college year in September," observed Gerald, finally setting aside his paper. "There must be work to be done on the house, you've only got to look at it. The Shorts have done nothing to it in the ten years they've been there. It'll need some money spending on it."

"Don't be silly, Gerald," scoffed Sheila. "Students won't have money to spend on doing it up. It'll simply go from bad to worse."

"I doubt if it's students actually buying the place, Sheila." Gerald sounded mildly exasperated. "Someone will have bought it with the idea of letting it out to students, and whoever it is will have to make it habitable."

"You mean it probably isn't decided that students will live in it yet." Sheila grasped at the straw. "Of course, you're right. If we act at once maybe we can convince the new owner *not* to let it to students at all, but to some nice professional people. The Circle isn't the sort of place for students to live."

"I'd have thought it was perfect for them," Gerald pointed out wickedly. "Five minutes' walk from the college, ten minutes to the leisure centre and three to the nearest pub."

"I shouldn't think the Ship and Compass'll want them. It's such a nice quiet pub."

"In the present economic climate I should think they'll welcome them with open arms," Gerald said gravely. "They'll be glad of the custom."

"And then they'll come home from the pub at all hours, drunk and rowdy," said Sheila, hotly. "I know I'm right, Gerald, we must do something. We should go round and see everyone this afternoon and warn them of the situation."

"You must do as you think fit," sighed Gerald, picking up his paper again. "I don't think you should meddle. And this afternoon, I shall be playing golf with Andrew Peters."

"Well, at least you can tell him," said Sheila, blithely ignoring his comment about meddling. "His mother lives alone in number one. She's ninety if she's a day; she'll be terrified of having a house full of students just across the road."

Gerald did not agree with this last statement. Madge Peters had insisted on living alone in her own home, despite anything Andrew could do to try to move her to somewhere smaller or more convenient, and he couldn't imagine her being terrified of anyone, let alone a bunch of students. But he had long ago learned the wisdom of keeping ninety per cent of his thoughts to himself and he did so now, merely remarking that he would mention the news to Andrew when he saw him this afternoon so that he could warn Madge if he wanted to. Another thought that occurred to him, but which he also prudently kept to himself, was that the students were an invention of Ned's, simply to worry Sheila. He wouldn't put such a piece of spite past Ned Short, but Gerald decided to say nothing, as Sheila would not find it a reassuring thought, it would just fuel her rage.

## Chapter Two

Ben Gardner sat at his desk and stared out of the window across the college gardens to the windows of the hall opposite. He had an essay on Richard III to hand in, in the morning, and he had only just begun to marshal his thoughts on how that monarch governed his kingdom, and already his mind was drifting again. Next year he had to find somewhere to live, he couldn't remain in hall for his final year and so far he had done little to find himself a room or a flat. There had been some talk earlier in the year that Madeleine Richmond's father was going to buy a house for her to live in for the rest of her time at college, and was going to rent out the other bedrooms in it to pay the mortgage. Madeleine had asked Ben if he wanted to go in with her, to take one of the rooms that would be on offer, and he had agreed. It seemed a good idea.

"Yeah," he said. "Why not? We get on all right. As long as I have a room to myself...and the rent's right of course," he added as an afterthought. "You asked anybody else yet?"

Madeleine shook her head. "Not yet. Got any ideas? No boyfriends or girlfriends though, too much hassle." She looked stricken for a moment. "You didn't want Angie to share too, did you? I mean..."

"No, I didn't," Ben reassured her.

"It's just that...well I mean, of course she's very welcome to visit any time, to stay over and things, but not to live. One of Dad's rules!"

"Don't worry," Ben said. "That arrangement suits me fine. Have you got anyone in mind? How big's the house? I mean, how many bedrooms?"

Madeleine laughed. "I don't know. We haven't found one yet!"

"Yeah, well when you have, let me know."

Occasionally after that, Ben would ask her how the house hunting was going, and Madeleine would grin cheerfully and say, "Nothing yet, but we're still looking." He hoped that they would find something suitable. He liked Mad Richmond, she made him laugh. They went around in the same crowd, as her present boyfriend, Dan Sharp, was another keen rugby man, and Ben thought she was always good company.

Now it was May, and if they didn't find a house soon he'd have to give up on Madeleine and make a determined effort to find something, somewhere. It wouldn't be easy, there were too many students chasing too little accommodation in the town, and only freshers were automatically found a place in hall. Ben sighed. He'd been relying on Mad Richmond, but it didn't sound as if she would definitely have a house ready for the end of September, and he had to be practical. He wondered what the others had decided to do. There were now three other students who were interested in sharing the house. Ben knew them as they were all in the same hall, and he liked them well enough, but he wasn't particularly close to any of them. He hoped the house would be big enough to give them room to breathe... if there was a house.

Ben was older than most of the students in his year as he had decided to go to university only after trying several other things first. He'd left it late and at twenty-five he was determined to get a good degree, but he was short of cash, he had no grant, only a student loan. To make enough money to live, he worked several evenings a week in the Flying Dutchman, a pub frequented mainly by students from the university. It was good working there because he was able to join in some of the social side of life from the other side of the bar. His girlfriend, Angie, often came and sat on the corner bar stool, making a half of shandy last most of the evening, and the Dutch, as it was known, was also the official rugby club pub, and Ben was a regular player in the Belcaster University first fifteen, the Belchers.

He knew that as a last resort there might be a chance of a room at the Dutch, but he didn't really want to live there.

"You can probably have the back bedroom," Joe Briggs the landlord had said when he heard that Ben was looking for somewhere for next year. "I haven't used it since we stopped doing B&B. Now it's only a dumping ground. It's not big, mind, but it would serve a turn if you wanted it. Be nice to have you on hand, in case you needed any extra hours."

"Thanks, Joe." Ben had been touched by the offer, but it certainly wasn't ideal as far as he was concerned. He didn't want to be "on hand" as Joe put it, called up whenever Joe and Jane were short-staffed. However, he did go up and look at the room. It was tiny, with no space for more than a bed and a desk, and there were no kitchen facilities. No, certainly not ideal, but it was an offer he could keep on hold to be accepted if he became desperate. "Thanks, Joe, I may take you up on it, but I'm still hoping Madeleine Richmond's dad is going to find a house in time."

Joe nodded. He liked Ben, he was a popular barman and good at the job, and he wanted to keep him. "No problem. It'd be much more fun for you in a proper student house, and that Mad Richmond is always a live wire isn't she? I mean, never quiet when she's in the bar, is it? But you know the offer's there if you want it."

"I can't see why you don't move in with me," Angie suggested when he told her about Joe's offer. "That seems the obvious thing to do. There'll be room in our house in September, because David will have graduated."

Ben shook his head. He had no intention of moving in with Angie for various reasons, but all he said was, "No, I don't think so, Ange. I don't want to live that far out of town."

"It's not far out," Angie said.

"Not for you," Ben agreed, "you've got a car."

"Or what passes for one," Angie agreed ruefully, thinking of the clapped-out Volkswagen Beetle she had bought with her summer vacation earnings. "You could always get a bike. Be good for your rugby training, biking in every day."

That was another bone of contention. Ben's rugby. It was all right in the summer when there wasn't any, but during the season when he went training mid-week and played matches every Saturday, sometimes miles away so that he wasn't home for the evening, there had been several mutterings about "you love rugby more than you do me", and on balance Ben thought that he probably did.

Anyway, he had lived with a girlfriend before and it was not an experience he was rushing to repeat. When he was twenty his girlfriend, Katie, had moved in with him and they had been a definite item for over a year. Gradually however, they had drifted apart and things had started to go wrong. Their circle of friends changed as Katie became more involved in her job and the people she worked with, and Ben seemed excluded. She had less and less time for the crowd he wanted to go around with and the recriminations began...Where have you been? Why are you so late? Who have you been with? By the time they had finally decided that their relationship was over and Katie moved out, the last flames of affection had been extinguished, the upheaval was enormous and the bitterness extraordinary.

"As bad as getting divorced," Ben told his mate Flintlock. "Watched my parents do that. Shan't get caught in that trap again!"

Flintlock had grinned. "Yeah, you will, with some other bird."

Ben had laughed too. "Well, maybe, but not for a hell of a long time. Love 'em and keep 'em at arm's length. That's what I say. Let them look forward to seeing you, not fall over them night and morning and," he added as an afterthought, "you can steer well clear when it's PMT time!"

Definitely, Angie was not a girl he wanted to move in with. He still liked his space. He looked forward to seeing her in the evenings all right, to going to parties with her, to going to bed with her, but she was not the centre of his life and they both knew it. Angie wanted that to change. Ben didn't.

He was just turning his attention back to Richard III when there was a banging on his door. Only one person knocked like that.

"Come in, Mad," he called and she exploded into the room, her face split into a beam. She grabbed him in a bear hug.

"Guess what," she cried, as she flung herself down on to his bed. "We've got it!"

"Got what?"

"The house, dumb-dumb, the house, and it's brilliant!" She beamed across at him. "You'll love it. It's in Dartmouth Circle, so it's right near the Union. Couldn't be better, could it?"

"Sounds great," Ben agreed.

"You are still on, aren't you? Like, to share, I mean? You haven't found anywhere else?" This had been worrying Madeleine. She knew the time for finding the house had run short. All the students needed to be certain of somewhere to live in September before they went down for the long summer holidays, and she had known that Ben was beginning to look around.

"No, sounds great," repeated Ben. "Is it definite?"

"Yeah, contracts exchanged today, and completion in a couple of weeks. But Mr Short, the guy who owns it, says we can go down any time and look at it. There's lots to be done on it, but Dad says he can have it all ready for the beginning of next term, no problem. Let's go out and celebrate."

"Have you told the others? Are they still on?"

"As far as I know, though I'm not sure about Mandy, I think she's been looking elsewhere. I came to tell you first, but I'm on my way to tell them now. Coming?"

Ben looked at the work on his desk. "Can't, not now. Got to hand this in tomorrow, but I'm working at the Dutch tonight. Bring them there and we'll celebrate then."

Mad got up from the bed. "OK," she said. "See you later."

"Oh, Mad, if Mandy has changed her mind, I know someone who might be interested in taking her place."

Madeleine paused by the door. "Oh, who's that?"

"Girl on my medieval history course, Charlotte Murphy. Her room's on Bottom East. She was saying the other day that her plans for next year have fallen through. You know her, tall willowy blonde, always wears lots of chains round her neck?"

"Yeah, I know the one. Nice, is she?" enquired Mad with a grin.

"Yeah, good kid. She's had to repeat her second year because she was ill. And before you go stirring it up with Angie, I see her at lectures, that's all."

Madeleine laughed. "Fine, no probs. If Mandy has found somewhere else we'll ask Charlotte."

"Charlie, she's called Charlie."

"OK, well, I must away. Back to your work my man, and we'll see you down the Dutch later."

Madeleine waltzed off down the corridor to spread the good news to the others. She could hear Cirelle's reggae music throbbing through her door and knowing she would never be heard above the beat, Madeleine didn't bother to knock, but simply went in.

Cirelle looked up and smiled. She was sitting on her bed braiding her hair. "Hi Mad," she said, and reached across to turn the volume of her stereo down a fraction. "What are you at?"

"The house," crowed Madeleine. "That's what. We've got it! Contracts exchanged today."

"Hey, man, that's great. Where is it? Is there room for us all as planned?"

"Yup, there're five bedrooms, or there will be when we've finished working on the place, so that's you and me and Mandy, and Ben and Dean."

"Not sure about Mandy," Cirelle said, her fingers nimbly plaiting and twisting her hair without pause. "Like, I saw her yesterday, and she said she couldn't wait for your dad to get somewhere, and she'd been offered a place with Billy Thomas and his crowd, you know down the Friary end of town? She might not have taken it yet."

"Well, if she has, too bad," shrugged Madeleine. "Ben says there's a girl on his course, Charlie Murphy, who's looking for somewhere. He says she's OK, so if Mandy's out we'll ask her."

"Where is this house anyway?" asked Cirelle.

"Dartmouth Circle. You know it? Just off Dartmouth Road behind St Joseph's Church. Couldn't be better could it?"

"Yes, of course I know St Joseph's," said Cirelle. "Sounds great. When do we get in?"

"Not till September for you. Dad says there's masses of work to be done on it, but you know he's a builder, so it won't be a problem. But it's got everything we need, or will have. We can all go and see it. Mr Short, who we're buying it from, says just to give him a ring and come round any time. I told Ben, and we're going to celebrate in the Dutch tonight."

Cirelle finished her hair and grinned across at Madeleine. "Great. I'm going to the gym before supper, but I'll be ready to go down the Dutch after that. Come and get me when you're going. Right?"

Madeleine jumped to her feet, already on her way to the door, before she darted back to Cirelle and hugged her. "Cool, eh?" she cried and rushed out to find Dean and Mandy.

There was a sudden emptiness as she left the room, almost as if she'd left a vacuum in her place. Cirelle smiled at the swinging door and got up to close it. She was used to the way Madeleine moved through the world, always rushing enthusiastically from one thing to the next; totally different from Cirelle herself, who liked to consider every move she made before committing herself to anything. Once committed, she was as enthusiastic as anyone else, but life had taught her that thought needed to be given to every action.

She had taken a long time to decide whether to take up the

place she had been offered at Belcaster University. Brought up the eldest of five children in a small house in Brixton, she had been very dubious about launching herself into the world of higher education instead of getting a job locally. She had never been away from home by herself except on one school field trip and only twice on family holidays when they had stayed in a rented caravan in Dorset. The idea of living the other side of the country, in an unfamiliar town where she knew no one, was daunting in the extreme.

"I'm not sure I'm cut out for student life," she admitted to her family, and her wide brown eyes were troubled.

Her parents, who had not been able to stay at school beyond their 'O' levels, had been encouraging and supportive.

"Of course you must go, Cirelle," her mother Phyllis had urged. "You've earned that place, girl, and you gotta go. It's the chance of a lifetime." She had smiled proudly at her daughter. "Fancy a daughter of mine going to get a degree."

"Hey, steady on, Mum," laughed Cirelle. "I only just got the place. Supposing I can't do the work when I get there?"

"What kind of talk is this?" reproved her mother. "Of course you'll be able to do it. You're a clever girl, Cirelle. Don't waste this chance to get on. And," she added with a twinkle, "it'll make Gary work harder. He'll be determined to show he's as clever as you!"

Cirelle smiled at that, thinking of her younger brother Gary about to do his GCSEs, and always keen to prove himself as good as if not better than his older sister.

"But I could be earning," she pointed out a little guiltily. "You know, helping with the bills and that."

Phyllis engulfed her daughter in a bear-like hug. "Sure you could, babe, but you don't have to. Dad and I can manage like we always have. You'll be able to get a loan, won't you? We'll all get by, don't you worry. Don't you think I'm proud as Punch being able to boast about you at work? My daughter, doing her degree in English at Belcaster University! And as for your granddad, he's nearly bursting with pride!"

Her father, always less demonstrative, just hugged her and said, "Go for it, girl. Wish I'd had the chance."

As the time for her to leave for Belcaster drew nearer, Cirelle found herself dreading it, going to a strange place where she knew no one, had no friends.

"Everyone will be in the same boat," her mother pointed out. "All the new students will be as nervous as you. Find a nice church in the area," Phyllis went on. "You'll make friends then, people who think as you do."

So Cirelle had arrived at Belcaster last year and been allocated a room in a hall of residence, and her life had taken off because the first person she had met that first evening was the girl in the next room, Madeleine Richmond.

She was very quickly absorbed into the group of students on her landing, and gradually got to know the others on her course. There were plenty of other West Indian students and though at first they gravitated to each other, they were soon all involved with any student who happened to have the same interests. There was no feeling of being a separate group, and her closest friends were those in hall with her.

When the time came to think about where they would all live in their second year, Cirelle had been pleased when Madeleine had asked her to come in with her in a house somewhere.

"It'll be great, Cirelle, you'll see," Madeleine had said. "I'd love you to share if you think you could live with me."

On the whole, Cirelle thought she could. She knew that she and Mad were quite different from each other, but had long ago decided that was why they got on so well together. Madeleine, exuding self-confidence, was impetuous and immediately affectionate; Cirelle, on the other hand, naturally more reserved, was cautious and less outgoing. Madeleine's relationship with her boyfriend, Dan, was constantly tempestuous, whereas Cirelle never had a "boyfriend" as such, but was happy to go out in a crowd. She had been to stay with Mad's family on a couple of weekends and had been made very welcome, slipping easily into the family circle. Over the year, a firm friendship had been forged, and Madeleine's invitation simply reinforced it.

In those first weeks, however, Cirelle had followed her mother's advice, and had discovered St Joseph's. Though she was nothing like as regular a churchgoer as her mother would have wished, she did sometimes go there to church and had offered to help occasionally making teas and coffees in the St Joe's drop-in day centre.

"It's mostly the elderly and disabled who use the centre," Frank Marsh, the vicar, explained, "so you'd be doubly welcome, a new face and someone who's young as well."

Cirelle found she enjoyed going and talking to the St Joe's customers and often wore the T-shirt Frank had given her with "Not just Holy Joes at St Joe's" on it.

"We can do with any publicity you care to give us," he said with a smile, "and you make a delightful model! Oh, dear," he added at once. "Is that sexist?"

Cirelle grinned at him. "No, Frank, it's a compliment."

The vicar looked relieved. "Oh, good," he said. "That's what it was meant to be, but you never know these days how people will take things. Don't worry about being on a rota, just drop in when you can, we'll be delighted to see you."

Cirelle had taken him at his word and when she had the odd half-hour she often spent it at St Joe's, serving teas, washing up or just chatting to the customers. She had an easy way with people once she'd overcome her initial shyness, and the regulars at St Joe's soon looked forward to her visits.

She thought now about the news Madeleine had brought. She was delighted that they had definitely got a house as she too had been thinking she must try and make other arrangements for next year if they hadn't found somewhere soon. It was in the perfect position, too. Dartmouth Circle was a nice area, just minutes' walk from the college union building and from St Joe's, as well.

"Sounds great," she announced to her room and switching

off her music she gathered up her sports bag and set off for her workout in the gym, feeling at one with herself. As she passed Ben's room she knocked and at his call stuck her head round the door.

"Heard the good news?" she asked. "About the house."

"Yeah, great, isn't it? Mad whirled through earlier."

Cirelle laughed. "She whirled by me as well, on her way to tell the others. She said we're celebrating in the Dutch tonight, so I'll see you there, unless you fancy coming to the gym now, you could do with a workout."

Ben pulled a face. "Can't," he said. "I must get this done for tomorrow."

"OK, see you then."

"Yeah, I'm working from seven, I'll see you there."

The Flying Dutchman was very busy that evening, and Ben was working at full stretch for the first hour or so of his shift, but by the time Madeleine and Cirelle came in, the rush had eased a little and he was able to chat to them over the bar.

"Where are Mandy and Dean?" he asked. "Are they still coming in with us?"

"Dean is," Madeleine replied. "He's dead chuffed we've got a place. He'll be in later."

"But not Mandy?"

Madeleine shook her head. "Don't think so. I did see her in the canteen earlier, and she said she thought she was going in with Billy Thomas. Said she couldn't wait while we got our act together and had virtually committed herself to Billy's house now." Madeleine shrugged. "She can suit herself. I wouldn't want to live over at Friary if I had the chance to live in Dartmouth Circle, would you?"

"Dartmouth Circle?" Jane, the landlord's other half, chipped in to the conversation. "Did you say Dartmouth Circle?"

Madeleine grinned across at her. "Yup. Isn't it great? We finally found a house for next year, and my dad exchanged contracts on it this morning."

"And it's in Dartmouth Circle, you say?"

"Yes. It's in a terrible state, so there's masses of work to be done on it before we move in in September, but Dad says we can get it all done. He says I've got to help with the decorating when the structural work is finished, but I don't mind that. I like painting, and I can't wait to strip off the grungy wallpaper and to paint over the sludge-coloured walls, they're... awful." Madeleine's voice trailed away as she saw a strange expression flood Jane's face. "Jane," she said uncertainly, "is there anything wrong?"

Jane shook her head as if trying to clear it and then smiled at her. "Not at all," she replied. "It all sounds wonderful, I'm sure you'll all be very happy there. Which number have you bought?"

"Number seven," answered Madeleine cheerfully. "Why? Do you know it?"

"Oh yes," Jane said, "I used to live there."

"In Dartmouth Circle?"

"In number seven."

A moment's stunned silence greeted this revelation as Madeleine reheard the comments she'd just made about the house and its decor, and then it was broken by a cackle of laughter from Jane herself. "Hey, Joe," she called over her shoulder, "come and hear this."

Joe came through from the other bar. "What is it, love?" he asked. "What's so funny?"

"Ned's finally sold the house. He's actually sold it, and do you know who to?" She jerked her head across the bar. "Our Mad, here. Our Mad's student house is going to be in Dartmouth Circle." She gave another shout of laughter. "I'd give anything to see the face of that cow next door when she hears she's going to have students as her neighbours!"

Madeleine and the others were still looking perplexed at Jane's reaction to the news of their house and Joe, seeing they weren't with what was going on, said, "Don't worry, Mad, it's just that Jane used to live there before her divorce, at seven Dartmouth Circle. It wasn't a very happy time for her there."

"Oh, I see," Madeleine looked awkward. "I'm sorry, Jane, I didn't realise..."

"And why would you, indeed?" Jane said cheerfully. "I'm delighted to hear the place has been sold. Maybe now I'll get some money out of the bastard. And don't worry what you said about the house either," she went on. "It was in a bad enough state when I left; I imagine it's quite desperate now." She winked at the amazed students saying, "I wish you joy of it," and went into the lounge bar to serve a customer.

"She means it, you know," Joe said, glancing after her. "She's glad it's sold at last, and she hopes you'll all enjoy living there."

"It'll probably be a mad house," said Madeleine, "but you can be sure we're going to have great fun."

Cirelle raised her glass to the others. "Let's drink to it anyway," she said, "let's drink to Mad's house."

"To the madhouse?" queried Jane appearing again on the other side of the bar. She gave a bitter laugh. "Seven Dartmouth Circle was certainly always that!"

"Hey," cried Madeleine in delight. "That's what we'll call it, The Madhouse. I was trying to think of a good name for it, and that's perfect, don't you think? Here's to The Madhouse, everybody. Cheers."

They all raised their glasses and at that moment Dean came in. He had come straight from the squash courts and was dressed in a disreputable tracksuit, his straggly hair still wet from the shower.

"Hi guys," he said, dumping his sports bag down with a thump. "Where's my pint? Jeez, I'm knackered."

"Coming up," said Ben, picking up a glass.

"This round on the house," Joe Briggs called across. "To celebrate the sale of The Madhouse."

"Hey, cheers, Joe," cried Madeleine, raising her glass. "Nice one."

"The Madhouse?" echoed Dean. "What the hell's that?"

"Mad's house...where we're all going to live next year?" Cirelle laughed.

"Is that what it's called?"

"It is now," Mad said cheerfully and took another pull at her drink.

"Now our only other problem is who is going to take Mandy's place. She's changed her mind," she explained to Dean. "Ben's suggested a girl on his course called Charlie Murphy, anyone got any other suggestions? Cirelle? Dino?"

They both shook their heads almost indifferently. "No, if Ben's happy about her she's probably OK," said Dean.

"We ought to meet her and see if we like her," Cirelle suggested. "I mean, maybe she won't like us. Don't you think?"

"Yeah," Ben agreed. "I'll probably see her tomorrow at a lecture, so I'll arrange a meet, OK?"

It was agreed and when Madeleine's boyfriend, Dan, arrived a few moments later, he found them all discussing The Madhouse in happy anticipation. With pint in hand, and his arm draped round Mad's shoulders, he joined cheerfully in the conversation. He was happy enough with Mad's new living arrangements, for although he was regarded by all as her boyfriend, and indeed regarded himself as such, Dan liked his freedom, to come and go as he chose, no questions asked, and he had no wish to live in The Madhouse.

## Chapter Three

Jill Hammond kissed her children goodnight, switched off the light and leaving them safely cocooned under their duvets in the glow of the night light, went downstairs to get supper for her husband, Anthony. Anthony was often not home before the children were in bed. Several days a week he commuted to London, and today was one of them. On London days, he normally rang to let Jill know which train he would be on, but so far she'd heard nothing.

Jill went into the kitchen and dialled him on his mobile.

"The vodafone subscriber you have called is unavailable," intoned the microchip sweetly, "please try later."

"Damn," she muttered and then called through to Isabelle the au pair who was laying the table in the dining room. "Did Mr Hammond phone before I got home?"

"Oh yes, Mrs Hammond, I am sorry. He telephone to say he takes the train at six-fifteen."

"Please, Isabelle," Jill said with exaggerated patience, "I've asked you before, please write down *all* telephone messages."

"Yes, Mrs Hammond. I have written it. The paper is in the hall. There are other telephones as well. I will get it."

While Isabelle scuttled downstairs to bring up the messages, Jill poured herself a gin and tonic and put the potatoes, peeled earlier by Isabelle, on to the stove. If Anthony had caught the six-fifteen, he should be home in the next half-hour. She was looking forward to a quiet evening alone with him. Isabelle had eaten her evening meal with the children and was going out somewhere with a German au pair, Heidi, whom she had met when collecting Sylvia from nursery school.

Jill and Anthony would be able to have a peaceful dinner, and then when they were settled with their coffee, she would broach the subject that had been simmering in her mind for so long. A job. She longed for a job even though she knew Anthony didn't want her to go out to work.

"There's no need, darling," he had said when she tentatively suggested that she return to teaching. "We always agreed you should be here for the children. Sylvia needs you to be here when she gets home from nursery, and you know you'd hate someone else to look after Thomas."

"Isabelle does that now," Jill pointed out mildly.

"Not really, not all the time," Anthony countered, "and always under your supervision and guidance. She has no responsibility for the way he develops."

"It would give me a little money of my own," Jill said, trying a different tack.

"But you don't need extra money." Anthony was surprised. "If you need more money you only have to ask."

"Yes," agreed Jill bitterly, "that's the problem. I have to ask, and I don't want to have to." She knew Anthony couldn't understand why that was important to her, but for the moment she had let the matter rest.

Then yesterday evening, after what seemed a pretty routine day, Jill had been confronted with the idea again. Sitting in the bath and scooping bubbles into mountains of foam, Sylvia had suddenly looked across at her mother, perched on the closed loo seat and said, "Zoë Carter's mummy goes to her office every morning and stays all day."

Jill smiled. "Does she, darling?"

"Yes. Why don't you go to your office?"

"I haven't got an office," Jill pointed out. "Would you want me to go to the office all day?"

Sylvia considered. "No," she decided. "Zoë goes to her nan's till her mummy fetches her. Our nan lives too far away."

"Yes, I'm afraid she does," Jill agreed, "both Granny and Nan do. That's why it's such a treat when we go and see them."

"Mmm." Sylvia gave herself a foam beard. "Granny makes chocolate cake and Nan does fudge. Today in news time we were telling what our mummies did, and Zoë said hers went to the office."

"And what did you say about me?" Jill asked cautiously.

Sylvia beamed at her. "I said you didn't do anything." She gathered up another dollop of froth and put it on Thomas's head. Thomas, aged two, shrilled his disapproval and splashed her, kicking hard with his feet. Before the bathroom could become totally awash, Jill scooped him out of the bath and snuggled him into a warm towel.

The conversation was over, but it stayed with Jill and she had mulled it over in her mind during the day. She was suddenly sure she needed to do something outside the home. She played golf, and that was good, it got her away to an entirely different environment one afternoon a week, but even with Isabelle's help, she felt bogged down in the daily routine of washing, ironing and shopping and meals.

What I need, she decided, is to do some part-time teaching, just mornings. It would mean relying on Isabelle even more, but Isabelle had let drop the other day that "Heidi works for more time for Mrs Vane, and has more wages. It is a good arrangement I think."

The more Jill thought about it, the more she agreed that it was, perhaps, a good arrangement. After Sylvia's comment last night, Jill decided to tackle Anthony again. A quiet dinner, a bottle of wine and a tactful approach was what she planned. She wouldn't spoil the meal, she would bide her time until Anthony was quite relaxed.

Isabelle reappeared with the piece of paper and Jill scanned the messages. There were four, timed and neatly written in

Isabelle's spiky French handwriting. Jill knew she owed the girl an apology, but perversely she didn't feel like offering one. Two calls were from friends of Jill's who had left only their names and said they would ring again. The fourth was from Anthony about the train, and the other one was a message to phone Sheila Colby.

"Did Mrs Colby say what it was about?" Jill asked Isabelle.

"No, but Mrs Colby did not telephone, she came to the house when the children have tea. She looks for you or Mr Hammond. I say you play golf and come home later. I say Mr Hammond works. She says please to telephone. I write the message."

"Fine, thanks," said Jill. "I'll phone her. Are you off now?"

"Yes, if I have ended."

"Finished," corrected Jill absently, still wondering what the dreadful Colby woman wanted.

"Finished," repeated Isabelle dutifully. "I go now. I have my key. I will see you tomorrow morning."

"Have a good time," said Jill, and pushing Sheila Colby to the back of her mind, turned her attention to the dinner.

Forty minutes later, when there was still no sign of Anthony, she left the supper in a low oven and poured herself another drink. He must have missed the train, she thought with irritation; but why hadn't he phoned? She thought too of Sheila Colby.

"I'm not going to ring her now," Jill decided. "It can't be that urgent. Tomorrow morning will do." Putting her feet up, she zapped the television into life and waited for Anthony.

When he finally came in, Anthony looked tired and strained. He shed his coat and briefcase on to a chair and pulled his tie loose.

"They say let the train take the strain," he complained as he took the drink Jill handed him and dropped into his chair, "but then they have points failure outside Swindon and we sit there for over an hour while they sort it out."

"Why didn't you ring?" asked Jill. "I was beginning to get worried."

"I couldn't get off the train," Anthony replied, "and somewhere along the line today I've lost my mobile. It may even be here at home, though I'm sure I took it this morning."

"Never mind that now," soothed Jill, switching off the television and heading for the kitchen. "You finish your drink and I'll put the supper on the table. I've opened some wine."

Anthony looked at her in mild surprise. "Are we celebrating something?" he asked. "What have I forgotten?"

"Nothing, silly," Jill laughed. "I just thought it would be nice, that's all."

They were just finishing the meal when the doorbell rang. "I'll go," said Jill. "Were you expecting anyone?"

Anthony shook his head. "Don't think so."

Jill went down to the front door and found Sheila Colby on the doorstep.

"Mrs Hammond! Good evening," Sheila gushed. "I'm so glad you are home. I did call earlier, but your French girl said you were playing golf." There was a faint emphasis on the last two words, implying criticism that a woman might so waste her time, and Jill took the inference with a compressing of her lips. She waited in silence on the doorstep and Sheila hurried on. "I did leave a message for you to phone me when you got in, but I don't expect you got it – these foreign girls..." She finished the sentence with a knowing shake of her head.

"Oh, yes, Isabelle did give me the message," said Jill, "only I'm afraid it hasn't been convenient to phone yet. I've had the children to see to and my husband's supper to get. In fact," she went on repressively, "we are still at the table."

Sheila Colby knew exactly what time Anthony Hammond had got home, because she had been watching for his car from her window.

"Oh, I'm so sorry to drag you from your dinner," she said, annoyed with herself for misjudging the timing, "but it's actually your husband who I've come to see. Do you think he could spare me a few minutes?" She was determined not to leave now she was here, but she added reluctantly, "Or I could come back in half an hour or so, when he's finished eating."

Jill, who had planted herself firmly in the doorway and kept hold of the door when she'd seen who her unexpected caller was, now stepped to one side, allowing Sheila to enter. "You'd better come up now," she said. "We've just about finished." She led the way upstairs into the living room. "Please do sit down. I'll just tell Anthony you're here."

She disappeared through a door in a wall that in Sheila's house wasn't there. Sheila looked round the room with interest; she'd never been into the Hammonds' house before. The design was essentially the same as her own, but instead of the living room stretching the width of the house as hers did, with a dining area next to the kitchen, the end section of the room had been walled off to make a separate dining room. Quite a clever idea, she supposed, except that she, Sheila, liked to sit in her chair and have light from windows at either end of the room. The sitting room in which she waited was nicely furnished, though there was a coloured crate of toys tucked behind the sofa and she noticed that the video recorder and all the ornaments were high on shelves, out of reach of small inquisitive hands.

Almost at once Anthony Hammond emerged from the dining room, and, coming across to her, held out his hand.

"Good evening, Mrs Colby. I understand you wanted a word with me. How can I help?"

Before Sheila could answer, Jill also appeared and said, "I'm making us some coffee, Mrs Colby. Would you like some?"

"No, oh no, thank you. Not in the evening. It keeps me awake, you know."

Jill nodded and disappeared into the kitchen, leaving the door open behind her, curious to know what the Colby woman was after.

Sheila turned back to Anthony Hammond. "I've come to see you, Mr Hammond, in your capacity as chairman of the

Residents' Association." She paused dramatically and Anthony said again, "I see. How can I help you?"

"I've some news that affects the whole Circle," Sheila went on. "Dreadful news, I think it is, and I want you to call a special meeting of the Association to see what action should be taken."

Again she paused and Anthony said patiently, "And what news is that, Mrs Colby?"

"Ned Short has finally sold number seven," she said, "and he's sold it to be a student house." She glanced up at Anthony to see if he had realised the enormity of what she was telling him. Not satisfied with his reaction, she continued, "You realise what this means, don't you? There'll be rowdy parties all the time, and comings and goings at all hours. The peace of the Circle will be shattered."

"Particularly yours," remarked Anthony seriously, "as you're in number six."

"Exactly!" cried Sheila, and then realising that made her motive sound more than a little selfish, she went on hurriedly, "But of course it isn't *just* us, is it? I mean, apart from the Redwoods who will be affected in the same way as we are, the whole Circle will be affected in some way or the other."

"I see." Anthony maintained his serious expression. "And what do you think the Association can do about it? Mr Short is entitled to sell his house to whomever he chooses, you know."

"I know that," agreed Sheila, "but Gerald says there may be covenants preventing any of the houses in the Circle being used for multiple occupancies."

Anthony shrugged. "There isn't any such covenant on mine," he said. "Is there on yours?"

"No. I mean I'm not sure. There might be. Gerald doesn't remember." Sheila was flustered. Gerald had refused point-blank to go to the bank for the deeds stored in their safety deposit box. He said he was certain there was no such covenant, but as always Sheila drew on his name to lend authority to her own pronouncements.

Anthony was not taken in by her pretended ignorance, he had had dealings with Sheila Colby before, so he said smoothly, "Well, I think we can be fairly sure there aren't any attached to any other property in the Circle. All the houses were built at the same time, and I imagine they'd have been dealt with in the same way."

Sheila recognised that she'd come to a dead end here and changed direction. "Anyway, we feel, Gerald and I, that a meeting should be called so that everyone can hear the news and we can decide a plan of campaign."

"Campaign?" Anthony repeated. "I'm sorry, but I don't quite see what sort of campaign would be appropriate, Mrs Colby."

"Well, perhaps we could start with a very firm letter," Sheila suggested, "welcoming them to the Circle, warning them that we expect certain standards of behaviour here and that we won't put up with drink and drugs and noise."

"That wouldn't be very welcoming," Anthony pointed out, "and it would probably be counter-productive. We don't know what, if any, trouble they may cause, but we can't just assume they'll behave as you suggest."

"I think you'll find they do," Sheila said darkly. "Most students do."

"You've had a lot of dealings with students, have you, Mrs Colby?" asked Jill sweetly, as she carried the coffee tray into the room. Recognising the dangerous sweetness of tone, Anthony flashed a warning glance at his wife. He was going to have enough trouble dissuading Sheila from following her plan without having her antagonised by Jill. Jill caught his glance and gave him a "yeah, yeah, I know" look, and began to pour the coffee.

"Here's what I think we should do," Anthony offered. "We should wait until these students have moved in and then perhaps have one of our Association social evenings. That way we can get to meet them and they can get to know us. The actual owner of the house will also be a member of the Association, so if necessary, and I mean only if there is a problem, *we* shall deal with *him* and *he* will deal with *them*. They, after all, are his tenants."

"Well I think they should know where they are right from the start," Sheila said and rose to her feet. "I shall be visiting every house in the close to suggest holding a meeting. I believe if enough members ask for one, you have to call one."

"Certainly if there is general demand," Anthony agreed, and Jill wondered how he could remain so unruffled. He stood up as well. "Thank you for coming to let us know the situation and for sharing your fears with us. I will certainly keep my ear to the ground and let you know if I hear any more myself. Let me show you down." He stood aside at the top of the stairs and she preceded him down to the front door.

"Dreadful woman!" Jill exploded as he came back. "Who does she think she is?"

"She's an old lady living in a peaceful backwater who's suddenly discovered she is going to have to share it with the twenty-first century," Anthony replied calmly, sinking into his armchair and picking up his coffee again.

"Oh Anthony, don't be so reasonable," snapped Jill, irritated.

"Well you can't have it both ways, darling." Anthony still remained unruffled. "You're upset with her because you think she's being unreasonable, though I think you might find her less so if it were us attached to the student house, and now you don't like me being *reasonable*."

"It's just so stupid. I mean she's going to go round to every house in the Circle and try to set people against these students before they've even arrived."

"I shouldn't worry about it," Anthony said. "We don't know for sure there are going to be any students. It's only a rumour, and I wouldn't be at all sure Ned Short hadn't started it just to wind her up. We'll just have to wait and see." He reached for the TV remote and switched on the evening news.

Jill looked across at him, still angered – almost as much by his equanimity as by Sheila Colby's prejudice. Her husband,

Anthony, was only thirty-five and yet all of a sudden he seemed to be positively middle-aged. There were lines of tiredness about his eyes and mouth, and his hairline had receded so far that his forehead extended to the top of his head. There were touches of grey over his ears too. Have I noticed them before, wondered Jill? Or are they new? How often do I actually look at him and really see him? How often does he look at me?

She sighed ruefully. In the early days of their marriage, his sense of humour would have had them giggling happily together over Sheila Colby's absurdity, but now somehow, life had become more serious. Of course he had the responsibilities of his home and his two young children. His job, working with a finance company, was a responsible one too, and on top of all that, he'd been elected chairman of the Dartmouth Circle Residents' Association at the last AGM. He hadn't wanted the job much, but the only other person prepared to stand had been Gerald Colby, and few of the residents had wanted him running their affairs. Almost everyone had realised that a vote for Gerald was in truth a vote for Sheila, and she already interfered with their lives enough.

A pity the chairmanship hadn't gone to Gerald, Jill thought angrily. Then *he* would have had to deal with this student business. She said as much to Anthony now, and Anthony shrugged. "That wouldn't have helped anybody," he said and turned his attention back to the news.

Jill sat watching too for a moment, and then with a wave of frustration she went out to the kitchen to wash up the supper things.

"Damn that woman!" she said aloud as she banged the pots and pans into the sink, "damn that interfering, busy-bodying bitch!" Jill knew now that tonight was definitely not the time to bring up the job idea. The carefully fostered mellow mood had been shattered by the doorbell and the intrusion of Sheila Bloody Colby! Jill could have wept with frustration and rage. Even as she had chatted to Anthony over dinner about her day,

Jill had been framing careful, non-confrontational phrases in her head ready to use when the moment came, when they were comfortably settled with their coffee, and now the moment wasn't going to come, not tonight anyhow.

She thought back over her day. Not a bad one as days went; the golf was always a bonus, and the rest of it run of the mill. Going with Thomas to the supermarket, dropping in for coffee with Alison Forrester at number eleven, doing chores until the children's bath time reminded her of Sylvia's innocent remark the previous evening…"I said you didn't do anything," and, though it was ridiculous, Jill knew she felt the same. On impulse she picked up the kitchen phone and dialled her mother, Nancy.

"Mum, are you about tomorrow?"

"Yes, I expect so. Why? Are you coming?"

"I thought I might, if it's all right. Probably just me and the children. I think Anthony will be working and it's Isabelle's day off."

"Of course it's all right, it'll be lovely to see you all. I'll make a chocolate cake."

Jill laughed at that. "Do," she said. "Sylvia loves them."

Feeling a little better for having done something positive, Jill went back into the sitting room. Anthony had fallen asleep in front of the television. She looked down at him for a moment. The lines of strain were etched into his face, so that even in sleep he looked tired. He's thirty-five, Jill thought suddenly, but he looks like an old man.

She woke him gently and said, "I'm going up for an early night, and you'd be more comfortable in bed than in that chair."

Anthony shook himself awake. "I've got some work to do before I turn in," he said.

"Leave it," Jill urged gently. "Come on, come to bed. Do it in the morning."

"No, I can't. I told you I had a meeting in the morning. It's got to be finished for that."

"But tomorrow's Saturday," objected Jill.

"I know, but I have to go. The man I have to see is only here now. He flies out to Hong Kong tomorrow evening. You go on up. I won't be long."

"All right. Actually, if you're going to be out tomorrow, I might take the children up to Mum's for lunch."

"Good idea," agreed Anthony reaching for his briefcase. "They'll enjoy that."

It had been easy, Jill thought as she went upstairs. She would have a chance to talk to her mother properly, and uninterrupted.

Jill loved her mother's home. She had never lived there herself, Nancy had only moved to Meadow Cottage in Over Upton after Jill's father had died, but she loved the quiet peace of the little house. It was set back from the lane, just outside the centre of the village and nestled into a dip in the hill, so that it was sheltered from the prevailing west wind. The garden surrounded it, with an orchard to one side and beyond that were the open fields and a view to blue hills in the distance. It was bathed in sunshine when they arrived, and Nancy was working in the garden, dressed in a pair of old corduroys and a man's shirt.

"Granny, Granny we're here," Sylvia shrieked as she catapulted from the car and struggled with the garden gate.

Nancy dropped her trowel and hurried to hug her. "So you are," she cried. "How lovely to see you." She opened the gate and gathered her granddaughter into her arms.

"Did you make a chocolate cake?" Sylvia demanded.

"Well now, I wonder," laughed Nancy. "We'll go and see in a minute. Just let me say hello to Mummy and Thomas." She set Sylvia down and reached for Thomas as Jill released him from the car seat. Thomas put his chubby arms round her neck and hugged her. "Cake?" he asked hopefully.

"Sorry, Mum." Jill was laughing. "Sylvia was talking about your chocolate cake all the way here."

Nancy laughed too. "Well," she said, "there is one, so we'd better go and find it."

Once the children had been given small pieces of cake with

the promise of more after lunch, Nancy poured drinks for herself and her daughter and they carried them out on to the terrace and watched the children playing in the sandpit Nancy had had built for them in the garden. For a while they watched, amused by the antics of the children, and then even as Jill was wondering exactly how to introduce the subject of the job, her mother said, "Well, now that we're comfortable, tell me what's wrong."

"Wrong?" Jill looked startled. "What makes you think anything's wrong?"

Nancy laughed. "You're my daughter, darling," was her only explanation.

"I'm bored," Jill answered. Now the initiative no longer rested with her she might as well be direct. "I'm bored and I want to go back to teaching part-time."

"But darling, you can't possibly," Nancy began.

"Why not?" broke in Jill. "Other mothers do. Lots of them *have* to."

"But you don't," replied Nancy. "You're lucky enough not to have to work. You don't have to give your children to a child-minder, and miss out each time they learn something new. Think of the children. Thomas is only two. They're young for such a short time." She looked fondly at her grandson as he filled a plastic bucket with sand, his tongue stuck out between his lips in concentration. "And Sylvia is only at school in the mornings, she needs you there to come home to, to spend the afternoons and evenings with."

"But I would be there in the afternoons," Jill explained. "I'd get a morning job somewhere and be finished at twelve. Isabelle can have Thomas for the mornings, and I'll be there for them both in the afternoons."

"What does Anthony think?" asked Nancy, trying a different tack. Her instinctive reaction to Jill's suggestion was to be against it. She believed very strongly that before children went to school full-time, their mothers should be at home with them.

"I haven't discussed it with him lately," Jill admitted. "He's so busy we hardly have time to talk any more." She sighed. "But I know he won't like it much. You know he's never wanted me to work even before the children."

Nancy did know. She had backed Jill in her stand to continue teaching until they started a family.

"I want to provide for you," Anthony had kept saying. "I want you to have time to enjoy your life."

"I *do* enjoy my life," Jill had protested. "I love teaching and I would hate to be at home all day."

Anthony had appealed to Nancy privately, telling her it was his place to provide for his wife. Nancy was sympathetic. She knew he felt so strongly about it because his own father had done a flit when Anthony was only two, and he had watched his mother struggle on her own to bring up her three children, while working full-time. He had never forgiven his father, and was determined that his own wife should lack nothing that he could provide.

"It is very commendable that you feel like that," she had told him, "but really it would be better for both of you if Jill went on working. She does enjoy her teaching, you know, and finds it both rewarding and fulfilling. When you start a family, she'll find that equally rewarding and fulfilling, but she needs to teach in the meantime." Nancy held firmly to this belief and Anthony, with reluctance, had agreed.

Now Nancy was equally firm with Jill. "Your place is with your children," she said. "Your first duty is to your family. I think you should rule any notion of going back to teaching out of your head until Thomas is at school full-time. Then maybe you could consider a little part-time work."

"My duty?" Jill echoed.

"Yes, your duty. It's a much maligned and underrated word in this day and age. Most young women of your age would give their eye-teeth for what you've got, Jill. A loving husband, two beautiful, healthy children, a nice home and enough money not to have to worry about the bills. You have an au pair to help with the chores and to give you some time to yourself, a car of your own, you lack for nothing and if it means you can't go back into the classroom for a few years, so be it."

It was a long time since her mother had laid down the law and Jill greeted her words with a moment's mutinous silence before she muttered, "Well thanks for the vote of support, Mum."

"Now, darling, don't get in a mood. You asked what I thought and I told you."

"I didn't actually." Jill was still angry. "I just wanted to talk things over, not be given a lecture. I'm not beginning to suggest that I work full-time, anyone would think I'd suggested that I went and ran ICI or something. I just want an interest outside the house. Didn't it drive you mad when you had to stay at home all day to look after us?"

"Sometimes," admitted Nancy, "but I had no help in the house, and with four of you I was kept pretty busy. If I'd tried to hold down a job as well, I think I'd have died of exhaustion. But in fact, I wouldn't have missed the day-to-day changes as you all grew up, for the world." She looked across at her daughter. "I think you and Anthony need a holiday. Why don't you have a couple of weeks away, just the two of you so you can find each other again? I can have the children, they'll be no trouble, especially if Isabelle comes to help."

"I don't suppose Anthony can get the time," Jill muttered, still annoyed.

Nancy smiled sweetly. "Why don't you ask him?" she said.

Anthony finished his meeting earlier than he had expected, and was already in the train on the way home when he thought he would give Jill a call at her mother's and suggest that they go out for dinner. Then he remembered that he had lost his mobile phone. He racked his brains as to where he could have left it, and then it came to him. Yesterday he had grabbed a quick cup of coffee as he waited for the morning train. Someone had rung him as he sat in the cafeteria and he had answered the phone sitting at the table. He'd had to get some papers out of his brief-case to answer a question, and he must have left the phone on the table, or maybe it had fallen on to the floor as he repacked his briefcase. He would ask when he got to the station, you never knew, someone might have handed it in.

When he reached the station he hurried into the cafeteria and asked at the cash desk if anyone had found a mobile phone. The cashier shook her head. "Nothing handed in to me, dear," she said. "Well, they wouldn't, would they? Not these days. Finders keepers these days. You could try the lost property I suppose."

Anthony thanked her and turned away annoyed. He certainly hadn't used the phone after the time in the cafeteria, so he must have left it and someone must have picked it up. As he went out to the car park he remembered a story he had heard about someone who kept having his phone stolen from his car, and an idea came to him, an idea which made him laugh. It probably wouldn't work, but it was worth a try.

As soon as he got in he made himself a cup of tea and sat down in the kitchen to write himself a script, then when he had read it aloud several times he decided he was ready. Picking up the telephone, he dialled the number of his mobile phone. The number rang, and after a moment or two it was answered.

"Yes?" The answer was male and gruff.

"Oh, good afternoon," Anthony said cheerfully. "I'm ringing on behalf of Radio Belcaster. You've been chosen by our computer in a random selection to win a TV and VCR set or £350 in cash if you can answer a simple question."

"What question?" The voice sounded slightly less gruff, younger than before.

"Can you tell me the name of the Honda garage in Pottage Street?"

"Just tell you the name of a garage?" The voice sounded suspicious.

"Yes, that's all. It's part of an advertising campaign for Honda."

"Windridge Motors," said the voice.

"Congratulations, sir," Anthony enthused, beginning to enjoy himself.

"That answer makes you a winner. Now if you would like to choose whether you'll take cash or the TV and video…?"

"I'll take the cash," said the voice.

"Certainly. Now if I might just make sure we have your name and address correct. It would be a pity if your money went astray…?" He ended his comment as a question and then held his breath to see if he would get a reply.

"Scott Manders. I live at Flat C, 19 Elmbank Close, Belcaster."

Anthony repeated the name and address and then said, "Thank you, Mr Manders, you'll hear from us in the next couple of days." He rang off and with a delighted laugh he phoned the police.

The officer who answered his call was less than grateful for the information Anthony gave him, it was after all very small potatoes, but said he would look into the matter and they would be in touch.

When Jill and the children arrived home for bath time, Anthony was sitting in the garden reading the paper. He greeted them with smiles and kisses and Jill remembered all of a sudden the man she had loved and married and she held him tightly in her arms.

"Mum says she'll have the children for a couple of weeks so we can get away on our own," she said. "Can you get the time off so we can have a real break?"

Anthony looked down into her face. "Definitely," he said and kissed her.

## Chapter Four

Nicholas Richmond turned into Dartmouth Circle and pulled up outside number seven. His daughter Madeleine, who was in the back of the Jag, pointed to the house excitedly.

"Look, Mum. That's it. Number seven."

Clare Richmond looked at the peeling paint and the cracked panes of the front door. Her eye ran over the frontage, taking in the general state of neglect and decay. She didn't know quite what she'd been expecting after the paroxysms of delight from Madeleine and the cautious admissions from Nick that "the place needs a lot spending on it, but has possibilities", but whatever it was, it was not the reality of number seven.

"So it is," she said noncommittally.

"What do you think, Mum?" Madeleine was scrambling out of the car. "Won't it be great?"

"Well," said her mother, opening the car door, "let me see it all properly, before I say any more." She paused on the pavement and glanced round the circle of the close. The houses had been built in the garden of a large old house, now demolished, and were grouped round an area of communal garden in the middle. It was a pleasant round of garden with flowering shrubs, two wooden seats set to catch the sun, and a tiny play area with two swings and a small slide. The whole was fenced off with a low white fence, not to keep people out, but rather to delineate it from the grass verge that surrounded it. There was no one in the garden now, and it looked very peaceful in the May sunshine.

"It looks a nice quiet area," she remarked, and Nicholas gave a shout of laughter.

"It won't be when Maddo and her crowd have moved in," he cried. "They won't know what's hit them." He pulled a bunch of keys from his pocket and walked to the front door. Clare followed, and as she did so her attention was caught by a movement in the window of the adjacent house. She could see no one, but the twitching of the curtain told her that their arrival had been observed by the next-door neighbour, anxious to see who was going to be living on the other side of the party wall. Clare paused again, glancing round the close to see if she could see any other surreptitious curtain-twitching, but the other houses stood quiet and still in the morning sunshine, their windows unoccupied and their curtains still. She turned back to number seven and glanced sharply up at the first-floor windows of number six. No one was there, the net curtains were now undisturbed, and the sun reflected brightly their innocence.

I suppose it's only natural to want to see who your new neighbours are, thought Clare as she followed her husband and daughter into the house.

As she crossed the threshold, all thoughts of inquisitive neighbours and twitching curtains vanished as she inhaled the smell of damp and mould and cats. Maddo was standing at the bottom of the stairs, hopping from one foot to the other, for all the world more like a ten year old than a young woman of twice that age.

"Come on, Mum, come and look." She started up the stairs.

Nicholas emerged from a door down the hall and said, "Let's start at the bottom and work up. Then you can explain to Mum what we thought we could do."

"Yeah, great." Madeleine led her mother into the room where her father stood. "This is going to be Ben's room," she said. The room had obviously been a study as there was still an old desk in it. It had a glass door to the garden. Though garden, Clare reflected, was hardly the term she'd give to the rubbish dump beyond the window.

"Have the others been here yet?" Clare asked. "Or did you decide who was going to have which room?"

"Oh, they've been here all right," Madeleine said. "Mr Short let us come down straightaway. He moved out as soon as the contract was signed." She waved her hand round the room. "Ben wanted to be on the ground floor, and the others didn't mind, so it was an easy decision. Dean's going to be in the new room...I'll show you in a minute...and us girls are going to be on the top floor."

They made their way up through the house, Clare inspecting the big living room on the first floor, identical no doubt to that of the curtain-twitcher next door, the diminutive kitchen, up another flight of stairs to the bedrooms on the second floor.

"This one will be mine," Madeleine enthused, pulling Clare into the largest, which had its view out over the gardens. "I'm going to paint it yellow and have bright curtains and a duvet cover to match."

Clare smiled at her daughter's enthusiasm, and finding it catching, suggested colour schemes for the other two upstairs bedrooms. These were smaller rooms, looking out over the close, but each could be made very comfortable.

"Will the boys have to come all the way up here to use the bathroom?" she asked. "It'll be a nuisance for Ben."

"No, no," Madeleine explained, "there's a downstairs loo on the ground floor, and Dad says we can easily put a shower in under the stairs. That's really for the boys, and then we'll be up here."

"Maddo, come and hold this tape for me," called Nick from downstairs. While Madeleine had been showing her mother round the house, he had been making notes and taking measurements in the rooms that they were going to alter. The biggest alteration was to create a new room on the living-room floor. The present living room stretched the width of the house, and could easily have a section partitioned off to make another bedroom, looking back over the garden.

Madeleine ran down the stairs and dutifully held the end of the tape measure, as her father worked out exactly where the new wall would go. Gradually they worked their way round the house, deciding what they wanted to do and how the alterations should be done.

"We'll have to do something about this kitchen, Nick," Clare called. "It's in a dreadful state. So's the bathroom for that matter."

"Don't worry," Nick called back. "We'll sort it all out, and when we've finished it'll be a really nice little house. I'll take care of the building and decorating side, you and Maddo will have to sort out furniture and curtains and all that sort of stuff."

By the time they left the house Nick had made copious notes about what he intended to do, and Madeleine and Clare had made other notes on what was needed for curtains and carpet and furniture for each room.

"Let's go to a pub for some lunch," Nick suggested, "and we can talk this through."

"I told the others we'd probably go to the Dutch for some bar food," Madeleine said. "I thought it would be a good idea if you met them all, Dad, because you've got to sort out the rent with them and all that. They're going to look in at about lunchtime to see if we're there."

"Fine," said Nick. "We'd better go then. Anything anyone else wants to do here?"

There wasn't, so they got into the car and Madeleine directed them to the Flying Dutchman.

The bar was quite busy, but they managed to get a table in a corner, and Nick ordered drinks while they decided what to eat. Before they had ordered the other four arrived and cheerfully squashed themselves into the corner, too.

Madeleine introduced them all to her parents. They had met Cirelle before, as Madeleine had brought her home on a couple of occasions, but the others were new to them. As they drank their drinks and chose their food, Clare looked round at them all and wondered how they would get on together in the house. They were clearly good friends at the moment, but would that friendship survive living in fairly close proximity? She knew Cirelle was a quiet girl, used to working hard. At first, when Maddo had brought her home, Clare had wondered what her daughter had seen in her, but as she got to know Cirelle herself, Clare had come to recognise her dependability, and the generosity of her nature. Far more concerned about the consequences of her actions than Madeleine would ever be, Cirelle, Clare decided, might be a good influence on Maddo, perhaps even exercising restraint on some of her more flamboyant doings. She smiled across at Cirelle now, and was treated to Cirelle's slow smile.

She really is a very beautiful girl, thought Clare. Her skin is exquisite, and those huge dark eyes...well, you could drown in the innocence of those.

The other girl, Charlie, was a tall slim girl with blonde hair and grey eyes. She was far less exuberant than Madeleine, but she smiled and joined in the conversation readily enough, with a gentle Irish accent that Clare found attractive.

"I'm reading History," she said in answer to Clare's question. "Unfortunately I had glandular fever last year and I missed so much I've had to repeat my second year. I can't wait to get out into a house for my final year. I was so pleased when Mandy changed her mind and Mad offered me her place in your house."

Clare laughed. "Mad? Is that what you call her?"

Charlie looked a little embarrassed. "Well," she said, "we all do. It sort of suits her. She says she's going to call the new house The Madhouse."

"Is she indeed?" smiled Clare. "Sounds most appropriate to me."

"We all call it that already," admitted Charlie. "Don't we, Dean?" Dean was another one Clare hadn't met before. He was small, not more than five foot eight, with faded mousy hair and a rather feeble attempt at a beard, but his rather ordinary face was redeemed by his dark blue eyes. They were wide-set and shone with a luminosity that lit his whole face, and when he smiled, as he was doing now, he had an endearing quality that made Clare like him at once.

"Says she's going to have a house sign made," he laughed.

"He's very easy-going," Maddo had told her mother. "Never gets stressed about anything. Should be an easy guy to live with."

"Provided he does his share," murmured Clare.

"Yes, well, we'll all have to do that," agreed Madeleine. "I must say his room's usually a tip, but that won't matter if he keeps his door shut."

"And if he doesn't leave the same tip in the kitchen," said her mother.

"He won't." Madeleine spoke in the long-suffering voice she kept for simple-minded parents. "He'll be fine, OK?"

Clare looked across at the last of them. Ben was obviously older than the rest, not just in years, but in experience. Clare thought him attractive. He was a big man, tall and broad with powerful arms, and Clare supposed if she could have seen them, powerful legs as well. She knew from Madeleine that he was a rugby player, and looking at him she could well believe it. He was good-looking, too. Not in a classically handsome way, but with a strong face, with deep-set dark eyes and a firm mouth and chin. He wore his thick, dark hair long, tied back in a pony-tail, though wisps of it curled forward round his ears. Clare was only gradually coming to terms with men who wore their hair in pony-tails, she always felt that it was rather effeminate, but there was nothing effeminate about Ben Gardner. The strength of his face was echoed in the strength of his body, he seemed charged with a masculinity that Clare could almost touch. She wondered if Maddo was as aware of it as she was. There seemed to be nothing but friendship between them, and of course Maddo had Dan, but Clare knew if she had the choice which of those two she would choose. As she watched Ben talking with Nick, she was struck by the confidence with which he conversed, treating Nick with the ease of an equal. He seemed much older than the others, not only in age where the difference was not really that great, but in experience where he seemed to outstrip them by miles. Would the difference in age and experience make for difficulty in the house she wondered? Something told her that Ben's room would not be a tip, nor would he tolerate fools gladly. There would be no rivalry between him and Dean, Clare was fairly certain, but, she thought, there would be no close friendship either.

Ben caught her studying him, and raising his chin he let his eyes run over her in an equally appraising fashion, finally holding her own with a quizzical smile. He waited for her to speak and eventually she said, "Maddo was telling us that you're a keen rugby player." Even to herself it sounded trite and rather patronising, but it was the best she could think of on the instant.

However, Ben answered easily enough. "Yes, I play for the university."

"Is it a good team?"

"Good enough."

The conversation suddenly seemed to be going nowhere and Clare was glad when Madeleine broke in to demand of Ben what he was going to eat and she was able to turn and speak to Cirelle.

While they munched their way through jacket potatoes stuffed with a variety of fillings, Nicholas explained to them all how the finances of the house would be run.

"There should be no problems if we all stick to a few elementary, but unchangeable rules," he said, and went on to outline what these would be. Most of them were simple common sense and everyone readily agreed to them.

"I shall get these written down as a sort of contract, so that we all know where we stand, and that part will all be safely on a business footing. Your own house rules are up to you!"

They parted outside the pub with the general feeling that everything was going to work out perfectly. Madeleine walked back to the car to see her parents off.

"I'll be getting my men over some time in the next couple of weeks," Nick promised her. "The problem is being so far away."

"Only an hour."

"Yes, but it's an hour at each end of the working day. It is just one more thing to be organised. But don't worry, we'll sort it out. They seem a nice crowd," he added as he gave her a hug. "I should think you'll have a lot of fun living with them."

"Though goodness knows what their neighbours will think," Clare said as they drove away.

Nick shrugged. "They'll just have to put up with them," he said.

## Chapter Five

The news of the student house percolated gently through the Circle and was met with various emotions ranging from unabashed delight from Chantal Haven aged fifteen through the complete indifference of several of the working couples to the fear and indignation of Sheila Colby.

"It'll be great to have some real guys living here," Chantal enthused to her sister Annabel when they heard the news. "Anything's better than the Crosshills' crowd."

Annabel agreed, adding in the silence of her own mind, except for Scott, and aloud to Chantal, "Not that they'll look at you, you're far too young."

"I am not," Chantal shot back indignantly, "and anyway they won't know how old I am if I don't tell them."

"And if I don't."

"You won't," Chantal said sweetly.

"Oh, really? And what makes you so sure?" asked Annabel. She, of course, had Scott, so that a houseful of students conveniently across the road was of little real interest to her; but if they did turn out to be a good crowd, she didn't want Chantal tagging along. She, herself, was just finishing her lower sixth year at Belcaster High, and in October next year would, she hoped, be entering the world of university somewhere. Chantal hadn't even done her GCSEs.

"Because if you so much as breathe anything about me, I might just let slip to Mum about Scott Manders."

Annabel was momentarily stunned as Chantal slipped this thrust under her guard, but recovering swiftly and with amazing control over her voice she managed to say carelessly, "Who?"

Scott Manders was the centre of Annabel's life. She ate, drank and slept Scott Manders, and with the connivance of her best friend Avril, she managed to spend much of her out-of-school time with him. He had never been home to Dartmouth Circle of course. Scott wasn't the kind of guy you brought home to meet your mother. She wouldn't understand someone like Scott, and certainly, Annabel knew, she wouldn't approve of him. He'd dropped out of the sixth form at Crosshills to start his life for real; he was cool and he was streetwise with stubble hair, stubble chin and an earring in his ear and Annabel adored him.

She had met him one Friday evening as she struggled home from school with a weekend's homework in her bag. As she passed the entrance to the park a small gang of Crosshills lads emerged and Annabel's heart sank. It was the Crosshills Pack. She recognised them only too well with their leader, a stocky red-headed youth, called Martin Collins. Teasing and bullying Belcaster High School girls was one of their favourite pastimes, and his face lit up as he saw her. Immediately they were round her, penning her in against the park railings.

"Hallo, darlin'," grinned Martin. He shoved his face into hers. "I could really fancy you!"

Annabel jerked her head away, pressing against the railings at her back. Emboldened by their leader, the pack began to torment her.

"All right, darlin'?"

"Want to feel my cock, do yer?"

"Needs a mouthful of cock, eh Denzer?"

"Nice tits!" The one addressed as Denzer made a grab at Annabel's breast: "Give us a feel, then."

Again she jerked away, shouting, "Go away! Leave me alone! Get lost!" But she was surrounded. Her bag caught on the railings and ripped so that some of her work fell out. With a whoop of delight, Martin pounced on it.

"What a good little worker," he crowed, tossing files and papers in the air. "Mummy's good girl. Ain't you got no time for fun, darlin'? We could show you a good time." He grabbed at her again, pulling her blouse out of her skirt.

Annabel did her best to fight him off, kicking out and screaming abuse at him, but the street was empty and her tormentors, discarding her bag and its contents, moved in on her – in a pack.

Suddenly she was not alone. Someone erupted from an old Bedford van parked across the street. Another guy, a little older and very much bigger than any of the pack tormenting Annabel, charged across the road, and picking up Martin Collins as if he were a doll, tossed him against the railings. He crumpled into a heap and lay still. The result was a moment of frozen astonishment and then the pack began to back warily away.

"Pick it all up!" the newcomer bellowed, and to Annabel's amazement the Pack, the Crosshills Pack, of whom all the younger children and the Belcaster High girls were terrified, had scurried into the gutter and over the fence into the park retrieving folders and sheets of paper and text books, and had stacked them neatly on the pavement in front of her. Scott stood in a silence more terrible than his explosive wrath until they had finished, then he prodded the still crumpled form of the red-headed leader and said, "Take him with you and bugger off. And remember if I see one of you fuckers within a mile of this woman again, you'll lose your balls. Right? Now, fuck off!"

There were murmurs of, "Yeah, Scott. OK man. Didn't know she was one of yours," as they dragged their leader to his feet and shuffled off down the road.

Annabel, still bemused at the speed and the weirdness of the whole incident, watched them disappear round the corner, and then turned back to her rescuer. She saw Scott Manders and fell in love.

"They won't come near you no more," he said. "'Ere, pack up your stuff and I'll take you 'ome."

Still in a daze, Annabel shoved the pile of books back into her ripped duffel bag, and at a nod from Scott climbed into the passenger seat of the Bedford. He drove to the entrance of Dartmouth Circle without saying anything else, and when he pulled up outside her house, Annabel stared at him.

"How did you know where I live?" she asked.

"Seen you around," Scott replied. "What's your name?"

"Annabel," whispered Annabel. "Annabel Haven."

"See you around then, Bel," he said, and reaching across her he opened the passenger door.

For one wild moment Annabel thought he was going to kiss her; his face was so close she could feel his breath on her cheek, but he simply pulled the strap that served as a handle and the door swung open. For a moment more, Annabel sat unmoving, then she slid out on to the pavement, reaching back for her bag, and closed the door behind her. She looked back at Scott through the open window.

He grinned at her. "See you little girl," he said, and she heard a voice quite unlike her own say, "See you, Scott." He nodded as if in confirmation, and then letting in the clutch, he pulled away, round the Circle and out on to the main road.

Annabel stood staring, long after the van had disappeared. It was April, she was seventeen and Scott Manders had entered her life. When she finally turned and went into the house, it was as if she were a different person. Everything looked familiar, but smaller somehow, and of no substance or consequence. She went upstairs to her room and with great care mended her school bag. She had no intention of mentioning the incident to Mum or Chantal. Her own world was still spinning round her, but of one thing she was certain, they should know nothing of Scott. He was hers and to share him and what he had done for her, putting him up to public view, would diminish him.

She looked at herself in the mirror, trying to see herself as he might see her, but her face looked the same. Her dark shoulder-length hair was scraped back off her face, and knotted into a careless bundle at the nape of her neck. The short side-pieces had escaped and hung round her face in untidy spirals. She wasn't allowed to wear make-up at school, and her face looked washed out. She had large dark eyes, which she considered were nothing until she had outlined them in heavy eyeliner and mascara. She stared hard at her reflection. Scott had warned the Pack to stay away from "this woman". Annabel had never been referred to as a woman before – girl, of course, young lady, all too often in that patronising way so many adults have, but woman? No.

She said the word aloud, slowly, letting it sit on her tongue: "Woman." And although nothing had happened to her physically, Annabel felt quite different.

So it began, Annabel's secret life, the life where she was Bel and she rode round in a clapped-out Bedford van; when 'A' levels were forgotten or dismissed as irrelevant. Not for Scott the wasted hours spent labouring over essays.

"Get real, Bel!" he laughed. "What good is mouthing off about Macbeth going to do me? No profit in that! Me, I'm going to be a millionaire by the time I'm twenty-one." Three years to go – Scott was eighteen, now living alone in a bedsit at the Friary end of Belcaster, and Annabel envied him the place of his own, his privacy and his independence. There was no one to nag Scott about tidying his room, or tell him what time he must be in, or that he treated the place like a hotel. Scott could come and go as and when he chose, and the difference that Annabel perceived between their lifestyles seemed to her a gulf the size of the Grand Canyon. Scott was a man, with the freedom of a man, while she was still a schoolgirl and generally treated as such.

Nobody else noticed the transition of which she was so aware. Mum and Chantal treated her as they always had done, and Dad, when she saw him, gave her hugs and treats and called her his beautiful girl, but he did that to Chantal as well, so it meant nothing.

The only person who saw her as she now felt herself to be, was Scott, and the fact that their meetings were spontaneous and casual made them even more addictive. Annabel woke every morning with the agonising uncertainty of whether today might be a "Scott day". Nothing was ever arranged between them, Annabel knew that wouldn't do for Scott, so she never knew when he might put in an appearance. Sometimes she didn't see him for days and she would wander round the streets of Belcaster after school in the hope of bumping into him. She never did, and he never offered any explanation for these absences. He just turned up again another day and waited, parked in his old Bedford van round the corner from the High, and in the mass exodus at the end of the school day, she would slip into the passenger seat and they would be away.

Sometimes they drove to the broad beach at Belmouth, where Scott was teaching her to drive; other times to somewhere he had "a meet". Then she would sit in the van while he did whatever business he had to do, and then drive home. She never questioned what his business was. It was enough to be with him for an hour or two; to exchange passionate kisses in the back of the van before he brought her home, dropping her at the entrance to Dartmouth Circle. Then with carefully adjusted dress, Annabel would revert to Belcaster High School girl, sling her disreputable duffel bag over her shoulder and slouch her way into the Circle and home to another evening of homework and kitchen supper.

There were some evenings when Annabel's lips felt so bruised that she was sure they must be swollen and her mother must see, but Angela had problems of her own and greeted the girls absently when she got in.

It worried Annabel sometimes that Scott never did any more than kiss and fondle her. He would sometimes take her blouse and bra off and nuzzle against her, but he never seemed to want to do *It*. At first the thought that he might, and that she might not do it right, scared her, but as they met more and more often and he still didn't do It to her, or even try, this worried her much more. Maybe he didn't find her attractive after all. She knew that other girls at school had done *It*, at least they said they had, and discussed with stifled laughter the different attractions of various types of condom – raspberry-flavoured, ribbed, or studded for extra pleasure. Annabel would join in cautiously, anxious to be included so that she could learn from their experience. She bought three different types of condom from a machine in the public loos in the shopping centre, and in the privacy of her own room got one out of each packet to compare them. She blew into each to see its shape, and rubbed them against her cheek to see how they felt. She touched the flavoured one with the tip of her tongue and a faint raspberry taste lingered for a moment.

"How do you get them on, for goodness sake?" she wondered aloud. "Do I do it? Does Scott do it himself?" Again, she was in agony in case when the time came, as she fully intended it to, she got it all wrong and Scott turned away, or worse still, laughed at her inexperience. However, she always carried one packet with her now, and not knowing which were the best, she chose the one that promised "Exquisite sensation for both partners". She kept it in the little bag in which she carried her Tampax and waited in an torment of anticipation and fear, as she slipped between her secret life, her Scott life, and the mundane life of home and school.

Avril, her best friend since infant school, was her alibi. Annabel had to confide in her to cover her meetings with Scott, but not even to Avril did she tell all. She simply told her enough to enlist her excited aid, but she did not, could not, speak of how she changed the moment she was with Scott; how she became Bel, with Annabel sloughed off like a constricting skin. All Avril knew was that Annabel was meeting a guy Angela Haven would not approve of, and overcome with the romance of it all, Avril was prepared to cover for her friend.

"I went round to Avril's to discuss our history project," Annabel would say to her mother, when Bel had actually been learning to control high-speed skids on the wide sands of Belmouth Bay. "We have to get it done by half-term, so we're dividing the research and sharing our findings."

Angela Haven believed her, she had no reason not to. Most evenings she wasn't home from work herself until six-thirty. Annabel was careful about time and so far Angela did not know that the daughter she found dutifully sitting at the desk in her bedroom, struggling with an essay on Keats, had scurried into the house and up the stairs only moments before her own arrival.

Chantal continued to smile sweetly at her. "Scott Manders," she repeated. "I've seen you get into his van."

"Oh him," Annabel said carelessly, "he just gives me a lift home sometimes."

Chantal looked at her pityingly. "I'm not *stupid* you know," she said. "I do notice when you only get home minutes before Mum."

"I go round to Avril's. We're working together on our history project."

"Yeah?" Chantal was unimpressed. "And I'm Pamela Anderson. Get real, Anna, I know you're off with Scott Manders. He's your bit of rough." Chantal was not exactly sure what this phrase meant, but she'd heard it on TV as a description of someone who looked remarkably like Scott and it seemed appropriate. She was not prepared for Annabel's reaction. Annabel picked up the jug of water she had just put on the supper table and with great deliberation, poured it all over Chantal's head. Chantal spluttered and shrieked with rage as Annabel grasped her by her wet hair and pulled her head back so that she had to look up at her.

"If you say one word to Mum, or anyone else, about Scott Manders or anybody I choose to go about with, I will tell her about Mike Callow's New Year party."

It was a dire threat and Chantal put up her hands in mock surrender. "OK, OK, it was a joke. You keep quiet about New Year's Eve and I won't tell Mum."

"Won't tell Mum what?" asked Angela, struggling into the kitchen, her hands full of supermarket bags.

"That I upset a jug of water over her," Annabel said smoothly as she refilled the jug and set it on the kitchen table in readiness for the evening meal. Then she relieved her mother of some of the bags.

"How on earth did you come to do that?" Angela asked wearily, surveying Chantal's wet head and clothes and the puddle on the kitchen floor.

"She was cheeky," Annabel replied lightly. "She won't be again."

"You mean you did it on purpose?" Angela was exasperated. "For God's sake, Annabel, grow up. Chantal, go and get dry. I really have got enough to do without having to act as referee to you two. Annabel, put the potatoes on and then put this shopping away."

Annabel, pleased to have escaped further explanation, changed the water in the saucepan of potatoes she had peeled before school that morning and put them on the gas. Since Dad had left and Mum had started to work full-time again, the girls were much more involved with household chores.

It was odd without Dad; Annabel was still not really used to it and missed his company with a dull ache of longing. She didn't like living in an all-female household, or being a statistical "one-parent family", but at least she could escape from time to time, escape from being Annabel Haven, lower-sixth pupil at Belcaster High, and become Bel, who was now a competent high-speed driver, who had a packet of condoms in her duffel bag and intended to put them to use in the very near future.

"Did you know that number seven is going to be a student house, Mum?" asked Chantal at supper.

"Is it?" Angela was not that interested. "From the university?"

"Yes, most of them have to live out after their first year. It'll be great having some people our age in this geriatric place."

"Hardly your age, darling," Angela smiled. "You're only just fifteen, and if they're second and third years they'll probably be in their twenties."

Annabel smirked across at her sister at this remark, but Chantal was undeterred. "Even so," she said, "it'll be nice to have someone between Jon Forrester and old Mrs Peters."

"There's always Emma and Oliver Hooper," Annabel said evilly and drew a look of loathing from Chantal.

"I'm sure you'll get to know them, darling," Angela said, unaware of the undercurrent around her.

At that moment the phone rang and Chantal jumped up to answer it.

"If that's David," hissed Angela, "say I'm busy. I'll call him back."

"Hallo." Chantal's face broke into a wreath of smiles as she heard the caller speak, then without covering the mouthpiece to protect anyone's privacy, she called out clearly, "It isn't David, Mum. It's Dad."

Later that evening, when Chantal had gone to bed and Annabel was in her room wrestling with a French translation, Angela poured herself a large whisky and ginger and curled her legs into the big armchair. The phone call from Ian had unsettled her and the phone call from David had not come.

It was over six months now since Ian had left and the wound of his going had only the softest of scar tissue protecting it. The cold empty space he had left in her life, in the fabric of her being, was as cold and empty as the day he had gone to move in with Desirée. When she had heard the name of her husband's mistress, Angela always used that word with its sordid overtones in preference to "girlfriend" which sounded cosy and romantic, when she had heard Desirée's name it drew a harsh laugh.

"Desirée! The desired one!" she barked. "How appropriate!"

"She pronounces it Deseray," Ian replied calmly.

"I don't give a toss how she pronounces it," Angela snapped. "You certainly desire her."

"I love her," Ian said simply.

"Don't try and dignify your lust with that word," raged Angela. "What about me? You love me, or I thought you did. And the girls – your daughters, remember? You're supposed to love them, this will break their hearts." Even as she brought Annabel and Chantal into the argument, Angela despised herself for doing so. None of this was their fault, they shouldn't become pawns in the bitterness of the fight which was about to erupt.

I won't use them as weapons, she swore to herself then. They are going to be hurt enough by his leaving without being drawn into the crossfire. For Angela intended to fight for her husband and her marriage; to her their life together had been a happy one, and she had had no inkling that Ian had found someone else until he dropped the bombshell. The feeling of betrayal engulfed her, drowning her in pain. It had never once crossed her mind to question the business trips and late work at the office, her trust in Ian and his love for her and their daughters had been absolute. They had still shared a bed, and though on reflection they had made love less often of late, she had put that down to his tiredness from pressure of work; and when they had, it had been as tender and satisfying as ever. She responded to his touch as she always had, and he had been as aroused. After all, she thought bitterly, men can't fake it.

She had no warning, no premonition that her life was about to collapse in jagged shards about her feet. Ian had simply said one day, "I have to tell you I'm moving out."

Angela stared at him, uncomprehending. "Moving out?" she echoed.

"Yes. I've found someone else." And that was that.

He moved out the same day, saying, "A quick, clean cut is best, easiest for everyone." And his quick, clean cut sliced through Angela's inner being. She had no protection against such a cut, for up till now she hadn't realised she needed one.

He waited only to see the girls when they came home from school, to try to explain why he was going. Annabel greeted the news with a blank stare of total incomprehension, and Chantal had shrieked in horror and rushed from the room to find her mother. Then he picked up the case he had already packed, dumped it into the boot of his car and drove off, leaving his stricken wife and daughters to comfort each other as best they could.

Gradually, over the months, the girls had adapted to his absence, each in her own way. Life continued for them as near to how it always had been as Angela could manage, and the girls came to terms with only having a weekend father. Outwardly, Chantal slowly settled back into her normal self, noisy, untidy, slapdash with her school work. The only outward signs of her inner turbulence were that she was much more argumentative and truculent than she had been, and occasionally when things went wrong, she dissolved into tears.

Annabel seemed to have become more aloof; she was working hard, as far as Angela could tell, but she no longer confided in her mother the trivial happenings of her daily round as she had used to do. She had withdrawn into herself behind an invisible wall. Outwardly, she was perfectly polite, well-behaved and hard-working, but lately some part of her had become private.

Now, Ian had phoned to say he wanted to discuss things. Would she have dinner with him tomorrow evening?

"No!" Angela had said fiercely, while aching to go and despising herself for that ache.

"A drink then," he persisted. "So we can relax a little and talk things over in a civilised manner."

I don't bloody feel civilised, Angela had raged to herself, but she had agreed to the drink. She didn't feel at all civilised and she was afraid; afraid of what he was going to say; afraid that the separation was going to become permanent with the official seal of divorce, but it would be worse not to see him. And David hadn't phoned as he'd promised.

David, recently encountered, had given Angela back a touch of self-respect. Clearly he admired her and the admiration in his eyes was balm to her soul. He had asked her to go away with him for a weekend and was supposed to ring her this evening for her answer. She still wasn't certain of that answer, but it piqued her a little that he hadn't phoned to find out. After Ian's phone call, she was even less sure of what her reply would be.

Angela sighed and downed the last of her whisky. Tomorrow she would see Ian and talk. There were things *she* wanted to talk about, too. Annabel, for instance. She was really worried about Annabel. It seemed to Angela that she was nursing some secret to herself. Often, although she was there physically, her mind kept slipping away.

I'll tackle her in the morning, Angela resolved. It's Saturday, so neither of us has to rush off anywhere, then maybe I'll have something more definite to tell Ian.

Her chance came next morning as they lingered over their breakfast together. Chantal had not yet put in an appearance and Angela decided to grasp the opportunity while it was there. She looked across at Annabel, whose eyes were unfocused, somewhere in the middle distance.

"Penny for them," she said casually. "You're miles away, darling. Problems?" Keep it light she adjured herself, keep it comfortable and easy.

"Sorry, Mum," said Bel, slipping back into Annabel's skin. "I was thinking about my history project."

"Were you now?" Angela was not convinced and didn't sound it.

"Really, I'm meeting Avril this morning to go over what we've got." That at least was true because what "they" had got was whatever Avril had got. Annabel had nothing to contribute yet.

"I see. Fine. It's just that you used to discuss your work with me too, and I don't even know what your project is this time."

"The effect of the First World War on the lives of women in the early nineteen-twenties," Annabel said. She gathered up her plate and mug and put them into the waiting dishwasher. "I must go now," she said. "I'm sorry if I haven't discussed it with you, Mum, but you aren't always there like you used to be."

Seeing the pain on her mother's face that this comment had caused, Annabel gave her an awkward half-hug and said, "I know it's not your fault, Mum. I know you have to work full-time now Dad's gone. You always look so tired when you come home, I don't like to trouble you."

"Never too tired to talk to you," Angela said. "We can always talk, you know, like we used to." She kept her voice gentle, as if dealing with a frightened animal. "I like to be involved in what you're doing, and if you do have a problem, any problem, I'm always here for you."

"I know that, Mum. I'll show you my project tonight if you like," Annabel promised, "when I'm really up to date with Avril." When I've at least a few notes on the subject, she thought.

She gathered her books into her bag and closed the front door behind her. Angela watched her from the living-room window, saw her slouch her way across the Circle and out to the main road. She sighed and poured herself another cup of coffee, feeling she had got nowhere, had indeed driven the wedge of silence deeper between them. Far from calming her fears, Annabel had excited them further. There had been something furtive in the way her eyes had slid from her mother's gaze and Angela was even more certain now that there was something wrong in Annabel's life, that she had a problem that she was keeping to herself, or at least the rapport they had always had was gone.

Maybe she blames me for Ian leaving, thought Angela for only the thousandth time. Maybe she's right, maybe it was my fault that he left. They always say it takes two to tango, but I didn't even know I was dancing.

Annabel turned the corner out of Dartmouth Circle. She scanned the main road for any sign of the Bedford van, and was none she trudged on to Avril's and the inev-
here was going to be when Avril discovered that
, had done none of the reading research she had

There was a toot behind her and the Bedford drew up at her side.

With a burst of guilty relief, Annabel put off the evil hour with Avril, and Bel climbed swiftly into the passenger seat before Scott accelerated into the Saturday-morning traffic.

*Chapter Six*

Oliver Hooper lay in bed in the downstairs bedroom of his father's house, staring at the cracks spreading like river deltas in the ceiling. He was fed up. School holidays should be spent at home or with his mates, not here in boring Dartmouth Circle in boring Belcaster with that bitch Annie going on at him all the time. Dad was out all day at work, Annie worked part-time and there was nothing to do and no one to do it with. He could hardly admit it to himself, but he found he actually missed his sister, Emma. It was never quite as bad at Dartmouth Circle when she was there. She seemed to get on all right with Annie and created a buffer zone around Oliver. But Emma was off in France on a school trip; she wouldn't be back for two weeks and he was stuck here.

Oliver didn't allow himself to dwell too much on why he wasn't at home with Mum for the Easter holidays, it made him too angry. She had gone away as well, to Tenerife, with her new man, Oslo. How could he be called Oslo, for God's sakes? Oslo was a bloody town in Norway! However, his name was Oslo, Oslo de Quinn and the stupidity of it made Oliver loathe the man even more.

"I'm sorry it's during the holidays, darling," Lynne Hooper had said, "but that's the time of Oslo's timeshare, so we have to go then."

*He* has to go then, Oliver raged inwardly. You don't have to bloody go at all!

"Why can't I come too?" Oliver demanded. "You said it was a villa, there must be room for me."

"Yes, it is a villa, and I'm sure you'll be able to come another time, darling, you and Emma, but this time Oslo's invited some other friends. Come on now, Ollie" – Oliver hated it when she called him Ollie, he'd stopped being Ollie when he started at prep school – "Come on now, Ollie, it's only for two weeks, and you'll be fine at Dad's."

Lynne didn't tell him that she had already asked Oslo to take him too, but had met with a direct refusal. She was not sure enough yet of Oslo and the continuance of their relationship to stand against him, and had given in.

"I'm sorry Lynne, but it's not possible this time," Oslo said firmly. "I have already invited some business associates and their wives to join us, it would be no place for Oliver, he would be bored." He didn't add, "And in the way," which is what he was thinking, but he softened his words by taking her in his arms and saying, "I'm afraid Oliver is going to have to get used to sharing you, my darling. He's going to have to get used to you having a life of your own."

Lynne returned Oslo's kisses and allowed the guilt she felt about deserting Oliver during his Easter holidays to be smoothed away by Oslo's persuasion, culminating in a murmured reminder that, "A boy needs to spend time with his father, it's important their relationship is strong."

Lynne agreed. She thought it would indeed be good for Oliver to spend some real time with his father, not just the occasional weekend. Let Stephen take some responsibility for him for a change, instead of always turning up like the good guy in the white hat, being the one who provided presents and treats and days out, who never had to nag about prep, or bedtimes or TV programmes or games kit. Lynne's indignation began to build. Let that bitch Annie deal with the soggy, filthy, rugby kit that smelled so high it almost crawled out of the kit bag by itself, except that it would be holidays and there wouldn't be any rugby kit, or any kit at all for that matter. Typical of Annie to get out of everything.

Encased in Oslo's persuasive reasoning and her own indignant righteousness, Lynne had smothered the last of her guilt, dropped Oliver off in Dartmouth Circle and flown off to Tenerife with a clear conscience.

"Goodbye, darling." She hugged him at the gate. "I won't come in, I'm running behind time" – not true and he knew it – "have a great time with Dad. I'll give you a ring on Saturday."

"I've only been here for half a day and I'm already fed up," he thought angrily. Then he brightened as he remembered that Dad had promised him this afternoon together at the County Cricket Ground to watch the opening match of the season, but even so he didn't rush to get up, there was too much morning to get through on his own. There was no one in the Circle remotely near his age, except on occasion Peter Callow and that stuck-up madam, Chantal Haven.

The thought of Chantal made him pull a face. There she'd been at the Callows' party at New Year, posing on, so cool yeah? With a glass of wine in her hand and puffing at a cigarillo thing. Oliver could see she didn't like the cigar because she never inhaled. He recognised the trick because it was one of his own when the need to smoke at school arose.

Chantal simply took smoke into her mouth and blew it out again, and twice he heard her coughing when she'd done it. Some coolth!

He'd offered to get her another drink and she, looking at him as if he were something the cat had brought in, shrugged her shoulders and handed him her glass. With another puff at the cigarillo, she drawled, "If you like, thanks."

Oliver had smiled and taken her glass to the kitchen where he half filled it with wine and then topped it up with vodka. When he took it back to her, she was talking to Max Davies, the son of the doctors who lived at number twelve. Oliver didn't know him very well, but handed Chantal her drink and stayed with them. Chantal accepted the drink without a thank you and took a large swig. She looked across at Oliver.

"Is this a different wine?" she asked.

Oliver shrugged. "Don't know," he said. "Maybe. It came from one of the open bottles in the kitchen."

Oliver's sister, Emma, and Peter Callow joined them and Max gently detached himself from the group, leaving the four youngsters together.

Chantal scowled at the newcomers. "Now look what you've done. He's gone. He didn't want to be with a bunch of kids; just when I'd got him interested!"

"Interested? Interested in what?" Oliver laughed derisively. "You? He's at least ten years older than you!"

"That's nothing these days," remarked Chantal airily, downing the rest of her drink. "I always go for the older man."

"You go for any man," muttered Emma.

Chantal glanced at her. "And men seem to find me attractive too," she said as if she hadn't heard Emma's remark. "They might go for you, too," she added, "if only you did something with your hair and got rid of your zits."

Emma went scarlet. The fact that she had bad acne mortified her, she already knew with a desperate certainty that no one could possibly find her attractive with spots on her face, and in a crowd, she often retreated into herself, rejecting herself before anyone else could reject her.

Seeing her flush, Oliver suddenly felt very protective of his sister. It was out of order for someone like Chantal to make remarks like that. He said stoutly, "Well. I think you look great, don't you, Peter?"

Peter Callow rose to the occasion. "Yes, I do," he said. "I was, like, going to say let's go in the disco." He took Emma's hand and pulled her towards the music which blasted up the stairs from the garage which had become a makeshift disco.

"Do you want to go down the disco?" Oliver asked Chantal.

"No," Chantal replied shortly, "but you can get me another drink if you like."

"OK," Oliver said easily. "Same again?" He was soon back with another glass of wine, spiked as before, and a glass of beer for himself. "Here you go," he said, meeting her eye.

At that moment, Peter and Emma reappeared. "Hopeless down there," Peter said. "Can't move and the music's crap. Me and Em's going to grab a few beers and go up to my room and watch a video. I've got *Vindicator*. Coming?"

Oliver shrugged. "It's a good movie. Coming, Chantal?"

Chantal glanced round the room. Max Davies was talking to some woman she didn't know, and there was no one else to take her interest. For a moment, the room seemed to slip out of focus, but Chantal blinked and all was clear again.

Gripping her glass tightly she said, "May as well." *Vindicator* was indeed a good film. Her mother hadn't let her see it at the cinema as it was an 18. She followed the others unsteadily to the stairs. As they passed the kitchen, Oliver picked up a six-pack of lagers and a newly opened bottle of wine, and they scurried up to Peter's bedroom where the TV and video sets stood in the corner.

"You're lucky to have your own TV and video," Emma said enviously.

"Christmas present," answered Peter, "from Dad, to keep here. No chairs I'm afraid." He pulled his duvet on to the floor. "Room for two on the bed and two here on the floor." He sank on to the duvet and pulled one of the rings on the lager. "Beer, Em?"

The others made themselves comfortable while Peter put the cassette into the video.

Chantal sat on the bed and leaned back against the wall. Oliver could see her tits outlined against the white of her shirt. He wondered what it would be like to feel them, how they would feel in his hands, pressed under his fingers. He knew from guys at school, that feeling girls' tits was exciting, made you feel powerful. Suddenly Oliver wanted to try – to see if they were right. Chantal had her eyes shut. The title music of *Vindicator* blared out. Oliver looked at Chantal's legs, encased in skin-tight jeans, and wondered what the skin on her thighs would feel like. He felt himself grow hot and he grabbed at a can of lager, pulled the ring, took a long pull, almost choking.

Emma and Peter were leaning against the bed wrapped in the duvet, eyes glued to the TV screen. Chantal still leaned against the wall, her eyes closed, wishing the room wouldn't spin and that the music wasn't so loud.

"Drink?" suggested Oliver to Chantal, offering the wine bottle.

"Girls relax when they've had a drink or two," Drew Elliott at school had told him. "Everything's much easier then."

Downstairs Oliver had spiked her drink because he was angry; angry with her stuck-up bloody superior pose, the way she'd treated him, the way she spoke to Emma. He'd wanted to take her down a peg or two, to show her she wasn't so bloody clever, no better than him or Emma or Peter, that she was just a posy kid. Now it was different, she didn't look like a dressed-up kid and he, Oliver, didn't feel like a kid either. He ached between the legs, he wanted to feel her tits and for her to take off her jeans. He looked down at his sister and Peter, staring at the screen, caught up in the terror of the *Vindicator*, Emma's hand already pressed against her teeth in horror, and he saw them both as kids – watching sex and violence, but having no feeling of it inside them, within their beings. Oliver felt both, and as he looked down at them gripped by the film, he saw them as children and knew that he was not. So, he offered Chantal more drink, not from anger any more, not to spite her, or to make a fool of her, but because he thought it might relax her and he wanted to take advantage of that relaxation.

Chantal opened her eyes and the world swung crazily past her. Oliver was holding out a bottle of wine towards the glass she still held clutched in her hand.

"I feel funny," she slurred. "Peculiar. Perhaps I'm drunk. D'you think I'm drunk, Oliver?"

"Nah." Oliver shook his head. "You've only had a couple of glasses of wine. Have some more, it'll make you feel better." He settled himself beside her, legs across the bed, back to the wall, and filled her glass up before setting the bottle on the bed-side table and taking a pull at his lager. He could feel the heat of her body against his, the heat of his own body burning from the heat of hers. He could feel himself grown hard and aching. He swallowed more beer.

"Drink up," he said, and obediently Chantal emptied her glass.

"Hot," she remarked vaguely. "Hot in here."

It was the opening Oliver had needed, been waiting for, offered to him unasked.

"Yeah," he agreed. "Take your shirt off."

As a suggestion, it lacked finesse and subtlety, but Chantal was past the subtle stage. She looked at him blearily. "Take my shirt off?" she repeated. "Too difficult." Her words ran into each other.

"I'll help." Oliver reached over and began to unbutton the shirt.

She pushed him away angrily. "I can do it," she said, enunciating her words carefully, "I can do it for myself." With great deliberation she undid and removed her shirt, pulling it down over her shoulders and off her arms, one at a time, until she had it in her hands. With a giggle she draped it over Oliver's head, but not before he had seen the rounded curves of her breasts pushing up from the lace cup of her bra. He pulled the shirt off his head and looked again. Chantal had closed her eyes again and was leaning her back against the coolness of the wall. Oliver reached out with both hands and touched the skin below the bra. He saw it quiver and the feeling of power, promised by Drew Elliott, flooded through him. He drew his hands upward and grasped the rounded flesh, pushing the lace of the bra downwards and squeezing the emerging breasts between his fingers. For a moment, he stared at the taut nipples, like ripe raspberries, jutting and inviting. He needed now to do more than feel and press – he bent his head to taste…and then, as far as Oliver was concerned, it all went pear-shaped.

Behind him the door opened and Mike Callow had appeared. Chantal, who had ignored Oliver's fumblings and graspings in an effort to fight the rising waves of nausea, gave up the fight and was suddenly and violently sick, all over Oliver's head, all over her exposed tits, all over Peter's bed, all over Emma and Peter, still unaware of anything except the Vindicator stalking the red-light district of Chicago.

Mr Callow had been pretty good about it really. He'd pulled Oliver unceremoniously off the bed, grabbed a towel from the rail and wrapping it round Chantal, had half-carried her into the bathroom, run a bath and told her to get into it. He went back into the bedroom and switched on the main lights.

"What the bloody hell do you think you're playing at, Oliver Hooper?" he demanded, as Oliver scrabbled with a pillowcase to get some of the vomit from out of his hair and the back of his neck. "Peter," he bellowed at his own son. "Turn off that bloody video and go into my shower and get cleaned up. Emma, go into the bathroom with Chantal. See she's OK and get clean yourself. Oliver, go with Peter. You'll have to lend him a shirt, Peter. Then get back in here and clean this room up. Strip the bed and put all the dirty stuff in the bathroom for now." He grabbed Oliver by one vomit-covered shoulder. "And if you don't want your parents to hear about this, you be back here tomorrow morning, eleven o'clock, to get this room properly cleaned. When you're washed and clean yourself, go home. I want no arguments or explanations tonight."

Mike Callow had been as good as his word. None of the various parents, Hoopers or Havens, heard a whisper of what had happened that night. Angela, in no mood for New Year celebrations, had gone home early. Steve and Annie had been to a

73

different New Year's Eve party and when they finally awoke on New Year's Day, they were nursing their own hangovers, and expressed only a passing interest in Oliver and Emma's evening.

Oliver admitted to Emma that he had spiked Chantal's drinks because she had been spiteful to Emma, and Emma, grateful for her elder brother's championship, had agreed that the incident should never be mentioned again. Indeed, she was a little hazy herself as to what had actually happened, as she had consumed several cans of beer, which would have been forbidden at home.

The following morning Oliver had arrived at Mike's at eleven o'clock, and he and Peter had scrubbed the floor and the mattress of Peter's bed. They had put the sheets and the duvet cover into the washing machine, they had hung the duvet and the pillows out to air. They spent the rest of the morning helping to clear up the party. Of Chantal Haven there was no sign. She had not been summoned to clear up the mess. Emma told him that Chantal had gone home in one of Mike's shirts over a pair of his jogging pants. Her clothes went home in a plastic bag.

"She was going to tell her mother someone spilled beer all over her and put them into the washer herself, so her mum wouldn't know it was sick and not beer."

Since that day, Chantal had given no sign that she even knew Oliver existed. If they did chance to meet, she passed him with her head in the air, ignoring him with a haughty indifference that infuriated him. They didn't often meet of course, because Oliver didn't really live in the Circle, but now as he lay on his bed, he wondered what would happen if he bumped into her this time. As there had been no repercussions from any direction, Oliver assumed that Chantal, too, had kept her mouth shut about that evening, and he found it gave him a strange feeling of power to know something about her of which she was ashamed. When the guys at school were discussing women these days, Oliver said nothing except to Drew Elliott; and to him he simply said, "You were right, Drew, it's great to have power."

When Annie had called him for the third time to get up and come up for breakfast, Oliver crawled off the bed and dragging on his T-shirt and jeans, went upstairs.

"Hurry up, Oliver, do," Annie snapped as he walked into the kitchen. "I want to get the kitchen cleared before I go to work."

Oliver pulled open a packet of Shreddies and piling them to overflowing in a bowl, slurped milk over them, splashing some on to the table. Annie's lips tightened, but she managed to bite back a retort and said instead, "There's a note for you from your dad. He had to leave early." She passed across a piece of folded paper. With a mouthful of Shreddies, Oliver unfolded the paper and reading it threw down his spoon in disgust.

"That's not fair," he muttered. "He promised."

"He says to tell you he's very sorry," Annie began. "He got a call from work this morning, some crisis or other. He said to tell you he'd take you on Saturday, instead."

Oliver pushed his unfinished cereal away. "Doesn't matter," he shrugged. "I didn't really want to go anyway." He picked up the note and ripping it across threw the pieces back on to the table.

"Oliver," began Annie, "He's very sorry…"

"Forget it," snapped Oliver. "I'm going out!"

"Where are you going?"

"Out."

"But you haven't finished your breakfast…" but Annie was speaking to an empty room, thudding feet on the stairs and a slamming front door.

"Bloody boy," she expostulated through clenched teeth, and sweeping the unfinished Shreddies into the dog bowl, she rammed the bowl into the waiting dishwasher and set it off.

Annie had never found either of her husband, Steve's, children easy. Emma wasn't too bad; with Emma she had an uneasy truce, Emma didn't actually set out to be awkward, but Oliver made her life as difficult as he could. Annie knew that, encouraged by his mother, Oliver blamed her for the separation and divorce of his parents. He believed that Annie had entered an idyllic marriage, where all was sweetness and light, and had ensnared his father, luring him away from his family. Annie knew it wasn't like that. Annie knew, because Steve had told her, that his life with Lynne had been hell on wheels. Unending rows and tears and recrimination for imagined slights; all because he was working every hour God sent to establish his business.

"You've no time for me and the children!" Lynne cried. "You leave me to cope with everything."

"No time for you and the children?" bellowed Stephen. "Why the hell do you think I'm working myself into an early grave if it's not for you?" The anger and the bitterness went both ways and ran deep.

Steve ran his own security firm, Hooper Security Consultancy, and like most men running their own businesses with all their financial eggs, plus many belonging to the bank, in one basket, he worked extremely long hours and took little time off. Business was steady rather than buoyant, but by working very hard he managed a comfortable living and was able to send his children to independent schools. Oliver was now in his first year at Chapmans, a large senior school outside Belcaster, and Emma had another year at Beechlands before she moved on to Belcaster High. The strain on his marriage, however, had become almost unbearable, Lynne wanted the lifestyle his dedication produced, but resented the dedication needed to achieve it. Thus it was that when Steve met Annie, a store detective, at a meeting with Harper and Hill, the big department store in town whose account he was trying to win, he was instantly attracted by her calm, quiet manner, so different from Lynne's bitter moaning.

After the meeting, he took her out to lunch, followed soon after by dinner and the quiet sanctuary of her flat. Steve had found himself a haven of peace, and it was a haven of peace to which he returned more and more often until he decided to make the break and stay for good.

The ensuing divorce proceedings had been bitter and vicious. Oliver and Emma ceased to be the children of loving parents, and became their pawns, moved across the chessboard of the divorce at the whim of either parent, used as weapons to wound and hurt. At the ages of five and seven, Emma and Oliver's world disintegrated round their ears and they, understanding nothing except that everything was wrong, were pulled and pushed about in a war of attrition.

Once everything was finalised, life settled down to some sort of pattern. They lived with Lynne, but visited Steve and Annie at weekends and in the school holidays. Recently though, there had been hints from Lynne that she thought the children ought to see more of their father.

"Oliver needs a father figure at his age," she would say, "and Emma was always Daddy's girl."

The present arrangement had suited Annie well enough, as she agreed the children needed to see their father. She had never wanted children of her own, but was prepared to do her best by Steve's. Not too difficult when they were younger, but the last few visits had not been at all easy, and she wasn't looking forward to Oliver's extended stay these holidays.

She knew he was disappointed that his dad had had to cancel their proposed afternoon at the County Ground watching Belshire play Essex, but it couldn't be helped. Work had to come first if you ran your own business, and Oliver, at rising fifteen, ought to recognise the fact. There was nothing to stop him from going to the cricket on his own if he wanted to; Annie had been about to offer him the money for his ticket when he had walked out.

She sighed, and having given the kitchen surfaces a quick wipe, picked up her bag and went out. She was already running late, not only because of Oliver, but because Mrs Colby from number six had been on the phone, something to do with students moving in to number seven. Mrs Colby had started off the rigmarole in great detail, but Annie had had to cut her short.

"I'm very sorry, Mrs Colby," she said, "but I'm late for work. Could we discuss this some other time?"

"Of course, Mrs Hooper," Sheila Colby said. "I quite understand. But what I'm telling you is quite important, if I could just pop over and see you and your husband some time..."

"Yes, any time," Annie agreed. "Just call round. I must dash now. Bye." With luck, Steve would be home when she did come and he could deal with her. Annie had little to do with any of her neighbours, but Sheila Colby she had long ago decided should be actively avoided.

She pulled the front door closed behind her, wondering as she did so whether Oliver had his key. Deciding that quite frankly she didn't care, she got into her car and drove to work.

From a seat in the gardens, Oliver watched her go. His anger and resentment still burned hot, and his toes curled up with rage. He hadn't got his key, and now he was shut out with no money and nothing to do all day. He heard voices across the Circle and saw Mrs Colby coming out to her car. Its front door was open, and having dumped her basket and handbag on the front seat, she went back indoors, still calling to someone inside.

Oliver got up and ambled across the Circle towards the car. The handbag was lying, unzipped, on the front seat and Oliver could see a purse stuck into the top. He approached the car casually, but his eyes flicked round the Circle and up to overlooking windows. In the next house, he caught sight of Mrs Jarvis, sitting in her window. She waved to him and he raised a hand in reply.

Christ! he thought, that was a close one. He hadn't actually extended his hand to snatch the purse, but if he had, she would have seen him. With his heart pounding he sauntered on to number ten, as if he'd always been headed there, and ringing the doorbell, asked Mike Callow if Peter was there.

"No," Mike answered shortly. "Sorry, Oliver, not expecting him this week."

As the door closed on him, Oliver turned on his heel and set off into town, slouching along the streets and peering into shop windows. He wanted new trainers, but Mum had told him to ask Dad. There were some in a basket outside a shoe shop and he stopped to look at them. They were cheap ones, not the expensive Nikes he wanted. As he stood looking at them, a woman with three small children, one in a baby buggy and the other two holding on to the handles, stopped beside him. The woman's handbag dangled from the back of the buggy. She peered into the basket of trainers and pulled one out.

"Come here, Nigel," she was saying, "let's see if these fit you. Put your foot up here." As she held the trainers against her son's foot, her daughter began demanding trainers too. Her attention was entirely taken up with the two of them as the little girl reached into the basket for herself and had to be restrained.

Oliver didn't hesitate. Smoothly he unhooked the handbag from the buggy's handle, slid it under his jacket and moved unhurriedly away. Once round the corner he legged it down a side street and dived into a gents' toilet. He went into one of the cubicles, and collapsed on to the toilet seat. His heart was pounding with exhilaration and he wanted to laugh aloud. He felt the usual surge of power sweep through him as he sat gripping the bag in his hands. It had been so easy.

Quickly he rifled the contents of the bag. There was a purse containing £55 in folding money and some silver and a bank debit card. He was about to throw this away as useless without the pin number, when he saw a diary. He thumbed through it and there, among the telephone numbers was one Cassie Carde 0743. Clearly not a phone number. God, this woman – he glanced at the name on the card, Mrs D. Hawkins – this Mrs Hawkins was as stupid as his mother, who had hidden her pin number in much the same way.

Oliver stuffed the cash into one pocket of his jeans and the card into another; then checking that there was no one else in the toilets, he emerged from the cubicle, wiped the handbag with a paper towel, dropped it into the bin and sauntered out into the sunshine.

Once back into the city centre, he went to a bank cash point and inserted the card. As the machine swallowed the card, Oliver felt a quick flash of panic. Surely the woman couldn't have reported the card stolen yet. Even so, Oliver kept a wary eye on the door of the bank, ready to run if anyone came out demanding to know where he'd got the card. Nobody did. He tapped in the Cassie Carde number. The machine accepted it. He asked for a balance. One hundred and ten pounds. Knowing that cards sometimes had a limit of a hundred pounds on them and not wanting to attract attention, Oliver drew out a hundred pounds and adding it to the cash in his pocket, continued on his way. Safely round the corner, he again felt the power course through him. It had been so easy. So fucking easy. He wanted to shout to the world what he had done, but he managed to contain his exhilaration and set off to find a sports shop that sold Nike trainers.

That evening Steve Hooper noticed the expensive trainers his son was wearing. "Those are new, aren't they?" he enquired. "Where did you get the money for those?"

Oliver looked up at him, ready for the question and ready with the answer. "Mum said to get some new trainers," he said. "She said you'd buy them for me. I saw these in a sale today, so I bought them before someone else did. Good value, eh? Half price!" His eyes met his father's, smiling easily as he lied. "I used the pocket money Mum gave me, I knew you'd pay me back."

"How much do I owe you?" asked Steve, reaching for his wallet.

"They were £99.99, reduced to £50," Oliver replied. He had decided on the amount he would ask for after some careful thought. It would be no good going for the full amount, Dad would know Mum hadn't given him £100 pocket money. They were top-of-the-range trainers, so their being in a sale was the way round that. "They were good value, weren't they?" he repeated.

"Even so, Oliver, they were too expensive really. Still, just this once, eh?" His father pulled out five ten-pound notes from his wallet and handed them over, saying as he did so, "Sorry I couldn't make the cricket today, Ollie. We will do before you go, I promise."

"Doesn't matter, Dad," Oliver said generously and putting his hand into his pocket he produced a penny. "Here's your change, the trainers were only £49.99, I wouldn't want to do you out of a penny."

*Chapter Seven*

Shirley and David Redwood turned off the motorway and took the main road into Belcaster. They were both tired as it had been a long journey, and they had been having interrupted nights ever since they had been in their daughter's home.

"It'll be nice to get home," Shirley said. "I can't wait for a cup of tea."

"I wonder how the garden will be," David mused. "Everything grows so fast at this time of year."

Shirley smiled. She knew David hated to be away from his garden for very long at any time of the year, but this trip away had been special. They had gone to be with their daughter, Melanie, for the birth of her second child, their new grand-daughter, Suzanne. However, they had stayed on longer than they had originally intended, to help with Todd, their three-year-old grandson, who, finding that a baby sister was a vastly overrated commodity, had been demanding all the attention that, until her arrival, had naturally been his.

"Do you think she'll cope all right?" Shirley wondered for the hundredth time. "It isn't easy at the best of times, but she does seem to be having difficulty...."

"She'll be fine," David reassured her as he been doing for days. "She's much stronger now, she'll be fine."

"Yes, physically she is," Shirley agreed, "but it's her mental state I'm worried about. I think it's postnatal depression. She doesn't seem to have any energy for anything, even looking after Suzanne."

"She'll soon get over her baby blues," David said cheerfully. "She'll have to now that we're not there to rally round. Peter gets home quite early some days, so he can deal with Todd at bedtime."

Shirley wasn't convinced, but she said no more. She knew David tended to dismiss "baby blues" as he called them, as all in the mind. It was not that he was unsympathetic towards his daughter, but he really believed that all Melanie had to do was pull herself together and everything would be fine. Shirley wished she could believe it too, but she was sure this was something deeper than just simple tiredness. She would keep in close touch with Melanie and see how things went. If necessary she'd have to go back, but for a few days it would be bliss just to be at home and slip back into their quiet, retired routine.

David swung the car into the Circle and pulled up on to their own drive. There was a red van parked on the drive of number seven with the words Nicholas Richmond, General Builder, on the side, and a man was puttying new panes of glass into the open front door.

"Look at that," said David. "Don't say Ned's having some work done on the house at last."

"The For Sale board has gone," Shirley pointed out. "David, do you think he's finally sold?"

"Don't know. I'll ask this chap." David got out of the car and spoke to the man mending the door.

"Hallo," he said, "has this place been sold?"

"Think so, mate. My boss has bought it."

"Oh, I see. Is that...?" David glanced again at the name on the van, "Mr Richmond, the builder?"

"That's right."

"Is he here, now I mean?"

"No, not today. Should be over tomorrow with the chippies."

"Chippies?"

"Carpenters, to do the stud partitioning."

"I see, well, thanks. I'll keep an eye out for him tomorrow. I'd like to meet him."

"Yeah, well, I'll tell him if I see him," said the man and turned his attention back to his glazing.

David collected their suitcases from the car and having carried them into the house and upstairs for his wife to unpack, he wandered out into his beloved garden to see how everything had fared in his absence, and was happily employed until Shirley rapped on the window, and held up a mug of tea to encourage him indoors.

When he went in, he found she had sorted the heap of post that awaited them into two piles, and he sat skimming through his pile as he drank his tea.

"There's a very odd note here from Sheila," Shirley said.

David looked up from his own post. "Sheila?"

"Sheila Colby."

"Hmm." David was not interested. He didn't like the woman, and couldn't imagine how Gerald put up with her.

"She says to phone her the moment we get back as she has some important news. What on earth can that be?"

David shrugged: "Can't imagine. Just her usual busybodying I expect. Ring her if you want to know."

"Not this evening," Shirley said firmly. "I'm too tired to cope with Sheila Colby today. If I ring her now I'll never get her off the phone. The trouble is, if she once sees we're back, she'll ring me." Shirley put down her mug with sudden decision. "Give me the car keys," she said.

David handed them over. "Where are you going?" he asked.

"To put the car in the garage," Shirley answered. "There's just a chance that she hasn't seen it yet, then she won't know we're back. I really don't feel up to her today."

Shirley hurried down to the car, drove it into the garage and hauled the door closed behind her. There had been no car parked outside number six, so perhaps Sheila was out and Shirley's strategy would buy her an evening's peace. She even considered taking the phone off the hook, but decided against it in case Melanie wanted to ring.

Whether Sheila did not realise the Redwoods were home, or whether she herself was home too late to call, they were left in peace that evening. There were no phone calls at all, so Melanie must be coping as well. Shirley and David had the first night's unbroken sleep they had had for more than three weeks, and when they woke in the morning, Shirley felt greatly restored and looked forward to getting back to her normal life.

After breakfast, she rang Mary Jarvis. They were not close friends, but they were both volunteers at St Joe's drop-in day centre, and Shirley wanted to let Mary know that she was back.

"Has Sheila got hold of you yet?" Mary asked when they'd finished discussing the St Joe's rota.

"No, she hasn't," Shirley replied. "But she has put a note through our door asking me to phone her the minute I got back. I must admit, I didn't phone last night when we got in, I was too tired. Do you know what she wants?"

"To spread alarm and despondency," said Mary wickedly.

Shirley could hear the laughter in Mary's voice. "What sort of alarm and despondency? Mary, you're laughing, what on earth is all this about?"

"I shouldn't laugh really," Mary said sheepishly. "It's not funny, at least what she's doing isn't funny. But it does affect you and David."

"Come on, Mary," Shirley expostulated. "Spit it out."

"Ned Short's sold his house," began Mary.

"I know that," interrupted Shirley, "we talked to one of the workmen yesterday when we got home. He said some builder has bought it."

"Indeed he has," Mary agreed. "Chap called Nicholas Richmond."

"So what's all the excitement about?"

"The builder, Nicholas Richmond, isn't going to live in the house himself. He's doing it up for his daughter," Mary explained.

"Well, it certainly needed some work done on it," Shirley said, "but I still don't see what the fuss is about. Why does Sheila want to talk to me about it? Doesn't she like our new neighbour?"

"She hasn't met him yet, as far as I know," Mary said. "But his daughter is at the university, and he's bought the house to be used as a student house. His daughter, I don't know her name, is going to live there with an undisclosed number of other students, and Sheila's got her knickers in a twist about the whole thing."

"Just a minute, Mary, let me get this straight. You're telling me we're going to have a houseful of students living next door?"

"That's right," said Mary, "as far as we know, unless Ned made the whole thing up!"

"Who discovered this?" asked Shirley. "I mean where does the information come from?"

"Ned Short told Sheila, the day he had signed the contract. Took great delight in telling her, I should add."

"Probably would have taken great delight in telling me, as well," Shirley sighed. "We weren't on the best of terms with him either, you know." She sighed again and Mary waited in sympathetic silence. "Well, this is a facer. I'd better go and tell David I suppose. I'll see you later at St Joe's."

Shirley cut the connection and went to find David. He was in the garden room they had built on to the back of the house, pottering contentedly with his plants as he always did. Shirley watched him for a moment, wondering how he would react to the shattering of their peace, which was certain if the news was true.

"I've found out what Sheila wanted us for," she began.

David looked up from what he was doing. "Oh yes, did she ring?"

"No, she didn't. But I rang Mary Jarvis about going to St Joe's and she told me."

"And?"

"It's about Ned's house."

"What about it?"

"The builder who has bought it is going to let it as a student house."

"A student house. You mean he's not going to live there but has just bought it as an investment."

"Not quite. Apparently his daughter is at the university and he's bought it for her and some of her friends to live in."

"Sounds very sensible to me," David remarked. "With the price of rented accommodation these days, and the scarcity of it in Belcaster, it seems a wise move."

"It probably is from his point of view," snapped Shirley, exasperated by his calm acceptance, "but from our point of view it could be a disaster. They're sure to be noisy, you know how loud these youngsters play their music these days."

"Well, if they do, we can ask them to turn it down," David said reasonably. "I understand what you're saying, of course I do, but I don't think we need to panic yet. They may be very nice kids. We must at least give them the benefit of the doubt until they prove themselves otherwise, don't you think?"

Shirley smiled ruefully. "Of course you're right," she admitted. "It would be most unfair to condemn them before they even move in. But I'm sure that must be what Sheila wanted to talk about, Mary said she'd got her knickers in a twist about it."

"Always got them in a twist about something," said David dismissively. "Well, now you're forewarned." He turned back to the seed trays he was pricking out. "Any chance of a cup of coffee?"

"Yes, of course. Do you want it down here, or will you come up?"

"I'll come up in a minute," David said. "I've nearly finished these."

As they were drinking their coffee in the window overlooking the Circle, a red van drew up on the drive of number seven, and a short thickset man climbed out and walked up to the front door.

"Looks like our builder," David said. "Definitely a different man from yesterday. Shall I go and introduce myself?"

"Yes, do," said Shirley, "then we can hear straight from the horse's mouth."

David set down his coffee mug and went down into the front garden. The builder was looking at the new panes in the door.

"Good morning," David said, walking across. "Are you our new neighbour?"

"Oh, hallo." The man smiled and held out his hand. David liked him at once. He had an open face, tanned from the outdoors, with grey eyes which met David's squarely and a handshake that was firm. "Nick Richmond. Yes, in a way, I am. I've bought the place, but my daughter, Madeleine, is going to be the one living here." He glanced across at the van and called, "Hey, Maddo, come and meet one of your neighbours."

David turned to see that there was someone else sitting in the van, a girl of about twenty. She scrambled out at her father's call, and David saw what an attractive girl she was. Not tall, but with a neat figure and a mass of dark curls tumbled all over her head. She wore the uniform denims and enormous sweater, and her small feet were greatly enlarged by the huge and heavy black boots, but even so she didn't look as scruffy as many of the students who lurched about the town. Her smile was broad, lighting her bright hazel eyes and mirroring her father's.

"Hallo," she said. "Do you live next door?"

"Yes, number eight. My name's David Redwood."

"I'm Madeleine Richmond." She held out her hand and her handshake was as firm as her father's. "Nice to meet you. You're the first of our neighbours that we've met."

"We've been away, Shirley and I. We only got back yesterday evening." Somehow, David felt he needed to explain why they hadn't met before, to make it clear that they hadn't been avoiding them.

"Well, we only got possession a few days ago," Nick said. He looked back at the house. "So we're getting to work at once.

There's a hell of a lot of work to be done before they move in, in September."

"I'm sure there is," David said. "I don't think Ned Short ever did anything to it, from the day they bought it." He turned to Madeleine again. "You hope to be in for the beginning of next term, do you? How many of you will be living there?"

"Five of us," replied Madeleine. "Two blokes and three girls. You'll like them, they're all great guys."

"I'm sure we will," said David, a bit taken aback by the news that there were to be five of them. "Five will be fairly close quarters won't it?"

"Not by the time Dad's finished," Madeleine said. "We're making new bedrooms, so everyone will have a room of their own, and then we'll share the living space."

"I see, well that sounds very good." David sounded doubtful and Madeleine laughed.

"When it's finished, the structural part I mean, I'll give you the guided tour," she promised.

David smiled. "Thanks," he said, "I'll look forward to it."

"In the meantime, I'm afraid things may get a bit noisy with all the work which has to be done," Nick said. "There'll be some banging and hammering, and various deliveries of materials. I'll apologise now for any inconvenience, but we'll try and keep it to a minimum. It's always difficult with these open-plan front gardens. If there is any problem," he felt in his pocket and produced a rather dog-eared business card, "that has my business number, home number and mobile. You should be able to find me somewhere, and I'll do my best to sort it."

"They seemed very charming," David reported back to Shirley, who had been watching from the living-room window. "The girl is a looker."

"How nice," Shirley said wryly.

David grinned at her. "Well, there are going to be two young men living there too, so keep your fingers crossed, you never know, you may find yourself a toy boy."

Shirley laughed. "Silly old fool," she said affectionately.

"Seriously though," David went on, "they were very pleasant. But I did discover that there are going to be five of them living there."

"Five," cried Shirley in horror. "Good Lord! How will they all fit in?"

"With a shoehorn I should imagine," smiled David. "Now I think you must know at least as much, if not more than Sheila, so you'll be able to hold your own."

"Well, I'm hoping not to see her today," admitted Shirley. "I'm off to St Joe's this afternoon, and I must do a supermarket shop this morning or we'll have nothing to eat. If she phones while I'm out," Shirley added sweetly, picking up her handbag, "you can deal with her."

"I just shan't answer the phone," said David carelessly.

"David, you must. It might be Melanie."

"If it is, no doubt she'll ring back. She knows we won't be far. Don't worry about Melanie, love, she'll be fine. Peter is sure to ring if he's worried about her." He gave his wife a little push. "Go on, off to Sainsbury's. I'll be in the garden, but I'll answer the phone if I hear it."

Shirley walked round to St Joe's after lunch. She always enjoyed going there, and had the double pleasure of knowing she was actually being useful. The day centre was held in the small church hall behind St Joseph's, a huge Victorian gothic church off Dartmouth Road, one of the main streets leading into the centre of Belcaster. It was a simple hall with a small kitchen off it, but it served cheap lunches and free cups of tea, and most of its regulars were elderly or disabled, lonely, and sometimes homeless. It was run by a capable woman named Mavis Hope who, with a band of faithful volunteers managed to keep it open five days a week. The Friends of St Joe's worked hard to keep it funded, and with a small grant from the local authority they just about kept their heads above water. It had been equipped with tables and chairs, there were a few packs of cards and it had some chess and draughts and domino sets. A bookshelf of tatty books stood behind the door, but they were well read, and as they finally disintegrated newer second-hand replacements were found. When Shirley got there she was greeted with delight by one or two with whom she regularly played draughts, and by old Vera Harris who waved at her and called out, "Thank gawd you've come back, Shirley. My knitting's all gone wrong and none of the other buggers here can put it right!"

Shirley laughed. "I'll be over in a minute, Vera, just let me say hallo to everybody."

Mavis was sitting at one of the tables helping a scruffy young man to fill in some complicated-looking form. She waved a hand of welcome to Shirley and then turned her attention back to the form.

Shirley went through to the kitchen where she found a West Indian girl tackling a pile of washing up. "Hallo," Shirley said, "I don't think we've met, have we? My name's Shirley Redwood."

The girl smiled at her. "Hi, I'm Cirelle Thomas."

"Nice to meet you, Cirelle. Do you want a hand with that?" Shirley looked round for a tea towel to help with the drying up, but Cirelle shook her head.

"No, really, I can manage here, I've got time to finish this. You go and help Mavis outside. There's a new pot of tea made if anybody wants some."

Shirley shed jacket and handbag, and went back to Vera.

"Now then, Vera," she said sitting down by the old lady, "let's have a look."

Vera had been labouring over a sweater for months now, determined to get it finished, but her hands were arthritic, and she found the work hard going.

"I'm not going to waste this wool," she would say. "I'll finish this bugger if it kills me."

Shirley swiftly disentangled the wool and gave her attention to the pattern. "Ah, I see. I'm afraid you've gone wrong right back here." She showed Vera the mistake. "I'm afraid you'll have to go back if it's going to look right in the end."

"OK, Shirl, whatever you say." Vera watched as Shirley ripped the knitting back to the mistake. "Where you been these last few weeks, then?" she asked. "I been stuck with this ever since the last time you was in. I brought it every day since in case you come back."

"I went to stay with my daughter," explained Shirley. "She just had her second baby."

"Lovely," said Vera. "Boy or girl?"

"Little girl, they've called her Suzanne."

"Lovely," Vera said again. "Got any snaps, have you?"

Shirley smiled at that. "Yes, lots!"

"With you?"

"No, not today, but I'll bring them next time if you like."

Cirelle appeared at their side. "Want another cup of tea, Vera?"

"Oh, yes please, luv. Never say no to a cup of tea, do I?"

Cirelle brought them tea, and as she moved on to another table, Vera said, "Nice girl, that one. Doesn't come in very often, but when she does she's always smiling. She's a student you know. Up at the university. Must be a clever girl. Told me she come from London."

Shirley smiled. "Does she? I haven't met her before today."

"Well, she won't be here much more now, 'cos she'll be finished for the summer, won't she? But she'll be back in September, she said. Going to live somewhere round here, she is, so she'll be in more regular. Nice to see a youngster about the place, isn't it?"

Shirley agreed it was, and looked round again for Cirelle, but she was back in the kitchen, and by the time Shirley was able to leave Vera to her now corrected knitting, Cirelle had disappeared.

"I haven't met Cirelle before," she remarked to Mavis as they snatched a cup of tea together in the kitchen. "She seems a nice girl."

"Yes she is," agreed Mavis. "She comes to church occasionally, and Frank suggested she might like to help here sometimes. Several students do, you know." She smiled across at Shirley. "I often think we don't give them enough credit for what they do, you know, we only notice the vandals."

Shirley, thinking of her own reaction to the news of the student house next door, had to agree. She felt ashamed of herself. David was right, they had to give them a chance.

Unable to restrain herself any longer, Sheila Colby phoned Shirley that evening.

"I don't know if you've heard the news," she said. "I did leave you a note to give me a call, but I expect you've been too busy."

"Yes, I have," replied Shirley sweetly.

"Well, the long and the short of it is, Ned Short has sold his house at last."

"Oh yes, we did hear that," said Shirley. "David met the new owner this morning actually. A very nice chap, he said."

"Well, it isn't the owner I'm concerned about," breathed Sheila, "it's the tenants. He's letting it to a load of students."

"Yes," agreed Shirley, "his daughter and some of her friends. David met her as well. A very attractive girl he said."

"I had heard a rumour that it was for his daughter," said Sheila, unwilling to admit that Shirley already had more information than she did. "I gather they are going to do a lot of work on the house over the summer. Gerald says there's sure to be an awful mess as they do the alterations."

"There's sure to be a bit," agreed Shirley, "but Mr Richmond gave us his card so we can call him if things get out of hand."

"Hmm, did he indeed? He hasn't given *us* one, and we're just as likely to be affected by the building."

"Well, David made a point of introducing himself, this morning."

Shirley maintained her sweetness of tone. "Perhaps Gerald should do the same if he gets a chance."

"Yes," agreed Sheila. "I think he should. I'll tell him. But I also wanted to tell you that I've seen Anthony Hammond about this, because I think it's something the Residents' Association should be aware of. Gerald thinks we may need to take some swift action."

"I expect he's right," said Shirley, deliberately misunderstanding her. "We gave a Circle barbecue when the Forresters moved in, didn't we? Perhaps we can do the same for the students, so that they can get to meet everyone. What a good idea of Gerald's. Though we'll have plenty of time to arrange it over the summer, won't we? I mean they aren't moving in until September, are they?"

"She didn't know what to say to that," Shirley told David that evening over supper. "I wish she wouldn't always blame Gerald for her unpleasant ideas."

"I expect he's used to it," replied her husband. "Any more pud?"

*Chapter Eight*

Madge Peters sat in her window and watched Dartmouth Circle waking up to its day. She was always awake herself by half past five these days and, knowing she would not go back to sleep again, she made herself a pot of tea and took it to the sofa in the living-room window. The position of her house, number one Dartmouth Circle, allowed her to see everyone who came in or out of the close as well as a small part of the main road beyond, and Madge enjoyed watching the comings and goings of her neighbours.

"When you're nearly ninety and don't get out much, you start to live your life through other people," she explained when her son Andrew teased her about being nosy and minding everybody else's business. "I like to watch them all coming and going and guess what they're up to."

"Really, Mother!" expostulated Andrew. "They're probably not 'up to' anything."

"Of course they are," Madge returned cheerfully. "People are always up to something, that's what makes them so interesting. That Sheila Colby for instance, now if you're talking about busybodying, she's a right one. She's been running about like a wet hen these last two weeks just because a few students are moving in to the house next door to her. Did I tell you that?"

"No, Mother," answered Andrew with exaggerated patience, "I told you. Remember, Gerald told me one afternoon when we were playing golf, and then I told you, because Sheila thought you ought to know."

"There you are then," said Madge triumphantly. "Why send *me* messages about *her* neighbours?"

"She was concerned about you, Mother. She was afraid you'd be nervous with a crowd of students living just down the road."

"Rubbish," Madge said tersely. "She just wants to draw attention to herself and feel important."

"I think you're a bit hard on her, you know. Anyway, from what Gerald says, I think she'll be coming in to see you soon," Andrew warned.

"She can if she must," Madge answered with resignation in her voice, but secretly she was pleased. Her visitors were few enough to make her welcome anyone coming to break up the day, even Sheila Colby.

Now as she drank her tea and watched the exodus to work from the Circle, Madge remembered Sheila was coming today. She had rung last night and invited herself to coffee this morning.

"Wonder what the silly woman wants," Madge said to Spike, her cat, who lay curled on her lap as he did every morning, listening to her comments on the world outside. She spoke a good deal to Spike. He was a sympathetic listener and never queried her dictums.

From the house opposite, she saw Paul Forrester leave for work, followed soon after by his wife, Alison, taking the children to school. Madge liked the Forresters. They were a sensible no-nonsense couple whose family life was how Madge felt a family should be, as her own had been. Paul went out to work, Alison did not. She stayed at home with the children to run the household and make it the place to which everyone was pleased to come home. The children were escorted to and from school, played with, read to and generally given their mother's attention when they were at home. They played in the Circle garden, laughed and shrieked and yelled and were generally rowdy like any other six- and four-year-olds, but they were not unruly and were very affectionate. Sometimes Madge was invited over for tea, and she really loved going. After tea they played games or had a story, and though Madge did not always participate in these pastimes, she always enjoyed watching them.

"That's the way a family should be," Madge had said to Mary Jarvis when she came to tea one day and they were watching Alison pushing Harriet and Jon on the swings. "Children and mother doing things together, not the children coming home with latch keys and left to their own devices."

"Happens more and more these days," Mary said. "Most young mums want to have a job. Let's face it Madge, most mums *need* to, to make ends meet."

"Maybe," said Madge darkly, "but it isn't doing their families any good."

"I agree with you," Mary said. "But we're old-fashioned, you and I. The modern thinking is that it makes the mother a more complete person to have interests outside the home."

"You sound like a women's magazine," sniffed Madge.

Mary laughed. "I probably read it in one," she admitted. "Still, some families manage very well with two working parents. We shouldn't be too critical, you know, just because it isn't how it was in our day."

"This is still my day," Madge replied tartly, and Mary laughed.

"Don't worry," she said, "we're not writing you off yet."

"I should think not, even if I *am* old enough to be your mother," at which they both roared with laughter.

Madge thought about this again as she watched Alison walking round the Circle holding Harriet's hand while Jon skipped happily beside her.

"I'm glad I'm old-fashioned," she remarked to Spike. She looked at the clock. "Now where are those Haven girls? They'll be late if they don't get a move on."

Even as she spoke, Chantal erupted from the house, followed at a more sedate pace by Annabel. Angela had left some time earlier, relying on the girls to get themselves off to school on time.

Sad that the husband upped and left, Madge mused. They had seemed a happy family, never any breath of scandal there, and then suddenly...They should keep an eye on that older girl though, Madge thought, watching Annabel trail past her window towards the main road. Madge had noticed how often she was later home than her sister. Two or three times Madge had seen her scramble out of an old van at the corner. Did her mother know about that van...or its driver? Madge wondered. Not my business, she thought, but she watched with interest nonetheless.

"I'm not a gossip," she said to Andrew. "It's only wrong if I talk about what I see, and I don't. But simply watching gives me something new to think about, makes me feel involved in life."

She saw Jill Hammond taking her little girl, Sylvia, to playgroup, and soon after watched the au pair setting off to town with young Thomas in the buggy.

She saw the two doctors, Harry and Fran Davies, leaving in their separate cars for their surgery in the health centre half a mile away. They had two other partners, Ella Garrett and James Durbin, as well, but so that the two Dr Davieses did not get muddled up, they were always referred to as Dr Harry and Dr Fran.

Madge was one of their patients and liked them both, but was particularly grateful to Dr Fran for encouraging her to stay in her own home as long as she could manage, despite her physical difficulties. Andrew had wanted to move her into sheltered accommodation in Belmouth, near where he lived, but Madge was determined to stay in her own home.

"I don't want a lot of people fussing round me all day," she said. "I don't want to go into a home. I've got a home, and it's here."

"No one's asking you to go into a home, Mother," Andrew said patiently, "but a nice little bungalow by the sea, with a warden on hand just in case you *do* need anything, instead of this great big house."

"Andrew," she replied equally patiently, "I have lived in this house ever since it was built, and I have every intention of staying in it."

"But it's on three floors, Mother," Andrew pointed out. "You have to do stairs every time you want to go out."

"And every time I want to go to the bathroom, or to my bedroom. I know. But I've talked to Dr Fran about it and she suggested we looked into getting one of those stair lifts."

"You'd need two," Andrew said flatly, wishing Dr Fran at Jericho.

"Then I'll have two," snapped his mother. "I can afford them, and with the other things Dr Fran has suggested, there isn't any reason why I can't go on living here at present."

"It worries me to think of you here on your own, that's all," Andrew said, and Madge knew the battle was won.

"I know it does," she said more gently, "and I couldn't wish for a better or more caring son, but this is my home. You don't have to worry about me. I have the entry phone on the door, I have the panic button round my neck, the neighbours are very good about popping in, and that Jenny from the Social comes three times a week to give me my bath. Mrs Price comes in two mornings to clean and do the washing, I have meals on wheels on weekdays and I manage very well by myself for the rest of the time. And let's face it, Andrew, I live bang opposite my own doctor. She can be over in a moment if I need her."

Yes, if she's there, and if you're in a position to actually call her and not lying on the floor with a broken hip or having a heart attack, Andrew thought, but he didn't say it. He knew when he was beaten, he had never in his life succeeded in getting his mother to do anything she didn't want to, and it was clear he wasn't about to start now.

He wondered whether he ought to offer to move in with her yet again. He had offered once, but his mother's refusal had been swift and absolute.

"Certainly not, Andrew. It's very kind of you, but it would never work. For one thing I wouldn't want you to give up your own home because of me, and for another we've both lived alone for too long to start living with someone else now." Her voice softened. "I love you dearly, but we couldn't live together comfortably now, we're both too set in our ways."

Andrew had really been relieved. She was quite right, he certainly didn't want to leave his own home in Belmouth. It had been his home all his married life, and when his wife died at forty-five nearly twenty years ago, he had stayed there alone.

No, living together still wasn't the answer. After all, he was getting on himself now, and he didn't want the day-to-day responsibility of looking after his ninety-year-old mother. He still would have preferred her to be closer at hand and in some sort of sheltered accommodation, but at least he had to agree she was very well organised where she was.

"All right, Mother," he conceded, "we'll get the lifts installed and see how you get on."

Now that she had no further problems with the stairs, Madge found her life very much easier than before. It didn't matter if she'd left her book by the bed, or if she'd forgotten to go to the loo before she came down, she could simply glide easily upstairs again; and if she wanted to sit in the Circle garden for a while, she no longer had to struggle with the stairs in either direction; her lift carried her downstairs and she simply let herself out of the front door. She didn't go much further than the garden these days, though occasionally Mary Jarvis took her in the car to St Joe's, and she always enjoyed that. She had been one of the founders of the day centre some years before, and she missed being able to go regularly, but at least she could still go into the garden by herself on warm sunny days if she wanted to. Her independence was very important to her. Even Spike was taken care of, he had a cat flap in the garden door, so she didn't have to bother about him, he could come and go as he chose. Everything was taken care of, and she managed very well.

The roar of a car engine drew her back to her view in time for her to see a red sports car pass her window and pause at the mouth of the Circle to pull out into the traffic. The roof was down, and Madge could see it was driven by a woman in her thirties, her hair tied back with a scarf and wearing a huge pair of sunglasses. Madge didn't know who the woman was, but she did know which house she had come from, for she had seen the car parked outside Mike Callow's the evening before. Madge's lips tightened. She didn't approve of Mike Callow, or his life-style. She knew he was separated and lived alone, but that was no excuse for the stream of women who passed through his house. Some of them even stayed when his children were with him, which Madge considered unforgivable.

"How he conducts his own life is his business," she remarked to Spike, "but he shouldn't involve his children in his goings-on."

Mike Callow worked from home and was often about the Circle in the daytime. If she were sitting in the garden when he walked by, he never failed to wish her good morning and often stopped for a chat, and Madge found herself responding to his charm, in spite of herself. She distrusted his dark good looks, his easy manner and his lopsided grin, but she always found herself smiling back at him, and realised how attractive he must be to most women, how easy it must be for him to find willing partners to bring home.

As the red car finally found a gap in the traffic, Madge sniffed. "Haven't seen that one before, have we, Spike?"

A red van turned into the close and Madge watched with interest as it pulled up in front of number seven. There was a builder's name on the side that she couldn't read from where she was, but she recognised it as the van which had come several times before. They must be working hard on the Shorts' old house.

"No doubt we'll hear all about it when Sheila comes later this morning," she remarked to Spike. "Now, I'd better be getting upstairs, Jenny'll be here before long for my bath." She tipped Spike off her lap and struggled to her feet. As she paused to get her balance, she looked out of the window again. Mike Callow was walking past, and glancing up he saw her watching him and he waved. Caught off guard, Madge found she was smiling and waving back.

When Sheila rang the bell soon after eleven, Madge was ready for her, and pressing the entry phone door release let her in. "Come straight up, Sheila," she called. "You don't need the lift, do you?"

"No, indeed I don't," Sheila said as she bustled up the stairs. "How are you this morning, Madge? Getting on all right?"

"Yes, of course," Madge replied. "Come right in, Sheila, and sit down. I've made the coffee, I'll just bring it in."

"Can I get it for you?" Sheila asked, turning towards the kitchen.

"No, thank you. I can manage. Make yourself comfortable. Just push Spike off that sofa if you want to sit in the window." Madge went into the kitchen where she had already laid out the coffee cups and some cake on the trolley. She wheeled it in and found Sheila at the window looking out over the Circle.

"You get a very good view of everything from here," Sheila said. "And facing south like this you get the sunshine nearly all day."

"Gets too hot sometimes," Madge said. "Do you take milk and sugar?"

"Just milk. Did you notice they've started work on number seven? They've got a lorry and a van there now. It's making getting in and out of our drive quite difficult. I told Gerald he should go out and have a word with them, but you know what he is, he wouldn't go."

"Have you met the new people yet? What are they called?" asked Madge, passing Sheila her coffee.

"The man's name is Richmond. He's the builder himself, but we haven't met him. David Redwood has, says he's nice enough, but he hasn't been to see us yet." Sheila sipped her coffee and accepted a piece of cake. "Of course it doesn't really matter, because he isn't going to be living there. He's bought the house for his daughter to live in. Amazing isn't it what the young have given to them these days. My father never gave me a house, even when I was getting married, let alone as a student."

"Were you ever a student?" Madge enquired.

"No, it wasn't the thing girls did in my day," Sheila said. "Even so, buying a house seems a little too much, don't you think?"

"I imagine he's bought it as an investment, and is letting his daughter use it while she's studying. He'll be taking rent from the other students, won't he? Do you know how many there are going to be?"

"David said five, though goodness knows how they're going to fit them in." Sheila sighed. "At least we'll have the summer in peace," she went on. "The house won't be ready until the beginning of September and then they'll move in for the autumn term. Shirley Redwood suggested that we might give a Circle barbecue, like we did when the Forresters moved in, but I don't think that would be the right thing in this case."

"Oh?" said Madge. "Why not?"

"Well, they aren't a family, are they? They aren't really going to be part of the community, are they? I mean they'll probably only stay a year and then move on."

"Even so, it would be nice to make them welcome, don't you think?" Madge laughed suddenly. "I know!" she cried. "I know just the thing. It's my ninetieth birthday on the twenty-third of September. I can give a party, have a barbecue like we did for the Forresters and I'll ask them all to that. We must meet them properly. I'll have a word with Anthony Hammond."

Sheila sniffed. "I've already talked to him," she said. "He wasn't much help. He said there was nothing the Residents' Association could do about them."

"Well, he's right," replied Madge. "What do you want to do about them? They're going to live here whether you like it or not, so far better to make the best of it and get to know them, don't you think?" She reached for her portable telephone and said, "I'll give Jill Hammond a ring now and ask if Anthony can call round some time."

"She's probably out playing golf," Sheila said. "You'll only get that French girl who doesn't take messages properly." But Madge had already dialled and the call was ringing.

The phone was indeed answered by Isabelle, and so that there would be no misunderstanding about the message, Madge spoke to her in French. The conversation, conducted in rapid and fluent French, was short and when she rang off Madge smiled across at Sheila's surprised face. "That's all right," she said. "It was the au pair, but I've left a message for one of the Hammonds to ring me some time."

"I didn't know you spoke French," said Sheila, clearly astonished by the old lady's fluency.

"Of course I do," Madge replied, mildly reproving. "My mother was French. My father was working in Paris in 1899, and they eloped. I was brought up bilingual."

"Well, I never," said Sheila. "I didn't know your mother was French. Fancy you speaking French like that."

Madge's eyes twinkled. "I speak German, too," she said. "I did modern languages at London University."

When Sheila had gone Madge gave serious thought to the idea of a barbecue to celebrate her ninetieth birthday. She had surprised herself with the idea as much as she had surprised Sheila. Indeed, she had only suggested it because she was irritated by the way Sheila had received the idea of a welcome barbecue for the students, but why not? The more Madge thought about the idea, the better she liked it. Andrew was sure to want to mark the event in some way, and she would far rather have a street party, than some dinner in a hotel.

"If I organise it myself I can have it exactly as I want it," she told Spike. "And I can invite who I like as well."

## Chapter Nine

Mike Callow saw Andrea Martin to her car and waited while she lowered the roof, while she tied a scarf round her hair, while she found her sunglasses, but she was no longer in his thoughts. As she roared off round the Circle, he was already back in the house, stacking the few breakfast dishes into the dishwasher and brewing a fresh pot of coffee. He had met Andrea at a dinner party the previous week and had made a date for last night which had ended, inevitably it had seemed at the time, in his bed, but though he had enjoyed his evening, he was in no rush to repeat it.

"You'll ring me then," had been her parting words, and he had agreed somewhat vaguely, while actually promising nothing. It was a technique he had perfected since he and Caroline split up, agreeing to everything, promising nothing, and as a man determined to escape all shadow of commitment, he had it down to a fine art. It was unlikely he would give the unfortunate Andrea more than a passing thought, and if she called him she would be greeted with the politeness of his answerphone.

The sun was shining brightly as Mike set out for the newsagents' on the main road to collect his daily paper. He went every morning. It was his only exercise and he enjoyed the walk. The colours of early summer were creeping back into the park and gardens he passed and Dartmouth Road itself was lined with flowering cherry. The pink fondant flowers were nearly over now, but the trees themselves alleviated the dull greyness of the main road and he appreciated the thought behind their planting.

As he reached the corner of the Circle, he glanced up at the living-room window of number one and saw Madge Peters watching him.

Nosy old besom, he thought affectionately, but he smiled and waved because despite her vigilance at her window, he liked her and respected her, admiring her determined independence. Hope I'm as with it when I'm pushing ninety, he thought.

Madge waved back, which made him smile. He knew she didn't approve of him, and from devilment, he always went out of his way to wish her good morning, and even stop for a chat if he came across her sitting in the gardens. Her innate good manners never allowed her to ignore him or snub him completely, and it amused him to see her disapproval warring with her upbringing.

He knew she would almost certainly have seen Andrea's car, and he knew she would have guessed from whose house it had come. Another black mark against your name, Michael, he told himself, and grinned as he strolled along Dartmouth Road. When he returned from the newsagents' with his paper, he looked up again, but the window was empty.

It was a beautiful morning and Mike took his paper into the Circle gardens and settled himself on the bench in the sunshine to catch up on the news. It was a favourite spot of his, for his garden didn't get much sun in the morning, and the Circle gardens were generally peaceful once the flurry of morning departures was over. This morning however, he could hear the hammering and general clatter of building work, and looking over to number seven, he saw a small truck being unloaded and building materials carried indoors.

He had heard, of course, of the advent of the student household from Sheila Colby. Now, she's another nosy old besom, he thought, but he felt no affection or respect for her.

"I'm sure you'll be alarmed to hear Mr Callow, that Ned Short

has sold number seven and it's to be used as a student house."
Sheila had called to warn him within days of hearing the news
herself. "I've spoken to Anthony Hammond about it, as chairman of the association." Sheila's tone seemed to be demanding
admiration for her efficiency and public concern. Mike Callow
felt none, rather he felt irritation that she should have taken it
upon herself to interfere in something perfectly legal and legiti-
mate and then try to involve him in her interference.

His reply was cool, almost indifferent. "Really Mrs Colby?
And what did he have to say?"

"Oh, you know, he was obviously concerned for the Circle at
large and for us as the immediate neighbours, but he felt there
was little the association can do before they actually move in."

"In which he was absolutely right, Mrs Colby. What had you
thought he could do?" Mike surveyed her with wide innocence,
but his voice had a sardonic edge, and Sheila, who always felt
very uncertain with this man, felt flustered.

"Well, you know, well Gerald thought maybe a letter, welcoming them of course, to the Circle, but explaining to them
what a quiet neighbourhood it was, and reminding them that
we'd like to keep it that way." She looked up at him to see how
he had taken to the idea. He had raised an eyebrow.

"I don't think that would be very helpful, Mrs Colby," he
replied. "If I were moving in to a house and was greeted with a
letter like that, I reckon I'd consider it a challenge." Mike's eyes
held hers for a moment as he added, "I certainly wouldn't want
to be party to such a letter. You say Anthony Hammond didn't
agree to write one?"

"No, he can do nothing before they move in."

"Well, I for one am glad to hear it," Mike said firmly. He
made himself smile at her. "Don't worry, Mrs Colby, I'm sure
we can deal with any problems which arise. Nobody wants a
rowdy house in a small close like ours, but we're not sure we've
got one yet, are we?"

As he listened to the banging and crashing emanating from

number seven this morning, Mike smiled. Sheila and Gerald Colby must be loving this, he thought.

His thoughts were interrupted by the arrival of his neighbour Alison Forrester with her daughter Harriet, who had come to play on the swings.

"Hallo, Mike," Alison called. "Lovely day isn't it?"

"It is," Mike agreed. "Hallo, Harry, how are you doing?"

"All right," Harriet called back as she headed for the swings. Alison paused beside Mike's bench and they chatted for a moment or two.

"How's Paul?" Mike asked casually. "I haven't seen much of him lately."

"He's fine," Alison replied. "Working all the hours God sends at the moment. Some sort of panic at the office, I think. He doesn't say much, and if I ask, he just says he doesn't want to bring his work home with him. To be honest I worry about him, he seems to be under tremendous stress just now. He left at crack of dawn this morning."

"Don't worry about Paul," Mike said cheerfully, "he thrives on it! Tell you what, I'll drag him out for a beer at the Ship one night this week, how would that be?"

Alison smiled at him gratefully. "That would be great," she said. "It'd do him good. You not working today?" she added.

"Should be," Mike admitted, smiling, "but I went out for the paper and then was tempted to sit in the sun and read it."

"I see they've started work on number seven," Alison said, glancing across. "I'm hoping some of the students may want to earn a bit of cash, babysitting. It would be great to have a couple of babysitters on tap."

"I hadn't thought of that," mused Mike. "It'd be useful to me too, when the children come." He sighed and repeated, "If they come."

"Don't they come any more?" asked Alison sympathetically.

"Less than they used to. Caroline always seems to have some reason why they can't."

"Mummy, come on," yelled Harriet, swinging herself on her tummy and trying to climb up by herself.

Alison glanced across at her, and Mike said, "Go on, she's waiting for you. I'll tell you all about it some time. I must get back anyway, for as you so rightly say, I ought to be working. I've a deadline for Monday." He folded his paper and got to his feet. They walked over to the swing and Mike scooped up Harriet and set her firmly on the seat. "Hold tight," he ordered and then swung the little girl, squealing with delight, high into the air. He smiled at Alison. "See you," he said, "and don't worry about Paul, I'll give him a bell later in the week."

As he left the gardens, he could hear Harriet's excited cries, and he knew a stab of regret. He really missed seeing his children, even though only Debbie was of a size to be pushed on the swing now. He looked up at number ten as he approached it and wondered why he still lived there. It was really much too big for him, but it had been the family home, until Caroline moved out, and he wanted the children to feel they were coming home when they came to see him; that they still slept in their own bedrooms and knew where everything was. He sighed and repeated to himself, "When they come." They hadn't been to stay with him for three months now, not since the night he had had them there and had brought home a girlfriend. Debbie told Caroline the next day that "Daddy had a lady in his bedroom," and Caroline had been furious and refused to let them stay ever since.

"I promise I won't do it again," he had pleaded. "It was a one-off. You changed the weekend they were to come and I already had a date. I fixed a babysitter so the kids were fine."

"That was bad enough," Caroline cut in. "When they come to stay with you, it's you they want to see, not a babysitter!"

Mike shrugged. "Yes, well it was a one-off. Then I had too much to drink to drive Francie home, so she had to stay the night."

"In your bed!"

"Well, there wasn't anywhere else, Caroline. The children were in their own beds and the babysitter was already asleep on the sitting-room sofa."

As always the row escalated into a screeching match, and Caroline ended up sweeping out of the house, yet again, this time vowing the children should not come and stay with him again, he could have them for days, and that was all.

It was the rows that had made Caroline leave. She hadn't found anybody else, or discovered about his occasional wanderings for that matter, but gradually over the years the arguments had grown from disagreements and tiffs into full-blown rows and fights. Sometimes after a major flare-up they wouldn't speak to each other properly for days, and the atmosphere in the house became quite appalling. They could both see that things were going from bad to worse, and it was having a definite effect on the children. At last, Caroline had done something about it. She had waited until the summer holidays so that the children's school lives would not be too disrupted and then made her announcement.

"I've found somewhere else to live," she told him when she came in one day. "The children and I are moving out at the weekend." She spoke quite calmly this time. There were no hysterics or shouting. "It's a little house in Belmouth. There's a good school just round the corner for Debbie and Carl, and Peter can start at Belmouth Comp instead of Crosshills. It's got a far better reputation anyway."

"I see you've got it all worked out," said Mike wearily.

"Yes, I have," Caroline agreed. "I'm sorry, Mike, but one of us had to do something. Dad helped me to find the house, and he's paid the first month's rent. You'll have to pay us maintenance of course, but that can be sorted. I can still get to work from there, so I shall have some income." She looked at him sadly for a moment and said softly, "Oh Michael, whatever happened to us?"

Mike shrugged. "One of those things, I suppose. We just grew apart. Don't worry, it's probably for the best. We'll sort out the finances somehow, and at least you aren't far away. I can still see the kids."

Perhaps it had been the uncertainty of his work that had contributed to their break. So many of the arguments had begun over money before they spiralled out of control. Working from home had made him feel shut in sometimes, and he'd felt the need to burst out, as if he were buried and had to fight his way out of smothering earth, and it was all too easy to put off switching on the computer and getting stuck in.

That had always been his problem, it was his problem now, even with Monday's deadline looming over him. He had promised the draft outlines of six more episodes of the sit-com he had written for a television company. The first series, written, ironically, just after Caroline had left, had been an instant success, much to Mike's and the TV company's surprise. What they had produced merely as a pot-boiler had caught the public's imagination and there were demands for more of the same.

When they had asked for the second series just before New Year, Mike had thrown a huge celebration party. He had invited everyone he knew, including everyone from the Circle. It was to be the beginning of his new life as a success. He hadn't felt much of a success since Caroline had left, despite the TV series. He wondered if it was worse to be left for another man, traded in for a new and improved model, or to be left because you were just too awful to live with and that even living as a single parent with three children was an improvement. He knew that the former had happened to Angela Haven across the road; Ian had found someone else and she had been devastated. Mike imagined he could sympathise with her, yet somehow simply being left seemed to him worse.

The party was in itself a success apart from a few minor irritations, like the younger Haven girl, Chantal, having too much to drink and being sick all over Oliver Hooper, who appeared to be exploring her attributes at the time. Luckily, her mother had already left, and he and the elder sister, Annabel, had cleaned her up, put her in Debbie's old room to sleep it off, and as far as he knew no word of the disaster leaked out into the Circle. He had seen the girl's grey-faced embarrassment when she had awoken in the morning and so he had refrained from teasing her. He had not taken Oliver to task either, except for making him help with the clearing up. Mike mentioned the incident to neither set of parents; there was no need to worry them with the teenage humiliations of their offspring and he had decided that the least said was soonest mended.

Living apart seemed in a strange way to bring Mike and Caroline closer together. There were no rows, hardly a disagreement even over arrangements for the children. Mike found he always looked forward to seeing her when he picked up the kids, and she always seemed pleased to see him too, often asking him in for a drink and occasionally a meal. He had even wondered, for a while, whether they might eventually get back together again, but he made no move in that direction and Caroline, hearing about his succession of girlfriends from the children and from old friends, drew away from him, and gradually any real chance of reconciliation slipped away. Mike was fairly certain now that she had found herself someone else. The children never mentioned anyone, but Mike never asked and Caroline, he knew, would behave with complete circumspection.

He sighed and, downing the last of his coffee, switched on his computer. He thought for a moment of Alison in the garden, pushing Harriet on the swing. Perhaps he should find himself someone like her, placidly comfortable with her family and her home, but even as he thought about it, he knew that much as he liked Alison, he would soon find her incredibly boring. Far better to play the field, enjoy life and feel no commitment to anyone. He smiled wryly as he returned to his sit-com where he could make anyone do anything he liked, and began to type.

Paul Forrester had indeed left for work early that morning. He wanted to be in the office in particularly good time to look over all the projects he had on hand. He needed to have everything at his fingertips, details of recent sales, properties under offer and new properties just on the market. He wanted to be certain that all his paperwork was up to date, and that he had left nothing undone that he ought to have done.

Last night a message had been waiting when he got back from showing a house in Over Stretton just outside Belcaster, that Mr Fountain, the senior partner, wanted to see him first thing in the morning, and Paul had the feeling that it wasn't going to be a pleasant interview. Whispers of business difficulties within the firm and the possibility of redundancies had been buzzing round the office for some time now, rumours which fed on themselves until everyone was in a state of unease and Paul was afraid it was he who was going to be told that Johnson, Fountain, Estate Agents and Auctioneers, no longer required his services. It was always the same, he supposed, last in first out, and he wished yet again he had not allowed himself to be head-hunted away from Frederick Jones and Co. where he had worked for the last ten years.

He had been introduced to James Fountain at a Round Table dinner, and they had had an informal chat about the work he was doing for Freddie Jones, about his family, about his prospects. When he thought about it afterwards, he realised he had been naïve to assume that the conversation had been merely a friendly exchange. When James Fountain followed it up with an invitation to bring Alison round for dinner, however, he realised there was more to it. They spent a very convivial evening meeting James's wife, Monica, and business was hardly touched on, but both the Forresters felt they were on show.

"Just making sure we don't eat our peas with a knife, do you think?" Alison asked dryly.

Paul laughed. "Probably. I wonder if we passed the test."

He was invited for a formal interview the following week and discovered that they had indeed passed the test.

"We're looking for someone young and enthusiastic, with

good qualifications to come into the firm," James said, leaning on his desk and studying Paul over his steepled fingers. "Someone who, all things being equal, would become an associate partner within the year. Someone who could turn his hand to any aspect of the business and perhaps take on the opening and running of a new office. Working for old Freddie, you've had just the experience we need. It's been an excellent training ground for you, Paul, and from what I've heard around the town, you've certainly made the most of it."

Paul found he was holding his breath and let it out as softly as he could, hardly able to believe what he was hearing, not daring to guess what might be going to come next.

"Don't you think it's time you moved on to bigger and better things?" James asked. "I assume you weren't planning to stay as jack of all trades to Freddie for ever, were you?"

"No, well, that is, I've been very happy working for Freddie," Paul admitted. "I hadn't really thought about any career moves." But he was definitely thinking about one now, and how they could do with the extra money which had been laid temptingly before him. Their comparatively recent move to Dartmouth Circle had stretched them a bit, but rather than lose the opportunity of living there, he and Alison had decided to go for it. If he moved to Johnson, Fountain, the pressure would be eased considerably. At the time it had seemed too marvellous an opportunity to turn down, a dramatic increase in salary and improved prospects as several of the older staff would soon be reaching retirement age. There had been mention of an associate partnership within a year or so, meaning yet higher earnings, and of opening and running a branch office in Belmouth, where Paul would virtually be his own boss. After long and excited discussions with Alison about this apparent upturn in their fortunes he had handed in his notice to Freddie Jones and accepted James Fountain's offer.

"I'm sorry to see you go, Paul," Freddie Jones had said and he had meant it. His firm was his own, a one-man band, and he had relied heavily on Paul as a negotiator, selling houses and doing surveys, while he himself carried out a few surveys, took the occasional auction and dealt with some local-authority work. "But, of course you must seize the opportunity, I'm afraid I can't match that salary, and I know how expensive a growing family can be. Alison doesn't work, does she?"

"Not at the moment," Paul said. "We don't want her to work again at least until the children have both started school. I shall be sorry to leave you, too, Freddie, but they've made me an offer I can't refuse."

Since he had made the change, however, there had been an unexpected but definite downward turn in the property market and Mr Fountain had been overheard talking about the economic situation and discussing "cuts", all of which fuelled the current rumours.

Paul hadn't yet told Alison of his fears. After all, they might come to nothing and there was no need to alarm her yet, but while maintaining a cheerful face at home, he worried more and more about what he was going to do if he were given the push. It was unlikely any other estate agent in Belcaster would employ him; they were all suffering from the drop in the housing market, and if a large company like Johnson, Fountain was experiencing difficulties, what must some of the smaller firms be going through?

As he waited to turn out into Dartmouth Road, he saw Mrs Peters sitting in her window and he gave her a wave. Paul liked Madge Peters. He admired her courage, living alone at her age, and occasionally, when asked, she had given him the benefit of her wisdom.

Perhaps he should go and talk his worries through with her, Paul thought. She had a cool way of looking at things and considered all the options with a detached view that allowed Paul to get things into perspective.

He had not discussed his move to Johnson, Fountain with anyone but Alison until it was an accomplished thing. Perhaps he should have, he thought now, as he drew out into the traffic, for when he had told Madge about it, he had been aware that she was not as delighted with the move as everyone else seemed to be. Of course she had not said she thought he was wrong in so many words, but she'd expressed surprise, and said, "It all sounds very exciting, Paul, I do hope it will all work out for the best." And for a moment the shine went off the enterprise.

Although Paul was early, he had little time in the office to himself. Mr Fountain arrived soon after.

"Ah, Paul, I'm glad you're here. Come into my office will you?"

Paul set aside the survey report he was working on and followed the senior partner into his office.

"Sit down, Paul," he said and seated himself behind the desk. "I expect you've some idea why I asked for a meeting this morning, haven't you?"

Paul had already decided to play the innocent and make James Fountain spell it out to him. "Not really, Mr Fountain, unless it was about the house at Over Stretton we're selling for your friends. I was over there yesterday showing some people round, and Mrs Standen said that she was disappointed there hadn't been more viewings."

James Fountain gave a short laugh. "No, it wasn't that, though I'm not surprised to hear Margaret Standen was after you. She expected to sell that house immediately, but it's overpriced; they want far too much for it. I've told them so, both of them, but of course they know better than we do. No, Paul, it isn't the Standens' house I want to talk to you about, though their situation is indicative of the problems we face at the moment." He looked across at Paul, and Paul held his gaze, saying nothing.

"You know yourself the market is down at present. Very little is moving except at the very cheapest and the most expensive ends of the range. People can't believe that their houses haven't gone up in value, and if they don't need to move they're staying put in the hope of an upturn, and this of course affects us."

Paul shifted uneasily in his chair. Here it comes, he thought, I'm out!

As if he had read Paul's mind, James Fountain smiled a quick smile and said, "Don't worry, Paul, I'm not giving you the boot. I'm delighted with the work you've been doing, but what I'm afraid I am saying is that we have had to shelve our expansion plans."

He went on to explain that there would be no new office opening in Belmouth, no new associate partners, and little chance of bonuses at the end of the year, but Paul hardly heard him, he was so relieved that he still had a job.

"So, you understand, Paul, that things will have to stay pretty much as they are for the foreseeable future."

Paul gave himself a mental shake and forced a smile to his lips. "Yes, of course, Mr Fountain, I quite understand."

"Unless you want to try your luck for a partnership somewhere else?" James Fountain raised an enquiring eyebrow. "Then, of course, although we don't want to lose you, we should have to let you go."

Paul shook his head. "No, thank you, Mr Fountain, I'd like to continue working here. Things may improve during the summer."

"Indeed, they may," agreed Mr Fountain, with a thin smile, "but I don't think we should count on it. I'm sure no one is expecting an upturn in the market in the short term."

"Was he hoping I would resign, do you think?" Paul asked Alison when he relayed the interview over the supper table.

"I don't know," she replied, "but you didn't, that's the main thing." She reached out and took Paul's hand. "Look at it this way, Paul. You're still earning more than you were with Freddie. You still have a job in one of the biggest firms in the area. We're all right. We don't need you to be a partner, nice as it would have been. We can manage as we always have done. We've done OK so far, haven't we?"

Paul returned the clasp of her hand. "You're right, of course.

Let's face it, this morning when I went into work I thought I might be coming home to tell you that I'd been made redundant."

"Ah, yes, well, that's another thing. You should have told me. If you are worried about anything like that, for God's sake don't keep it to yourself. OK?"

Paul smiled ruefully. "OK, I promise. Another time I'll tell you."

"Let's hope there won't be another time," Alison said with feeling. A comfortable silence enveloped them for a few moments and then Alison said, "I saw Mike Callow in the gardens today. He seemed to be fairly low. He says Caroline won't let him have the children to stay. It's sad, isn't it? He was pushing Harry on the swing, and you could see he was really missing his own kids."

"They're not Harriet's age," said Paul.

"No, I know," agreed Alison. "But that doesn't stop him missing them. Can you imagine only seeing Jon and Harriet on alternate weekends?"

Paul shook his head. "Doesn't bear thinking about," he said.

"Tell you something else, while I was in the gardens with Harriet, I was watching the workmen at number seven. They seem to be doing a lot of work on that house. There was tremendous banging and hammering. They put a huge skip outside. It takes up the whole of their side of the drive."

"I bet that pleases old Mother Colby!" laughed Paul.

"I didn't see her," Alison said, "but Shirley Redwood was cleaning her car the other side. She says David has met the new owner. He's called Nick Richmond and is very nice. His daughter is called Madeleine and she's going to live there with some other friends from college. I said to Mike, I hope some of them might want babysitting work."

"Doubt if they will," said Paul. "Students go out drinking in the evenings, then come home rowdy and drunk."

"Paul!" Alison cried in disgust. "You're as bad as Sheila Colby. You've no idea what they'll be like. At least give them a chance."

As they lay together in bed later on, Alison thought over what Paul had told her about his job. She snuggled closely against him and said softly, "I really wish you'd told me about the problems at work."

Paul grunted. "Hhmm."

"No, I mean it. Listen – are you quite happy staying there now the job isn't what you thought it was? I mean if you wanted to tell them to stuff it because they hadn't kept their end of the bargain, you could, you know. We'd manage somehow. I could always get a job."

Paul reached his arm round her, holding her even more closely against him. "Darling, I'm sorry, I should have told you. I just didn't want to worry you, that was all. I'm quite happy to stay at Johnson's. If I hang on in there, I should be in line for the partnership when the market turns the corner. It will in the end, just later rather than sooner, that's all. We can easily manage without you getting a job. I really don't want you to work while the children are so young."

"I know, and I agree, one of us should be at home for them, but it doesn't necessarily have to be me, does it?"

She felt Paul's incredulity in every line of his body, and then he relaxed and laughed. "Make me into a house husband, would you?"

Alison laughed too. "Not unless I have to, but we can keep the idea up our sleeves, can't we?"

"Doesn't *fit* into my sleeve," Paul said with feeling, and they both laughed.

It'll be all right, Paul thought, still smiling. We'll cope, we did before, and at least I've got Alison. Unconsciously his arm tightened round her now sleeping form. He remembered what she'd said about Mike Callow missing his children, and thought that he must be missing having a woman he loved beside him too. Poor old Mike, he thought, and despite his worries Paul drifted into sleep feeling a comfortable content.

*September*

*Chapter Ten*

Madeleine Richmond closed the door of number seven, Dartmouth Circle, The Madhouse, and let the silence settle round her. She leaned for a moment against the front door, her eyes closed, listening to the quiet peace and privacy of her first "own home". The others were not due back for a couple of days and she felt a surge of proprietorial pleasure at being the first to live in the new house, entirely and completely her own person; answerable to no one. All the responsibilities of the house were hers, but her pleasure at being in charge of herself and her life far outweighed any worries she had about those responsibilities. She felt she was on the edge of something new and exciting, that over the horizon, only just out of sight, was something amazing, and she only had to stand on tiptoe to get her first glimpse.

"No more cash from me, Maddo," her father had said. "You get your rents in and you'll be better off than when you were on the allowance I was giving you last year, even after you've paid all your outgoings. Don't forget all the bills are in your name, so it's up to you, girl, to get it all sorted."

Maddo and a friend from home, who was in need of some extra cash, had spent three weeks painting and decorating the altered house. They hired a skip and filled it with all the rubbish Ned had left in the garden and the garage, so that though the garden was not exactly a garden yet, and Madeleine had plans for that, at least it was no longer the tip it had been, and the garage now actually had room for a car.

She and her mother had combed the second-hand shops for furniture, sturdier pieces than the flat-packed conti-board items offered in the DIY shops, pieces they hoped would stand up to life among students. They had adapted old curtains and made new ones where necessary, and Maddo's pride in her new house was in direct proportion to the effort she'd put into it herself.

Her parents had helped her move in, carried boxes and bags up to the bedroom on the top floor that Madeleine had chosen for her own, and now they were gone.

She opened her eyes and walked down the corridor to the downstairs bedroom, Ben's, a simply furnished as yet uncluttered room, waiting for him to make his mark on it, to make it truly Ben's room. Newly painted like the whole interior of the house, it bore little resemblance to the damp-smelling study belonging to Ned Short. The windows looked out at the wilderness that was still the garden, but they were new and without the overlay of grime that had covered their predecessors. Maddo opened the door to the downstairs cloakroom and then moved on to the walk-in cupboard under the stairs, now occupied by a shower cubicle, a washing machine and a tumble dryer. Maddo smiled at her mother's insistence that the house should be equipped with these last.

"They must have somewhere to wash and dry clothes, Nick," Clare had said. "With five of them in the house there's no way they can dry everything in the bathroom or over radiators."

"Perfectly good launderette in Dartmouth Road," Nick pointed out.

"But quite apart from the inconvenience of having to cart everything to the launderette," Clare said, "in the long run it's cheaper to pay for the electricity here in the house."

"Cheaper for them, maybe," grumbled Nick, but he had acquired a second-hand washer and reconditioned dryer, both in reasonable condition, and had them plumbed in, as Madeleine had known he would once her mother's aid was enlisted.

Closing the door on what her father had nicknamed "the

extravagances" she went upstairs. The kitchen, newly fitted and pristine, with gleaming surfaces, awaited the arrival of its cooks and bottlewashers. A box of groceries stood on the floor ready to be stowed in Maddo's private cupboard and on Maddo's shelf in the fridge. She put the kettle on for a cup of coffee and continued her tour of the house.

Dean's room had been created by chopping off the end of the living room. It, too, stood waiting for its occupant. The sun streamed through the window, a shaft of light with dancing dust motes. Up the second flight of stairs was the refurbished bathroom and the three girls' bedrooms. Standing in her own bedroom doorway, Maddo hugged herself.

"Right," she announced to the empty room, "cup of coffee and then time to get settled in before Dan comes round."

Madeleine had been going out with Dan for several months. He was tall, broad and handsome, built like the rugby player he was, with dark hair, dark eyes and a flashing smile. Madeleine loved him dearly and though she knew that most of her friends found him attractive, and he was always eyeing up the talent, she was determined they should stay together. Their relationship was often stormy, but it tended to be Dan who did the storming, usually when he'd had a pint too many, but he seldom stayed away long and Madeleine was always there when he came back.

"Don't know how you put up with him," Cirelle had often said in disgust, and there were times when Maddo wondered herself, but the thought of him not being there filled her with such imagined loneliness, that she always took him back.

She had been afraid there might be a row when she told him about the house. He was about to start on his last year at the college and was well established in a gloomy flat above an office not far from the cathedral, which he'd shared with two mates since their second year. This didn't mean, however, that he might not jump at the chance to move in to a more modern, rejuvenated house much nearer the college. Luckily for Madeleine, he didn't show any inclination to do so, because one of the stipulations her father had made when agreeing to buy her the house, was that she did not share it with a live-in boyfriend.

"I don't mind it being a mixed household," Nick had said, "but life could get much too complicated if you start actually living with someone. If the relationship goes wrong, you're in trouble. You must have a place to escape to, your own space round you."

Madeleine knew it made sense; she knew that relationships could get claustrophobic, she'd seen it with Ben and Angie, and didn't want hers and Dan's to go the same way. It wasn't that she and Dan didn't sleep together, they did, and she was pretty certain that her parents knew they did, though nothing had ever been said, but in moments of clarity she recognised they both needed their own space.

However, she'd promised to cook dinner for the two of them to celebrate her occupation of the house, and she didn't anticipate he would be going home to the gloomy flat that evening. She was really longing to see him as they'd been apart for most of the summer. He'd been away working at a beach restaurant in the south of France, and their only contact had been a few hasty phone calls and a couple of scrawled postcards. Madeleine knew there must have been girls in France; she had to be realistic. Dan wasn't the man to resist a bikinied French girl with plenty to offer, and the beach was no doubt swarming with those, but she was anxious to re-establish their relationship, to slip back into the acceptance that they were a couple as they had been before.

By the time Dan arrived, she had sorted out her own room and the kitchen, made a pot of spag bol and showered and washed her hair. When the doorbell rang, she was waiting and when she opened the door, there was Dan, face tanned, teeth brilliant white in his flashing smile.

For a moment she looked at him and her face creased into its familiar grin. "Hi," she said.

"Hey, Mad," he drawled, "you're looking great." He hugged her and then kissed her, and she knew as she returned his kiss that everything was going to be all right. Dan was back.

Dean Joseph directed his mother into Dartmouth Circle, and they pulled up outside number seven.

"Looks a nice house," Janice Joseph said, looking up at it.

Dean was looking at it too, in amazement. Last time he had seen the place it was decidedly scruffy with flaking paint and cracked window panes. Now it was newly painted, the windows were clean and the front door stood open as if in welcome.

"They've done a lot of work on it," he said. "You should have seen it before!"

They got out of the car and walked up to the front door. Dean pushed it gently and leaning inside called up the stairs, "Hallo! Anyone there? Mad, are you there?"

"Well, goodness, look at that!" Janice was looking at the house's nameplate beside the front door. "The Madhouse. Is that's what it's called?"

"She really has had a nameplate done!" Dean laughed in delight. "She said she would. Yes, it's called The Madhouse, because it's Mad's house. Come on let's go in. Mad may have popped out, that's why she's left the door for us. I said we'd be here some time this afternoon."

He led the way into the house and up the stairs to the first floor. One quick glance into the kitchen showed him the improvement in the kitchen with its new work surfaces, gleaming sink, and what were clearly a new cooker and a new fridge.

"Hmm, that looks nice," said Janice peering over his shoulder. "Wonder how long that'll stay looking like that."

Dean ignored that comment. "Here's the living room," he said, leading her into it. "See, they've cut off the back part to make another bedroom; it all used to be one big room."

He opened the new door to reveal a bedroom that looked out over the back garden. It was furnished with a bed, wardrobe and desk. A small cabinet stood by the bed and there was a shelf for books running the length of one wall. The carpet flowed in from the living room.

"This is my room, Mum," Dean said and went and sat on the bed, bouncing up and down. "Bed's quite comfortable."

"It's a nice room," agreed his mother, going to the window to look out. "Pretty curtains. The garden's a bit of a mess, isn't it?"

"That's our next job," said a voice from the door. "Hi, Dino." Madeleine came into the room and gave him her usual bear-like hug. "Do you like your room?"

"Yeah, great. Mad, this is my mum. She's brought me down with all my stuff."

"Hallo, Mrs Joseph," said Madeleine. "Nice to meet you. Would you like a cup of tea? I'll just put the kettle on." She led the way back to the kitchen.

"Hey, Mad, this is an improvement," Dean said, as she filled the kettle and plugged it in. "This kitchen was a nightmare before."

"Come and see the rest of the house while the kettle boils," Madeleine said. "Dad's done a fantastic job. You won't recognise any of it."

They went up the second flight and proudly Madeleine showed them the three bedrooms there.

"Look good, don't they?" said Madeleine. "Mine's this one, over yours... so keep the noise down."

They all laughed, and Janice said, "I should think you'll all have to keep the noise down. I don't envy your neighbours, specially if you all have your music as loud as our Dean does at home."

"Oh, we'll be careful," promised Madeleine. "My mum's been on at me too. Look, here's the bathroom. New bath and shower and a new loo. You guys have got your shower down on the ground floor, and a basin and loo as well, so you'll only need to come up here if you want a proper bath. Come down and see Ben's room."

They trekked back down to the ground floor and inspected

Ben's room, as yet unoccupied, and the "downstairs ablutions" as Mad referred to them. "We took the very end off Ben's room to make a passage to the garden door. Now we can get into the garden without going through his room."

"It all seems very cleverly organised," Janice remarked as they sat in the living room with their cups of tea. "Your dad must have spent a lot of time and effort on it."

"And money," said Dean. "You should have seen it before, Mum, it was horrendous." He turned to Madeleine. "When do the others come back, Mad?"

"Ben and Cirelle are coming tomorrow, and Charlie comes on Friday. It's a good thing we'll all be here by the weekend, because we've been invited to a party, look." She reached for an invitation that was standing on the mantelpiece. "Madge Peters, from number one, it says, is going to be ninety on Sunday and is having a barbecue in the garden to celebrate, and we're all invited."

"In the garden? What garden? Hers?"

"No, the one in the middle of the close. Dad's been invited to join the Residents' Association, and this party is something to do with them. This Mrs Peters who lives at number one has arranged this party for her birthday with the residents' club, and we're all invited so we can get to know our neighbours."

"What a lovely idea," said Janice, taking the invitation from Madeleine and reading it.

Dean pulled a face. "I'm not sure I want to go to a barbecue the first weekend back at college," he moaned.

"It's all right, it won't interfere with any plans you've got," laughed Madeleine. "It's Sunday lunchtime. You won't even miss your Sunday lie-in after your Saturday night on the town. Anyway," she went on, "you don't have to go if you don't want to, but Dad says I ought to go as they've made the effort to invite us."

"I'm sure he's right," Janice said firmly. "You should go too, Dean. It's only manners."

"Hmm, I'll see," Dean said noncommittally. "Come on, Mum, we'd better get the car unloaded. You've got a long drive home again."

All three of them carried Dean's belongings into the house, and what with stereo equipment, two lamps, boxes of books, and a supply of food, it took them several journeys.

"Don't look now," Madeleine said to him as they went out for the second load, "but her indoors next door in number six is watching from the window. She's always snooping out of that window."

Dean flicked his eyes upwards and saw the shadow of some-one standing behind a lace curtain, watching them. "I'm going to wave," he said, and suiting the action to the word, he looked up at the living-room window of number six and raised his hand in cheerful greeting. The shadow instantly disappeared and there was no return wave. Dean laughed. "She's gone," he said in mock surprise.

Madeleine giggled. "We haven't met the ones on that side yet," she said, "but the ones on the other side are called David and Shirley Redwood, and they're OK."

By the time the car was empty, Dean's room looked like a second-hand shop, with boxes and bags stacked up, and an armful of clothes dumped on the bed.

"Well, I must be on my way," Janice said. "Nice to have met you, Madeleine, I hope you'll all be very happy in your Mad-house. I love the sign, by the way."

"Thanks," said Madeleine. "I'm sure we will."

"Now, I thought you might not have time to go shopping before this evening," Janice went on, "so I've put a pot of chicken curry into the fridge. I don't know how you're going to work the food between you, but there's enough there for the two of you this evening if you want it. All you need to do is warm it up and to boil some rice. There's a packet of rice in one of Dean's food boxes."

"Hey, thanks very much, Mrs Joseph," Madeleine said. "That's really kind of you."

"Yeah, thanks, Mum." Dean gave her a peck on the cheek. "Now you ought to be going or Dad'll think you've piled up on the motorway."

Janice laughed. "It's all right," she said, "I'm going." She turned again to Madeleine. "I think you should call me Janice," she said. "Mrs Joseph sounds a bit stiff if you're living with Dean, don't you think?"

They saw her into the car, watching and waving as she drove off round the Circle.

As they walked back into the house, Dean waved again to number six's living-room window. There didn't seem to be anyone there, but as he said to Mad, "You never know, and you wouldn't want them to think we weren't friendly, now would you?"

That evening, when they had done justice to Janice's chicken curry, Madeleine went out to meet Dan, but Dean stayed in to sort his room out. When he had the house to himself, he wandered round it slowly, just as Madeleine had done, going into every room again and looking at it. It would seldom be quiet like this again. It would be a good place to live, he decided, and set about unpacking his belongings and making his room his own. The first thing he set up was his stereo, and for the rest of the evening treated himself to Pink Floyd. Remembering his mother's comments about noise, he didn't have it as loud as he would have chosen, but even so it was a good thing that the Colbys were out, or Sheila would have been certain her worst fears were being realised.

Luckily the doorbell was shrill, for Dean did actually hear it above his music. He went down to the front door, wondering if one of the others had decided to come back a day early after all, or if Mad had had yet another row with Dan. When he opened the door, however, he found a girl on the doorstep. She was tall and slim, with long auburn hair hanging round her shoulders. Her long legs were shown off to advantage in the mini-est of mini skirts, and her eyes were glowing in her face.

"Hallo," he said in surprise.

"Hallo," she replied, "I'm Chantal."

Chantal had practised to herself in the mirror, what she was going to say when he opened the door. She tried, "How do you do, I'm Chantal Haven, and I live at number four," but that seemed terribly formal and also rather schoolgirlish, and the last thing she wanted was for him to think of her as a schoolgirl. She tried a super-casual "Hi, Chantal's the name," but somehow the words didn't come out right when they were said aloud. Finally she settled for the simple, "Hallo, I'm Chantal," and practised it several times to introduce the right husky tone into her voice. Then she had to wait for her mother to be busy catching up on the ironing in front of the television, and for Annabel to be working in her room. At last they were properly occupied and she could slip out of the house and walk round to number seven. She had seen Dean emptying the car earlier. He wasn't desperately handsome or anything, in fact he looked a bit small and ordinary and she wasn't sure she liked his beard, but she was determined to meet him and have an introduction to the students before Annabel did. After all, even if this one wasn't anything special, he could introduce her to the others, and there might be one...She knew of course that she was going to meet them at old Mrs Peters's barbecue on Sunday, at least she hoped they would come, but there would be lots of people there, almost the whole Circle probably, and she might not be remembered afterwards. Much better to get in ahead of the crowd. She put on her make-up carefully, quite aware that it made her look several years older than her actual fifteen, chose an outfit to dazzle, and set out.

"Hi, Chantal, I'm Dean. Are you looking for Mad?"

"Mad?" Chantal looked blank.

"Madeleine Richmond...who lives here?"

"Oh, no." Chantal felt confused and at a disadvantage. "No, well, yes sort of. It's just, well, I live at number four and I thought I'd come over and introduce myself, you know, and say welcome to the Circle."

"The Circle?" It was Dean's turn to look confused.

"Yeah, the Circle, this road, Dartmouth Circle. It's known as the Circle."

"Oh, well, thanks very much. Ahem, do you want to come in? I'm afraid the others aren't here. Mad is out, and the others arrive tomorrow or Friday, I'm not sure which." Dean stood back in the doorway and Chantal walked in past him. She stood at the bottom of the stairs and looked round.

"They've done an awful lot to this place, it was pretty crappy before. Is that your music?"

Dean nodded. "Yeah. Do you like Pink Floyd?"

"Yeah, cool."

"Come up if you like," Dean said, "and I'll make some coffee, or there may be a beer." Chantal turned at once and set off up the stairs and as Dean followed he was treated to an extended view of her legs right up to the little white panties which stretched tight across her bottom.

Jeez, thought Dean, who on earth was this amazing girl who'd virtually invited herself into the house and was now wandering upstairs as if she owned the place?

"Oh, that's clever," Chantal said when she saw how the new bedroom had been created. "Is that your room?"

From the safety of the kitchen Dean called, "Yes it's mine. I'm just sorting out my stuff. Did you say beer or coffee?"

Chantal was about to say beer, because she thought it sounded more grown up, but remembering the effect drink had had on her before she settled for coffee. After all, students drank coffee, didn't they?

While he was making the coffee, Chantal wandered round the living room looking at things. She saw the invitation on the mantelpiece and picked it up. It was addressed to "All at number seven".

"I see you've got an invitation to old Ma Peters's barbecue on Sunday," she said to Dean when he came in carrying two mugs of coffee.

"Yeah, Mad showed me. Do you take sugar?"

"No thanks. Are you going to go?"

Dean shrugged. "Don't know. Expect so." It was certainly more likely than it had been before, if Chantal was going to be there. "You going?"

"Probably," she replied casually. She was actually looking forward to it, but it might not be cool to sound too enthusiastic. "Should be lots of food and drink, at least."

"Well, Mad's going, I know, so I expect we'll all show up as well. What's she like, this Mrs Peters? She must be quite a character if she's throwing a party for her ninetieth, Jeez, imagine being ninety!"

A silence lapsed over them as they drank their coffee, and Chantal wondered what to say next. The Pink Floyd CD had finished and the silence threatened to engulf them.

At last, Dean thought of something to say. "You a student too?" he asked.

Chantal was ready for that one and her much-practised answer came out as smoothly as she could have wished. "No, just finishing up at Belcaster High."

Dean nodded. Must be about eighteen, he thought, but before he could say any more he heard a key in the front door and the sound of Madeleine coming upstairs. She wasn't alone, Dan had come home with her. She stopped at the top of the stairs in surprise.

"Hi," she said.

"Mad, this is Chantal," Dean explained. "She lives just down the road."

"Number four," said Chantal, but she wasn't really listening; her eyes slid off Madeleine on to the face of the man with her. This was more like it, much more the sort of person she had hoped would be coming to live in number seven. As he appeared up the stairs she saw he was well over six foot tall, with dark, wavy hair and a strong face. His eyes, a dark chocolate brown, swept over her and came to rest on her face, but not before Chantal had seen him take in and approve of her long legs extending from under their mini skirt. He was behind Madeleine, so she didn't see his appraising look, but Dean did and his mouth hardened. He didn't like Dan much at the best of times. Dean was very fond of Mad and didn't like the casual way Dan often treated her, and he certainly didn't like Dan's cool appraisal of Chantal, as if Mad wasn't even in the room.

"I just thought I'd come round and introduce myself," Chantal said, "and say welcome to the Circle."

"That's Dartmouth Circle," put in Dean.

"Great," said Mad cheerfully. She waved a hand at Dan. "This is my boyfriend, Dan. Do you guys want more coffee or a beer?"

"No, thanks," Dean said shortly. "I'm going to finish my sorting." He got to his feet. "See you Sunday, I expect, Chantal."

"Yeah, great." Chantal was disappointed that Madeleine had claimed Dan as her boyfriend, still, there would surely be others coming to the house. As long as she got to know these, she would soon meet their friends. She, too, got to her feet. "I must get back too. Are you coming on Sunday?" she asked Madeleine, but the question was directed at Dan as well.

"To the barbecue? Yes, we'll be there, at least I will. Dan hasn't decided yet." She grinned. "He's not a proper resident."

"But you'd be very welcome," Chantal assured him hastily, "everyone's invited."

"Oh, I expect I'll come and keep you company," he drawled, and gave Chantal the faintest of winks. He was well aware of the effect he had on women, and he could never resist trying out his charm. He was rewarded with a faint blush from Chantal, who, with her heart beating a tattoo said, "Well, anyway, I must be going. See you on Sunday." She went downstairs and let herself out, closing the front door behind her. Neither Mad nor Dan offered to see her out, and in a way she felt this was a compliment. It meant, she thought happily, that they already regarded her as a friend who didn't need such niceties. She might have been less happy had she heard Dan's comments when she had gone.

"What a peculiar girl," he said, dropping down on to the sofa. "What made her come round out of the blue?"

Mad shrugged. "Just wanted to be friendly, I suppose. The other people we've met already have been." She passed him a can of lager from the fridge and sat down beside him on the sofa with her own. "I suppose we'll get to meet most of them on Sunday."

Cirelle arrived the next morning before the other two were awake, and being discovered in her pyjamas by Cirelle's father, Mad was pleased that Dan had decided to go home last night. She was quite sure that all their parents knew and to some extent accepted that they all slept with their boyfriends, but she was glad that they hadn't had their suspicions confirmed, particularly as she'd not yet met Cirelle's parents and had the feeling they were rather strait-laced.

"Sorry to wake you up," Cirelle cried as Mad opened the front door. "Mad, this is my dad. Dad, this is Madeleine, whose dad owns the house."

Mad, still rubbing the sleep from her eyes, held out a hand. "Nice to meet you, Mr Thomas. Sorry, I had rather a late night last night. Give me a couple of minutes to get dressed and I'll give you a hand in with your stuff."

Cirelle's father looked at the tousle-haired girl and grinned. "Don't worry, Madeleine. We can manage." He turned to his daughter. "You know where to go, girl?"

"Yeah, Dad, no worries. We'll just prop the door open and carry everything in."

While they went back out to the car for the first load, Madeleine shot upstairs to get dressed, As she passed Dean's door she thumped on it heavily, before opening it to hiss, "Rise and shine, Dino, Cirelle's here, with her dad!" Once back in her own room she threw on some jeans, a T-shirt and some train-ers, and scurried downstairs again to help Cirelle. As she went out to the car, she instinctively looked up at the windows of the houses next door. Shirley Redwood, who was sitting in the window with a cup of coffee in her hand, waved cheerfully, but the other window was innocently empty.

Cirelle's luggage was soon unloaded and her father was made to sit and have a cup of tea before he set off home again, but as soon as he had finished it he got to his feet.

"Well," he said, "it was nice to meet you both, but I'd better make tracks. I gotta get the car back and be back for my afternoon shift."

"Dad borrowed my uncle's car to bring me," explained Cirelle, "but he needs it back this afternoon."

The girls went down to see him off, and as they stood chatting by the car, Shirley Redwood came out of her front door. She stopped when she saw them and smiled. "Hallo," she said. "Welcome to Dartmouth Circle. I'm Shirley Redwood and I live here, in number eight."

Madeleine introduced herself and then Cirelle and her father. Shirley shook hands with each, and then looking at Cirelle she asked, "Haven't we met before? Didn't I see you at St Joe's drop-in centre?"

Cirelle returned her smile. "Maybe," she replied. "I do go there to help sometimes. But I haven't been since the end of the summer term."

"Well, I'm sure they'll be glad to see you back," Shirley said warmly. "You too, Madeleine, if you wanted to come. We love to see new faces."

"Yes, well, maybe," Mad hedged unhappily. She wasn't at all sure, from what she'd heard, that St Joe's was her scene.

Just then a car swung into the Circle and pulled into the drive of number six. Sheila and Gerald Colby looked out at the assembled group and slowly got out of the car.

"Ah, here are your other neighbours," Shirley was saying and immediately called over to them. "Sheila, Gerald, come and meet our new neighbours."

There was no escape for them, Sheila thought, and anyway, it had to be done some time. They came over and at once Shirley made the introductions.

"Hallo, Mrs Colby," Mad said brightly. "I'm sorry we haven't met before, though I have seen you at your window sometimes and waved."

"Well, of course, Gerald and I have been meaning to pop round," Sheila said, "haven't we, Gerald? But somehow, if you're busy people like us, the time just flies by. Still, now you've moved in…you have moved in now, haven't you?" Mad nodded. "Well, now you've moved in we must get to know one another."

She had shaken hands with both girls and Cirelle's father, but now she backed away a little. Gerald did not shake anyone's hand, he simply raised his own in a general greeting and nodded genially.

"Cirelle, girl, I have to go," said her father, and giving her a final hug, he slipped into the driver's seat. "Look after yourself and have a good time. Phone your mother, OK?"

"Yeah, Dad. I will."

"We'll see you soon, I expect," murmured Sheila, and she and Gerald returned to their car to unload their shopping. By the time they had done so, Mr Thomas had driven away.

"Well, I'm not really surprised," Sheila said as she packed away the shopping.

Gerald, already ensconced with the crossword, looked up. "Surprised at what?" he asked.

"That one of them is black," replied Sheila.

"Does it matter?"

"No, of course not," Sheila said. "I'm just sorry for the girl herself, that's all. I mean, this isn't an area where blacks live, is it? She'd probably be much happier living with people of her own sort."

"Now, Sheila, don't start making problems where there aren't any," Gerald began.

"Problems? I'm not making problems. It doesn't matter to me. I shook hands with both of them, just as I would with anybody. It isn't a problem for me, it's her I'm worried about. She may feel out of place."

"Well, she won't if we make sure she doesn't," Gerald said, and returned to his paper.

*Chapter Eleven*

Sunday's weather behaved itself perfectly, and the sun crept over the rooftops, promising a beautiful autumn day. Madge Peters sat as usual in her window and watched the gardens come to life as the sunlight struck russet and gold in the trees and added brilliance to the rainbow of dahlias in the Hoopers' front garden. Spike stalked up the stairs and with a graceful leap landed on her lap.

"My birthday, today," she told him as she stroked his fur. "Ninety. Imagine being ninety, Spike! I don't feel ninety. It's funny, I don't feel any particular age, but I certainly don't feel ninety." She continued to stroke him as he set up a rumble of purring. "It's going to be a beautiful day," she remarked. "Everything's been organised, so let's hope it all goes with a swing."

Anthony Hammond had thought Madge's idea of a ninetieth birthday party combined with a welcome barbecue for the new student house was a marvellous compromise.

"I think it's a wonderful idea," he said to her when she suggested it. "It'll be your party of course, but it means we have a reason to introduce people in the Circle to the students and get to meet them in an informal way." He smiled a quick smile. "It also gets Mrs Colby off my back for a while," he admitted, "because if it's your party, it is technically nothing to do with the Residents' Association, and she can't complain about it. But of course we'll give you all the help you need with the arrangements. Will Andrew want to do the barbecuing, do you think?"

Madge laughed. "Good Lord, no. I should think the idea would horrify him," she said. "And anyway, I wouldn't deprive Mike Callow and Steve Hooper of their fun. They're always great behind the barbecue, aren't they?"

"They always seem to enjoy themselves," Anthony agreed. "Will you ask them, or would you like me to do it?"

"No, I'll do it," Madge said. "I want to organise this myself as far as I can, it'll give me something to do and something to look forward to."

"Well, if you run into any difficulties, don't hesitate to come and say," Anthony said, "and we'll get it sorted. Of course we'll provide the manpower on the day."

Madge had great fun organising her party. She had few people she wanted to ask herself apart from Andrew and one or two from St Joe's. "Most of my friends are dead," she pointed out when Andrew asked her if she was quite sure she wanted this sort of celebration for her ninetieth. "The people in the Circle are the ones I know best now. Of course if there's anyone you want included you only have to tell me. Don't worry, Andrew," she said, seeing worry lurking in his eyes, "I'm *enjoying* myself."

Andrew knew this was true and was very pleased she had found something to occupy her. The party was some way ahead, but it was certainly giving her something to look forward to, and appeared to involve him very little.

"All you have to do, darling," she told him, "is turn up on the day."

Before she sent out her invitations, Madge canvassed everyone in the Circle. She invited each of the wives round to tea or for coffee and either press-ganged or charmed them into making her a pudding or a salad for the day. She invited Mike and Steve in for a drink and asked them if they would take charge of the barbecue as they usually did on such occasions.

"We'd be honoured, Mrs Peters," Steve Hooper said gravely. "Would you like us to sort out the setting up of the barbecue on the day, get all the charcoal, that sort of thing?"

Madge dazzled him with a smile. "Well," she said as if she hadn't intended that they should all along, "that would be absolutely marvellous. Would you mind? I'll order all the meat from Footwell's in the Dartmouth Road. They're very good there, they'll cut it all up and deliver it here the day before."

Madge looked across at the student house. There was no sign of life from there yet, not that she had expected there to be. She had heard some of them come home the night before, and it had been quite late. They were all in residence now. Madge had watched with interest as each one had arrived, carrying boxes and bags, cases and rucksacks into the house, until she wondered if it could possibly hold any more stuff.

What had pleased her most, however, was that yesterday she had had a visit from Madeleine Richmond, the girl whose father actually owned the house. Madge had been dozing in her window when she'd been awakened by the buzz of her entry-phone. She reached for the receiver and called, "Yes?"

"Mrs Peters? It's Madeleine Richmond from over the road. Can I come up?"

"Yes, of course." Madge pressed the door release, delighted to have an unexpected visitor. She heard footsteps running up the stairs and the girl came into the room. Madge didn't get up from her chair, but she held out her hand in welcome and the girl crossed the room immediately and grasped it warmly. Madge liked her at once. She had a cheerful, open face, framed with dark curls, partially caught back with a clasp, and she was grinning broadly.

"Hallo," she said, "I'm Madeleine. I've come to thank you for the invite to your party tomorrow. We'd all love to come, if that's all right. It isn't too late to accept, is it? Ben didn't move in until yesterday, and I wasn't sure how many we'd be."

"Of course it's not too late," Madge said cheerfully. "It'll be lovely to meet you all." Her eyes twinkled. "I've been watching you coming and going from my window. Now have you time for a cup of tea with me?"

"Oh, yes please," said Mad. "Shall I put the kettle on?"

"Would you? It'll save me getting up." Even as she said this, Madge wondered why it was so easy to accept help from this young student, when identical help offered from Sheila or Shirley or even Andrew always irritated her.

"You'll find cups and things in the cupboard, Madeleine," she called through to the kitchen.

Madeleine appeared at the kitchen door. "Do call me Mad or Maddo, everyone does, except my Great-aunt Molly."

Madge laughed at that. "Then I shall certainly call you Mad, I don't think I want to be classed with Great-aunt Molly if she's referred to in that tone of voice. And you," she went on as Mad carried a tray into the room, "must call me Madge, if you can manage it. Not many people left in the world these days to call me Madge, at least," she added with a wink, "not to my face!

"Now, pour out the tea, and then tell me all about the students in your house. Then when I meet them tomorrow, I shall have some idea of who is who."

Mad had stayed for nearly an hour, and the two of them had got on like a house on fire. Mad found Madge surprisingly easy to talk to, and Madge thought Mad's zestful way of speaking both endearing and refreshing. Both were surprised when they looked at the time.

"Hey, I must go," Mad said, jumping to her feet. "We're all meeting at the Dutch later. But I'll come and see you again, shall I?"

"That would be lovely," Madge smiled. "And you must make sure I meet them all tomorrow," she added. "I'll want to know who I'm watching through my window in future!"

Mad laughed and promised to bring each of her house-mates over to be introduced. "I'll try and bring them one at a time," she said, "so you can really work out who everybody is!"

"I can't see us having any problem with them," Madge remarked to Spike, "if they are all like young Mad."

Spike agreed. Mad had put down an extra saucer of milk for him in the kitchen before she had left, and he felt extremely well disposed towards her.

By the time Madge had had some breakfast and dressed herself, there were the beginnings of activity in the Circle below. Steve and Mike were sorting out the big barbecue made from half an oil drum, which was kept for such occasions in the Hoopers' shed. This they set up on the pavement outside Mike's house. Paul Forrester had borrowed some trestle tables and he and Alison were covering them with sheets ready for the food to be laid out. Anthony Hammond was setting up a bar on another table in his drive, while Jill took glasses from a cardboard box and put them in neat rows beside the cans of beer and bottles of wine.

Andrew was supposed to be coming to fetch her down into the Circle just before twelve, but suddenly Madge wanted to be there now, to be part of the preparation. It was her party, after all, why should she miss out on all the fun of setting it up? After all, she might never have another party. Tipping Spike off her lap, she got up and went to the top of the stairs, settled herself in the seat of the lift and glided down to the ground floor. As she let herself out, she saw Dr Fran coming out of her house, carrying a huge bowl of raspberry and meringue.

"Morning, Mrs Peters," called Fran, "and happy birthday."

"Thank you, Doctor," replied Madge, "I'm having one. I just thought I'd come down and see what was going on. What a scrumptious-looking pudding."

"Thank you. It's usually a favourite." Fran slowed her pace to match Madge's and they strolled into the garden. When they reached the bench Fran said, "Why don't you sit here and direct operations, it's your day after all."

Madge smiled at her gratefully, she hated to admit how much walking anywhere tired her these days. "Yes, what a good idea, I think I will. It's such a lovely morning."

Everyone came over to speak to her, to wish her happy birthday, to consult her on where she wanted the food tables. Jill and Alison went into her house to collect the meat that had been delivered the day before. Even Sheila Colby who had been against the whole idea seemed to be entering into it now. She came up to where Madge was sitting, carrying a huge cake.

"I've made you a birthday cake," she said, and, leaning down, showed Madge the enormous chocolate cake, decorated with little chocolate roses and an iced message, "Happy Birthday Madge, Ninety Today." Round the edge were nine candles. "Not ninety, I'm afraid," Sheila said, "but one for each decade."

Despite her habitual feeling of irritation whenever she saw Sheila, Madge was touched by her kindness in making a cake. She had considered getting one made herself, but had decided against it, thinking people of ninety didn't need birthday cakes. However, now she saw Sheila's offering, she found that they did, and feeling the tears pricking the back of her eyes, she said with true sincerity, "Sheila, how kind of you, it's a beautiful cake. Thank you very much indeed. You know how much I love chocolate cake."

Sheila flushed with pleasure. She was always a little afraid of Madge Peters, but she could see that the old lady was really pleased and it made the effort she'd put into the cake well worthwhile.

"I'll go and put it on the table with the puddings," she said and bustled off, pausing to warn Isabelle not to let the children she was minding, Hammonds and Forresters, play near the food table. As she moved on, Isabelle pulled a face at her back and gathered the four children, who were nowhere near the food table, to come and say happy birthday to Mrs Peters.

The invitation had said twelve, and by half past nearly all the residents were out in the Circle, either in the garden or on the road itself with glasses in their hands, chattering and laughing in the comfort of their own private community. As soon as Andrew Peters had arrived and parked in his mother's driveway, Mike Callow and Dr Harry had put their cars across the entrance of the Circle, so that the party was cut off from the outside world.

"We'll move them if necessary," Dr Harry promised Anthony, "but we don't want cars sweeping in to the Circle and ploughing into the party."

"Anyway," Mike added, "everybody's here. We're none of us expecting anybody else, and there shouldn't be any casual traffic on a Sunday."

The smell of the barbecue wafted across the Circle and in through the windows of number seven. Most of the inmates were just emerging from their beds, but the smell of barbecuing meat hurried them to the windows.

"Shit!" said Dean peering out. "The whole street is out there."

"Well, it's a street party, dumb-dumb, what d'you expect?" cried Mad. "Come on, Dan, I'm going out to have some breakfast."

Dan, who had spent the night at the Madhouse, sniffed. "Yeah, maybe, in a minute. Put the kettle on, eh?"

Madge was delighted with her party. She sat in the sunshine with a coffee table beside her, thoughtfully provided by Mary Jarvis. On this, she had her lunch and a glass of wine, and as she ate, she watched her guests enjoying themselves.

The Callow boys, Peter and Carl, and the two young Hoopers, had put rugs on the ground in the garden and were sitting round eating barbecued sausages and spare ribs in their fingers. Oliver and Emma were living with their father now, but Madge had made a point of inviting the Callow children with a separate invitation from Mike's. It hadn't escaped her notice that they visited their father far less often than they used to, and she wanted them to be at her party. She had asked Caroline as well, since she always had been part of Dartmouth Circle before she left with the children. Caroline had allowed the children to come, but declined for herself. Probably for the best, Madge thought with a sigh. She didn't want any rows or scenes at her party.

Young Debbie Callow was playing with Tom and Sylvia Hammond in the sandpit, enjoying being the big one for a change. She'd said to Jill, "I'll mind them for you, I like little children."

Jill had smiled and said, "That would be a great help, Debbie. Just give me or Isabelle a call when you're tired of them."

Debbie played with the younger children quite happily. She liked coming to see Daddy, and she thought this party was great fun. Dad was busy cooking of course, but he'd promised to take them swimming when it was over.

Madge's eyes wandered round the groups of adults as they shifted and changed. Angela Haven was here with her two girls. Annabel, Madge thought, was looking very peaky, obviously working too hard for the exams the young were burdened with these days. She seemed to have made little effort to dress up for the party. She wore the regulation jeans and a T-shirt with an outsized shirt over the top. In contrast, Chantal had obviously given a lot of thought to her appearance. Though several years younger than her sister, she didn't look it. In comparison with Annabel's wan face, Chantal looked blooming. Her make-up heavy, with thickly applied mascara and heavy-handed eyeliner, was startling, but it had been painstakingly done. Dressed to catch the eye, Chantal was wearing a crop-top and the shortest skirt Madge had ever seen, and though it was really very warm she had long boots on that came up over her knees. It certainly had the desired effect; no one could possibly miss her.

The sisters were talking to Isabelle, but even as they did so Chantal's eyes were scanning the other guests, as if searching for someone more interesting. The students no doubt, Madge thought with a wry smile. She had no illusions about Chantal Haven.

Angela was talking to Fran and Harry Davies. She looks tired too, thought Madge. Can't be easy when your husband ups and walks out.

David and Shirley Redwood were sitting with Mary Jarvis

and Sheila and Gerald at a picnic table at the edge of the garden. They had two bottles of wine on the table and seemed to be in fine spirits. The Hoopers and the Forresters were gathered round the barbecue with Mike Callow, and Jill and Anthony Hammond were standing by the bar on their front drive.

Andrew came and sat down beside her, a plate piled high with barbecue and salad in one hand and a pint of beer in the other.

"Good party, Mother," he said. "Everyone seems to be enjoying themselves. Can I get you anything?"

"No, Andrew, you eat yours. I'll wait for a pudding."

Across the Circle a door banged and out of number seven streamed Mad Richmond and the other residents of The Madhouse. They were all talking and laughing and at once made a beeline for the bar, all except Mad. She looked round the groups, and seeing Madge sitting with Andrew in the garden, came straight across.

"Happy birthday!" she cried and dumped an envelope in the old lady's lap. "There's a card from all of us. I'm sorry we're a bit late, but we had rather a late night last night." She looked at the elderly man sitting next to Madge and said, "Hi, you must be Andrew. I heard all about you yesterday when I came for tea." Hardly pausing for breath, Mad went on, "That food looks good, I'm starving. See you in a minute, Madge, I'll bring the others over as soon as I can drag them away from the bar."

"Who was that?" asked Andrew, startled.

"Madeleine Richmond," replied his mother. "It's her father that's bought number seven, remember? As a student house?"

Andrew grinned. "Yes, I remember. Sheila was horrified."

"Still is, as far as I know," smiled Madge. "But Madeleine, or Mad as she's called, seems a very friendly girl. She came to tea with me yesterday and was great company."

Mad went up to the others at the bar and claimed a glass of wine.

"We're supposed to be meeting everyone," she said. "I gather it's one of the reasons for the party." She grinned. "I want to introduce you to our other next-door neighbours, coming, Dino?"

"Yeah, in a minute," said Dean, who had just spotted Chantal. "Just got to speak to someone first." He wandered off.

Ben was already talking to Jill Hammond as she poured him a pint, and so Mad gathered up Cirelle and Charlie and went across to the picnic table.

"Hi," she said, "we've come to introduce ourselves properly." She smiled at David Redwood. "We've met, haven't we? You live next door in number eight."

David half got up. "Indeed we have," he said. "You remember my wife, Shirley?"

Shirley smiled up at the girls and fluttered her fingers in greeting. "Welcome to the Circle," she said. She looked at Cirelle. "I know I met you and your father the day you arrived. You help at the day centre, don't you?" she asked. "At St Joe's?"

Cirelle smiled back shyly. "Yes, that's right."

"Yes, I remember now, when I first met you there you said you were coming to live in the area, but I hadn't realised you were one of the students moving in next to us." She waved a hand towards Sheila and Gerald. "You remember your neighbours on the other side," she said. "Gerald and Sheila Colby, and this is Mary Jarvis from number five. She helps at St Joe's too, so you'll soon get to know her."

"And you haven't met Charlie Murphy," Mad said. "She's in her final year, like Ben, who's over there." She waved vaguely in the direction of the bar where Ben was standing talking to Anthony Hammond.

The Colbys nodded at the girls and murmured something about looking forward to getting to know them better, and Mary Jarvis reached across and shook hands with all of them.

"Do go and help yourselves to some food," Sheila suggested. "There's still plenty on the barbecue and the salads are over there on the table."

Taking this as their dismissal, the girls moved away. "Well, that's done," said Mad, relieved. She had promised her father that she would introduce them all properly to her immediate neighbours as soon as she could and now it had been done she could go on round and meet the rest of the Circle.

"Let's get some food," Charlie said. "I'm starving." They crossed to the barbecue, where Mike and Steve, having seen the students arrive, had just put on some more chops and sausages.

"There's plenty here," Steve called as they approached, and Mike looked up to see who was coming.

He had heard of a *coup de foudre*, but had never believed in it. Now as he looked up and saw Charlotte Murphy coming towards him, it happened to him. Brash, confident, suave Mike Callow was struck, as if by lightning, at the sight of a young girl walking towards him. She was tall and slim and carried herself easily. Her long fair hair hung down on either side of her face like a curtain, and her wide grey eyes were amused as she glanced across at Debbie and the younger children playing in the sandpit. As she reached the barbecue she smiled at the two men who were cooking, and Mike felt as if he had been pole-axed.

"What can we get you?" Steve Hooper was asking. "Chop? Sausage? Spare rib? All three?"

"All three please," Mad answered, and Cirelle said the same.

"What about you?" Mike spoke to Charlie in a voice he hardly recognised as his own. "What would you like? I'm afraid I don't know your name."

Charlie directed her smile straight at him and said cheerfully, "It's Charlie, and I'll have whatever's going please." It was clear she had no idea of the effect she was having on him, and for that at least Mike was grateful.

He drew in a deep breath and scooped up a couple of sausages, a chop and a piece of spare rib. "That do to be going on with?" he asked.

"Fine," Charlie said. "Thanks." She turned away, moving towards the table where all the salads were laid out. Mike forced himself to turn his attention to the other two girls.

Steve was dishing out sausages, chops and ribs, saying as he did so, "Nice to meet you girls, I'm Steve Hooper, I live at number two, next to Mrs Peters, and this reprobate," he waved a barbecuing fork towards Mike, "is Mike Callow, of number ten. Welcome to Dartmouth Circle."

Dean carried his drink over to where Chantal was sitting with her sister and Isabelle on the grass outside the Havens' house.

"Hi, Chantal," he said, dropping down beside them, "how's it going?"

Chantal greeted him with a smile, pleased that he had remembered her name and come over to speak to her. It must be clear to Annabel that she already knew the occupants of number seven. She had, very carefully, not mentioned her visit earlier in the week, so that she could casually acknowledge the students when she saw them.

"Hi, Dean," she replied, and then not knowing quite what to say, said rather grudgingly, "This is my sister Annabel and this is Isabelle. She's the Hammonds' au pair." Even as she spoke, Chantal's eyes drifted away, skimming the Circle to see if the tall guy, Mad's boyfriend, was with them. As she couldn't see him, she returned her attention to Dean, who had begun to talk to Annabel.

"You at the college?" he asked.

Annabel shook her head. "No."

"Going to college somewhere else?"

"Next year. Maybe."

Pretty monosyllabic, thought Dean, not sparkly like her sister, so he gave up. He took a pull at his beer and then got to his feet. "Think I'll get some food," he said.

"I'll come with you," said Chantal, jumping up, and together they wandered over to the barbecue.

"Not very chatty, your sister," Dean remarked.

"No, like, she's been in a funny mood lately," said Chantal. "Come on, I want to meet the others in your house."

Dean allowed himself to be introduced to Steve and Mike,

collected himself some food and, followed by Chantal, went to join the girls who were sitting on the grass near Mrs Peters.

"Here's another of us," cried Mad cheerfully as he flopped down beside them. "Dean, this is Madge, whose birthday party this is."

"Hi, happy birthday. Great party."

"I'm glad you could come," Madge replied.

"Hi," Chantal said to the girls. Her eyes rested on Mad. "We met the other night, didn't we? I'm Chantal, from number four."

"Hi, yes, I remember, this is Charlie Murphy and Cirelle Thomas." Mad waved a hand at the others.

"I thought there were five of you," Chantal said innocently, still hoping the hunky Dan would put in an appearance.

"Yes, Ben's over there." It was Charlie who answered, nodding in the direction of the bar where Ben still stood, pint in hand, chatting now to Jill Hammond.

Angela Haven went over to the bar for another glass of wine. She wasn't driving anywhere today and decided an extra glass wouldn't hurt and might give her some dutch courage. As she waited for Anthony to open a new bottle she looked across at Annabel, still sitting on the grass with Isabelle.

She looks exhausted, thought Angela, not at all herself. There's something wrong, I know it.

Angela had been worrying about her elder daughter for some time now. She had become more withdrawn and evasive than ever. She did whatever was asked of her about the house, but she spoke only when spoken to, and disappeared up to her room as soon as supper was over, presumably to work. She never lingered over another cup of coffee after supper as she used to, or talked about her day, the way Chantal prattled on. She appeared to be doing her school-work properly now, after the row there had been about her progress and attitude during the early part of the summer term, but she no longer seemed friendly with Avril. They were certainly not combining on a history project any more, and neither visited the other at home.

Annabel seemed to have no friends, she had stopped going out and had no visitors.

"I'm fine, Mum," she had said, when Angela had tried to talk to her. "There's a lot of work to catch up on. I'm a bit tired, that's all."

She had never told them about Scott, even when they were raging at her about her having done no real work for weeks. She had just shrugged and refused to say where she had been and what she had been doing.

Annabel sat beside Isabelle watching the party. Chantal seemed determined to make herself the centre of attention, sitting with the students, making extravagant gestures, laughing loudly and flashing her darkly encircled eyes. Then, Oliver Hooper, who had been sitting with his sister and the Callow boys, suddenly got up and wandered over to where Chantal was holding court. He flung himself down by Chantal and grinned at her.

"Hi," he said to the group at large. "Hi, Chantal," he said. "Get you another drink?"

Chantal stopped in mid-flow, glowered at him. "No," she snapped, and turned her back on him.

Oliver laughed and said, "Come on, Chantal, don't be like that. We had good fun together at the New Year's party."

"No, we didn't," she replied between her teeth, "and I hope I never see you again."

"Oh, I'm afraid you will," Oliver said, lazily pulling at the grass. "Me and Em are going to live at Dad's now. My mum's got married again so we're living here." He got to his feet. "See you around." He grinned down at her, pleased with the way he had delivered his awful news, ignoring Chantal's retort, "I'm not surprised she doesn't want you to live with her, no one would." He wandered off as if he hadn't heard, but he stored the remark in his memory with revenge in mind. He knew that Chantal was afraid of him, and he enjoyed the knowledge.

"Oh no," muttered Chantal.

"Problem?" asked Mad casually.

"No." Chantal shook her head. "That's Oliver Hooper. His dad's doing the cooking? He lives at number two. Him and Em, his sister, used to live with their mum, now they're coming to live here."

"Is that bad?" asked Cirelle.

"Yeah, he's a real creep. Em's OK, she's over there," Chantal pointed, "but I *loathe* him."

At that moment, Dan emerged from the house and having collected a beer, wandered over to join them. He flopped down on the grass beside Mad, but his eyes ran appreciatively over Chantal and he grinned at her. "Hi," he said, "didn't we meet the other night?"

Trying to match his casual tone, Chantal said, "Yeah, I'm Chantal, from number four." She got to her feet to give him the benefit of her long legs and mini skirt, and said, "I'm going to get another drink, can I get one for anyone?"

No one else wanted one, and Chantal didn't either, but she'd made the move now, so she went across to the bar and asked Anthony for another Coke. Jill Hammond was talking to the only other student that Chantal hadn't yet met, so she joined them with her refilled glass.

"Hello, Chantal." Jill smiled at her. "Have you met Ben yet? He's in the student house." She turned to the tall man next to her. "Ben, this is Chantal Haven."

Ben said hello, and then continued with what he'd been saying before she'd joined them. "So I'll be finished this summer and then out looking for a job."

As he went on talking Chantal was able to study him. She approved of his dark good looks, his thick hair caught into its pony-tail, but he was a bit old, and he was taking no interest in her. Nor was Jill, so after a moment or two she moved away and went back to the student group in the garden.

Mike Callow went over to her. "I'm taking my lot swimming after this, Chantal. Want to come too?"

"Is Oliver coming?" Chantal asked, seeing him sitting with Emma and the Callow boys.

"I don't know," Mike replied. "I think Emma is, but I don't know about Oliver." He looked at her speculatively. "Does it matter?"

"No, of course not," Chantal replied quickly, feeling her face redden. "Thanks anyway, but I've got some homework to do," and she turned away.

Mike watched her go back to the student group. He had seen the colour flood her face and was sorry for her. He hadn't realised how much the fiasco at the New Year's Eve party had affected her. He'd assumed she would shrug it off and it was best forgotten, but now he wondered if he ought to have told Angela and Steve what their children had been up to. It was too late now, of course, but he decided to keep an eye on young Oliver himself, since he was now living in the Circle on a permanent basis. He looked across at where Peter and Oliver were sitting, laughing together and wished, not for the first time, that they weren't such good friends. There was something unpleasant about Oliver, and he didn't want him around Peter too much.

Just then, Andrew called for attention. Everyone gathered round and Sheila brought out Madge's cake. Andrew proposed a toast and they drank her health and sang happy birthday, while she sat, beaming, among them.

"Thank you all for coming," she said. "You've made my birthday a very special day. I think I'm a very lucky person to be surrounded by such good friends and neighbours. I'm going back inside now, but do go on enjoying yourselves. I shall be watching you from my window."

"As usual..." commented Mike Callow in a loud aside, and everyone laughed as Madge agreed. "As usual, Mike Callow. So behave yourself!"

Soon after she'd gone in, however, people did begin to drift away.

Mike took the promised swimming party and Isabelle took

over the care of the younger children again as the Forresters, Hammonds and Hoopers began to clear up. Annabel disappeared indoors, but Chantal sat around with the students as they finished their drinks.

"We're going to the Dutch this evening," Dean said to her. "Want to come?"

"The Dutch?"

"Flying Dutchman. You know, in Francis Street?"

"Yes, I know it," Chantal agreed, though she'd never been inside it. "What time?"

"'Bout half seven to eight I suppose. Shall I pick you up?"

"No." Chantal tried to sound casual. She knew there was no way her mother would let her go to the pub with a crowd of students so much older than her, but she would get round that problem in her own way. "No, don't worry, I'll see you there."

## Chapter Twelve

Jill and Anthony cleared the last of the bottles away and Jill stowed them in the boot of her car to take to the bottle bank in the morning. It had been a good party, she thought, as she slammed the boot shut, and as far as she could tell it had achieved its aims.

They had well and truly celebrated Madge's ninetieth birthday, with excellent food and drink, and more to the point Madge had thoroughly enjoyed herself, talking to everyone, and cutting the beautiful chocolate cake that Sheila had made. Everyone had congratulated Madge and chatted with her until she had finally admitted she was a little tired and allowed Andrew to take her back into the house and people had begun to drift away.

They'd also had a chance to meet the students in number seven. Jill hadn't met all of them, but she had spoken to Madeleine, whose house it was, and the pretty little West Indian girl and the older of the two young men, Ben, with the pony-tail and the penetrating dark eyes.

"I told one of the students," she said to Anthony casually when they were finally indoors, "Ben, I think his name was, that we could probably give him some gardening work. He's putting himself through university and needs some extra casual work."

Anthony was already reaching for his briefcase. "Fine," he said absently, extracting a file and opening it.

Jill felt a stab of hot anger at his disinterest; it was almost as if he had heard her speak, but had no idea what she'd said.

Stock answer number one, she thought angrily, suitable for ninety per cent of the comments I make! She was tempted to say, "I've decided to have an affair with him." Would that get stock answer number one, "Fine," or stock answer number two, "Oh, really?" or would Anthony actually hear her if she said anything so outrageous? However, she simply said, "Anthony, you're not listening to me."

He glanced up at the sharpness of her tone and said, "Yes I am, darling. You want Ben to help you with the garden. Fine. You fix it up with him." He gave her a quick smile and his eyes returned to the paper in his hand.

Frustrated, Jill left him to it and went into the kitchen, but a shepherd's pie was already made for supper, cauliflower washed and cut ready in a saucepan, and there was nothing for her to do there.

She went upstairs and looking out of the children's bedroom window, she saw Isabelle and the children still playing in the Circle garden. For a moment Jill leaned her hands on the windowsill and laid her forehead against the cool glass of the window. She felt so useless – no one needed her. For a moment she allowed this idea to nestle in her mind, then she gave herself a mental shake.

"Don't be so damn stupid, Jill!" she said aloud. "Anthony needs you, the children certainly need you and self-pity is going to get you nowhere." She turned away from the window and went into her own bedroom. On the dressing table stood a photograph of her and Anthony together on a hilltop that summer in Ireland. Anthony had an arm round her shoulder and she was laughing up into his face. Jill picked up the photo and looked at it, recalling the day that it had been taken.

Nancy had been as good as her word and moved into Dartmouth Circle for two weeks in June. Jill and Anthony had taken the car across to Ireland on the Swansea–Cork ferry and meandered their way around Cork and Kerry, bed and breakfasting wherever they ended up each night.

At first Jill missed the children dreadfully and found herself looking round for them, but this quickly slipped into an uneasy feeling that she'd mislaid something, then after a few days she gave herself up to the freedom of having no one to think of but Anthony and herself. They could drive or stop, sightsee or swim, walk or sunbathe, entirely as the mood took them and as they did all these things, they gradually rediscovered each other. To begin with they were very careful to ask, "What would *you* like to do today?" but after a week they had regained their ability to decide things together without more than a suggestion, a word or a look.

The day of the photograph they had been in West Cork. The weather had been perfect, she remembered, and they had set off from the B&B where they were staying, in their walking boots with a picnic in the rucksack. There was an iron-age fort on the top of a hill above the village, from which the views of the coastline were said to be stupendous. They had left the coast road and scrambled up a track through gorse, heather and the occasional bog and finally reached the top.

The fort was a complete circle of stones, piled like dry-stone walling, shoulder-high and four feet wide. A small gap in this allowed them to wander inside, where they found a souterrain, an escape passage down through the hill. The entrance to it was blocked with a grating, but they peered down through the bars to the darkness below.

Jill shuddered. "I'd hate to have to go down there," she said.

Anthony laughed and hugged her. "Bet you'd go fast enough if the enemy was clambering over the walls behind you," he said, still holding her in his arms. He kissed her nose and then hand in hand they wandered outside again. The view was even more stunning than promised, the sea shimmering blue, the coastline edging it in smooth sweeps of green and jutting rocky headlands. On the top of one in the distance, a lighthouse gleamed white in the sunshine; inland were fields and farms and beyond them the misty grey of distant hills.

"You really couldn't be taken by surprise here, could you?"

remarked Jill. "You have the most amazing view on every side." Coming round to the seaward side again, they sat down on the grass looking out at the sea, the sun warm on their faces, the countryside below them ablaze with golden gorse.

"This is just beautiful," Jill breathed, lying back on the grass and closing her eyes. The warmth soaked into her body and she wriggled her fingers in the cool grass beside her.

Suddenly she felt Anthony unlacing her boots and her eyes flew open as he pulled off first one then the other and then her heavy walking socks. She saw he had already discarded his own and now he lay beside her and kissed her gently.

"Can't make love in walking boots," he murmured as he slid his hand inside her cotton shirt.

"Anthony," she protested feebly as she felt her body respond to his fingers on her breast, "we can't make love here."

"Why not?" he whispered as he undid her shirt buttons and let his lips take over from his fingers, which had moved to the waistband of her shorts. "Seems the perfect place to me."

"Someone might come," Jill said weakly even as she reached for him.

"Let them," he said huskily as he eased her free of the last of her clothes, "and they'll see how much, how very much, I love my wife."

All resistance gone, they both surrendered to a perfect giving and taking of love, passionate, tender and satisfying, and when at last they lay side by side once more, relaxed on the grass in the shelter of the age-old fort, Jill felt she had never been as happy in her whole life. She raised herself up on one elbow to drink in the view, to remember exactly how it had been.

Suddenly, some way below, where the path dipped through a clump of bushes, she saw a movement and realised people were coming up the hill.

"Someone's coming, Anthony," she giggled and poking him with a finger said, "Get dressed! Come on, quick, before they get here."

Anthony opened one eye and glanced down the hill. A man and a woman were negotiating the boggy patch before the last climb up to the fort.

"Suppose you're right," he said reluctantly, and gathered up his scattered clothes.

By the time the newcomers reached the fort, Jill and Anthony were sitting decorously side by side, admiring the view, fully clothed except for their boots and socks. The other couple said good morning and disappeared inside the stone circle. When they came out again, the woman approached them carrying a camera.

"Would you mind?" she asked, indicating the camera. "Would you take a photo of us together up here?"

"Of course," Anthony got to his feet and the couple posed beside the entrance to the fort.

Jill rummaged in the rucksack and produced their own camera. "Perhaps you could take one of us," she said smiling, "with the view behind us." The photo was taken and the other couple wandered off down the far side of the hill.

"If it comes out well," Jill said, "I shall have it enlarged and framed, and then every time I look at it I shall remember today." She put her hands on his shoulders and reaching up, kissed him gently. "I do love you, Anthony."

The holiday continued its blissful way; the weather stayed perfect, long sunny days with the light lingering until eleven or later. Their happiness in each other's company was completely re-established, and though Jill longed to discuss her need to be more than "just a housewife" she was reluctant to spoil their new-found happiness and she said nothing, putting the conversation off, leaving it for a better moment; but in Ireland that moment never came. Their two weeks away together, away from home, away from the office, the telephone, the fax machine, had brought them closer than they had ever been. There seemed to be a new understanding between them, and Jill decided to wait until they were home again before bringing up the subject of a job.

She sighed now, as she replaced the silver-framed photo on

the dressing table. It had been a mistake, she'd been wrong to wait, for the moment they'd got back, Anthony was sucked into the morass of work that had accumulated in his absence. The closeness they had known dissipated in the routine of family life and normal living. There were times, but for the photo, that Jill would have thought that the day at the hill fort had been a dream. She remembered his words, "they'll see how much, how very much, I love my wife".

"But not enough to let me be myself," Jill muttered resentfully.

She had finally seized the moment one evening, when, sitting on the floor, leaning her back against his legs, she said, "Anthony, I really do want to go back to teaching…part-time of course." She felt him stiffen, and turning round she laid her arms on his knees and looked earnestly up into his face.

"I can't spend all day in the house, Anthony, it's driving me mad. I must get out, do something."

"It's too soon," Anthony said firmly. "The children need you."

"And the children have me!" Jill cried in frustration. "I'm *here* when they need me. Isabelle's here for them too. I need to do something out of the house. I need to contribute something to life."

"Your contribution is being a wife and mother," protested Anthony. "What greater contribution could you be making?"

"I know that," said Jill, fighting to sound calm and reasonable, "but it isn't enough. I don't feel fulfilled as a person. Other women have jobs and families, other wives cope with both."

"Yes, but you don't have to. I don't want a wife who's a part-time worker and a part-time mother. I want a full-time wife for me and a full-time mother for my children."

"But what about what I want?" demanded Jill. "They're *our* children, not just yours, and I think I'd be a better mother to them if I felt fulfilled myself."

"Perhaps we should try for another baby," suggested Anthony.

Jill felt a flash of anger. "I don't *want* another baby, Anthony," she said between clenched teeth, "I want a job."

"Well, it's too soon," Anthony repeated stonily. "We agreed, not until both the children were at school." He put his arms round her shoulders and touched his forehead to hers. "I thought we'd sorted this out in Ireland."

Jill drew back and stared at him in amazement. "In Ireland?" she repeated. "We never mentioned it in Ireland."

"I didn't think we had to, not make an issue of it. I just thought you understood how I felt, how I want our family to be. We were so close there, I thought..." Anthony's voice trailed off.

"You thought if you told me you loved me, I'd do everything your way. Be a good little wife and do as I'm told." Jill pulled away from him, got to her feet and turned away. She was near to tears, but she was determined not to let them fall, not to cry. When she cried her voice didn't work properly and she felt the urgent need to finish this conversation, now that at last it was being held at all.

"Jill, don't be absurd." Anthony was exasperated. "Don't put stupid words in my mouth. I loved being with you in Ireland, having you to myself, being just the two of us like when we were first married, but here at home it's not like that. Here we have two lovely children, we're a family and the children need you. You're their mother and you should be there for them."

"You're their father," Jill snapped back, "they need you too, but you go out to work, full-time."

"That's different."

"Yes," replied Jill bitterly, "it always is!" And she had walked out of the room, knowing bleakly that this question was never going to be resolved.

She was right, it wasn't resolved; it wasn't even mentioned again. Jill spent the rest of the summer trying to be what Anthony wanted her to be, but all the time the resentment bubbled. Gone was the special closeness they'd experienced in Ireland, gone the usual comfortable ease they knew at home, and in its place was the coolness of acquaintances.

Without the knowledge of the other, each of them consulted

Nancy, but she was far too wise either to give advice or take sides; all she said was, "Give it time and remember how important your children are to both of you."

So, they had coasted along, each waiting for the impossible, a change of heart in the other. Occasionally they made love, but their lovemaking seemed routine, lacking the fire and delight of their time in Ireland. Perhaps Anthony was too tired, he certainly was working extremely hard these days, or perhaps Jill herself was uninterested, for she seldom initiated their lovemaking any more. She hadn't really given the matter much consideration. It probably happened to all couples after a while and was perfectly natural. Then, today at the party, she had come face to face with Ben. She had been pouring drinks at the makeshift bar and he had come over for a beer.

"Hallo," he said, "I'm Ben."

"Hi Ben," she replied. "Want a beer?"

"Yeah, please." His dark eyes rested on her face for a moment and then he smiled. Suddenly his dark rather saturnine good looks were illuminated and Jill's heart skipped several beats. He was a very good-looking boy with his dark hair and his dark eyes – except of course he wasn't a boy, but quite definitely a man. He was much older than the other students, probably only three or four years younger than she was, and the look he was giving her was frankly sexual. She saw him assessing her and realised with a jolt that she was doing exactly the same to him – her eyes taking in the breadth of his shoulders, the strength of his legs encased in their blue jeans, and at this realisation, colour flooded her face and she laughed up at him, a little guiltily. His smile changed to a genuine grin of amusement and he took the glass from her hand.

"Thanks," he said and as their fingers touched round the glass Jill felt a frisson shoot through her. She pulled her hand away and said in a voice which sounded, to her at least, quite unlike her own, "So what are you studying, Ben?"

He had stayed to chat and she had promised him some

gardening work. But there had been something, a sharp recognition that had flashed between them, and in the calm of recollection, Jill wished she hadn't offered him work. She could still see the gleam of assessment in his eyes and a surge of heat flooded through her.

"This way madness lies," she said aloud and looked again at the Irish photograph. She saw herself and Anthony sharing the secret of their loving and suddenly she wanted it to happen again. She hurried downstairs to find Anthony. He was sitting at the computer in his study and didn't even look up as she came in. Slipping her arms round him from behind she pressed her cheek against his and then whispered in his ear, "Hey, handsome, let's go to bed!"

He was startled. "What, now? The children'll be back in a minute!"

"And Isabelle can give them their tea. Come on," she nibbled at his ear lobe, "be a devil!"

"Isabelle will know what we're doing," protested Anthony.

"Then she'll know how much, how very much, I love my husband," murmured Jill.

Anthony spun his chair to face her and gave her a quick hug. "I must finish this," he said, "I'll be up later."

Jill stared at the computer screen of figures for a moment and then said, "Yes, of course, later," and left the room.

It was several days before Ben came over to take her up on her promise of gardening work. It was late on a Tuesday afternoon when she was alone in the house. Normally she played golf on a Tuesday, but it had been raining nearly all day and the game had been cancelled. Isabelle had taken the children over to the Forresters for tea as she did most Tuesdays. Poor Paul had apparently had to take quite a pay cut to avoid redundancy and Alison had had to find herself a part-time job to help make ends meet.

"I really hate having to work when the children are so young," Alison had sighed to Jill, "but we can't manage without the money." They had been sitting in her kitchen having a coffee and she'd looked at Jill across the kitchen table. "Would you mind if I asked you something, Jill? It's a bit of a cheek really..."

"Go ahead," said Jill cheerfully. "What's the problem?"

"Well..." Alison was hesitant.

"I won't bite," promised Jill.

"Well, I wondered if I could sort of share Isabelle with you. You know, pay her a bit and ask her to help look after Harriet and Jon. Not when you need her of course, but perhaps there are times when she could have all four children together?" She watched Jill, trying to gauge her reaction. "I mean," she went on, "there are days when Isabelle is looking after yours, like when you're golfing, and I wondered, well, I just wondered..."

She trailed off and Jill finished the sentence for her, "If she could have all the children together." She smiled at Alison. "I don't know. I'll ask her. I know she'd be glad of the extra money, but if she worked for you as well it would certainly cut into her free time, and she is supposed to be studying too, you know."

"Yes, I realise that," Alison said quickly, "but you don't mind, in principle, sharing her sometimes."

"As long as she's there when I want her," Jill agreed. "But it would have to be at set times, so we all know where we are."

Isabelle had been delighted at the prospect of extra money for relatively little extra work, and on several days a week she either had the children in the Hammonds' home or the Forresters', and the arrangement seemed to suit everyone.

It's bloody ironic, Jill thought, fuming, that Alison should have to go out to work when she doesn't want to, and here am I going stark staring mad, stuck here at home. Sod's law, I suppose.

She shouted these thoughts down the phone at Nancy, who listened quietly, making sympathetic noises, ignoring the juvenile wails of "it's not bloody fair", but offering no solution.

The rain had stopped and Jill decided to have a bonfire. She donned her old jeans and sweater, tied her hair back with a scarf and set to work. There was a pile of old cardboard boxes in the garage which she carried down the garden, and then she set to work raking the fallen leaves and dumping them in the wheelbarrow and trundling them over to the bonfire. Ben arrived just as she was setting light to it.

"Hi," he said, coming up behind her and making her start. "I rang the bell but there was no reply, so I just walked round the back. Hope that was OK."

Jill, suddenly breathless, said, "Yes, fine. You made me jump, that's all."

"Sorry." Ben looked unrepentant. "It's just that you said you might have some gardening work, and I came round to see if you have."

Jill had been regretting the offer and hoping he wouldn't take her up on it. She waved her hand vaguely round the garden. "I'm afraid there isn't very much at the moment, really," she began, "just the leaves and clearing up."

"Shed could do with a coat of creosote," said Ben, nodding towards it, "and your conservatory needs painting. Trouble with wooden buildings is they need a lot of maintenance. I could do those for you."

Jill looked uncertain and said, "Maybe, I'll talk to Anthony, see what he says."

"Yeah, great, whatever."

They stood for a moment in silence, watching the flames creeping through the bonfire, crackling and taking hold of the dry cardboard at its base. Jill could feel the heat on her face and was glad, for she knew her cheeks would be burning anyway.

"I've always liked bonfires," Ben remarked, picking up the rake and poking at the fire so that the sparks flew up in a shower. "I love the crackle and the smell of them. They always make me think of Guy Fawkes Night when I was a kid."

"Mmm, me too," murmured Jill, still gazing at the leaping flames, not looking at Ben.

Ben is like fire, she thought suddenly, fascinating, but dangerous. I mustn't play with fire. For, despite all she knew and felt for Anthony, for her children, she was suddenly intensely aware of the man beside her, the strength of his attraction for her, an animal magnetism which was dragging her into unreality. She wanted to reach out and touch him, to feel the warmth of his hand on hers, the strength of his body against her own. It was an impulse so strong that she had to hold her hands tightly together to stop one of them reaching to him of its own volition. For a moment she felt she was sliding, slithering down a steep and slippery slope, with nothing to grab on to, to slow her fall.

"Would you like a cup of tea?" she asked abruptly, knowing she had to say something to bring back the semblance of normality. "I was just going to stop for one."

"Yeah, thanks." Ben put the rake across the barrow. "These live in the shed?" he asked, grasping the handles.

"What? Oh, yes, thank you. If you'd just put them away, I'll go in and put the kettle on."

She turned towards the house and as she did so, her attention was caught by movement in the window of the house next door. Must be one of the Hooper children, she thought, waving vaguely, and let herself into the house.

Upstairs in the kitchen she plugged in the kettle and found some mugs and the teapot, then she heard Ben calling from downstairs, "Can I come up, Mrs Hammond?"

He was already halfway up the stairs when she replied, "Yes, come up...and please, just call me Jill, not Mrs Hammond."

"Jill," he repeated. "Where's your family, today?"

Jill explained about Alison and the sharing of Isabelle. "But they'll be home soon, and Anthony too I expect." Now why on earth had she said that, she wondered? Anthony wasn't due home for hours, but even as she wondered, she knew the answer.

I'm afraid, she thought, afraid of being alone with Ben. I don't trust him and worse still I don't trust myself!

As she acknowledged the reason to herself, she heard the

front door open and Anthony's voice calling, "Anyone home? I'm back."

With the most amazing feeling of relief, Jill called, "In the kitchen," and when Anthony strode up the stairs she said quite smoothly, "Hallo darling, you're nice and early. You remember Ben, don't you? He was at Madge's barbecue."

Anthony kissed her and said, "Yes, of course I remember. Looking for odd jobs, weren't you?"

"Yeah, gardening and the like."

"I was just saying to Ben that we haven't really got much to do in the garden at the moment..." began Jill, as she poured Anthony a mug of tea.

"Not much really," Anthony agreed, "but have you ever done any decorating?"

"Some," said Ben. "Painting, not papering, I was saying to Mrs Hammond that your shed could do with some creosote, and your conservatory. The wood's all drying out."

"Yes, you're right." Anthony nodded. "Well, you could do those for us anyway, and then maybe paint the children's bedroom. That's been on the agenda for some time now, hasn't it darling?"

"Yes, but they're quite big jobs," Jill objected. "Ben has his college work to do too."

Anthony smiled. "Well," he said, "I'll leave it up to you. Actually, I've got to go out for a meeting in half an hour. I just came in to pick up some papers I'd forgotten. See you, Ben. I'll be in the study if you want me, Jill."

Clutching his mug of tea, he disappeared downstairs to the study, leaving Jill and Ben in the kitchen to finish theirs.

"Well," Jill began brightly, "you can begin with the shed and we'll see how you do. If that's OK you can go on to the conservatory. What's the going rate for the job do you think?"

They agreed a price, per job, Jill decided, rather than per hour, and Ben downed the last of his tea.

"I'll make a start tomorrow," he said. "Thanks for the tea."

He handed Jill his mug and as she took it her hand touched his. It was as if a jag of electricity had jolted through her, and she snatched her hand away.

"Hey, steady," Ben laughed, sounding anything but steady himself, and reaching for her hand again he held it briefly against his cheek before letting it go and grinning at her. "See you tomorrow," he said and laying a finger to her lips to forbid an answer, he turned and ran down the stairs.

And so it began.

He arrived the next morning whistling cheerfully and carrying the creosote and brushes they'd agreed he should buy. He set to work on the shed at once and the walls were soon covered. Jill watched from the dining-room window, carefully hidden behind a curtain.

What am I doing? she demanded furiously of herself. I'm behaving like a lovesick teenager, and she turned angrily away from the window, but she couldn't stop herself returning to watch him again. As if he knew she were there, Ben glanced up at the window and smiled, before he disappeared round the shed to start on the far side.

Forcing herself away from the window, Jill made herself clear up the living room, carefully putting away the toys Sylvia and Thomas had had out before school. It was Isabelle's job really, but because the morning was fine and bright, Isabelle had taken Thomas to play in the park. When she had finished, she went up to make the beds. From her own bedroom window she could see Ben, dressed in old jeans and a torn rugby shirt, painting round one of the window frames. Behind him, the bonfire was still smoking feebly, a drift of grey colouring the air, and her analogy of Ben with the fire came back into her mind.

"I mustn't play with fire," she murmured aloud, but even as she said it, she knew that that was exactly what she was going to do. As Ben had stuck the rake into the fire yesterday, prodding it into life and making it blaze, she knew she was going to risk doing the same thing. Without further ado she went down into the kitchen and put the kettle on. When it was boiling she opened the kitchen window and called down, "Ben, coffee."

He waved a brush at her and within moments she heard him open the garden door and come inside. As he came up the stairs to the kitchen, Jill knew a moment's panic. What am I doing, she cried inside, and as he came into the kitchen, she stepped back, holding her coffee mug in front of her as if it were a shield.

"Hi," he said, reaching for the mug of coffee waiting on the counter. "This one mine?"

"Yes," she replied, her voice a croak, and she watched him wide-eyed as he reached, not for his own coffee, but for the mug she held in her hands. Taking it from her, he set it carefully down on the counter next to his and then pulled her to him. For a fraction of a second she tensed against him, pulling away in refusal, he felt it and she felt it, and then she relaxed into his arms. His kiss was strong and searching, but hers was no less so. Her arms were round his neck, pulling his head down to her; she could feel the length of her body against his, straining against his, rubbing against him, and she could feel his undoubted response. His hands were swiftly under her sweater, caressing the smooth skin of her shoulders and back even as he continued to explore her mouth with his. Her arms slid down from his neck to tug the rugby shirt from the belt of his jeans and then to match his caresses with her own.

Even as she allowed him to pull her sweater up over her head, she thought, What am I doing? I can't be doing this! But she also knew that she was beyond stopping, her body was crying out for Ben and Ben was there urging it on. His rugby shirt was discarded and then her bra, and her breasts fell free and eager as she arched away from him and he transferred his lips to the tautness of her nipples. He felt for the zip on her jeans and slipping a finger in under her panties knew she was as eager and ready for him as he was for her. As he stroked her, she started to moan.

"Hello, we are here," Isabelle's voice cut through and for a split second they froze. They could hear the sound of the French girl manoeuvring the buggy in through the front door, and Thomas's piping voice announcing he wanted to get out now and go and find Mummy. "Shit!" muttered Ben and, grabbing his shirt, dragged it on over his head. Jill grabbed her bra, but having no time to put it on, she simply pulled on her sweater, and stuffed the bra into the nearby fliptop bin. They could hear Thomas coming up the stairs, one-step-one-step, and as he triumphantly reached the top and ran into the kitchen, they were standing on opposite sides of the room, each clasping a mug of coffee.

"Hello, darling," Jill managed, though her voice sounded breathless, "have you had a nice time in the park?"

"Yes, but I fell over, so we comed home." He displayed a grazed knee. "I've got a poorly knee," he explained to Ben.

"So you have!" Jill bent down to hug him and to inspect the damage, which was slight, and said admiringly, "You must have been very brave. I think we should give it a wash, don't you, and perhaps a plaster?"

Thomas was agreeing and demanding the special stuff to put in the water, when more footsteps sounded on the stairs, and Isabelle appeared at the kitchen door.

"Oh, Mrs Hammond, I am so glad you are in," she said.

"I hear poor Thomas fell over," said his mother, glancing up at her.

"Yes he was running and his feet went too fast," Isabelle explained. "It is not much, but I think it is best that we come home to wash."

"Very sensible," agreed Jill. "I'll just take him up to the bathroom and bathe it." She waved a hand in Ben's direction and said, "Ben and I were having a coffee, the kettle's still hot if you want to have one."

As Isabelle reached for a mug, Ben downed the last of his coffee. "I'll get back to the shed now, Jill," he said. Then pausing at the door he enquired innocently, "Did you say you wanted me to take the rubbish down?" For a split second, they both looked at the fliptop bin.

"Yes," Jill said levelly, and she pulled out the binbag and handed it to him. "And burn it please, Ben."

"Burn it?"

"Yes, please. We always have far too much for the bins. As the bonfire is still smouldering, you might as well burn some of it. There may be more in the shed, I'll come and see when I've sorted Thomas out."

Ben disappeared with the bag and Jill said, "Come on then, Tommy, let's have a go at this knee."

She ran warm water into the basin and dutifully put in a capful of "stuff" as Thomas had asked. As she watched it turn the water milky, she wondered what on earth would have happened if Isabelle and Thomas had come home just five minutes later. Her skin felt suddenly clammy at the thought of it and she found she was shivering. Would they have been caught having it off against the kitchen cabinets, or writhing around on the living-room floor? She buried her face in her hands at the horror of the thought, and it was only Thomas, tugging at her, that brought her to her senses in time to turn the water off before it flooded on to the floor.

"Sorry, darling," she said laughing awkwardly, "Mummy was thinking about something else. Now let's have a look at you."

When Thomas's knee had been bathed and covered with a huge pink piece of plaster, she took him back downstairs. Glancing out of the window, she could see Ben poking the bonfire into life with a stick.

"Keep an eye on Thomas, Isabelle," she said casually, "it's his programme in ten minutes, I'm just going down to tell Ben what to burn from the shed."

"OK, Mrs Hammond." Isabelle carried her coffee into the living room and turned on the television, and Jill went down into the garden.

As soon as he saw her, Ben stepped into the shed. She followed him, but not knowing what she was going to say. Ben didn't allow her to say anything, he pushed the door shut behind her and pinning her against the wall with one strong arm, he began to kiss her.

For a moment she responded, then she pushed him away, saying firmly, "No, Ben."

He released her but stood in front of her, barring her way from the shed. "Come, on Jill," he said huskily, "we can't stop now!"

"We can, we must," she said. "If they'd come home just five minutes later..." She let her words trail off and shuddered again at the enormity of what might have been.

"Yeah, yeah, I see that," Ben said soothingly, his fingers stroking her cheek and neck, "but I want you Jill...and you want me, you know you do." His fingers were wandering down her throat, and she stood still and quivering, unable to deny what he said. As his hands moved over her breasts, feeling them moving, unrestrained, beneath the thin wool of her sweater, he lowered his head to kiss her again.

"No, Ben, no," she murmured against his lips.

"Yes, Jill, yes," he teased, his tongue darting round her mouth.

"Ben, for Christ's sake, not here!" She forced herself to pull away.

He looked at her quizzically. "Where then?"

She tried to slip from his arms, but he held her firmly and repeated his question. "Where then, Jill? If not here?"

"I don't know, I don't know."

"You could come to my room," he suggested. "It's just across the road."

"Oh Ben, don't be stupid," she snapped at him, "that's as bad as our house. Anyone could see us."

Ben ignored her burst of temper and said gently, "Then where? Jill, I want you." He began to caress her again. "You've got a fantastic body and I want to...make love to you." The slight hesitation in his words told Jill that he had altered the words he'd been going to say, but she found she didn't care. All she could feel was the magic of his fingers as they roved at will, setting every nerve end jangling.

"What about that place, out by the dunes at Belmouth?" she whispered. "That motel place. Anthony's away tonight. I could go to the pictures, I often do when he's out."

"I'm working tonight, at the Dutch."

"What time do you finish?"

"I could probably get off about ten if it's quiet."

"I'll see you there then," she said. "Come to the chalet with my car parked outside."

And he had. She was sitting on the bed in the dingy little room nervously watching the television, and wondering if she should leave, when the door opened and Ben stood framed in the doorway. She got to her feet, but didn't move towards him. He closed the door softly behind him and crossing the room placed his hands on her shoulders, looking down into her face. With one hand he zapped the television into silence and then slid both hands down around her back.

"Ben...I'm not..." she began, but he closed her mouth with his, and they moved together.

It was sex as she'd never experienced it. At first it was urgent, taking up from where they had been interrupted that morning, and they were soon on the bed, their clothes strewn about the room as they had scrabbled them off, then suddenly, Ben pulled away, easing his body away from hers and looking down at her.

"Hey, slow down," he breathed, one finger tracing a line round her breasts and along her ribcage. "Slowly." He drew the word out. "Slowly."

"Ben," she heard herself moan, "don't make me wait!"

He grinned at her wolfishly, "Yes...wait," and he began his teasing work again. By the time they finally came together, she was gasping for him, and his need of her was as great. Almost at once, he was asleep, his body half across her so that she was trapped on the bed, but Jill couldn't sleep; she lay wide-eyed in the semi-darkness.

Oh God, she thought, what have I done?

She knew that she wasn't in love with Ben, and there'd been little tenderness, but there was a chemistry between them, an animal need that had driven her on even as she knew she would regret it later. Lust, she thought, that was the only word for it, lust, and it mustn't happen again. Her resolve lasted for as long as Ben was asleep, but when he turned over and began to kiss her again, she was lost once more.

She decided, when she was safely back at home, that he was like a drug. There were times when she didn't think about him at all, well hardly at all, and then it was as if a fix had worn off and the craving for him returned. Whenever she could slip away, on the pretext of golf, or going to the library, or visiting a friend, they would meet at the Bellevue Motel, if only for an hour. Every time Jill vowed it would be the last, but whenever there was a chance for them to meet, Jill took it.

Burdened with guilt, Jill transferred it to Anthony's shoulders. If he hadn't insisted that she couldn't have a job, she wouldn't have had time for any of this; she'd never have looked at Ben if Anthony had had more time for her and the children, and of course she'd been very careful, so that the children wouldn't suffer – she was always there when they needed her.

Ben continued to do the odd jobs that she found for him, but she never let him touch her in her own home, and much of the time anyway, Isabelle and the children were there as unwitting chaperones. He painted the conservatory and redecorated the children's room in colours that they all went together to choose from the DIY shop. Isabelle and the children got used to Ben being about, and though Isabelle might wish he'd pay some attention to her, and often dressed with him in mind, no one gave his continued presence a second thought.

*Chapter Thirteen*

Angela Haven tapped on Annabel's bedroom door and opened it without waiting for a reply. Annabel was sitting at her desk, a half-finished essay in front of her, but she had no pen in her hand and when she turned round as her mother came in, it was clear she hadn't been working.

Angela paused in the doorway. "Hi, love. Can I come in?"

With a slight shrug of her shoulders Annabel said, "Yeah, if you like," and swivelled her chair away from her desk.

Angela closed the door carefully and moved over to the bed, where, watched by her daughter, she made herself comfortable. Angela took some time settling herself, plumping up the pillow behind her back and wriggling into the softness of the duvet. Now the moment had come, the moment of confrontation and truth, she didn't know how to begin. The carefully rehearsed phrases slipped away and she ended up speaking far more abruptly than she had intended.

"Annabel, darling, what's the matter?"

"Matter...?" repeated Annabel, almost indifferently. "Nothing's the matter, Mum."

"Well, I'm sorry, darling, but I don't believe you." She held Annabel's gaze, maintaining the eye contact until it was Annabel who finally looked away.

"You look exhausted," Angela resumed. "Pale and washed out. Are you finding the work too much – is that the problem? You're doing three big subjects, you know – is it all getting on top of you?"

"No, the work's OK," Annabel said.

For a moment the silence was like an invisible wall between them, neither quite knowing how to scale it. Then Annabel took a deep breath.

"There is something, actually...I was going to tell you soon anyway, but since you're asking now...well I'm pregnant."

"What?!" Angela stared at her in horror. Of all the things that she had considered might be causing Annabel's depressed, lethargic state, pregnancy had never crossed her mind. There had been no sign of a boyfriend, ever, as far as Angela knew. "Oh, Annabel, you're not!"

"Yes, I am." Annabel spoke flatly.

"But how? I mean who? When? Oh God..." Angela drew a deep breath, trying to control her tumbling reactions and emotions; trying, not to become calm because that was impossible, but at least to become focused on what she had just heard. "Just tell me what happened," she said lamely.

"What happened is that I had sex with a guy and now I'm pregnant."

"Just like that? What guy?"

"Just a guy."

Clearly Annabel wasn't going to give the father's name at present, so Angela said, "When? I mean when is the baby due?"

Annabel shrugged, absentmindedly swivelling her chair rhythmically from side to side. "End of January some time I suppose."

"You suppose...don't you know? Haven't you seen anybody – a doctor I mean? Haven't you been to Dr Fran?"

"No."

"Oh, Annabel, why not? I mean...Oh God, why on earth didn't you tell me sooner?"

"I wanted to keep it," Annabel murmured. The she looked up sharply. "I didn't want an abortion."

"An abortion! Oh darling, I wouldn't have made you have an abortion." She looked at her daughter in despair. Had they really drifted so far apart over the last few months that Annabel could think that she, Angela, would force her, or even encourage her to destroy a baby? "All I'd have insisted on upon would have been a thorough check-up with Dr Fran and proper antenatal care." She crossed over to Annabel who still swung her chair, left right, left right, and kneeling beside the chair, Angela put her arms round her, gathering her awkwardly against her and holding her tight. Gradually the swivelling ceased and Angela felt Annabel relax against her, eventually felt her arms slip round her shoulders and tighten convulsively.

"Oh God," prayed Angela silently as they clung to each other. "Help me to know what to do and what to say. Don't let me say the wrong thing. Don't let me blow it!"

It seemed to her that now was the time to say nothing, just to be there – so she stayed still, kneeling uncomfortably on the floor, her cheek against Annabel's, clasping her tightly in her arms.

"I'm sorry, Mum." Annabel's whisper was so low, it was little more than a breath, and then Angela felt Annabel's tears wetting her cheeks, and her own sprang at once to mingle with them.

"Come on," she said, "come on, darling, let's sit on the bed and be comfortable." She got up and pulled Annabel over to the bed, then sat down beside her and took her hand.

"Now then, start from the beginning," Angela said.

There was another silence as Annabel assembled her thoughts and decided exactly what and how much to say. She'd already realised that she couldn't keep her secret much longer and had been considering how much she would have to reveal. Now the moment had come she was almost ready with her story.

"There was a guy I was meeting after school...end of April, beginning of May. We only did it once – had sex I mean and then I didn't see him again."

"You mean he dumped you when he heard you were pregnant," Angela said flatly.

"No," Annabel answered sharply, as if in his defence. "No, he doesn't even know."

"So, why isn't he…about?" Angela finished the question lamely.

Annabel shrugged. "I don't know. He just stopped coming round." She glanced up, trying to assess how her mother was reacting, what she was thinking. Would she accept this rather feeble explanation, "he just stopped coming round"? It sounded feeble in Annabel's own ears, but nothing would induce her to change it, to give her mother any inkling as to the real reason for Scott not being there, not knowing. Having got the confession of her pregnancy off her chest after so many days of trying to pick the right moment, she felt almost light-headed with the relief of it.

Angela was still holding her hand, but was staring into the middle distance as all the questions, all the consequences of Annabel's bombshell surged through her mind in confusion. What would they do with the baby? Who would look after it? Would Annabel want to keep it herself? What about adoption? What would the school say? What about her exams? What would Ian say? How would they manage with her working full-time? A new baby, time-consuming, demanding. And Annabel must say who the father was. He ought to be told, ought to face up to his responsibility in this and contribute to the care of the baby…his baby for God's sakes…except they were probably better off without him, whoever he was, using her daughter and dumping her once he'd got what he wanted. She knew she was being a touch melodramatic, but she *felt* melodramatic, damn the man…whoever he was.

In the silence that enfolded them, Annabel was equally far away, remembering, reliving yet again, the day it had happened; the day that stood out above all others in her eighteen years.

It was the Saturday when she had been on her way to admit to Avril that she hadn't done any of the promised research on their history project. Scott had drawn up beside her in the van, and with relief at putting off the interview with Avril, Annabel happily climbed in beside him.

Immediately she could tell he was different. All he said was, "Hi Bel," as she clambered into the passenger seat, and pulled out into the Saturday-morning traffic, but there was a tenseness about him. Normally he drove with one hand on the wheel, the other elbow resting on the open window, but today both hands gripped the steering wheel and his eyes were constantly flicking to the mirrors, darting sideways at intersections.

They cleared the city centre and finally pulled into the car park at Belmouth. He drove to the far end, away from other cars and parked looking out across the slate-grey expanse of sea. Scott switched off the engine. Keeping his hands on the wheel, he straightened his forearms, pushing back against the seat, staring out through the windscreen. Silence enveloped them, broken only by the ticking of the cooling engine.

At last Bel said tentatively, "Scott...?"

He turned his head and looked at her. "Got a job to do this morning, Bel," he said. "Wanna help?"

"Sure." Bel shrugged. "What do you want me to do?"

"Drive," he replied and got out. Bel slid across to the driving seat and Scott got in the passenger side.

"I've got to collect something. Drive back into town."

They headed back into Belcaster and joined the sluggish Saturday-morning traffic.

"Keep in the left-hand lane," Scott instructed, "and drive right round the one-way system."

Bel did as she was told, concentrating on the heavy traffic. Scott was wound up like a coiled spring, and his tension clamped Bel as well, so that her movements felt awkward and stiff.

"Keep going round until I tell you," Scott said, glancing quickly at his watch before scanning the traffic yet again. At last, he said, "Turn left here."

Bel turned into a narrow one-way street that served as a twisting short cut from one side of the one-way system to the other. It was called Bells Street, and wound a tortuous route round the back of the cathedral and the Sovereign Shopping Centre, before emerging once again on the Belmouth side of town. Fifty yards down on the left was Bells Yard, a narrow dead-end alley, serving the back entrances of the shops on the main road.

Scott glanced down the alley and said, "Stop here, back up into the alley."

There was no one behind her, and Bel manoeuvred the van expertly into the mouth of the yard.

Scott looked across at her. "Wait here," he said. "Just going to collect some stuff. Back up to the door when I wave – and keep the engine running – I shan't be long."

He got out of the van and went round to open the rear doors, then he walked swiftly to one of the service doors. Above it, Bel could see a red and white sign proclaiming it as "Belcaster Computers Ltd". She watched through the open back of the van as Scott produced a key from his pocket, and, after one more quick glance round the yard, opened the door. He disappeared inside for a moment and then reappeared and signalled to Bel, who eased the van backwards to the door. Even as she put the brake on, he was heaving boxes into the van, boxes of different shapes and sizes, some light and easily handled, others obviously heavy and awkward. The speed at which he worked told Bell all she needed to know. She stopped watching Scott and glued her eyes to the open end of Bells Yard.

More and more boxes thudded into the back of the van, and then Bel saw him; a policeman alone on foot appeared on the corner of Bells Yard and looked down towards them. Scott was manhandling a large cardboard crate into the van and Bel, turning sharply, hissed "Scott! Police!"

He glanced up and with a quick nod slammed the doors of the van shut, closed the shop service door, sauntered round to the passenger side and climbed in.

The policeman, meantime, had turned into the yard and was walking unhurriedly towards them.

"Drive!" Scott hissed, "and whatever happens, don't stop!"

Bel slammed the van into gear and it leapt forward. The policeman held up a hand, but she ignored him and kept going, so that he had to jump out of the way. He lost his footing and fell clattering against some dustbins.

At the end of the alley, she had to wait for two cars to pass and should have waited for a third, but Scott craning out of the window saw the policeman back on his feet and running after them, and shouted "Go! Go!" so Bel went, forcing herself in behind the second car and causing the third to ride up on to the pavement to avoid her, his hand blaring the horn.

"Shit!" breathed Scott. "Keep going, he's using his fucking radio. Just drive."

Bel did as she was told, following the two cars ahead as they wound their way round the cathedral. As they approached the one-way system, the Saturday traffic was still moving sluggishly and they heard the wail of a siren.

"Shit!" Scott's voice rose. "Right! Turn right!" and immediately Bel wrenched the wheel round, into another narrow street.

"I'm going the wrong way!" she shrieked. "It's a one-way street."

"Keep going!" yelled Scott.

There was a car coming towards them, the driver flashing his lights furiously to warn them they were in a one-way street. Bel flashed back and adrenaline took over as she accelerated towards him. Realising she wasn't going to stop, the driver, pale-faced and swearing, yanked his wheel over and mounted the pavement, giving Bel just enough space to squeak past him. She reached the end of the street and turned out into the traffic. There was no real gap and more angry horns blared as drivers hit their brakes to let her in.

"Left-hand lane," snapped Scott, and then they heard the siren again.

"Police car's coming up behind us," Bel shouted.

"Stay cool!" ordered Scott. "Change lanes."

Bel veered across the traffic and raced across the lights, just turning amber against her. The police car was now in hot pursuit, headlights flashing, blue light flashing, siren wailing. It jumped the red light and continued close on her tail. With her hand on the horn, Bel swerved in and out of the traffic.

"Right!" shouted Scott. "Turn right!"

Bel swung round a traffic island and accelerated down a side street. There were cars parked on either side, narrowing it to one lane wide where it had a right-angled bend to the right. Bel had to slow to negotiate the bend and in the mirror she saw the police car turn in behind her.

"Sharp right into the lane," yelled Scott. She only just saw the opening in time, another alley serving high street shops, but curving sharply, so that the moment they were into it, they were invisible from the street behind.

"Slow down," said Scott, and Bel eased to a walking pace. They heard the siren note change as the police car sped past the end of the alley.

Scott got out of the van, and pulling a pair of number plates from under the seat, quickly changed them for the plates on the van. Those he buried in a skip outside one of the service entrances. From the glove compartment, he stuck a huge snowboarding sticker across one of the back doors and then went round to the driver's side and opened the door. He jerked his head. "Shove over," and as she did so, he took Bel's place at the wheel. From under the dashboard, he produced a pair of fluffy pink dice which he hung from the mirror. Then he looked across at Bel and grinned. "Cool, huh?" he drawled and then added, "Let your 'air loose." Without a word, Bel pulled the scrunchy from her hair and, shaking her head, let her hair fall over her shoulders. Scott nodded his approval and, turning the van round, they emerged cautiously on to the street. There was no sign of the police car. Scott eased his way into the traffic and then cut across to the Belmouth Road. From there it was two minutes' drive before they were lost in the maze of a housing estate, and within five they were in a little yard outside a row of three lock-up garages. The yard was empty, and there was no sign of anyone taking the remotest interest in them. Scott backed the van up to the door and between them they quickly unloaded the boxes. As the last box was safely stowed, he pulled the garage door down and locked it carefully.

Suddenly Bel found she was shaking, her knees wouldn't hold her and she slumped against the van.

"Stay cool, Bel," Scott said, "and get in."

Bel pulled herself into the van and Scott drove to the dunes outside Belmouth. Then, hidden in a hollow surrounded by buckthorn and maram grass, he pulled her into his arms and began to kiss her. Her response was instant and passionate.

"Get in the back," Scott said huskily, and together they clambered over the front seats. The he kissed her again and Bel knew that this time it was *It*. He held her against him and for the first time she could feel him erect and strong, pressing against her, needing her. There was no time for condoms, raspberry-flavoured, studded or otherwise. After the excitement of the chase, the excitement of each other was demanding, consuming, entirely uncontrollable. They pulled at each other's clothes, their mutual need leading to an aggressive, almost violent coupling. As Scott pumped inside her, Bel thought, "This is it. I've done it." She knew a moment of pain and then a small flowering of pleasure, before, with one final gasping groan, Scott collapsed over her, panting. She lay there, half-smothered by the weight of him, and thought, Now I really am his woman.

After a few moments Scott heaved himself up on to one elbow and said, "You was great, Bel, really great." But she didn't know if he meant the escape or the sex, and she didn't dare ask. She wanted to try the sex bit again, more slowly this time, but when she reached up to touch his face, Scott moved away and said, "Better get sorted, Bel," and began to pull his clothes on.

She did the same, but her disappointment was somewhat lifted when he said, "We'll go back to my place."

He had never taken her there before, had always refused to tell exactly where he lived, so it cheered her to realise she must have passed some sort of test; that after today and her reaction to their morning's work she had been elevated to a new level of trust.

She tested it by asking, "What was in the boxes, Scott?"

"Computer stuff," he replied casually.

"But how did you know it would be there?"

"Mate of mine works there. They always have a delivery on a Saturday morning, see, but they're too busy usually to do more than stack it downstairs. He give me a key."

"But won't they suspect him?"

"Why should they? He'll have been working hard in the shop all morning. I told him I'd come at twelve, see, and he could make sure he was seen all the time, serving customers, nothing to do with a hit on the storeroom."

"But they'll know you had a key," Bel pointed out anxiously.

Scott shrugged. "I was supposed to give the lock a bash before we left," he admitted, "but we left in a bit of a hurry. Still, they can't prove nothing."

They climbed over into the front of the van and Scott said, "We'll get a pizza."

"Anyway, the police have got the wrong number plates," Bel said as they backed out of the dunes on to the road.

"Yeah, took them off a scraped Bedford. Always useful. I'll go back and collect them later."

They pulled up at a Pizza Hut on the seafront and got a take-away. All of a sudden, Bel found she was ravenously hungry.

"Let's eat it here," she said, so they sat looking out over the sea and stuffed themselves with a large pizza each.

Bel still felt on a high. What a day! She'd taken part in a robbery, driven the getaway car in a high-speed chase, lost the pursuing police car and lost her virginity at last. She glanced at

Scott, still munching the last mouthful of his pizza and put a hand on his thigh. He grinned at her.

"You're some girl, Bel," he said, and Bel felt a stab of pleasure shaft through her.

"Come on," he said. "Let's get back."

They drove sedately back into Belcaster, the pink fluffy dice dancing in the windscreen, the snowboarder careering across the back door.

Halfway along the Friars End Road, Scott turned into a side road and was just turning into a cul-de-sac when, with an exclamation of "Shit!" he jerked the wheel back and drove straight on. Bel looked into the little street and saw a police car parked outside one of the houses.

"Get out," Scott ordered sharply, and as she turned to stare at him he shouted, "Out! For fuck's sake get out and go home."

"But..." began Bel.

Scott leant across her and opened the door. "Out, Bel."

"Will I see you?" Bel asked, not yet moving.

"Yeah, some time. Don't know when. Get out, Bel!" He gave her a push and she slid out of the van. As the door closed, he accelerated away and disappeared round the corner. Bel stood for a moment, staring after him, and then turned slowly and walked back to the Friars End Road to find a bus. As she passed the cul-de-sac, Elmbank Close, she glanced down it to where the police car stood. Was it the one that had chased them earlier? She hadn't a clue, but even as she was wondering, she saw two policemen emerge from a house with a green front door, a young man hustled between them. Her heart almost stopped; even at this distance he was incredibly like Scott, same height, same build, same cast of features. What the hell is going on, she thought? Then, anxious not to appear conspicuous, she hurried on to find her bus. Scott would explain it all next time she saw him.

But he hadn't, because she'd never seen him again. The days had stretched into weeks, and then months, and there had been no sight of him. Everywhere she went, Annabel's eyes scanned the streets for the familiar van, searched the crowds of shoppers for his familiar figure. Several times, she even made her way to Elmbank Close, to the house with the green front door, but there was no answer to her ring and no sign of either Scott or his van. As time went by, she slid into a dull recognition that she wasn't going to see him, and she began to live with the ache of her loneliness.

The storm caused by the school work for her exams, or rather the lack of it, washed over her leaving her unmoved, a rock battered by a rising tide and still unchanged at that tide's retreat. To please her parents – Dad had been drawn in to reinforce what Mum and the school were saying – she did begin to give her attention to her studies; after all, she no longer had Scott to give it to.

When she had at length discovered she was pregnant, Annabel had been stunned. It had never crossed her mind. Her periods were so irregular anyway that several extra weeks without one had rung no alarm bells, nor even raised a query. It was only after she noticed that the smell of cigarette smoke and the smell, or even the sight of an onion made her feel sick, that she began to count the weeks and realised that she must be expecting a baby.

She made one more effort to find Scott. She went to Elmbank Close and rang the bell beside the green front door. This time somebody answered, a small tired-looking woman who replied in answer to Annabel's question, "Scott Manders? Yeah, he used to live here. Gone now."

"Do you know where?" asked Annabel. "Did he leave a forwarding address?"

The woman gave a cracked laugh. "Doesn't need to, ducky," she said. "Care of 'er Majesty, 'e is." Then seeing Annabel's puzzled look, added, "In prison. 'E's inside. Picked up by the fuzz, 'im an' 'is brother."

Annabel nodded and managed to whisper, "I see, well, thanks

anyway," and she hurried away to consider what she'd just learned.

With the woman's words repeating themselves in her ears, Annabel sat in a café in the Friars End Road, drinking coffee and considering her options. Scott must have been arrested for the computer job, but he obviously hadn't told the police about her. The young man she'd seen being arrested was clearly his brother. She wondered how they had got on to Scott, where he was in prison and how long he would be there. Why hadn't he got a message to her somehow? But he hadn't, or he hadn't bothered and she was on her own now.

She was definitely pregnant, she'd bought a pregnancy home-testing kit and it had shown two positive blue lines. She was determined to keep the baby, it would prove the reality of her few weeks as Scott's woman. She had never been in favour of abortion in the abstract, and now it was definitely a practical option she still wasn't in favour. She'd cope somehow. Mum would help her cope – when she knew.

Now she does know, Annabel reflected, her thoughts return-ing to the present as she sat beside her mother on the bed, but still I shan't tell her about Scott. Of course, Chantal would guess who the father was, Annabel realised, and must be silenced. Probably easy enough to do that, given how she had reacted to the sight of Oliver Hooper at the barbecue, still it had to be done and fast.

"Mum," she said, breaking into the heavy silence, "will you let me tell Dad and Chantal? I'd rather tell them myself."

Angela nodded. "Of course if you want to, but you must do it in the next few days so we can make some decisions."

"I'll ring Dad tomorrow," promised Annabel, "and I'll tell Chantal."

Later, downstairs, Angela poured herself a very large scotch and sitting curled up in her favourite armchair, considered what must be done. Annabel had promised to tell Ian, but as soon as he knew, they would have to get together and make some collective decisions. Annabel having a baby wasn't something she, Angela, wanted to cope with on her own. She sighed and took a long pull at her drink. She hadn't seen Ian since that awful week at half-term in the summer, when it all came out how little work Annabel had been doing, that her project was non-existent, that there was no way she would even achieve a pass unless she got her act together fast. In the light of this evening's revelations, it was clear why Annabel had let her work lapse, and now the chance of her being able to take her 'A' levels next July seemed even more remote. How could she look after a baby properly and study for exams? She wouldn't be able to take the baby to school, and there was no one at home to leave it with.

If only *I* didn't have to work full-time to make ends meet, she thought wearily. Maybe we could trace the father…but it doesn't sound as if he could contribute much, a student or something by the sound of him. One night's fun and off on his merry way. Angela knew the familiar taste of bitterness at the fickleness of men. Well, first things first. Tomorrow Annabel must get an appointment with Dr Fran and have a thorough checkup. Tomorrow the whole pattern of their lives would begin to change yet again and all due, yet again, Angela thought, to simple lust. Tomorrow was indeed another day, and it was going to start early, that was for sure.

It was far easier than Chantal thought it would be. She simply told her mother that she'd been asked round to the student house for coffee and with a light-hearted promise given "not to be late", she had closed the front door behind her.

Knowing Angela was still safely upstairs in the kitchen at the back of the house and couldn't see her from the window, Chantal made no pretence of crossing over to The Madhouse, but headed straight for the Dartmouth Road and into town to the Flying Dutchman. Dean had said they'd be there from around eight. It wasn't quite eight yet and Chantal was suddenly nervous. She realised she didn't want to go alone into the pub, where she would recognise no one, where she might have to wait by herself until they came – if they came. She walked more slowly, delaying her arrival in Francis Lane. Supposing they didn't come? Supposing they'd changed their plans? They wouldn't think to tell her. Only Dean knew she might be coming, and even to him it hadn't been definite.

By the time Chantal actually stood outside the Flying Dutchman, she was a mass of indecision. She didn't want to be first, that she considered would be well embarrassing, and she didn't, she realised, hastily moving onwards, want to be found loitering outside plucking up courage to go in, that would be worse! A flashing green sign caught her eye. Almost opposite the Flying Dutchman was a café. It was not much more than a snack bar, but the flashing green light announced "Sandwiches all day", and glancing in through the window Chantal could see a few, small, Formica-topped tables, some of which were occupied. There was an empty one in the window. At once she went in, bought herself a Coke and carried it to the table. From there, she could keep her eye on the arrivals at the pub opposite without much chance that she herself would be noticed. She was glad she had, because no one she knew arrived at the pub until after twenty past eight. She had finished her second Coke and was on the point of having to order a third, when she saw the tall figure of Mad Richmond's boyfriend, Dan, turn into Francis Lane and head for the door of the public bar. Chantal felt hot relief flood through her at avoiding a disaster. She had only been into pubs with her parents or more recently with her dad and Desirée for pub suppers. She would have gone into the lounge bar and been waiting in the wrong place.

Probably, thought Chantal as she left the café, the others were there already and Dan had come from somewhere else. It doesn't really matter if they're not, she thought, Dan knows who I am and he's a really fit bloke.

She paused for a moment outside the door and then, with a deep breath, pushed it open and walked in.

The bar was noisy and crowded with students. It was brightly lit, but hazy with smoke. The pool table at one end was busy, and the two or three tables with chairs and the bench seat round the window were all full. For a horrifying moment, Chantal could see no one she knew, then she saw Dan. He was standing at the bar, with a girl, not Mad Richmond, perched on a bar stool at his elbow, and behind the bar was the student with the pony-tail, the one called Ben. Only Ben looked up as she paused on the threshold, but he didn't seem to recognise her, as his smile was the sort he might have for any new customer.

Chantal was committed. If she turned round and left now, she couldn't come back in, and though there was no sign of Dean or the girls whom she knew better, she fixed a smile on her face and walked over to the bar.

"Hi," she said in a voice that didn't quite sound like her own.

"Hi." It was Ben who replied and added, "What can I get you?"

Chantal had already had to buy two Cokes in the café and her money was dwindling. She had no idea how much more, if any, she might need for the evening. It would be all right if she wasn't expected to buy a round.

Trying to sound casual, she replied, "Diet Coke please," and when Dan turned at the sound of her voice, she said, "Hi Dan, is Dean around? We said we'd meet here."

"Here soon I expect," said Dan, giving her mini skirt and boots an appreciative glance.

"They said they were all coming," Ben said, poised with the Diet Coke can and a large glass. "Pint?"

Chantal, already awash with unwanted Coke, nodded, not liking to ask for less. She paid for her drink, and as Ben handed her the change, he said, "Sorry, I think we met today, but I can't remember your name."

Chantal treated him to a dazzling smile. "Chantal. Chantal Haven. I live at number four."

"Oh yeah," Ben said, apparently unaffected by the smile,

"I remember. This is Angie," he added, nodding towards the girl on the bar stool.

Dan hooked a free bar stool towards her with his foot. "Here," he said, "have a seat."

Ben turned away to serve another customer, and Chantal picked up her pint of Coke. She wished the others were there. Now she was with Angie and Dan she didn't know what to talk about, her mind had gone blank. She took time tasting her drink and setting it down again, suddenly very aware of Dan's eyes resting on her exposed thighs.

"Hallo, Chantal," said a surprised voice behind her, "how are you?"

Chantal turned to find herself face to face with Jane Short, Ned's wife.

"OK thanks," Chantal mumbled, wondering what on earth Mrs Short was doing in a bar full of students, then she took in the tray of dirty glasses Jane was carrying and realised she must work there.

At that moment, much to her relief, Mad, Dean, Cirelle and Charlie burst in on a wave of laughter and loud voices and with a smile in their direction, Jane moved back behind the bar with her load of empties.

When he saw Chantal, Dean said cheerfully, "Hey! You made it! Great! What are you drinking?"

Chantal, whose relief at seeing him was enormous, treated him to a huge smile and said, indicating her pint of Coke, "I've just got one in, thanks."

Ben was busy at the other end of the bar and Jane came up to serve them. In the general order Dean said to her, "And a rum to put in Chantal's Coke."

"Sorry," Jane shook her head. "I can't serve rum to Chantal, she's under age."

Chantal felt her face flood with crimson mortification and said, her voice coming out as a croak, "Only just, Mrs Short."

Jane, knowing that this was certainly not true from what she remembered, smiled but said briskly, "Even so, I'm afraid I can't serve you rum."

Dean grinned at Chantal entirely unfazed. "Sorry," he said, "I should have ordered it from Ben. I suppose she knows you."

Chantal's embarrassment had given way to anger and she said tightly, "She used to live opposite, in your house." Then in a cooler voice, she added, "I don't drink rum anyway, thanks all the same."

For a while Chantal let the talk and laughter swirl about her. She longed to be part of it, but didn't know what to say and was terrified of making a fool of herself. Dean stood beside her stool, ensuring she was part of the group, and Ben came up to join in over the bar whenever he wasn't serving, but they were all talking about people and events that Chantal didn't know, and for once the one thing Chantal didn't want to talk about was herself.

Gradually the talk drifted round to Madge's barbecue, and they began to describe it to Angie, who hadn't been there.

Then Mad turned to Chantal and said, "Chantal can tell us who everyone was, spill all the local scandal. We only knew our neighbours before today."

"Oh, Sheil and Shirl," Chantal began dismissively.

"Sheil and Shirl?" Mad gave a hoot of laughter. "Is that what they're known as?"

Chantal shrugged. "By me and Annabel, anyway."

"Go on," urged Mad. "Tell us about them."

"Well, Sheil," said Chantal, warming to her task, "that's Colby at number six, she's a right cow. Got her nose into everybody's business and always moaning on about stuff. Shirl's OK though."

"Old Madge seems cool," Mad remarked.

Chantal shrugged. "Dunno. Don't see her much."

"Who were the guys doing the barbecue?" Charlie asked casually.

"Mike Callow and Steve Hooper. Mike's separated or

divorced or something and lives alone 'cept when his kids come over or he's got a bird in, which is mostly. Steve's married to Annie and's got Emma and Oliver. Emma's OK, but Oliver's really skanky."

"Who were the people with the bar in their drive?" asked Ben.

"Hammonds. They're well snooty. Got an au pair called Isabelle. She's cool, she's French."

"Might have known you'd notice the au pair," sniped Angie. She was hurt she hadn't been included in the barbecue invitation, especially when she discovered that Dan had been there. She didn't like Dan and never felt at her best when he was one of the group. Now they all laughed, but Ben was well aware that the comment hadn't been as light-hearted as it had appeared. He was getting tired of Angie's gibes and they were becoming more frequent these days.

"Well," he said in a mock French accent, "she was very sexy!"

"Didn't look at you, though," teased Charlie.

"Didn't look at any of you," grinned Cirelle. "You guys must be losing your touch!"

The bar closed at eleven and they all wandered back towards the Circle. There was a great deal of laughter on the way and Chantal felt a shaft of pleasure run through her as Dean draped an arm over her shoulder as they walked.

Now I'm really one of them, she thought, and she leaned against Dean a little, to let him know she liked his arm there. As they walked, she planned what she would say when they got back to the Circle, and so when Dean said, "Coming in for coffee?" she was able to reply casually, "Can't I'm afraid. Early start tomorrow, and still got work to do."

Dean accepted it without query and when they reached her house she slipped out from under his arm, saying, "See you around."

"Yeah, see you, Chantal. Glad you came."

As quietly as she could, she let herself into the house, but she knew it wouldn't be any good, Mum would never have gone to bed with her still out somewhere.

She was right. Angela was still sitting in her chair battling with Annabel's news and its implications. She heard the sound of the front door closing gently and roused herself from her thoughts. Chantal! Surely she was already home. Swamped by Annabel's news, she had quite forgotten that Chantal had been over to the student house for coffee. It was past eleven now, she should have been home hours ago.

"Chantal! Is that you?" she called sharply. "Do you know what time it is? Where on earth have you been?"

In the split second before answering Chantal decided that her mother hadn't checked at the student house and risked, "Over at number seven, Mum." She even managed to inject a note of injury into her voice as she replied. "You *said* I could go."

"Yes, I did, but I also said not to be late. It's past eleven and it's school tomorrow."

"Sorry, Mum," Chantal said, "I forgot the time."

"Yes, well, go straight to bed now, and another time I shall expect you home by ten at the latest. Understand?"

They kissed each other goodnight, and Chantal, surprised and glad to have got off so lightly, went upstairs, to be greeted by yet another surprise. Annabel was waiting on the landing, and with a finger to her lips beckoned her sister into her room.

"What's up?" asked Chantal as Annabel closed the door softly behind them.

"We've got to talk," Annabel said. "Sit down."

Chantal did as she was bid, and waited expectantly as Annabel sat swinging on her chair. "Well, what?" she said at last.

"I've been talking to Mum," her sister began, "and, well, I've told her...I'm pregnant."

"Pregnant!" echoed Chantal, amazed. "What? You?"

"Of course, idiot, otherwise I wouldn't say it, would I?"

Chantal stared at her wide-eyed, but as she said nothing more Annabel went on hurriedly, "Mum wants to know who the father is, but I'm not going to tell her, not now anyway, and I want you to swear you won't tell her either."

"But I don't know who…" began Chantal, and then as light dawned she said, "unless… is it Scott Manders?" She saw Annabel's lips tighten and said, "It is Scott, isn't it?"

"I'm not telling you who it is," Annabel said firmly. "Then if they ask you if I've told you, you can say no and it'll be the truth."

"But I can guess," pointed out Chantal.

"I know, and that's what I'm asking you not to do. Please Chantal, it's important to me, just say you don't know. Please?"

"OK," agreed Chantal, "but what are you going to do? Are you going to have an abortion?"

Annabel shook her head. "No, I'm going to have the baby. I want to have it."

"But will you keep it or have it adopted?" Chantal was nothing if not direct. "What's happening about your exams?"

"I don't know. I'm going to keep it. I don't want to give it away, but nothing is decided yet, about anything. Look, Chantal, all I'm asking you to do is to play dumb. When they ask, say you haven't a clue who the father is, that I never discussed him with you; which is also true!"

Chantal got up and gave her sister a hug. "Don't worry, I won't say a word. I know you'd do the same for me, that's what sisters are for, eh!"

Annabel returned the hug. "Bless you, Cha, I won't forget."

Chantal punched her lightly on the shoulder and said, "I must go to bed. Mum's already well annoyed that I'm in so late."

Annabel looked at her watch, "Not surprised," she said. "Where've you been?"

"Out with the students," Chantal admitted. "It was great."

"Yeah? Well you just be careful, they're all much older than you."

"Hey, get you!" mocked Chantal. "You're a fine one to talk!"

## Chapter Fourteen

"Well, that all seemed to go very well," Shirley Redwood said as they closed the front door behind them. "I think Madge thoroughly enjoyed herself, don't you?"

"Looked like it," agreed David. He headed for the garden door at the end of the passage.

"Cup of tea?" Shirley called after him.

"Yes, please. Will you bring it out? I just want to do a few things in the greenhouse."

"Won't be long," promised Shirley and went upstairs to the kitchen to put the kettle on. As she waited for it to boil she looked out of the window and watched David as he pottered in and out of his greenhouse. She felt a sudden and great surge of love for him as she watched him working methodically among his plant pots.

From the window she could see across the wilderness next door to the Colbys' garden beyond, neat and tidy, but somehow not cherished like David's, and it made her think for a moment about the Colbys.

Does Sheila feel about Gerald as I do about David, she wondered? They never seem quite at ease together. There's no easy banter as there is between us, their minds don't seem to run in tandem, there's no harmony. It's sad, Shirley thought. It's as though they live side by side rather than together. And yet they've been married at least as long as we have. Perhaps it's because they haven't any children.

Sheila had never talked about having no children, at least not to Shirley, but Mary Jarvis had once said that she thought Sheila wasn't able to.

"You'd think they'd adopt," Shirley had remarked, unable to conceive of a life without a child.

"Maybe they didn't want to," Mary said gently. "For some people that seems a risk."

"You don't know what you're getting, you mean?"

"Well, you don't, do you?"

"No," Shirley considered. "I suppose not. Even so, I think if *I* couldn't have had children I'd have adopted."

Mary smiled. "I think I would too," she said. "But maybe they didn't want any. I don't think Sheila really likes children very much, you know."

"If they hadn't wanted any, Sheila would have said just that," Shirley said firmly. "She would never have admitted that she couldn't have any."

"Maybe not, but she may have been disappointed about it for all that."

Shirley made the tea and carried two mugs down to the garden. David emerged from the greenhouse and they sat together on the bench in the late-afternoon sun.

"They seem a nice enough bunch next door," Shirley said. "Let's hope they don't make too much noise. I could hear their music last night."

David laughed. "So could I, but not when I had the television on. You're getting to sound like Sheila!"

Shirley laughed too. "Heaven forfend!" she said. "But I was thinking about her just now. She doesn't quite know how to talk to young people, does she? I mean, she always sounds a bit awkward. Probably because she's never had teenagers of her own!"

"Lucky her!" David said with feeling.

"Oh David! How can you? You don't meant that."

"No, of course I don't," David soothed, "but there are occasions when children seem to be more trouble than they're worth."

"And you don't mean that either," scolded his wife.

"Probably not," David grinned, "but I thought when they were grown up and off our hands, we wouldn't have to worry about them any more."

"You always worry about your children," Shirley said. "It's just different worries when they're grown up."

As if on cue the phone rang and Shirley got up to answer it. "That'll probably be Melanie now," she said as she went indoors. "She said she'd ring some time today."

"Mum?" Melanie's voice cracked as she heard her mother speak, breaking on a sob.

"Mel, darling, what is it? What on earth's the matter?"

"I can't…" Melanie's voice failed her again as she began to cry.

"Can't what? Melanie…what can't you do?" The sobbing continued. "Melanie, for God's sake tell me what's the matter?" Shirley spoke sharply. "I can't help if you can't tell me. Has something happened? Is it one of the children?"

Melanie still seemed unable to control her voice enough to explain.

"Is Peter there?" Shirley asked. "Mel, is Peter in the house?"

"No," Melanie managed. "He's had to go away. Mum I can't cope. I just can't!"

"All right," Shirley said, thinking quickly as to what was best to say and do in the situation. "Calm down and tell me quietly what the problem is. Come on, love, get a hold of yourself."

She heard her daughter blow her nose noisily and then take a deep breath. "Peter has had to go up north, to one of the factories there. There's some problem with some plant or other and they've sent him to sort it out."

"How long has he gone for?" Shirley asked.

Melanie sniffed. "Don't know. He doesn't know. As long as it takes, he says."

"And when did he go?"

"This morning. Mum, I rang you at lunchtime, but you were out." Her tone was accusing.

"Yes, we were at a barbecue in the Circle," Shirley said, and *not* saying that they did have a life of their own and didn't simply sit waiting for their daughter to phone.

"It's been a dreadful day," Melanie wailed. "Todd's been awful, throwing tantrums, and Suzie won't stop crying. I think she's teething. And I didn't sleep last night worrying about Peter going, but he said he had to go. He said I must get a grip and start coping, but I can't, Mum, I just can't." The tears began to flow again. Shirley said nothing for a moment or two while she considered what it was best to suggest.

It's always so difficult on the end of a phone, she thought despairingly. Words of comfort are useless and somehow whatever I say is wrong. If I'm sympathetic, she cries all the more, and if I'm bracing, she thinks I don't care.

"Listen Mel, darling," she began carefully, "try not to cry and listen..." but from down the phone she heard a shriek, and the receiver was obviously dropped and dangling. She could hear the sound of children crying and Melanie shouting, of chaos cascading.

At last Melanie came back to the phone and in a voice choked with tears said, "Mummy, I can't cope any more. Please come."

"It's all right, darling," Shirley promised, "I'm on my way."

Very carefully, very gently, she replaced the receiver. She closed her eyes and drew a deep breath, before turning back towards the garden and David.

"That was Mel," she said as he looked up. "I've got to go."

"Go?" repeated David, "go where?"

"To Mel's. She's in a dreadful state."

"What on earth's the matter now?" demanded David.

"Peter's had to go away on business, and she can't cope."

"Of course she can," David said. "She'll have to. Probably just what she needs to pull herself together. Let's face it, Suzie is more than six months now, Melanie ought to have got over the baby blues or whatever they are by now."

"You didn't hear her on the phone," Shirley told him. "She's obviously at the end of her tether, and if only for the children's sake I've got to go."

"Well, if you feel you must, then of course you must," agreed David, "but I don't think I can drive you, I'd be over the limit." He looked across at her speculatively. "Are you fit to drive?"

"Yes, I think so, I only had a couple of glasses of wine."

"Do you want me to come?" he asked.

"No, I can manage, in fact it may be better if I go on my own. I'll just put a few things in a bag and be off. I can be there in a couple of hours."

"Ring me when you get there," David said as he saw her into the car. "And if you want me to come up, I will."

Shirley kissed him. "I know, but I'll see how things are. If I need you, I'll call, don't worry."

"Yes, well take it steady," he said.

He watched Shirley drive out of the Circle and drew a deep breath. Of course, he had meant it when he'd said he'd go with her if she liked, but he was more than a little relieved when she said she didn't need him. He found Melanie very hard to cope with when she was in a state like this. He didn't know what to say to her, how to react. He wanted to be supportive, but found that he was quickly irritated by what he thought of as her moodiness, and though he realised that anger was the last thing to help Melanie just now, he found it quite difficult to bite his tongue and say nothing. With a sigh, he went back into the house to find himself another cup of tea.

Shirley drew up outside Melanie's house soon after seven. The lights were on upstairs in the bathroom and the children's bedroom, so Melanie must be putting them to bed. That seemed a hopeful sign. Shirley rang the bell, but when there was no reply she used her own key and let herself in.

"Mel," she called. "Melanie, I'm here." She could hear the baby crying and then there was the sound of running footsteps on the landing. Todd appeared at the top of the stairs, peering round the banister, thumb firmly in his mouth.

"Hallo, Todd," Shirley said gently. "It's Granny. Is Mummy upstairs?"

Todd didn't reply. But when Shirley began to mount the stairs, he disappeared and she heard him running back along the landing.

There was no sign of Melanie, and no answer when Shirley called again, so she went into the children's bedroom and looked in. It was a tip. Todd's bed was unmade and there were toys and clothes all over the floor. The cot side was down, and there was no sign of the baby. Shirley could still hear Suzie crying so she wasted no further time there, but strode into Melanie and Peter's room. There the picture was much the same, bed unmade, clothes overflowing from the dirty clothes basket in the corner of the room. Todd was standing by the bed, thumb firmly plugged in, and on the bed lying face downwards was Melanie, snoring gently. Shirley took it all in with growing horror. She could hear Suzie screaming, but for a moment couldn't see the child. Crossing quickly to the bedside, she found her, her face red with rage, lying on a pillow wedged between her mother and the bedside table.

"Melanie! Melanie!" Shirley, registering the empty whisky bottle on the bedside table, reached out and shook her. For a moment, there was no response, but then Melanie stirred, and opening her eyes said slurrily, "Hallo, Mum."

Seeing that Melanie was drunk, but otherwise all right, Shirley scooped up the yelling baby and knew at once that she needed changing. "Suzie's dirty," she said. "I'll go and change her. Will you show me where the changing mat is, Todd?"

Todd led the way towards the bathroom. Shirley paused at the door. "You'd better get up now, Melanie," she said. "It's time Todd had his bath."

When she got Suzie on to the changing mat, Shirley found that her nappy was soaking and filthy; it should have been changed hours ago.

"Now then, darling, we'll soon have you clean and comfy, won't we. Poor old girl, what a horrid nappy!" Talking softly to her, Shirley cleaned the child and, taking a clean nappy from the pack, made her comfortable. Gradually the yells subsided, and Shirley rocked her until, exhausted from her crying, Suzie fell asleep.

Throughout this, Todd stood and watched her, silently, thumb in place.

"It must be your bath time, Todd," Shirley said cheerfully. "I'll just pop Suzie into her cot and then we'll run the bath, shall we?"

With Suzie safely in her cot, Shirley went back to the bathroom where Todd waited for her. A glance into the other bedroom told her that Melanie hadn't moved, so Shirley decided to leave her to sleep it off while she dealt with the children. Todd made no protest as she undressed him and lifted him into the warm water, he allowed himself to be soaped and rinsed, but made no effort to help himself or to play with the bath toys that Shirley had dumped into the water. There was no splashing and laughter as there usually was when Todd was in the bath, and as soon as he was ready, Shirley scooped him out of the water and wrapping him in a warm towel sat him on her knee and hugged him. Normally it was impossible to dry him properly, as he wriggled and jiggled, slippery as an eel, but this evening he sat still on her knee, his little body curling against her. Gently Shirley rocked him as she had Suzie, and wondered what on earth had been happening since she last saw them all.

Her thoughts were interrupted by a little voice saying, "Can we have tea now, Granny? I'm hungry."

Shirley's head jerked up. Good God, hadn't Melanie even fed them? "Of course we can, darling," she said. "Let's get you into your pyjamas, shall we, and then we'll go and see what we can find." She carried him back to his room and while he was struggling with the pyjamas she went back to Melanie.

"Melanie, when did you last feed the children?" she asked.

Melanie was awake now, but still lying on the bed, her eyes open, gazing vacantly at the ceiling. Slowly she turned her head and focused her eyes on her mother. "Lunchtime," she said. "Todd had fish fingers for lunch."

"And Suzie?"

"Same. Her bottle's in the fridge."

"I'll find it," Shirley said, glad for once that Melanie had not wanted to feed Suzie herself, and that she would happily take a bottle.

An hour later Shirley turned out the light in the children's room. She paused on the landing. Boiling an egg and making Marmite toast for Todd had been easy, and there had been one last filled bottle waiting in the fridge for Suzie. Both children had eaten hungrily and when finally fed and warm, they went into their beds happily enough.

"I'll see you in the morning," she promised Todd as she tucked him in, and he snuggled down with Tedder, his teddy bear.

Now to deal with Melanie, she thought, and turned purposefully towards her daughter. At that moment, the phone rang. Melanie made no move to pick up the receiver in the bedroom, so Shirley answered the hall extension. It was David.

"You didn't phone," he said. "I thought maybe you'd been held up."

"No, I'm sorry. I forgot to phone. As soon as I arrived, I had to deal with the children. Melanie had passed out on the bed..."

"Passed out?" cried David. "What's the matter? Is she ill? Have you called the doctor?"

"No, she's not ill, not in that way anyway," Shirley reassured him. "She's drunk. There's an empty whisky bottle beside her. I don't know how much she's had, but she's pretty dopey. I've got the children fed and to bed and I was just going to see how Melanie was when you rang."

"Good God!" exclaimed David. "Are you sure you can cope?"

"No," Shirley managed a rueful laugh, "but I'll decide what to do in the morning. Don't worry, love, I'm fine for now. I'll ring you in the morning."

"Sure you don't want me to come?" David was anxious.

"Quite sure, I'll be fine, really."

When they had rung off, Shirley went back upstairs to tackle Melanie. Melanie was lying on her bed, apparently not having moved since her mother had arrived earlier. She opened her eyes as Shirley came in, and they immediately overflowed with tears.

"Mummy," she whispered, "I can't do this."

Shirley sat down on the edge of the bed and took her hand. "Can't do what, darling?"

"Can't be a mother."

"Of course you can," Shirley replied gently. "You were doing it perfectly when you just had Todd. Now with Suzie as well, it's a bit more difficult, I agree, but you'll manage. It's just a question of getting a routine up and running."

Melanie said nothing for a moment, then she announced, "I'm drunk. I feel awful. I think I'm going to be sick."

Shirley helped her to the bathroom and when she had been sick, wiped her face and helped her back to bed.

"The best thing for you to do is to sleep it off," Shirley advised, "and then we can get things sorted out in the morning. Try not to worry. Get a good night's sleep, and we'll talk in the morning."

Obediently, Melanie closed her eyes, and murmuring, "Thanks for coming, Mum," drifted off to sleep.

Once she was sure Melanie was really asleep, Shirley gently withdrew her hand and got to her feet. Quietly she gathered up the dirty laundry from both bedrooms and took it downstairs. She needed to be doing something. Her mind was racing as first she loaded the washing machine and then made herself some cheese on toast in the kitchen.

What on earth are we going to do, she thought? How can we deal with this? Obviously Melanie can't cope at the moment. She needs help, professional help of some sort, and in the meantime, the children need to be looked after properly. Who do I consult? The doctor?

As she was eating her toast, the phone rang again. It was Peter, ringing from Sheffield.

"Shirley?" He was amazed to hear his mother-in-law answering the phone. "What are you doing there? I didn't know you were coming."

"I wasn't," Shirley told him, "but Mel rang, she was..." Shirley tried to choose her words carefully, "not feeling herself, so I came up to help."

"What's the matter with her?" Peter asked. "She was all right when I left this morning."

"No, Peter, I don't think she was," Shirley said quietly, "I don't think she's been all right for some time. She really can't cope with the children at the moment, and I don't think it is a case of her having to snap out of it, I don't think she actually can."

"But what do we do?" Peter demanded. "I can't take time off work just because she's got the baby blues."

"I think it's more than what you call the baby blues," Shirley said, trying not to sound critical, "I've thought so all along, but now it has come to a head, Peter, and with the best will in the world she can't cope."

"But what can we do?" Peter repeated. "If I started taking time off, and being unavailable for trips like this one, I could well lose my job. Then we really would be in trouble."

"I don't really know the best way forward," Shirley admitted, "but in the morning I shall contact your doctor and take advice. If necessary, she and the children came come to me for a while, while we get things sorted out. How long do you think you'll be away?"

"I don't know for sure," answered Peter. "About four or five days. I'll be back at the weekend anyway."

"Yes, I see. Well, some action has to be taken before then. When I got here this evening, Melanie had finished whatever was in the whisky bottle and had passed out on the bed. Has she been drinking lately?"

"Drinking?" Peter sounded incredulous. "You're telling me Mel was *drunk*?"

"Yes, I'm afraid so. It's all right, the children were fine. She knew I was on my way, so I expect she just thought she'd have a drink to keep her going until I got there, and perhaps on an empty stomach, you know…"

It was exactly the same excuse Melanie gave herself, the next morning when she finally faced her mother.

"I knew you were coming, Mum. I just thought I'd have a whisky, there wasn't all that much in the bottle, it must have gone straight to my head because I hadn't really eaten any lunch."

Not that much in the bottle. Shirley heard what Mel said with disquiet. Peter had told her he had bought a new bottle of scotch only the week before, that as far as he knew it was unopened in the cupboard. Shirley had had a quick look when they had rung off, and could find no whisky at all. Melanie couldn't really have consumed a whole bottle last night, so perhaps she'd been drinking steadily, unknown to Peter.

"I'm very sorry, Mum, really I am," Melanie was saying, "I was so stressed out by the kids that…well I thought it would calm me down, you know?"

"Well, luckily there was no harm done," Shirley said. "But I am concerned about the state you'd got yourself into, Mel. We've got to get you sorted out, you know. You can't go on like this, it's not fair to the children, or to Peter, or to you for that matter. I've rung the doctor and got you an appointment for this morning, so we'll see what he says."

"He'll just say that I'm depressed and give me Prozac or something," Melanie said gloomily.

"Well, maybe Prozac or something is what you need," Shirley said. "I think you probably are depressed and do need something, and the sooner we sort it out the better."

"But, Mum, I don't want to be on pills all the time," protested Melanie. "I don't agree with this idea that drugs solve all your problems."

"Nor do I," agreed Shirley, "but there are times when it may be necessary for a little while. You really can't get as desperate as you were yesterday again. This is what I think we should do…"

Shirley explained what she had decided in the night as she had lain awake churning everything in her mind. "Go to the doctor this morning…"

"He won't have an appointment," Melanie interrupted.

"I've already got you one," Shirley said patiently. "They always keep one for an emergency."

"I'm not an emergency," snapped Melanie.

"Darling, I think you are." Shirley spoke gently, but firmly. She was determined not to budge on this; Melanie should see a doctor today. "Then, as I believe these pills take a week or so to take effect, I'll take you all home with me. You can look after the children, get a routine sorted out, and I'll be there to help when you need me. It'll give everybody a break, a change of scene. Dad will enjoy having the children, and we can give you all the support you need. Peter can come at the weekend, and when you're feeling better we can take it from there."

"You've got it all worked out," Melanie said tartly. "Do I get any say in this?"

"Of course you do, but I've had time to think about it all overnight, and this seems to me to be the best solution."

"Couldn't you stay here?" suggested Melanie. "Stay and help me here?"

"I could," said Shirley unwillingly, "but to be honest, Mel, I don't want to. I'd rather have you in my own home, where I can help you and carry on with my other commitments too." And have David beside me for moral support, she thought, because this could be a long haul, I don't think we're going to get this all sorted for quite a while.

Melanie went, reluctantly, to see the doctor and while she was out of the house, Shirley bathed Suzie and packed up clothes and toys for the children. She also rang David to put him in the picture.

"I really wish that I could have gone with her," Shirley said. "I want to be certain that the doctor really understands the depth of the problem, and I don't really trust Melanie to tell him the whole story." She sighed. "But of course I couldn't insist. Anyway, I'm bringing them home with me, I can't leave Mel to cope on her own, but I don't want to stay here, I'd rather have them in my own home."

"How long for?" David asked.

"As long as it takes," Shirley replied. "Peter can come and join us at the weekend, and we'll have a discussion all together then. But for now we have to give Melanie our support, and I think this is the best way to do it."

"Fine," David agreed, though his heart was sinking at the thought of the invasion. "Whatever you think is best. What do you want me to do?"

"Well, can you put the cot up, ready for Suzie? And perhaps go to the supermarket and stock up on some of Todd's favourite things, you know, sausages, fish fingers, ice cream. Just stick them in the freezer." She smiled into the receiver, visualising David's face as he heard these instructions. "Thanks, love. If all goes well at the doctor's this morning, I hope to be with you about tea time, anything different and I'll give you a ring."

When Melanie got home again, the coffee was waiting on the stove and her mother sat her down to hear what the doctor had said.

"He said a change of scene would do me good," Melanie said. "He thought going to stay with you for a few days would help."

"And did you ask him for something to relax you a bit so that you can cope with the children more easily?"

"Not exactly," answered Melanie, and she wouldn't meet Shirley's eyes.

"Oh Mel," said her mother, exasperated, "that's what you went to see him for."

"It wasn't," snapped Melanie. "I don't want pills, Mum, OK?"

She glared at her mother. "He said I needed counselling and that when I get back from staying with you he'd try and get something arranged, someone would come and see me and assess me."

Shirley felt the fury boil up inside her. I *wish* I could have gone with her, she thought. I knew this would happen. Still, she resolved silently, I shall get Dr Fran to have a chat with her and see if she can't help in some way. She forced herself to speak calmly and said, "Well, I've put some things ready in the hall, so when you've sorted out what you need and we've checked I've got everything the children need, I thought we'd have an early lunch and then crack on home."

They finally turned into Dartmouth Circle at about five and found David working in the front garden. He greeted them all with a huge smile, swinging Todd up into the air and hugging Melanie. Suzie, who still just fitted into the carrycot for travelling, was fast asleep and he carried her into the house with Todd trotting at his heels. As they were unloading the car, Cirelle Thomas came out of the students' house next door, a sports bag over her shoulder.

"Hi," she called.

"Hallo, Cirelle," said Shirley. "You haven't met my daughter, Melanie, have you? Mel, this is Cirelle from next door."

The two young women exchanged greetings. "You look as if you've got your hands well full," remarked Cirelle, as Todd emerged from the house again, swinging on his granddad's hand. Todd stopped and looked at her, and his thumb went into his mouth.

"Hallo," said Cirelle. "My name's Cirelle. What's yours?"

Todd eyed her from behind his granddad's back, but didn't answer.

"This is Todd," said Shirley. "They've all come to stay with us for a little while. Aren't you going to say hallo to Cirelle, Todd?"

Todd still didn't answer, so Shirley said gently, "You left

Tedder in the car, Todd, have you come to fetch him?" Shirley reached into the car and brought out Todd's teddy bear and held it out to him. The little boy reached for him and hugging him tightly took refuge once more behind his grandfather.

"Well, I'm off to the gym," Cirelle said cheerfully. "If you need any help with babysitting, don't hesitate to ask."

As she turned away, a thought struck her and she turned back. "I meant to ask you," she said, "who lives in number nine? Are they away? I've never seen anyone there."

"The Smarts," replied Shirley. "They are away, and have been for six months. They're visiting their daughter in Australia. Why?"

"It's just that I saw someone going round through their side gate, earlier today. Youngish bloke, didn't see his face, but when I saw his back disappearing through the gate, I suddenly thought that the house might be empty and he shouldn't be there."

"I'll take a look when we've got this lot unloaded," David promised. "We've got a key, if necessary. Thanks for mentioning it. You didn't recognise him, I suppose."

Cirelle shook her head. "No, but I only saw him from the back. He was in jeans and a bomber. Could've been anybody."

"Well, thanks anyway," David said.

Cirelle grinned at him cheerfully. "No probs," she said. "See you all," and she jogged off round the Circle.

"She's a lovely girl," Shirley told Melanie. "She helps out at St Joe's sometimes. Her babysitting offer is a good one, Mel, we might want to take her up on that."

Melanie nodded. "Yes, whatever," she said absently.

While the two women finished carrying the luggage indoors, David went across to the Smarts' house. He wanted to check that everything was all right there. The front looked as it always did, and so he went to the side gate and pushed it open. It wasn't latched as it should have been. He walked down the side passage and into the back garden. All was still and quiet and there was certainly no intruder there now. He looked up at the windows, but they were all closed, and there was no sign that anyone had tried to open one. Similarly the garden door was shut and undamaged.

Probably one of the Callow boys hit a ball over and had come to fetch it, David thought. He peered in through the kitchen window, but the little he could see appeared undisturbed. He walked back round the house, and noticed, in a muddy patch by the back gate, the print of a trainer, quite fresh and distinct. Well, he thought, Cirelle was right, someone has definitely been inside the gate recently. Perhaps he would just give Mike Callow a ring and see if his boys had been there today. If not they should keep a sharp look out in case someone had been casing the house.

He went home and found the children having their tea. Shirley had taken charge, but she encouraged Melanie to give Suzie her bottle and later to bath Todd, while she, Shirley, cooked the supper.

"I must see Fran," she said to David when he came into the kitchen. "I shall pop out after supper and see if she's at home."

"Do you think she'll be able to do anything for Mel?" David asked.

Shirley shrugged helplessly. "I don't know," she sighed. "But at least she's known her for years and might be able to talk to her as a friend, if not a doctor."

"Don't you think Mel might think you're going behind her back?" David asked.

"I suppose I am really," Shirley admitted. "But it's for her own good."

"She may not see it like that," David warned.

"No, I suppose not. Still, I could at least *talk* to Fran, don't you think? I really am worried about Mel, you know."

"I know you are, all I'm saying is, don't make things worse."

Shirley didn't go to see Fran that evening; she decided to wait a couple of days and see how things went, but the next day, on her way to do a stint at St Joe's, she bumped into Fran in the Dartmouth Road.

"Fran, can I talk to you some time? In confidence?" she asked.

Fran looked at her keenly and said, "Of course, Shirley. Do you want me to come over when I've finished today?"

"I'm not sure, it's a bit difficult. It's about Melanie, and she's staying with us. Honestly Fran, I'm so worried about her."

"Would you rather come over to me?" suggested Fran.

"In a way. The thing is I don't want her to think I'm going behind her back."

"Even if you are." Fran smiled, taking any sting out of her words.

Shirley laughed ruefully. "Exactly."

"Well, why don't I pop in later, casually? I'll think of a reason, and then we can take it from there."

"Would you? Do you mind doing it like that?" Shirley was apologetic. "It's just that I feel in need of some advice."

"I'm always ready to listen," Fran said. "As to advice, well, let's wait and see. Melanie isn't my patient, remember."

"No, but I am," Shirley said, "and I'm the one who needs the advice...about Mel."

"I can see you're worried," Fran said, "but try not to be. I'll drop in later this afternoon. What time will you be back?"

"I finish at St Joe's at about half past four," Shirley said.

"Fine, it'll be after that, then."

Shirley went on to the day centre, and found that when she was busy with the regulars she managed to forget about Melanie for a while. There was only one other volunteer there, the co-ordinator, Mavis Hope, so they were both kept fairly busy. Wrestling with Vera's ever-recalcitrant knitting and playing dominoes with old Fred Barnes, making and pouring numerous cups of tea, helped Shirley keep her mind occupied. Only once did she think of her daughter and that was when Vera called across to her, "'Ow's that baby, then? Getting on all right, is she? Did you bring them snaps you promised?"

"Oh, Vera, I'm sorry," Shirley replied. "I put them out ready and then came without them." Because Melanie didn't want me to come and leave her, she added silently. For goodness sake, David was there! And in all the fuss, I forgot the photos.

"Do you *have* to go, Mum?" Mel had wailed. "Couldn't you miss it just for once?"

"No, Mel, I couldn't," Shirley said firmly. "They rely on me."

"I'm relying on you, too," Melanie said pettishly.

"I shall be home by about half four," Shirley said soothingly. "Suzie's asleep and Todd's got the toy box out in the dining room, you can play with him. And make your father a cup of tea at about half past three, will you? He usually stops for one about then." She gave her daughter a hug. "And don't worry, Mel, you'll be fine, and I'll be back soon."

So she had left without the photos and without the books she'd collected to add to the bookshelf in the centre.

Towards the end of the afternoon, Cirelle came in.

"Hi," she said cheerfully. "I've got half an hour before I'm due at a tutorial, so I thought I'd look in. Anything I can do?"

Shirley smiled at her. "Well," she said, "would you mind tackling the washing up in the kitchen? They were short of helpers at lunchtime and there's still a pile in the sink."

"Yeah, no probs!" Cirelle turned to the kitchen.

"I'll be in to help you in a minute," Shirley promised.

As soon as she could, Shirley went in to help Cirelle clear the kitchen. "I'm glad you came," she said. "I wanted a quiet word with you."

"Oh, what about?"

Shirley hesitated, wondering if she were being disloyal to Melanie, and then deciding she couldn't help it. "It's my daughter, Melanie," she began.

"The one I met yesterday?"

"Yes." Once she had decided to speak, all Shirley's words came out in a rush. "The thing is she's not been very well lately and is finding the children too much for her. That's why she's come to us, really, so we can help out. But we're not getting any younger and I wondered, well, I wondered if you would like to help out with the children at times. We'd pay you of course, and it could be fitted round your college times. Would you be interested?"

"Yeah, very," Cirelle said at once. "I like kids. There's lots in our family and I often help with them. What sort of thing d'you want me to do?"

"It would probably be Todd, mostly," Shirley said. "Taking him into the Circle garden to play, coming over and giving a hand at bedtime, that sort of thing. Perhaps we can link up with the Hammond and Forrester children so that he has other children to play with. If they stay any length of time, I'll want to take him to the local toddler group. To be honest," she went on ruefully, "I don't really know. We'd have to play it by ear. I haven't discussed it with Melanie yet, so I don't know what she'll think of the idea, but when you mentioned babysitting yesterday, she didn't seem to mind." Shirley sighed. "The trouble is, you never quite know what's going to upset her just at the moment."

"Yeah, well if you want me, like, just give me a call," said Cirelle. "It's the sort of job I'd enjoy, and to be honest too, I need to find something, I need the cash."

They finished the dishes chatting easily and then Cirelle went off to her tutorial, leaving Shirley to go back into the day room, feeling a little more optimistic.

The rest of the afternoon passed all too quickly and, before she knew it, Shirley's clients had gone and she and Mavis had cleared up and were ready to go home.

Mavis looked at her critically. "You look tired, Shirley," she remarked.

Shirley managed a smile. "Didn't sleep so well last night," she admitted. "We've got Melanie and the children staying for a few days."

"Oh Shirley, you should've said," Mavis scolded. "I could have managed on my own this afternoon."

"No you couldn't," Shirley returned. "And anyway it did me good to get away for a couple of hours."

Mavis smiled. "Well, thanks anyway. See you soon."

As Shirley came into the Circle she heard the sound of children playing in the Circle garden, and looking over the fence she saw David pushing Todd on the swing, while Isabelle played with Tom and Sylvia in the sandpit. She went in and was greeted by David, still pushing the swing.

"Hello, love. Look Todd, here's Granny."

"Hello, you look as if you're having fun." Shirley spoke to Todd, but her eyes flicked to David, who said, "Yes, we thought we'd play out here until you got home again, didn't we, Todd?"

"Everything all right?" asked Shirley anxiously.

"Fine, but it was too nice a day to stay indoors." David let the swing slow and then catching Todd in his arms, lifted him off. "There you go, young man, go and give Granny a kiss."

Todd ran to Shirley and she bent to hug him. "Have you had a good time with Granddad?"

"Yes, I swinged very high!"

"I saw you," Shirley agreed. "You were very high. Shall we go and find some tea now?" She took his hand and they all three walked back to the house. "Where's Melanie?" Shirley asked David.

"Indoors, reading," he replied. "Suzie was awake for a while, and Melanie changed her, but I think she's put her back in her cot now. How was your afternoon?"

"Quite helpful actually," Shirley said and told him briefly of her conversations with Fran and Cirelle. "So Fran will drop in later and we can ask Cirelle to help if we need her."

Melanie looked up as they came up the stairs. "Hello, Mum."

"Hello darling, nice afternoon?"

"Yeah, not bad."

"Good. Will you put the kettle on while I just pop upstairs? I'll be down in a minute and we'll have some tea."

While they were eating, the doorbell rang and hoping it was Fran, Shirley said, "Answer the door, Mel, will you?"

Melanie went to the entry-phone. "It's Doctor Fran," she reported.

"Fran? How nice, tell her to come on up."

"Melanie," Fran cried as she came up the stairs, "I heard on the grapevine that you were here and I thought you wouldn't mind if I popped in to see this new baby I've heard so much about." She gave Melanie a hug. "Hello, everyone. Hello Todd, how are you? You are getting a big boy."

"Fran, how lovely to see you," cried Shirley. "Cup of tea?"

"Oh, yes please, just a quick one." She turned to Melanie again. "So, where's Suzie? Can I see her?"

"She's asleep," Melanie said.

"Well, I won't wake her, but could I have a peep?"

"OK." Melanie shrugged and led the way upstairs to where her daughter was in her cot. Suzie wasn't asleep and waved her fists at Fran as she bent over the cot.

"May I pick her up?" asked Fran, and when Melanie shrugged again she reached into the cot and lifted the baby out, cradling her in her arms. Fran looked across at Melanie, smiling. "She's beautiful, Mel," she said. "You must be very proud of her."

Melanie managed a small smile. "Yes, I am."

"You're looking tired, though," Fran said gently. "Does she cry a lot? Is she getting you up much at night? I remember being terribly tired when I brought Carol home. Max needed me as he always had, but all I wanted to do was sleep!"

She held Suzie out to Melanie, but Mel shook her head. "Put her back in the cot, I'll see to her after tea."

Fran did as she was asked, but immediately Suzie started to grizzle. She was tired of being in her cot and wanted to stay up in someone's arms.

Melanie looked at her for a moment, making no move to pick her up again, then all of a sudden her face crumpled and she began to cry. Fran at once gathered her into her arms and held her as she sobbed and sobbed.

When at last her sobs died away, Fran led her to the bed and sat her down, still holding firmly on to her hand. "Now, Mel, come on, tell me what's the matter? What's this all about?"

"I just can't cope with the children," Melanie blurted out. "Todd's OK, except he's so demanding, but Suzie...it's all too much. I can't seem to make the effort. That's why I'm here now, with Mum and Dad, because things at home were just awful! Mum wants me to go on Prozac or something, but I don't want to. She made me go to the doctor at home, but he didn't say much, just I need counselling and more time. It's hopeless, I don't know what to do."

"What about Peter?" asked Fran gently.

"He does what he can, but he's away so much with his work. He says he has to go, and I know he *does*, but it doesn't make it any easier. Then Mum came up to fetch me, and when I knew she was coming I had a whisky to keep me going, but I had too much and now she thinks I've got a drink problem as well, I know she does!"

"And have you?"

"No! At least I don't think so, though I have had a few drinks lately when it's all got beyond me. But I don't go round looking for it all the time. The odd drink just helps me get through." She looked earnestly at Fran. "What am I going to do, Fran? I don't know what to do."

Fran squeezed her hand. "The first thing to do is to stop worrying. Oh, I know that's easier said than done," she added as Melanie began to protest, "but all this can be sorted, you know, and you'll be back to your usual self. Now, what I suggest we do is take things a step at a time. Your doctor recommended counselling. Well, at my surgery we have a counsellor who can help you. You could see her while you're staying here. She's very nice, her name's Jackie Spencer. What do you think?"

Melanie shrugged. "I could try," she conceded.

"That's my girl," smiled Fran. "I'll make an appointment for you to see her as soon as possible and we'll take it from there. In the meantime, do as much as you can with both the children. Don't be afraid to accept help, but don't rely on other people entirely. They'll want to help, but gradually you'll find you can begin to cope without them. OK?" Fran fished in her pocket and produced a handful of tissues.

Mel nodded and taking the hankies blew her nose. "You don't think I need to go on to anything?" she asked, anxiously. "Pills, I mean?"

"No. Certainly not yet, anyway. I think that would be very much a last resort. Let's have a go with counselling and support first, eh?"

Melanie managed a smile and nodded.

"Good girl. Now, I think you need to change your daughter's nappy. From the whiffs I'm getting, I think she's been busy while we've been talking. Then we'll take her downstairs and you can tell Mum what you're going to do."

When the baby was clean and comfortable, they went downstairs and joined the others at the tea table.

Shirley was longing to know what had been said upstairs, but she managed not to ask and soon Melanie said casually, "Dr Fran's suggested I see the counsellor at her surgery, Mum. I think it's quite a good idea, don't you?"

"Yes, I do. It sounds a great idea, darling." She beamed across at both of them. "Do you want me to give Suzie her bottle while you drink your tea?"

"No, thanks," Melanie said. "I'll do it."

*Chapter Fifteen*

Oliver went with the swimming party that followed the barbecue, not because he wanted to swim particularly, but
because he couldn't think of anything else to do and he didn't
want to go home. Home! He wasn't going home any more.
Home was with Dad and that bitch Annie now and everything
in his life had changed. Mum had married that creep Oslo de
Quinn, and at his say-so they had been shunted off to Dad.

"Much the best for you, young man," Oslo had said. "You'll
be able to come and stay with your mother from time to time,
but there really isn't room in our flat for you to be here all the
time, and anyway you wouldn't want to live in London."

Oslo and Lynne had moved into Oslo's London flat, getting
rid of the house in Belcaster where he had been living when
they had met, and Lynne had sold the house in Belston St Mary
where she and her children had lived since the divorce.

"Are you really going to let him throw us out?" Oliver demanded angrily. "Don't you care about me and Em any more?"

"Yes, of course I do," Lynne had said in her most reasonable
voice. "I care very much. That's why I think you should stay in the
same area, where all your friends are. I've got to go to London to
be with Oslo, but I don't want to uproot you two; and living with
Dad for a while, you'll be able to get to know him better."

"Like I don't know him already?" shouted Oliver. "Me and
Em have been there enough as it is. Don't we get any say?"

"And I shall be very busy from now on," Lynne carried on,

ignoring his outburst. "Working with Oslo, entertaining business people. It really is for the best, darling. We shall see lots of you, at weekends and in the holidays. You'll be able to come up to London and we'll be able to go out to see the sights and go to shows…"

"You're talking to me as if I were about six!" Oliver shouted.

"Well, darling, you're rather behaving as if you were," his mother replied wearily. "I know it will feel strange at first, but you'll soon get used to it. Emma seems quite happy."

"It's all right for her," Oliver fumed. "She's staying at Beechlands for at least another year, I've got to leave Chapmans and go to Crosshills bloody Comp. It's not fair. I could still go to Chapmans from Dad's, there's a school bus from town."

But his dad said he couldn't. He was sympathetic but firm. "I'm sorry, Oliver, I just can't afford it any longer. I'm afraid you'd have had to leave Chapmans anyway, wherever you lived. I simply can't afford the fees."

"What about Em then?" Oliver growled resentfully. "Why's she still going to Beechlands?"

"She won't be, not after this year. She's doing her last year at Beechlands and then she'll be joining you at Crosshills." He laid a hand on Oliver's arm and said, "It's not what I want for either of you, son, but there's no alternative with the business in the state it's in, so we'll have to make the best of it."

"At least he'll be starting his GCSE course at the beginning and not swapping schools in the middle," Oliver had heard Annie say, "and he'll soon make new friends in the area."

It was comments like these that fuelled Oliver's rage and resentment.

GCSEs, he thought explosively. Who cares about those? They're just fucking exams. What about me? No one cares about me. No one cares how I feel about things, I'm never consulted. "You wouldn't want to live in London!" they say. "You wouldn't want to be uprooted!" How do *they* know? They've never even bothered to ask *me*.

He felt he had absolutely no control over his life and the anger boiled inside him. What was worse was that Emma didn't seem to care that they were being shunted round.

"I don't mind much," she admitted when he taxed her with it. "I loathe Oslo, and I don't want to live with him in London, I'd much rather stay here with Dad."

"And that bitch Annie?" Oliver's lip curled. "Imagine what it's going to be like living with her full-time!"

"She's not so bad," Emma said. "She says I can redecorate my room if I like, choose the colours and have some new curtains. We're going into town later, to look for material."

To Oliver this was the final treachery. Even Em wasn't on his side. She'd been bought...by new curtains.

The first day at Crosshills had been awful. The only plus about the place was that the pupils there didn't have to wear school uniform. There was a uniform and everyone was encouraged to wear it, but it wasn't obligatory and Oliver made the most of the fact. When he arrived the first morning, he was wearing jeans and a granddad shirt hanging loose over a T-shirt and his trainers. He joined the steady flow of children streaming in at the gate. He had refused point blank to let his father go with him.

"For Christ's sake, Dad, I'm not a two-year-old! I can perfectly well go by myself."

"Well, on your first morning you have to go in by the front door and ask for the headmaster, Mr Curtis."

"Head teacher, Dad," Oliver corrected him belligerently. "I don't go to a school where there's a headmaster any more. Remember?"

Steve understood how bitter Oliver felt, and he ignored his son's rudeness. "You ask for Mr Curtis and he'll have someone ready to...show you around." Steve had nearly said, "To look after you," but had hastily altered the words. He and Oliver had already been to the school and met Mr Curtis, and as Oliver was adamant that he should go by himself, Steve decided to let him.

"You'll be in year ten, Oliver," Mr Curtis had said. "Mr Dawson'll be your tutor. Any problems, you go to him. I'll have someone waiting to show you where to go on the first morning."

The person waiting had been a boy called David Hicks, short with smooth fair hair; he was wearing dark school uniform trousers and sweater, and carrying an old briefcase. Oliver disliked him on sight, but he followed him to the classroom that was to be his tutorial room and there he met Mr Dawson, who greeted him cheerfully and introduced him to the rest of the group. Oliver didn't like Mr Dawson either, indeed the only person he did like that day was another boy in the group, whose name was Jay Manders. He was small and wiry, with long hair that curled on to his shoulders, and a broken front tooth. His eyes were sharp and darting, and he picked up immediately on Oliver's resentful expression. He didn't wear school uniform either.

At first break he came up to Oliver and said, "OK, mate?"

Oliver shrugged. "Fucking awful place!" he said.

Jay grinned. "Not when you got it sussed, mate," he said. He jerked his head, "You stick with me, you'll be OK." And so it seemed. No one else came near them, which suited Oliver, and as he got his bearings he began to recognise something familiar in Jay. He was so completely different from Drew Elliott, and yet there were echoes; the same subtle feeling of power came from each, that fugitive power Oliver craved yet only tasted from time to time; and each appeared to be in charge of his own destiny, which Oliver was certain he was not. The others in the group, both girls and boys, seemed to steer well clear of him, and David Hicks, seeing his charge taken over by Jay, left him to it.

Even on that first day, Oliver came to realise that hanging out with Jay was a good move. Jay, with Oliver in tow, walked to the front of the queue in the canteen, and collected his food without waiting in line. Oliver did the same. There was no protest from those whom they'd queue barged, they simply relinquished their places to Jay and his friend.

They carried their trays to a table by a window. Two other

boys were already sitting there, but they moved up and made space at once.

"Oliver 'Ooper." Jay waved his fork in Oliver's direction. "Jackie Farmer, and Doss Eldon." He stuck his fork into a sausage and chomping the end of it off, asked, "How much so far?"

"'Bout twenty-five," answered Jackie, and pulling a fistful of money from his pocket slid it across the table. It was all in change, 20ps, 10ps, the occasional 50p or £1 coins among them.

"All pay up?"

"Mostly, a couple needed reminding. They'll pay tomorrer."

Jay looked at Oliver. "We look after some of the younger kids, see?" he said, scooping the money into his hand and putting it into his pocket. "Don't allow no bullying. They pay up on a Monday, regular, an' we look after 'em."

Oliver held his gaze for a moment before he shrugged and nodded. "Sounds fair," he said, and began to eat his own sausage and chips.

"The only guy you 'ave to watch out for is Martin Collins," Jay warned him, pointing out a red-headed youth across the yard. "But when he goes in the summer, the place'll be ours."

Over the coming days Oliver got to know quite a lot about Jay Manders. He was feared by most of the younger children in the school, and commanded a healthy respect among many of the older ones, and even Martin Collins and his gang left him alone.

He lived with his mother and his brother Barry, in a council flat on the Crosshills estate. "Me dad don't live with us no more. It's me, Bazzer, an' Mum, an' 'er boyfriend, Wayne. He's a right tosser an' all. She's welcome to 'im. I'm off, soon as I get out of 'ere."

"Where will you live?" Oliver asked.

"Got two bruvvers, see," Jay answered. "Scott, what's inside just now, and Bazzer. Bazzer'll stay wiv Mum, but not me. Might live wiv Scott. 'E's got a place." He was clearly very proud of his eldest brother. "They was 'ere, Scott an' Baz, at this school. Most of the older kids remember them," he grinned knowingly, "from when they was younger an' Scott looked after 'em, like I do now."

"Why's Scott inside?" ventured Oliver.

"He was like, running a business, see? 'Ad some stuff stashed round 'is place and the filth come round an' found it. I told you, 'e don't live at home no more, and Baz was round 'is place when they come. 'E nearly got done, an' all, for 'avin' a stolen mobile. Took down the nick 'e was, but they knew it weren't 'im what lived there, so they give 'im a caution for the phone an' let 'im off. When Scott got 'ome they was waitin'. Done 'im for 'and-lin'. He got nine months."

"What sort of stuff had he got?" Oliver asked intrigued.

Jay shrugged. "TVs, videos and the like. An' a lot of small stuff, out the supermarkets. Got a crowd of women working for 'im. They get the stuff and 'e buys it off 'em."

Oliver was very interested in this. After his success with the stolen charge card in the Easter holidays, he had tried his hand at shoplifting. He hadn't realised how easy it would be if he was careful. Over the summer holidays, he had been working all the main stores in town, all except Harper and Hill, of course, where Annie was one of the store detectives. Even that he put to his advantage though, asking her about her work and how she spotted shoplifters.

"How do you know who's stealing and who's just looking?" he asked innocently, and Annie, anxious to establish an easier relationship with him, explained many of the tricks of the shoplifter and how she countered them. Oliver stored the information away for future reference. Information was a type of power, he decided, and he would use it to his advantage.

Over the weeks, he had gathered a fair amount of stuff that he needed to offload somewhere. At the moment it was mostly small items, things which could be easily concealed under a jacket or in a pocket, and these he'd hidden for the time being in the shed at number nine.

Both the Smarts and the Redwoods had corner plots and so

had slightly larger gardens than the other houses. Between these was a small footpath that cut through to a narrow rutted track beyond. This track had originally given back access to Dartmouth House before the Circle had been built in its grounds. Edged on the other side by allotments, it now ran behind the houses on the south side of the Circle before emerging some half a mile away between two buildings on to the Crosshills Road. It was a short cut from the Circle to the Crosshills district of Belcaster, and as such, Oliver used it every day on his way to school. The cut, as it was called, ran between the garden fences of numbers eight and nine, and it was while slouching home from school one day Oliver had seen the shed in the Smarts' garden and was suddenly hit by its possibilities. As he emerged into the Circle, all was quiet, so he slipped through the Smarts' side gate and went to have a look. The shed had one small window, and a sturdy door with a large bolt, but to Oliver's surprise there was no key or padlock securing the bolt, and he drew it back easily and looked inside. There he found a work bench with some tools, a lawn mower, a strimmer and a hedge trimmer. There was plenty of space as well, however. Clearly the shed was new and the Smarts hadn't begun to accumulate all the rubbish one would expect to find in there.

It wasn't long before Oliver had a system going. Anything he wanted to hide in the shed, he put into plastic carrier bags and dropped over the bottom fence. The shed itself shielded him from the windows of Dartmouth Circle, and provided no one else was on the track or in the allotments, he knew he was entirely unobserved. Then later, when it was getting dark, he would slip into the Smarts' garden, retrieve the carrier bags and stow them inside the shed. He even left an old rugby ball tucked behind a bush, in case he was seen and needed to have an explanation for being in the garden at all. It would be fine while the Smarts were still away, but he'd have to clear everything away before they got back, and that's where he hoped Scott might come in.

"When's he get out?" Oliver asked casually.

Jay shrugged. "Dunno," he said. "Some time soon. 'E'll only do 'bout four months if 'e keeps 'is nose clean. Why?"

"Sounds a real guy," Oliver said. "Like to meet him."

"Yeah? Well, I'll tell 'im, when 'e come out."

Having heard about Scott, Oliver decided not to tell Jay about his stash. He thought he'd rather deal with Scott, but he did decide to increase what he had to offer. He got a real buzz from working the shopping centre. He'd got more adventurous and had occasionally taken stuff from unlocked cars including two handbags complete with cheque books and cards. He couldn't use them of course because they belonged to women, but he added them to the varied selection of clothes, blank videos, batteries, toiletries and even some bottles of booze that he had stashed in the Smarts' shed. He was certain from what Jay said that Scott would know what to do with them.

Gradually he settled in to life at Crosshills. He didn't make any other friends, being a friend of Jay's set him aside from the other guys, but he didn't care. There were reasonable sports facilities at Crosshills and when made to choose a major sport, Oliver opted for rugby. He'd always enjoyed it at Beechlands, and at Chapmans he'd been in the under-fourteen team, and here he found, in spite of himself, he still enjoyed playing. He did enough work to keep the teachers off his back, though it was nothing like the workload he'd had before and to all intents and purposes he settled into the school well. His father was both pleased and relieved, but unknown to him Oliver had an agenda of his own. When he went into business with Scott Manders, as he fully intended to, he would make enough cash to leave home the moment he was sixteen. He wouldn't live with Dad and bitch Annie or Mum and creep Oslo; he'd live on his own and take charge of his own life, and *no one* would tell him what to do.

"They can't make you come 'ome when you're sixteen," Jay had told him when outlining his own plans. "You don't 'ave to go to school no more."

As part of Jay's gang, Oliver took his turn at parting the

juniors from their money. He liked to see the hunted look in their eyes as they handed over the money. They were afraid of him and he enjoyed their fear. Jay gave him a cut of the take, as he did the others, but Oliver was not interested in the cash, it was the power to take it that gave him the buzz.

It was about three weeks later, just before half term, that Jay came into school one day and said, "'Ere Oliver, Scott's come 'ome yesterday. I told 'im you was interested in doin' a bit of business, and 'e said 'e'd meet you at the Rec after school today."

"Cool," Oliver agreed, feeling his mouth go dry.

Scott was waiting at the entrance to the playground, lounging against the fence idly watching the young children playing on the swings. He turned as Oliver and Jay approached, surveying Oliver.

"Hey, Scottie, this is Oliver who I told you about," Jay said.

"Yeah, OK." Scott nodded at Oliver and indicated with a jerk of his head that Jay should disappear. With only a look of disappointment for argument, Jay said, "Yeah, well see you later," and loped off towards the town.

"Jay said you had some business for me," Scott said, glancing round casually as if to check for watchers. Oliver did the same, but could see no one except the mothers and children in the playground, and an old lady walking her dog.

"Yeah," Oliver replied, "got some stuff to shift."

"Like what?"

"Good car boot stuff mostly." Oliver hadn't known where Scott sold his goods on, but had guessed car boot sales were a probability, and from the flicker in Scott's eyes when he said this he was pretty sure he'd guessed right.

"Like what?" asked Scott again.

"Like, clothes, toiletries, tools, garden stuff, you know. Oh, and a couple of switch cards and driving licences if you know where to unload those."

Scott looked at Oliver with new respect. He hadn't been that keen on meeting Jay's new posh mate on his first real day out, but he wanted to get back into business as soon as possible, and this would give him a start. He still had the lock-up with the proceeds from the computer shop robbery, but that had never been pinned on him and he didn't want to start unloading that stuff just yet, as he was fairly certain the filth were going to be keeping an eye on him. He'd sold his van that very morning and was in the process of finding a replacement, but Oliver's stuff could be very useful for some quick cash.

"You better show me," he said, drifting off towards the main road. Oliver followed.

"Where d'you keep it?"

"In the shed of an empty house near us."

"Don't the neighbours notice nothing?"

"No, there's a track down the back of the garden," Oliver explained, "and I just dump everything over the fence. Then when it's quiet, I just go in the garden and stash the stuff in the shed."

"Show me," ordered Scott, liking the sound of Oliver's stash. He might make use of it himself until he was sure it was safe to go back to the lock-up.

Oliver took his usual way home and they were soon on the track behind the Circle.

"'Ere, what houses are these?" Scott demanded as they approached.

"Dartmouth Circle," Oliver replied. "Why? There's a foot-path through from this track."

"I'll go over the fence at the back," Scott said, "and meet you in the garden." He had no wish to be seen anywhere near Dartmouth Circle.

"OK," Oliver shrugged, "I'll do the same. The shed'll shield us from the back windows of the houses."

With a glance round to make sure no one was in the allot-ments or on the track, Scott swung himself easily up and over the fence, dropping down into the Smarts' garden behind the shed. Oliver scrambled over after him and the two peered in the window at the back.

"I don't usually come here till it's getting dark," Oliver said quietly.

"Who lives in the houses?" asked Scott. "Will they be at home?" He needed to look at the stuff properly and was considering the risk of slipping round the shed in broad daylight.

"Yeah, I guess," Oliver replied. "The guy next door works at home and the lot on the corner are retired. But there's some bushes near the front of the shed. Should be OK."

"You go round and get the door open," ordered Scott, "and then I'll come after. If you see anyone at the windows, do your rugby ball routine, and I'll go back over the fence."

Oliver peered round the side of the shed. There was a light on on the ground floor of Mike Callow's, but his upper windows seemed empty, and the Redwoods only had one window giving a clear view of the shed. Oliver decided to risk it, and within moments, he and Scott were inside the shed.

Scott quickly sorted through the stuff he was being offered and nodded with satisfaction. "This'll do," he said. "Give you a hundred for this lot, including them tools." He jerked his head at the Smarts' strimmer and hedge clipper.

Oliver was disappointed, he'd hoped for a lot more. "That's not much for all this," he objected.

Scott shrugged. "'S what it's worth," he said. "Take it or leave it!"

"What about the switch cards and driving licences?"

"'Nother fifty," Scott offered. He actually knew a bloke from the young offender centre he'd just left who was in the market for those. "Any social books?"

"Yes," Oliver remembered. "One child allowance and one pension." He'd forgotten those.

"Give you another fifty for those," said Scott.

"They must be worth more than that," scoffed Oliver, determined not to be done down.

"Only if you know where to shift 'em, mate," grinned Scott. "And you ain't taking none of the risks, see?"

Oliver thought rapidly. It was a start, and he could always get more, find out exactly what Scott could deal in best.

"OK," he agreed, "you're on. Where's the money?"

"I'll bring my van round the back here on Friday, right? About 'alf seven, when it's dark. You 'ave the stuff ready by the fence. I'll have the cash with me."

Oliver agreed, and within moments the shed was bolted and they were back on the track.

"Friday at 'alf seven," repeated Scott as he turned away, "and be there ready. I shan't want to 'ang about!"

Oliver watched him jog off down the track and then made his way back into the Circle via the cut.

Yes! he thought, punching the air. I've done it! Now I can really make money. Scott must be going to sell that lot at a boot sale or market somewhere over the weekend, and he'd need more. Yes!

As he came into the Circle, he saw Annabel Haven coming up from the Dartmouth Road end. She was at the Tech now, doing her 'A' levels, not at Belcaster High. Oliver knew that her sister, Chantal, was still at the High, and he felt a moment's fellow feeling for Annabel. He knew what it was like to see your little sister still going to a proper school while you had to make do with Crosshills Comp or the Tech.

"Hi," he said as they passed.

"Hi." Annabel raised an apathetic hand in acknowledgement. Oliver opened his mouth to say more, but Annabel was already turning into her own house and clearly not interested in him, so he snapped it shut and slouched on.

Silly cow, he thought, just like her sister. Getting fat, too. Fat and ugly. He grinned. She'd never embark on a life of crime. She was a good girl, doing her 'A' levels. Silly cow! And he laughed aloud as he went home.

Friday came, and as soon as it was dusk Oliver crept into the Smarts' garden and transferred everything behind the shed, ready to pass over the fence to Scott. Spot on half past seven, a small van edged along the track and stopped by the fence.

"OK?" Scott hissed as he opened the van doors.

"Yeah, all here," replied Oliver and began passing the stuff over the fence. Within minutes it was all stowed in the van. Oliver heaved himself over the fence and handed Scott the cards and social security books. Scott stuffed them into the pocket of his jeans and gave Oliver a fistful of notes.

"'S all there," he murmured. "Let me know when you got somethink else. Tell Jay."

"Yeah, OK," Oliver whispered, putting the cash into his pocket. He turned to go, but Scott called him back.

"'Ere mate," he said, "do us a favour. Put this note into number four."

"Number four?" Oliver queried. "You mean the Havens'?"

"Yeah, that's the one. Cheers mate!" Scott got quickly into the van and pulled away into the darkness.

Oliver went quickly through into the Circle and by the light of a street lamp looked at what Scott had given him. It was a crumpled brown envelope, addressed to Annabel Haven. He wondered what it was. What the hell would a guy like Scott Manders have to do with Annabel Haven? Oliver put it in his pocket and went home to open it and find out.

The envelope was badly sealed and Oliver soon eased it open. Inside was a small piece of lined paper on which was written:

Roxy Café. Monday 4.30. Scott

Oliver stared at it for a moment. Something's going on, he thought, and I'm going to find out what. Carefully, he resealed the envelope and put it in his pocket. Should he wait and catch Annabel somewhere outside her house, or should he just deliver it as asked? He decided on the latter course. He didn't want Annabel to tell Scott that she hadn't got the note straightaway, or he might guess that Oliver had read it first and realise he knew about their meeting. Much better to act as messenger and keep watch to find out what was going on. Information like that might well come in useful some time. It would be good to have a hold over Scott Manders, Oliver thought, even if he wasn't sure exactly what it was yet, and so he slipped out of the house again to deliver the note. As he walked to the Havens' house, he decided he'd ring the bell and ask for Annabel. If she wasn't there he'd wait and deliver the note in person some other way.

In fact, it was Chantal who opened the door, and her face tightened with anger when she saw who was on the step.

"What do *you* want?" she asked rudely.

"I want to see your sister," Oliver said.

"I don't expect she wants to see you." Chantal began to close the door, but Oliver jammed his foot in the way.

"Just ask her," he said calmly.

Chantal turned away and called Annabel. "Oliver Hooper's here, says he wants you?"

Annabel came to the door. "Yeah?"

"Got a message for you," Oliver said, watching her closely. "From Scott Manders." The reaction was there, but Oliver wasn't quite sure what it conveyed.

"Who?" Annabel had been stunned, but hastily retained her control.

Oliver proffered the note. "Scott Manders. He asked me to give you this."

Annabel took the note, and sticking it in her pocket said, "I don't know anyone called Scott... whatever."

Oliver just grinned. "Yeah," he said. "Whatever. Night." He turned on his heel and walked away. As he heard the front door close behind him, he punched the air. Something was definitely going on there, and he meant to find out what it was. He needed Scott Manders at present, and to have something on him might ensure that he continued to give him his help.

## Chapter Sixteen

Annabel trudged into the Circle. She felt exhausted, it was pouring with rain and she was longing to get home. Since she had left Belcaster High School she had found her days very long. She had further to travel to the technical college where she was now finishing her 'A' levels and though life there was, in many ways more relaxed and the students were treated as students and not as schoolgirls, she found it difficult to settle down. She didn't have to be at college unless she had a lecture or a tutorial, and because there were no other subjects to be studied, or extra-curricular activities to be undertaken such as choir or games or drama as there had been at the High, Annabel often found time hanging heavy on her hands. It was an effort to do anything.

As she reached the front door, she fumbled for her key in her duffel bag. It wasn't there. Huddling against the door, trying to get out of the rain, she searched through her bag again, and then her pockets, but with no success. Then she remembered, she had taken the key out of her jeans the night before.

"Oh shit," she wailed, "I must have left it on my desk." She stared out into the darkening rain-filled evening in dismay. She knew her mother was working late that evening and that Chantal was visiting a friend after school, and realised she wouldn't be able to get in for at least another hour. "Shit!" she muttered again, "Shit and double shit!" Then she remembered that Mary Jarvis had a key, so she hurried across to number five. The house was in darkness and though she rang the bell, she was not at all surprised that there was no reply. Now she wouldn't be able to get in until one of them came home. In a fury of frustration, Annabel crashed the knocker against the door in an angry tattoo.

A voice sounded sharply from a window above. "Mrs Jarvis is not at home."

Annabel stepped away from the door and looked up to see Sheila Colby leaning out of her window.

In the light that spilled from her window, Sheila saw who it was and said, "Oh, it's you, Annabel. Why are you banging like that on Mary's door? She's not at home, you know."

"I only wanted to get our spare key," explained Annabel sullenly. "I'm locked out."

"I see. Well, you'll get very wet standing out there. You'd better come in here and wait. I'll open the door, just push and come up." With that Sheila shut the window and disappeared.

Annabel sighed, it was the last thing she wanted to do, to go and sit with Sheil until Mum got home, but there was nothing she could do about it now, and there was no point standing out in the rain. She went across to Sheila's front door, and finding the catch already released, pushed it open.

"Close the door and come on up," Sheila called from the first floor. "I've put the kettle on, I expect you'd like a cup of tea."

Annabel climbed the stairs and looked into the kitchen. Sheila was busying herself with teapot and mugs, and putting biscuits on a plate. She glanced up at Annabel.

"Take your coat off and get warm by the fire," she said. "The tea won't be a minute."

Annabel did as she was told, glad to be in the warm even if she did have to put up with Sheila. She sank into a chair by the gas fire and held out her hands to get warm. She was suddenly exhausted, and when Sheila came in with the tea and biscuits she was shocked to see how pale and wan the girl looked.

"My dear," she exclaimed, setting down the tray, "you look whacked! Are you all right?"

"Yes, thank you," Annabel said, managing a smile.

"Well, this'll warm you up," Sheila said and handed her a mug of tea. "Have a biscuit."

Annabel took the tea gratefully and then reached over for a biscuit. When she looked up, she found Sheila was studying her and she coloured, raising her chin in her new and now ever-ready defiance, half-prepared for what the older woman said next.

"I hear you're having a baby," Sheila said abruptly. "I expect you'll think it none of my business, but I did hear you were planning to have it, not have an abortion I mean."

"It isn't your business," began Annabel defiantly.

"You're quite right," Sheila said smoothly, apparently unruffled by her interruption. "All I wanted to say was that I think you're very brave to keep it, Annabel. I admire you for it."

Annabel, who had expected only condemnation from someone like Sheila Colby, was stunned at this, and could think of nothing to say. Sheila went on, "It can't be easy for you. Even in these permissive days, people are always so ready to judge."

"No, it isn't," murmured Annabel, and to give herself time to think of something else to say, she took a mouthful of the tea.

It certainly hadn't been easy. A few days after she had told her mother she was pregnant, they had gone together to tell Mrs Harman, the headmistress at the High.

They were shown into her office and offered coffee, and while they were waiting for it to come, Mrs Harman told Angela how much better Annabel had been doing.

"When I heard you wanted to see me," she smiled, "I spoke to each of Annabel's teachers so as to have an up-to-date report for you, and I must say it's very encouraging."

Angela took the plunge. "I'm very pleased to hear you say that, Mrs Harman," she began, "because we've got a problem, and we are both hoping you will be able to...well, to treat it sympathetically."

"I'm sure we can sort it out whatever it is," cooed Mrs Harman, and she glanced across at Annabel herself for explanation.

"I'm pregnant," said Annabel simply.

Mrs Harman's face froze, and as for a moment she said nothing, Annabel went on, "The baby's due at the end of January."

"I see." Mrs Harman's voice was icy.

"We want to arrange for Annabel to continue her studies so that if possible she can take her exams as planned in the summer," explained Angela, but her heart was already sinking. It was quite clear that Mrs Harman was going to show no sympathy for Annabel's predicament at all.

"Then I suggest she transfers to the technical college as soon as she can. I'm afraid there is no place in this school for unmarried teenage mothers."

Stung by this, Angela almost snapped, "What about married ones?" but she bit the words back. The last thing she wanted was to antagonise the woman. She said nothing.

Mrs Harman sat back in her chair and studied them for a moment across her desk before she went on, "This school maintains certain standards. I know it's not fashionable these days to have high standards of morality, but we at Belcaster High do not bow to fashion. I'm afraid there is no longer a place for Annabel here, she must leave us today. I will arrange for all her work to be sent on to you, with her assessments so far. I think you are lucky in that the technical college follows the same syllabus as we do for most subjects, so the transfer should not be too difficult."

"I see." It was Angela's turn to be icy. She had been hoping that Mrs Harman would be able to keep Annabel at the school until Christmas at any rate, and then be persuaded to have her back in February, after the baby was born, but clearly the headmistress was not entertaining the idea.

"And now of course," Mrs Harman continued, "there is the question of Chantal."

"Chantal?" Angela was startled.

"I'm prepared to keep her on for the moment," Mrs Harman said, "it would be a pity to move her just as she's starting her GCSE course."

"I don't see this has anything to do with Chantal," began Angela angrily. "Why should she be penalised for a mistake her sister has made?"

"I was only thinking of the child herself, the embarrassment she may face in the circumstances," replied the head smoothly.

There won't be any embarrassment unless it comes from *you*, thought Angela hotly, but again she managed to bite back the words. She didn't want to have to take Chantal away from the school as well, for the only alternative for her would be Crosshills Comprehensive, and Angela didn't want her to go there.

"I am happy to keep Chantal," Mrs Harman was saying, "provided, of course, that she maintains the standards we expect."

"I will discuss it with my husband," Angela said with all the dignity she could muster, "and we'll let you know what we decide." She got to her feet, and facing the headmistress across the desk said quietly, "I'm sorry you feel unable to stand by one of your pupils when she is in trouble, Mrs Harman. But as you can't, I'd be grateful if you could indeed send on all Annabel's work with any reports and assessments that have already been done, so that I can pass them over to the technical college. Good morning." Annabel got up too, and together they walked out of the office. As they reached the door, Mrs Harman's secretary arrived with the coffee tray.

"I'm so sorry to have troubled you," Angela said to her, "but I'm afraid we haven't time to stay for coffee. Good morning to you."

"Mum, you were brilliant," Annabel said as they walked to the car.

"I didn't feel brilliant," Angela said. "I'm still shaking. Let's go and find a cup of coffee somewhere else and decide what to do next."

They found a little café off the High Street and carried their cups to a table in a corner.

"Well, you seem to have left school," said Angela as they sat down. "We'd better go and see the people at the technical college. You realise that this may mean you can't do the exams this summer after all, don't you? If you have to change syllabuses or examining boards or something."

"I know. I'm sorry, Mum."

Angela smiled ruefully. "We'll manage something," she said. "I just wish I'd been able to tell that Harman woman that Chantal was leaving as from today too, then she'd have lost two lots of fees! Stupid cow!"

"Mother!" Annabel exclaimed in surprise.

"'We at Belcaster High do not bow to fashion,'" Angela mimicked the headmistress's prissy voice, and they both laughed. "But I can tell you this, Annabel, if there'd been *anywhere* else to send her apart from Crosshills, I'd have removed Chantal today. Still, that's not your problem, I'll discuss it with Dad. And you must talk to Dad this weekend as well," her mother added.

"Yes, I will, I promise," Annabel said. "I'll ring him this evening and arrange to see him." She looked across at her mother, and noticed for the first time the tired rings round her eyes and the drawn gauntness of her face and reaching out took hold of her hands. "Thank you, Mum, for standing by me."

Angela returned her grasp and said quietly, "What else did you think I'd do, darling? Try not to worry, we'll see it through together." She downed her coffee. "Now, come on, we have to go to the Tech, and see what they say."

"What happens if they won't have me either?" wondered Annabel.

"We'll cross that bridge when we come to it," replied Angela, "but I'm sure they will."

She had been right. That part of the arranging had been comparatively easy. The courses she was already studying were also being offered by the Tech, and though some of the work they had covered she hadn't and the other way around, the tutors were confident that she would be ready to take the exams in the summer provided she worked hard. She was to start immediately, and arrived for her first lecture the next morning.

Telling her father had not been easy either. As she promised, she rang him that same evening and arranged to meet him. She hadn't seen him for ages – still angry with him for leaving she hadn't wanted to – but when he heard her voice on the phone he sounded very glad to hear from her.

"Polly, what a lovely surprise!" His use of his private name for her caught at her heart and she realised how much she had missed him. Tears pricked her eyes and she said, "Can we meet up, Dad, at the weekend? Saturday perhaps?"

"It would be lovely to see you, pet," he said. "We'll have a pub lunch and catch up on everything. Just you, or is Chantal coming too?"

"Just me I'm afraid, Dad. I wanted to discuss something with you." She hesitated. "Can it be just us, Dad? Not Desirée too? It's sort of private."

"Fair enough," he agreed cheerfully. "She's away this week-end anyway. Shall we meet in the George and Dragon?"

"Yes, fine, or I could come round to your flat." Annabel wasn't at all sure she wanted to tell Dad about the baby in a public place. She felt the need for privacy.

"No, no," he said hastily, "the pub would be far better. I'll be there from about twelve. See you then, pet."

"See you, Dad," answered Annabel, but her father had already rung off.

When Annabel got to the George and Dragon on Saturday, it was full of cheerful lunchtime drinkers. She pushed her way through the crowd to where her father was standing at the bar.

"Hi Dad."

"Polly!" His face lit up at the sight of her and he gathered her into a bear-like hug, before holding her away from him to look into her face. "Let me look at you. It's great to see you. What do you want to drink, pet?"

"Orange juice and lemonade please," replied Annabel.

"Nothing stronger?" He was surprised. She usually drank lager, but when she shook her head he ordered the orange juice and lemonade and then said, "I've booked a table in the back bar for quarter to one. It always gets crowded in here on a Saturday and I wanted to be sure we could sit down." He handed her her drink. "Cheers," he said and took a pull at his own pint.

Annabel was determined she wasn't going to say anything about the baby until they were safely sitting down in the comparative quiet of the back bar, and she was relieved that Dad didn't ask her straight out why she'd wanted to see him. He waited for her to speak.

"Chantal sends her love," she began.

Her father smiled. "Does she? That's nice. How is she?"

"Oh, very excited. There is a house full of students at number seven, you know Ned Short's old house..." and to pass the time until they could sit down, she launched into an account of the goings-on in the Circle ending with a description of Madge's ninetieth barbecue.

"She really is an amazing old biddy," Ian said. "Hope I'm as good as that when I'm ninety." A silence fell, enclosing them in a bubble from the hubbub of noise about them, and then Ian asked casually, "How's your mum?"

"She's fine," Annabel said. "Busy, you know, working full-time."

"Still seeing that chap, what's he called...David?"

Angela was not seeing David, or anyone else for that matter, but Annabel was feeling very protective of her mother just now and she decided that Mum's pride must be protected. "Yes, he's around all the time," she lied. "Seems very keen."

"Do you like him?" asked Ian. "You and Chantal?"

"Yes, he's great fun." Feeling she had said enough and not wanting to get drawn too deeply into a web of lies, she said, "Are we going to eat soon? I'm starving."

Ian glanced at his watch. "Yes, let's go through."

When they were settled at the table and had ordered their food, Ian looked across at Annabel and said encouragingly, "Well, Polly, this is a treat."

Annabel decided it was now or never, so she said, "Dad, I've got something to tell you. I'm sorry to spring it on you, but there's no other way. I'm pregnant."

Her father put down his glass and looked across at her for a long moment before saying quietly, "Oh Polly, what have you done?"

Annabel felt the tears in her eyes and blinked hard. "I'm sorry, Dad," she whispered. "I didn't mean it to happen."

"No, I'm sure you didn't," he said dryly. "When's it due?"

"End of January."

"So you're going to have it, then?"

Annabel nodded dumbly, hating the look of disappointment in her father's eyes.

"And keep it? Or have it adopted?"

"I want to keep it, Dad. I don't want to give it away."

"And what does your mother say?"

"Mum says we'll cope somehow, between us."

"And who's the father? What about him? What does he say?"

At that moment the food came, and while the waitress put the plates on the table, brought them sauces and warned them that the plates were very hot, Annabel had time to phrase her answer.

When they were alone again, she said, "It was a man I met, went around with for a while. It only happened once and then..."

"He dumped you?" Ian fought to control the anger in his voice.

"Not really, he...well, he moved away. I don't know where he is and he doesn't know about the baby."

Ian looked at her sternly. "Then we must trace him, tell him what's going on. What's his name?"

Annabel lowered her eyes and simply shook her head.

"For God's sake, Annabel," her father exploded. "It's no good just shaking your head. We have to have his name. He has to be told."

"Why?" cried Annabel. "Why does he have to know? He has nothing to do with it."

"Nothing to do with it," repeated Ian incredulously, "it took two of you to start this baby...it's his baby too you know, quite apart from his responsibilities towards it, he's entitled to know. He'll have to contribute towards its keep, it's not just *your* baby, Annabel, it's his as well."

It was not the reaction Annabel had been expecting from her father and tears finally flooded down her cheeks. Over the months, she had felt herself hardening towards Scott, even though he seemed to have protected her from the police. She wished she'd never met him and genuinely didn't want anything more to do with him. She'd never thought of the baby as Scott's baby, it was hers, and she never wanted to see Scott again.

The room was filling up round them and seeing her distress, Ian pushed his plate away untouched. "I'm not hungry, are you?"

Annabel shook her head miserably.

"Come on, then," he said, "let's get out of here. We'll go back to the flat where we can discuss this properly and in private."

He paid for the uneaten food and marched out to the car park. They drove in silence to the flat where he now lived and let themselves in.

"We'll have to eat something," he said. "I'll heat up some soup and we'll have it with bread and cheese."

While he was in the kitchen, Annabel went the bathroom. When she came to wash her hands, she noticed that only her father's washing things were beside the basin. One toothbrush hung in the rack, his shaving kit was on the shelf with the toothpaste, but there was nothing of Desirée's. Before, there had been rows of pots and bottles, all her lotions and potions, deodorant, talc, make-up remover and other creams; now there was nothing. There was only one towel on the rail and her bathrobe was no longer hanging on the back of the door.

Of course, she's away for the weekend, Annabel suddenly remembered, drying her hands, Dad said so.

When they had drunk their soup and eaten some bread and cheese, Ian asked quietly, "What does Mum say about the baby?"

"She's been great," Annabel said. "She's upset, of course, but she hasn't really said so. She's been helping me to get things sorted out," and Annabel went on to tell him about Belcaster High and the Tech. Ian was less surprised at Mrs Harman's reaction than Angela had been.

"Of course she can't keep you there," he said. "How would she explain it to the other girls and their parents? I just hope she doesn't take it out on Chantal and make her life hell."

"Mum said she'd move her today if there was anywhere else but Crosshills to send her."

"Hmmm, well we'll have to give that some thought," Ian mused. "However, in the meantime I think we must all get together and have a proper conference on what's going to happen. I mean about when the baby's born. We have to consider all the options, and it's a decision that we all have to be in on, as it affects us all. I'll give Mum a ring and arrange a time to discuss things, OK?"

Annabel nodded. "Thanks for being so understanding, Dad."

"Yes, well... In the meantime you must give some thought to telling us who the father is. I assume your mother doesn't know? No, well we're going to have to find out in the end. You give it some thought, eh?" He looked at her for a long moment and then putting his arms round her said, "Oh Polly, how on earth did you let this happen? It's going to change your life!"

For the briefest span, Annabel considered telling her father the whole thing, including the robbery and the car chase, but her nerve failed her and she just said miserably, "I wish it hadn't happened, Dad, really I do, but it did."

For a moment they sat in silence, then Annabel pulled free. She had noticed as they'd been eating that most of the CDs were missing, as was the hi-fi itself. Now she looked into her father's face and asked, "Dad, where's Desirée?"

He looked uncomfortable and replied with a shrug, "She's away for the weekend, I told you."

"Just for the weekend, Dad?" pursued Annabel.

Ian sighed. "I'm not sure," he admitted.

"You mean she's left you?"

"I honestly don't know." He hesitated for a moment and then admitted, "She left last weekend, and I haven't heard from her since."

"But what about her things, what'll she do about those?"

"She took them with her," Ian said. "I was away all last Friday until late evening, and when I got home she'd gone."

"And taken everything with her, clothes, books, what?"

"Everything of hers and much of what we'd bought together." Ian sounded weary.

Annabel put her arms round him again. "Oh Dad, poor Dad, how awful for you, are you very sad?"

He returned her hug and then got to his feet, pacing to the window and back before saying, "To tell you the truth, Polly, no I'm not. Things hadn't been right for some time, and I think she'd found someone else. I'm not really expecting her back."

"So you're all on your own. Have you told Mum?"

"No, I haven't," he replied and added sharply, "and you're not to, either."

"Oh Dad, why ever not? Perhaps you could…"

"No, Polly," he cut her off. "It isn't as simple as that. We've changed, both of us. We aren't the people we were before Desirée came on the scene, and we can't just put the clock back. Our lives have diverged, and we've moved in different directions."

"But she ought to know," pleaded Annabel. "It's not fair not to tell her, 'specially now I know."

"I'm going to tell her…I will tell her, but in my own time."

"You mean if Desirée doesn't come back!" Annabel said bitterly.

"No," he answered patiently, "when I've thought things through. And in the meantime, Polly, I really don't want you to tell her, or anyone else for that matter, about Desirée leaving."

"Did she leave you a note?" demanded Annabel.

"Desirée? No."

"Or her door keys?"

"No."

"Then I should have the locks changed," remarked Annabel, bleakly.

When Ian dropped Annabel back to Dartmouth Circle, she tried to persuade him to come in, but he was adamant.

"No, pet. I'll ring Mum tomorrow and we'll arrange an evening to talk." He gave her a hug and then holding her at arm's length, he looked at her seriously. "Please, Polly," he reminded her, "don't tell her about Desirée, not yet. I'll tell her myself, I promise, when the time's right."

So she had promised, but the knowledge was burning a hole inside her.

"I'm glad you're not having an abortion," Sheila said, breaking in on her thoughts. "I know you'll think I'm an interfering old woman, but it's not something I think any woman should put herself through unless it's an absolute necessity."

"No, well I'm not having one," Annabel said firmly, and tried to think of some way to change the subject. "Look, Mrs Colby, I really don't want to discuss this with you. What I've decided I've decided, and it is, as you said, none of your business!"

Surprisingly Sheila nodded and said, "Quite right. But I just wanted to tell you something that very few people know. Just Gerald and myself now, I suppose." She set down her teacup and looking squarely at Annabel took a deep breath. "When I was your age I got pregnant too. In those days it was considered a dreadful thing to be a single mother. The father, not Gerald, of course, was a student who was lodging with my family. I didn't dare tell my parents, they wouldn't have been able to stand the shame of it, so, George – that was the student – he found a place where they would do something about the baby, no questions asked, for £200." Sheila had Annabel's full attention now.

"A back-street abortionist?"

"A back-street abortionist. I just turned up, they gave me an anaesthetic and when I came round again it was all over and they sent me home. Only, of course it wasn't all over. Later that evening I started to bleed, and I was so frightened that I had to tell my mother." For a moment Sheila's eyes became distant as she remembered the awfulness of that night and her mother's reaction, then she looked again at Annabel. "Well, to cut a long story short, I had to go into hospital and they saved my life, but after that I couldn't have any more children." She glanced across at Annabel's horrified face. "Of course abortions aren't like that these days, but it isn't just the physical side of it, you know. A day hasn't passed that I haven't thought about that baby, and wondered what he or she would have been like. That child would be forty-eight if it were alive today, but I killed it because I was too ashamed to let it live, to give it the love it deserved. I killed my own chances of having more children, deprived Gerald of the chance of being a father, and I have to live with those regrets."

Silence fell round them and then Annabel said in a small voice, "This is your secret. Why are you telling me this?"

"To encourage you," Sheila answered quietly. "I assume the pregnancy was a mistake?"

Annabel nodded.

"Well, so it was, but you're brave enough to let your baby be born, Annabel, and though it will be very difficult for you, I'm sure when he or she is laid in your arms you won't have any regrets about your decision."

"What happened to George?" asked Annabel.

"George? My parents kicked him out of the house and told him they never wanted to see him again."

"And you? Did you want to see him again?" Annabel spoke in a low voice.

Sheila shook her head. "No," she said. "No, I didn't want to see him again. He blamed me for the baby, and all he did was find the money for the abortion and then disappear." She looked at Annabel speculatively and asked, "What about the father of your baby. What does he think?"

"He doesn't know," her eyes met Sheila's, "he's disappeared as well."

"I see."

"But my parents are standing by me. I'm not facing this on my own." She gave Sheila a shy smile. "Thank you for telling me, Mrs Colby. I'll keep your secret and I'll remember what you said."

"Well now," Sheila said briskly, "that sounds like a car." She went and looked out of the window. "Yes, your mother has just pulled in, so you'd better be off, or she'll be wondering where you are. Look after yourself, young lady." The intimate moment between them had passed and Sheila reverted to the stiff awkward woman that Annabel recognised. Annabel got to her feet and picked up her bag.

"Thank you for the tea," she said awkwardly, "and, well, everything."

"Make sure the door shuts behind you," instructed Sheila from the top of the stairs.

"Yes, I will," promised Annabel, and did so, very carefully.

Ian Haven had been as good as his word and had rung Angela the day after he had seen Annabel.

"I think we should get together to discuss exactly what we are going to do," he said. "I'd like to come round one evening this week, if that's convenient, when you are all three there."

"Of course," Angela agreed. "Why don't you come on Thursday? Come for supper if you like."

When he arrived, he went into the living room where the fire was alight and the curtains drawn against the autumn evening.

"Supper won't be long," Angela said, returning to the kitchen. "Pour yourself a drink, and one for me too, please."

"Where are the girls?" Ian asked.

"Upstairs doing their homework," Angela replied. "I said I'd call them when supper was ready."

Ian poured the drinks and carried them into the kitchen, where Angela was straining pasta and putting it into the oven to keep hot.

"What do you really think about Annabel?" he asked. "Be honest. We all have to be honest if we are to cope with this."

"Honestly?" Angela put down the pan and looked at him. "Honestly, I'm horrified. She's rising eighteen and she's going to be saddled with a baby. She refuses to say who the father is, and she's determined to bring up the child herself. I'm not sure what this evening is really going to achieve, Ian, because she seems to have made up her mind on all the main issues already. I suppose they are her decisions, but I doubt if she can carry them through without our support. She'll live here of course, but that will affect Chantal as well."

"Yes, well, I've had an idea about Chantal," Ian said. "I know you aren't happy with her staying at the High…"

"Well, she's not going to Crosshills," interrupted Angela, "so we've no choice."

"We might have," Ian said. "Chapmans have started to take girls this term. They've had them in the sixth form for a while now, but from this term they have taken girls in other years too. Of course, most of them are thirteen, but I've spoken to the headmaster and he tells me there are several other girls who are starting in the GCSE year. I sounded him out and he's prepared to take her if we want her to go."

Angela stared at him. "Chantal go to Chapmans?"

"Yes."

"What, straightaway?"

"Yes."

Angela was staggered. "But how's she going to get there every day? There's no way I can drive her out there every morning, it's a twenty-mile round trip! She can't possibly go."

"You wouldn't have to drive her there," Ian replied. "There's a coach that does a pick-up of day children from various places in town. She could go on that."

"Perhaps she doesn't want to move," suggested Angela rather aggressively. This idea of Chapmans coming out of the blue had thrown her. She didn't want Chantal to stay at the High, but now Ian had come up with what seemed to be a viable alternative, she found it made her unaccountably cross.

"It's up to her and you," Ian said reasonably. "All I've done is find a good school, within reach, that will take her. She might like the idea of a mixed school."

Angela was sure she would, but all she said, rather ungraciously, was, "I'll think about it. Please don't say anything to her just yet."

"All right," agreed Ian, "but I do think the sooner we canvass the idea the better. The term's already started and we don't want her to miss too much."

"You make it sound as if you've already decided," Angela said.

"Not if you're seriously against the idea," Ian responded, "but I think it's worth serious consideration, especially if you really want to move Chantal anyway. It's all part of our forward planning, don't you think?"

Angela stirred the sauce thoughtfully. It might be just the answer, but she had the feeling she was being bounced into a decision and she didn't want to be. "Can we afford Chapmans?" she asked. "It must have higher fees than the High."

"That will be my problem," Ian said. "If you want her to go and she wants to go, then I'll manage it."

Angela sighed. She was completely knocked sideways by his suggestion. "Let me think about it," she said at last. "If I think we should bring it up this evening, I'll introduce the subject."

"Fair enough," Ian said. "I'll take your lead."

She turned back to the cooker and said over her shoulder, "Give them a call, will you? Supper's ready."

Ian went to the stairs and called, while Angela took a large gulp of her drink. What on earth was Ian up to? How come he could suddenly afford the fees at Chapmans? Of course they were no longer paying fees for Annabel at the High, but even so they were going to need any money saved that way to help support her and the baby when it arrived. There had been little enough cash to go round when they had split up and he had two homes to run, that was why she'd gone back to full-time working, simply because she didn't want the girls to suffer for what their father had chosen to do. Perhaps he'd been promoted and was now much better off. It was something she was determined to tackle him about, but not this evening, this evening they had other things to discuss and plan.

It was a strange evening all round, Annabel thought. It was as if they were in a time warp, sitting at the table having supper as they had always used to. By common consent they didn't begin to talk about Annabel and the baby during the meal, though Annabel told them what it was like at college.

"In some ways it's much better than at the High," she said. "They treat you like an adult. You're told what to do and you get on and do it. There aren't silly rules about what to wear, what you can and can't do about the place. You just turn up for lectures, there's no extras like hockey or religious studies and things. You don't have to stay if you don't have a tutorial or a lecture, you can just walk out. D'you know Dad, it's really weird, when I walk out of the gate I feel I'm skiving!"

"Well you certainly set the High on fire," remarked Chantal. "Like, everyone keeps coming up to me and saying, 'Is your sister really up the spout?'"

"Chantal!" exclaimed her mother. "What a frightful expression! Don't let me hear you use it again."

Chantal shrugged. "It's what they say," she said.

"Well it's not what *you* say," said Angela fiercely.

"Are they giving you a hard time?" Ian asked her casually.

"Nah, not really," Chantal said. "Some of the staff are a bit iffy."

"Iffy?"

"Yeah, you know," Chantal adopted a condescending tone: "'And how is poor Annabel?...what a dreadful thing! Such a waste. I just tell them we're all delighted."

"Oh Chantal, that isn't very helpful."

"Well, I get fed up with them. Mrs Harman had me in today. I didn't tell you, did I, Mum? She sent for me and said she hoped I was working hard because she'd heard some disappointing reports of my work recently, and it was up to me to maintain the honour of the family! I ask you! She really is losing the plot, you know, Mum."

Angela glanced at Ian and then said, "Well, actually Dad had an idea he wanted to put to you, Chantal."

"Oh," said Chantal through a mouthful of pasta. "Like what?"

"I just wondered if you'd like to change schools, and go to Chapmans."

"Chapmans!" cried Chantal dropping her fork, all thought of food forgotten. "But it's a boys' school, Dad."

"Not any more, it's gone co-ed."

"And I can go there?"

"If you wanted to, it could be arranged," her father agreed.

"But what about the fees? We can't afford them."

"You don't know what we can afford," replied Ian.

"Well, I don't know what *you've* got," said Chantal bluntly, "but *we* haven't got any money, that's why Mum goes out to work full-time instead of mornings only, like before." She looked fiercely at her father. "If you've got more money, Dad, you should be giving it to Mum!"

He nodded seriously. "I know, Chantal, and I will be. I've changed jobs at the office and I'm earning more. Mum won't have to work full-time any more if she doesn't want to."

Angela was speechless at this announcement. How dare Ian spring such a thing on her in front of the girls! He should have told her privately, so that she could give the new situation long and hard consideration. He could at least have mentioned it when they were discussing the question of fees before supper, but even as she thought this she realised that he hadn't been going to tell them that just now, but had been pushed into it by Chantal's reaction to his suggestion. Before she could think of anything to say that wouldn't provoke a scene, Chantal had jumped in again.

"Does Desirée know?" she demanded. "Is she going to let you give Mum more money?"

"Yes, she knows," Ian said.

Now, Dad, now! thought Annabel. Tell them there isn't any Desirée any more. But though she fixed him with her eye and willed him to speak, he simply gave her the faintest of shakes of his head and said no more about her.

"We won't make any decisions about schools, this evening," Ian said to Chantal, "but think about it. Talk to Mum about it, and then if you want to do any more, we'll go and have a look at Chapmans. All right?"

"Yes, Dad, OK," Chantal answered, but she knew she'd already decided. If there really was a chance of going to Chapmans, she was going to leap at it. A mixed school! Heaven! The others at the High would be so jealous!

When they'd finished eating they all continued to sit round the table and Ian said, "Now, we must decide how we are going to help Annabel and her baby." He looked across at his daughter. "We need to decide a few basics and work from there, agreed?"

Annabel nodded, wondering what he meant exactly.

"Now, I am right in assuming you mean to keep this baby when it's born. You aren't going to put it up for adoption?"

Annabel shook her head. "No adoption. I want to keep it."

"That's fair enough in some ways," Angela said, "as long as you've considered it from every angle, and that's what Dad and I want to be sure of." She reached across and took Annabel's hand. "The thing is, a baby is a lifelong commitment. If you decide to keep it, you will be struggling to bring it up on your own. Oh, I don't mean we shan't all be here to help, but it will be your responsibility. You will have to look after it, earn enough to keep it, give your entire life over to it for the first few years anyway." She smiled ruefully at her daughter. "You're only just eighteen and you are going to be tied down by this child. It isn't just a lovely warm pet, like a puppy … no, hear me out, darling," she said as Annabel tried to interrupt indignantly, "it's a whole new person and deserves the very best chance in life. What you have to decide, however difficult that decision may be, is whether what you can give it is best for the baby. Can you be both father and mother, or ought you to be standing aside and letting some couple, dying to have children of their own, take your place? They will lavish it with love, give it things perhaps you would want to but can't, and bring it up in a secure family."

"My baby is not going to be adopted," said Annabel firmly. "I know what you're saying, Mum, but it's my baby and I'm not about to give it away."

"Supposing, in a few years, you wanted to get married?" asked Angela gently. "The man you wanted might not want to take on a child that wasn't his."

"Then *I* wouldn't want *him*," retorted Annabel.

"Easy enough to say…" began Angela.

Annabel broke in, "Look Mum, I hear what you're saying, yeah? You think I should have the baby adopted, but I'm not going to, OK? I'm not going to give away my baby. If you'll all be there for me, fine, but if not I'll manage by myself, OK? Mum, OK?" Her voice rose as she spoke, and she pulled her hand away.

"Steady, Annabel," admonished Ian gently. "Mum's only trying to be sure you've made your decision for the right reasons." He looked across at Angela, who nodded wearily. "Right, well, you seem to have made that decision, so the next thing is to come on to some of the practicalities."

"I have thought it through, Dad," Annabel said more reasonably. "I will go to college as long as I can, and then try and work at home for the first few weeks after the birth. There's a crèche there, so that when I'm fit enough I can take the baby with me when I go for lectures and stuff."

Inevitably, the question of the father came up. "We need to

know who it is, Annabel," Ian said. "He should be contributing towards his child's keep."

"I don't know where he is," Annabel maintained, "and he doesn't know about the baby."

"But if you'd only tell us his name, perhaps we could find him," persisted her father.

"He's irrelevant," Annabel said stonily.

"Of course he isn't!" snapped Ian. "This child is his too."

Annabel felt the tears welling up in her eyes and she allowed them to spill down her cheeks. Her father was immediately contrite, and said, "Well, we'll leave it for now, but if you're thinking of claiming any sort of benefit, I think you'll find the DSS will expect you to name him."

The evening ended then, with Ian getting to his feet and saying he must get back. Annabel and Chantal saw him to the door and waved as he drove away. As they returned to the living room, Chantal sighed and said wistfully, "It was nice having Dad here like usual."

Angela gave her a hug. "I know darling, but we can't change the way things are."

Annabel had to fight the urge then, to tell them things had changed, that Desirée wasn't there any more. She'd promised Dad to let him tell them in his own time, but it was proving to be an extremely difficult secret to keep. But tonight she'd won her battles, and for the moment she was content with that. No one was going to take her baby away, no one.

## Chapter Seventeen

Annabel was extremely relieved that her mother had been out when Oliver had delivered the note from Scott the following day. She realised, of course, that Oliver didn't believe that she didn't know Scott Manders, but there was nothing she could do about that. When she went back upstairs, Chantal, who was curled in front of the TV, said, "What did he want?"

"Oh, nothing. He'd found a book in the Circle garden and thought it was mine. It wasn't." Even in her own ears this sounded a pretty feeble reason for his coming, but Chantal appeared to accept it and remained glued to her television programme, which enabled Annabel to disappear upstairs to read the note.

Feeling safest where there was a lock on the door, Annabel went into the bathroom and drew the bolt across before she opened the grubby envelope Oliver had brought.

Roxy Café. Monday 4.30. Scott

It was Friday evening and she had the whole weekend to decide whether to go or not, and her decision changed from moment to moment. By the time Monday morning came, she had almost decided not to go. On the way to college, she turned into the side street where the Roxy Café was. It was a small coffee bar, at present serving breakfasts, but advertising lunches and afternoon tea. She stared at the place for a moment and then went on to college.

Four-thirty saw Annabel back outside the Roxy. The windows were steamed up and the lights were on, but she couldn't see if Scott was already inside. Still, she had to see him. During the day, she realised she had come to the decision gradually over the weekend. She would go and meet him and see what happened.

When she opened the door she thought at first that he wasn't there, but then she heard him call from a table in the corner. "Bel!"

She made her way across to him and sat down.

"You want tea or something?" he asked, and seeing he had a thick, white china cup of tea in front of him she said, "Tea, yeah, thanks."

He collected it from the counter and as he waited for it, she was able to study him unnoticed. He seemed to have changed, wasn't how she remembered him at all really. He was much smaller somehow, less formidable, more insignificant. He was dressed in his usual jeans and bomber jacket, with the usual stubble on his chin, but he looked different.

Maybe it's his eyes, thought Annabel as she watched him. They were forever shifting around the room, flicking to the door, as if he were afraid of being trapped in the café. He came back with the tea and putting it on the table in front of her said, "There you go."

For a moment or two they were silent, and to cover the awkwardness, Annabel drank a mouthful of tea. It was strong and so hot that she almost had to spit it out again. She felt it burn her all the way down the back of her throat, and she coughed.

"You OK, Bel?"

"Yeah, just the tea was too hot."

"No, I meant, you been OK? While I weren't 'ere?"

"Yes." She looked at him levelly. "Where have you been, Scott?"

"Inside," he answered shortly. "Done for 'andling."

"Why didn't you contact me?" she asked.

"Why would I? You knew the score."

"Did I?" She pondered this for a moment. "Yes, I suppose I did, but not until that last day. Not really. And I didn't know what had happened to you. I tried to find you. A woman at your house told me what had happened. Said you didn't live there any more, and told me where you were."

"And now I've come back. Chrissy, the woman you saw? She always keeps my room for me when I ain't there, but she don't tell no one, see? That's why she didn't let on to you."

"She said your brother was arrested too," Annabel said.

"Bazzer? 'E was, stupid git. It was all 'is fault, an' all. 'E nicked a mobile phone and then when someone rings 'im up and tells 'im 'e's won some cash, 'e give my name and address so that Mum don't get 'er 'ands on it. The filth come round and find 'im at my place with the phone, but they 'ad a warrant and turned my pad over an' all. Found some of my stuff. Bazzer got off with a caution and I got sent down." He took a long pull at his tea and then said, "What did you want me for anyway, Bel? You wasn't in trouble, was you? They didn't know about the computer job, still don't for sure, but I know they're watchin' me."

"So now they've seen me with you," Annabel said tightly. "Won't take them long to put two and two together, will it? That policeman must have seen it was a girl driving."

"Nah, no one on me tail today," Scott said cheerfully. "I seen to that."

"Except perhaps Oliver Hooper," Annabel said. "The envelope wasn't stuck down properly. I'm sure he'd read your note."

"Forget about 'im." Scott laughed. "'E ain't nobody important. 'E don't know nothing."

"Well," said Annabel, taking the plunge, "he'll know something pretty soon, because he lives in our road and he'll see it for himself."

"What?" Scott's eyes narrowed. "What'll 'e see?"

"That I'm pregnant," said Annabel bluntly.

Scott stared at her blankly for a moment, as if he hadn't heard, then he said, "Whose is it?"

"Whose is it?" repeated Annabel incredulously. "Whose do you think it is? It's bloody yours of course. That's why I came to find you."

"Mine? Can't be." Scott was emphatic.

"Well it is," said Annabel coldly, "because I've never had sex with anyone else."

"'Ow do I know that?" demanded Scott.

"Because I'm telling you," snapped Annabel. "I've only done it once, in the back of your van, and now I'm pregnant."

"Well you would say that, wouldn't you?" retorted Scott. "Did you get rid of it?"

Annabel was almost overwhelmed by the rage that possessed her at that moment, but she fought it down and replied in a voice that was ice, "You're not listening to what I'm saying, Scott. I said 'I'm pregnant', not I *was* pregnant, I am pregnant and the baby's yours...was yours. It isn't any more, it's mine, just mine. My baby hasn't got a father and won't have one." Her hands were gripping the table as she sought to control her anger. "I came here today to tell you about it. I thought you ought to know, but now I wish I'd never come. I haven't told anyone who the father is, though my parents are still asking, but now of course, Oliver Hooper will soon work it out and then everyone will know."

"Don't 'ave to worry about 'im," Scott said roughly. "I'll sort 'im out, no problem. Listen, Bel, I'm sorry, I shouldn't of said what I did. I was, like, caught surprised, see? I believe you. Still we have to do something about it now, don't we?" He looked at her hopefully. "OK?"

"No," Annabel replied calmly. "It's not OK. I'm having *my* baby, and neither of us will have anything to do with you, Scott. You don't want us, and we don't want or need you." Suddenly Annabel felt much older and more mature than Scott. She looked across the table at him and said quietly, "You mean nothing to me, Scott. For a while I was one of your women, oh, yes, your friend Chrissy told me about those, but not any more." She got to her feet, pushing her chair away behind her. "I don't want to see you again, Scott, ever. If you ever had any feeling for me, which I doubt, leave us alone now. Thanks for the tea."

"Bel! Wait!" Scott called, but Annabel didn't hesitate or turn back, she simply walked out of the café door into the evening gloom. She continued to walk, ignoring the buses that ran along the Dartmouth Road, and as she walked the tears began to stream down her cheeks. By the time she reached Dartmouth Circle, she felt shaky and weak and the tears were still flowing. She knew she couldn't go home like this and so she slipped into the Circle garden and sat down on the bench to try and recover her self-control. It was beginning to get cold, but still Annabel wouldn't go into the house, she felt completely wrung out like a limp rag and she knew her face was blotchy and tear-stained.

Suddenly she was aware of someone standing beside her and looking down at her in concern. It was Charlie Murphy.

"Are you OK?" Charlie asked tentatively. "Is there anything I can do?"

The kindness in her voice made Annabel begin to cry again, and Charlie immediately sat down beside her and gently put her arms round her and held her close.

"You know," she said at last, "things can't really be that bad. Will you come in to our place for a while to get warm? You're shivering. Come in with me and have a cup of coffee, and tell me what's wrong. OK? I don't think anyone else is home, but if they are we can go into my room and be private."

Annabel didn't reply, but she sniffed, wiped her eyes and nodded. She hardly knew Charlie, but she was in sore need of someone to talk to. Together the two girls crossed out of the garden and went to number seven. Annabel glanced across at her own house and saw that the lights were on and Mum's car was in the drive, which meant she ought to go home, but she couldn't face it yet. Following her glance Charlie said, "If they'll worry, you can phone."

There was no one in the living room when they went up, but they could hear Dean's music thudding from his room next door, so Charlie said, "We'll go up to my room so we shan't be disturbed."

They carried mugs of coffee upstairs to Charlie's room. It was the smallest of the bedrooms, but she had made it very cosy, with a kingfisher-blue throw over the bed and cushions, so that it could double as a sofa in the daytime. Her work was spread out on a desk by the window, and there was a pile of clothes on a small armchair. These Charlie dumped unceremoniously on the floor in the corner. "Have a seat," she said, waving towards the chair, while she dropped on to the bed.

For a moment or two, they sipped their coffee and then Charlie smiled encouragingly at Annabel. "So, what's the problem?"

Once she started to tell, the whole story came flooding out of Annabel. There was no one to whom she had told the entire story, no one, until now, that she had felt she could trust. It's odd, she thought even as she was relating the getaway drive, how much easier it is to speak to someone you hardly know. She held nothing back; it was as if a dam had burst and everything was carried out on the flood.

"We managed to lose the police car," Annabel said, "and then Scott changed the number plates as we drove round through the city centre. It was scary, I can tell you. I was sure we'd be picked up. Anyway, we went to a lock-up garage Scott's got off Camborne Road, and unloaded the stuff there. Nobody saw us. It's a little yard with three garages in, and his was the one in the middle. There wasn't anyone about. After that...well we went to the dunes, and that's when it happened. It only happened once. We'd kissed and stuff before, you know, but never, well done it properly." She looked across at Charlie. "It was the excitement of the chase that did it," she said. "I don't think Scott could get it up properly before, but after that police chase...well he couldn't hold back. Know what I mean?"

Charlie said nothing, but listened without interruption until Annabel finally came to a standstill. "And you've just left this Scott bloke now?" she asked at last.

"Yeah." Annabel nodded. "Somehow I kept my cool while I was with him in the café, but after, when I got outside, like,

I just seemed to go to pieces." She brushed her hand across her forehead. "I'll be OK in a little while, I just didn't want to go in home while I was still so upset. Mum would've sussed straightaway that there was something wrong."

"But you said she knows all about the baby."

"Yeah, she does, except who the father is." Annabel sighed. "She'll know soon enough now, because Oliver Hooper will soon work it out. He's an evil boy. He's been absolutely foul to my sister. I think she's like really quite scared of him, you know? And now he'll know something about me, too."

"He may not say anything," Charlie said consolingly. "He may not even put two and two together."

"Oh, he will," Annabel assured her, "and I really don't want my parents to know what sort of person Scott really is, you know? It's bad enough about the baby, though they're being really good about that, but, well to be honest, it was an awful shock seeing Scott again today. He wasn't at all like I thought." Annabel's voice cracked again. "I can't think what I was doing! It's like I was hypnotised or something, you know? I couldn't wait to see him. I was a different person when I was with him, like, someone else, he was so exciting. Then, like, today he wasn't exciting at all, he was just…ordinary, you know?" She buried her head in her hands.

"I do know, exactly," Charlie said softly, "really I do, because it happened to me too."

Annabel looked up. "What did?"

"I fell for someone, just as awful as your Scott. I got pregnant and his reaction was just the same as Scott's, i.e. was it his? And if it was he didn't want to know."

"What did you do?" asked Annabel.

"Same as you're going to. I had the baby."

"But where…I mean, like, what happened to it?"

"My daughter, Kirsty, is safely at home in Ireland, being looked after by my parents."

"Your parents? Don't they mind?"

"Well," said Charlie philosophically, "they'd have preferred it not to happen of course, but they love her like one of their own and she's just an extra daughter for them. I'm the eldest, you see, and I've seven brothers and sisters, so my youngest brother, Declan, is only four years older than Kirsty."

"But does she know? Kirsty I mean?"

"That I'm her mother? No, not yet, she's far too young, she's only one. When the time comes I'll tell her."

"Only one! But I thought you were at college here…"

"I was, but no one here knows why I stayed home in Ireland for a while." She smiled ruefully. "I tell them glandular fever. They don't query that. I had to repeat a year, I finish in the summer."

"And did you never think of having an abortion?" asked Annabel.

Charlie shook her head. "No. I'm a Catholic. There's no way."

"But the father…" Annabel asked hesitantly, "he wanted…"

"He was much older than me, married of course, and so *he* wanted everything sorted, without any fuss." Charlie gave a bitter laugh. "He offered me the money for an abortion. I told him what he could do with it."

"So he knows that you had her."

Charlie shrugged. "He must assume I did. I've had no contact with the bastard since he told me to get rid of her. I certainly didn't tell him when she was born. I have seen him a couple of times in the distance, shopping with his wife. Been very tempted to go and accost him then and tell him, just to see his face. Wouldn't be fair to his wife though, poor woman, would it? But you know, I look at him and I think, how could I have loved *that*?"

"Like me today," mused Annabel, "like I was seeing Scott for the first time…and I felt…nothing." She looked across at Charlie, sympathetically. "Do you miss her?"

"Kirsty? Like hell, but I know she's in the best place for her. She's loved and looked after. What more could I ask for her?

I don't want to be a struggling single mum over here, when there's a home and family for her over the water. Anyway, my parents were determined I should get my degree. They persuaded me to come back and finish. 'You'll get a far better job with a good degree,' they told me, 'and if you aim to provide for Kirsty in the future that's what you need.'"

"They must be wonderful parents," Annabel said.

"They are, so," Charlie agreed, "but aren't yours as well? Aren't they standing behind you, now?"

"Yeah, but it's not so easy for Mum, with Dad having gone and everything. It'd break their hearts if they found out what I was doing with Scott, that I'm a criminal, you know."

"I should wait and cross that particular bridge if you come to it," advised Charlie. "For now go on as you are, and maybe they'll never know. Didn't Scott say he'd take care of this Oliver boy?"

"He did," said Annabel, "but whether he really can or not, I don't know."

"Look, it sounds to me as if Scott can take care of himself and his own interests, and it's in his interest not to be linked with you, isn't it?"

"Yeah, I suppose so," answered Annabel dubiously. She picked up her coffee mug, only to find that it had gone cold. "Oh hell!" she cried, leaping to her feet. "I never rang Mum, she'll be frantic."

"Better go then," Charlie agreed and got up too. "But if ever you want to come over for a chat, just come, OK? I'll be here, and if not, not far away. Don't forget I really do know what you're going through. Oh, but my house-mates don't know...about Kirsty I mean."

"Don't worry, I shan't say anything to anyone," promised Annabel, "but thank you for telling me, it does help to talk to someone who's been through it all, you know."

When she'd gone Charlie sat on her bed thinking, remembering her own rage, impotence and misery when she'd found herself pregnant. She thought of Kirsty's father, Duncan, a wealthy and respected professional man in the town, and felt the usual stab of anger at his callousness. Since she'd returned to college she had steered well clear of anywhere she might run into him, but on the odd occasion when she had seen him in the distance, she found that her original impotent rage had cooled to contempt. She'd actually seen him a couple of days ago, and he, seeing her, had turned away, stalking off in the opposite direction. Now she gave a mental shrug and said aloud, "It's your loss, Duncan, you'll never know Kirsty."

Charlie had settled in to the Madhouse very easily. She hadn't known her house-mates well before she moved in, and that, to her, was a plus. She wanted to have a complete change in her last year at college, keep away from her old haunts and make a new set of friends. She'd repeated her second year, she explained, because she'd been at home in Ireland with glandular fever and had missed too much of the course, so that made it easier to meet new people. When she'd come back she'd attended different lectures and was at a different stage in her studies from the crowd she'd started with, but Charlie had always been a bit of a loner and it suited her very well.

She liked the other Madhouse inhabitants, particularly Mad and Ben, and living in a house like this meant there was always someone to do things with if she wanted to. She liked Dartmouth Circle as well. It was ideal for the university, but quiet, on the edge of the town.

Charlie sighed and picked up the letter home she had started earlier in the week. She had just an hour before she was due to babysit for Mike Callow, and she really ought to finish her letter and get it into the post. As a family, the Murphys weren't good letter writers, and Charlie knew she should have written long before this, but somehow the days passed and she kept putting it off. Still, she always justified herself, Mam was as bad, she hadn't written either! She reread the letter as far as she'd got.

Dear Mam,

I'm safely back here and settling in to the house. It really is called the Madhouse, tell Declan, there's even a sign on the door!

It's in a lovely little cul-de-sac with a central garden, off the main road. The house is quite nice and I like the guys I'm sharing with, though they're majorly untidy and the kitchen is a tip! Still, we have organised a rota now for the clearing up, so it may get a bit better, but I'm not putting my loan on it! My room's OK though, so when I can't stand it I go up there. We had a great party here the first weekend we got back, no not in the house, though I think Mad is planning one for her birthday in December, but in the gardens of the Circle, as this street is known. It was some old lady's ninetieth birthday, think she lives at number 1, and all the people who live in Dartmouth Circle had a BBQ to celebrate…a real street party! We were all invited too, and it was a good chance to meet our neighbours. The ones next door are pretty dire, at least one side they are, but the other side don't seem bad and there are some quite nice families too. Have been able to pick up some babysitting too, which is great, as always could do with the cash!!

Charlie paused here, thinking about the babysitting she'd done for Mike Callow, well not babysitting exactly, but he'd asked her several times to come over and give a hand when he had his children visiting. Though the boys didn't need her much, they always seemed pleased to see her, and she had become quite fond of Debbie. On two occasions, Mike had asked her to go with them to the swimming pool.

"It's so much easier to have someone else there," he explained, "especially as I can't go into the ladies' changing room with Debs."

So, she had gone with them to the pool, to be with Debbie in the changing room, to help her shower and wash her hair after the swim, and she found she enjoyed going with them. Mike had an easy relationship with his children and she found herself comfortable with them all and slipped easily into the family group.

She picked up her pen to finish her letter.

> There's this guy who lives opposite, and I help him when he has his children to stay (he's separated and they live with their mum usually). It isn't just babysitting, sometimes I go with them swimming to help the little one, Debbie, to get changed. Isn't it grand to be getting paid for having a free swim?
>
> Must stop now and do some work, lots of reading to catch up on! I'm really glad that I'm in my last year now. College is OK, but I can't wait to get back to you all for good. Give my love to everyone, a special kiss for Kirsty and say I miss you all. Write soon.
>
> Lots of love, Charlie. xx

As she sealed and addressed her letter at last, Charlie thought about Mike and his family. She knew that she was being less than honest with her mother about her growing friendship with Mike. She was beginning to look forward to her outings with him and his family, but she didn't want her mother to get the wrong idea. She knew Mum would worry if she thought Charlie was getting involved with another man, another older man, a divorced man.

Not that I am getting involved with him, Charlie thought defensively, I'm just the hired help, lending a hand when I'm needed. He certainly hasn't given *me* a second thought. It's just a comfortable friendship. There's no way I'm going to fall into the Duncan trap again.

She went downstairs and found Cirelle in the kitchen grabbing a sandwich before going over to help with Melanie's children.

"The kids are great," Cirelle told her, "and the grandparents, you know, but that Melanie is a pain. You never know where you are with her. One day she's all over me and the next she hardly speaks to me. She's having counselling of some sort, but it doesn't seem to be doing much good. Still the money's good, hey?"

"Always useful," agreed Charlie. "I'm sitting for Mike this evening too. Doesn't often have his kids to stay in the week, it must be a special occasion."

"It's Dad's birthday," Debbie explained when she arrived, "so we're all going out for a pizza. Dad said you could come too!"

"You told me babysitting," Charlie said to Mike.

He looked a bit sheepish and said, "I promised Debs I'd ask you, as a surprise."

"I haven't even got you a card," Charlie said.

"Doesn't matter," cried Debbie, grabbing her hand, "we're going for a pizza and we're going to sing the birthday song in the restaurant. Hurrah!" And sing they did, to the amazement of the other pizza-eaters.

Mike dropped Charlie off in the Circle before running the children back to Belmouth; they weren't staying the night because there was school in the morning.

As Charlie lay in bed that night, she thought about the pizza party and was touched that she should have been included.

# Chapter Eighteen

Charlie and Annabel had become quite good friends after they had talked that first evening. Both of them were determined to do well in their studies and they were prepared to work hard to make up for what had gone before, but what really drew them together was their shared secrets.

Charlie found it a great relief to have someone to talk to about Kirsty, someone she could tell of Kirsty's new achievements and the exploits she got up to, speaking openly and not pretending, as she normally did, that she was speaking of a younger sister. She had finally received a long letter from her mother with all the news about everyone at home, and Charlie read it over and over, and longed for the time when she could see Kirsty on a daily basis and not have to hear of her progress second-hand.

Similarly, Annabel, having confided in Charlie about Scott and the robbery, went on to confide in her about her father.

"Dad's on his own again now," she told her. "The dreadful Desirée has buggered off, thank God, but Dad won't tell Mum that."

"How do *you* know?" Charlie asked.

"I was round at Dad's and when I went into the bathroom, I realised that her washing stuff wasn't there, you know? The bedroom door was shut, but I looked more carefully in the living room, and there was only Dad's stuff there. I challenged him about it and he admitted to me that she'd left. But the thing is, he made me promise not to tell Mum. I don't know if they'll ever get back together again, probably not, but the trouble is if I don't talk to someone about it I shall burst."

"Then tell me," laughed Charlie, so Annabel did. Each was the confidante that the other one needed and their friendship grew.

Charlie was still happy enough in the Madhouse, but she didn't go out much as she had little money to spare for having fun. She was very grateful for the extra cash she earned from Mike Callow, but even so she wasn't able to save as much as she would have liked. She had bought her air ticket home for Christmas well ahead of time, buying an apex fare, which, though it was non-refundable, was very cheap.

It was several days before Mad's birthday that the phone call came. Charlie was working in the library and it was Cirelle, about to leave for a lecture, who took the call.

An Irish voice asked urgently if Charlie was there.

"No," replied Cirelle, "sorry."

"Will you take a message?" asked the woman.

"Yeah, of course. What is it?"

"This is her mother speaking, who am I speaking to?"

"It's Cirelle, Mrs Murphy, her house-mate."

"Well, Cirelle, please tell her that her … sister, Kirsty, is ill and would she phone home as soon as possible."

"Yeah, sure. I'll write it down so that she gets the message as soon as she gets in. OK?"

"Yes, thank you. Do you know when she might be in?"

"Sorry, she didn't say."

"Never mind. If you could leave the message somewhere where she's sure to see it as soon as she comes in. It is urgent."

When they'd rung off, Cirelle wrote the message out and propped it up against the phone. She did think of going to see if she could find Charlie, but she was already running late, so she decided not to make herself any later. After all, Charlie would see the message the moment she got in.

Thus it was several hours later that Charlie had found the message by the telephone. She read it through...her sister, Kirsty. Charlie grabbed the phone and dialled.

"Mam! What's happened?"

"Charlie? Is that you? It's not your mam, it's me, Barbara. Your mam's at the hospital with Kirsty, I'm minding the little ones."

"Barbara! What's happened? What's wrong with Kirsty?"

"They think she may have meningitis," Barbara said carefully.

"Meningitis!" cried Charlie in horror. "How is she? I mean, what do they say? Oh God, Barbara, I must come home!"

"That's what your mam thinks," Barbara agreed. There was a sound from the other end of the line and then Barbara said, "Hold on a minute, Charlie, that sounds like your dad come in now."

Charlie's father came on to the line. "Charlie, it's Dad."

"Dad, what's going on? How's Kirsty?"

"Not good, I'm afraid, Charlie. The doctors say it's touch and go. Your mother's at the hospital now and I'm just going to join her." He paused and then said gently, "We think you'd better come over, Charlie. We have to prepare ourselves for the worst."

Charlie heard the break in his voice and the tears streamed down her own cheeks. "I'm on my way, Dad," she sobbed. "I'll fly. I'll ring you from the airport. Will you pick me up?"

"I will, of course," her father said. "Just let me know the time. And Charlie..."

"Yes, Dad?"

"I've been to see Father Ryan, they're praying for her at the church."

"Thanks, Dad. I'll ring you." Charlie put the phone down, unable to cope with her father's obvious distress on top of her own. She sat gripping her fingers so tightly that the nails bit into the palms of her hands. She'd told Dad that she would come at once, that she'd fly, but she'd no money. Her overdraft was at its limit and her savings had gone on the ticket she'd already bought to go home at Christmas, and it couldn't be exchanged. There was no one in the house, but even if there had been, she doubted if anyone would have had the money to lend her for a normal airfare.

Annabel, she thought. I could ask Annabel, at least she knows why I have to go. Perhaps she's got some money saved for the baby – I could pay her back. As soon as she'd thought of it, Charlie was on her feet and off across the Circle to number four. Annabel was working in her bedroom, and when Chantal opened the door, Charlie went straight up.

"Hi, Charlie..." Annabel began.

"Kirsty's got meningitis," Charlie burst out.

"What?" Annabel was horrified.

"Kirsty...she's got meningitis, at least they think she has. Annabel, I *have* to go home, but I've no money for the airfare. Have you? Have you got any money you could lend me? I'll pay it back by Christmas, I promise..." Her voice trailed away as she saw her friend's face.

"I'm sorry," Annabel began, "if I had any cash at all I'd let you have it, honestly..."

Charlie buried her head in her hands. "Oh, Annabel, what am I going to do? I must get home. Dad says it's touch and go." The tears began streaming down her face again, and Annabel put her arms round her, the only comfort she could offer.

"I don't know who to ask," sobbed Charlie.

"What about Mike Callow?" said Annabel, suddenly inspired. "Ask Mike. Surely he could lend you the money. It would only be for a short while, wouldn't it? You get on well with him. He might let you work it off next term, so that you don't have to find the actual cash at all." The more she thought about the idea, the more Annabel warmed to her theme. "You know him quite well enough to ask, and I'm sure he'd help you if he could." She looked out of her bedroom window, into the gloom of the November evening. "Look, his lights are on so he's at home now.

Go over. Go over now and ask. After all he can only say no, but I bet he doesn't." She pulled a wad of tissues from the box on her dressing table and pressed them into Charlie's hand. "Go on," she urged, "go and ask Mike."

Charlie said, "Annabel, you're brilliant!" She blew hard on the tissues and then, giving Annabel a quick hug, rushed back downstairs and across the road.

When he heard the doorbell ring, Mike cursed inwardly. He had set the evening aside to work so that he would have the weekend clear for the children, and though he wasn't actually in his study yet, he didn't want to be disturbed. He pressed the entry-phone and said in a voice calculated to deter visitors, "Yes?"

"Mike? It's Charlie."

"Charlie!" Mike's voice and attitude changed on the instant. "Come on up!" He pressed the buzzer and as the door opened he was at the top of the stairs to greet her. One look told him that everything was far from well.

He tried to keep his immediate concern out of his voice, and simply said, "Charlie, what a nice surprise. Will you have a drink?" and led the way back into the living room.

Charlie managed a wan smile. "No thanks, Mike." She followed him and sat down on the sofa, while Mike dropped into the armchair opposite.

"Well then," he said, "what can I do for you?"

"Please, Mike," she began, but her voice was croaky and she began again. "Please Mike, can you lend me some money?" Then her words came flooding out. "I'm sorry to have to ask you and I wouldn't if I wasn't desperate. I'll pay you back as soon as I can, or I could work it off next term, whichever you liked..."

"Hey! Hey!" Mike laughed. "Hold on. What's all this about? Look," he smiled across at her, "start again and tell me from the beginning, OK?"

Charlie had another blow on the tissues she was still clutching in her hand and then raised her eyes to meet his.

"It's my sister…" she began, but then something made her stop. If she was going to beg money from him, Mike was entitled to know the truth. "That's not true," she whispered, "it's my daughter…"

"Your daughter," echoed Mike, "but I didn't… I mean…"

"She's at home in Ireland, being brought up by my parents."

"I see…"

"No, you don't," said Charlie, "but it doesn't matter just now. The thing is my mother rang to say that Kirsty, my daughter, well they think she has meningitis, and she's only one, and they think…they think she might…" On the word die Charlie broke into sobs again. Instantly Mike was by her side on the sofa. He gathered her into his arms and held her against him. As he let her sob on his shoulder, he murmured to her soothingly, "Charlie, Charlie, sweetheart, don't cry, my darling, don't cry. We'll get you there, I promise, we'll get you there." He stroked her fair, silky hair as he had longed to do for so many weeks now, and then he kissed the wet tear-stains on her cheek. As he did this, she raised her face to him in surprise, and he looked into her eyes, still welling with tears before he, very gently, kissed her on the mouth. For a moment her lips were closed and dry, and he lifted his head, but as he saw the tremulous smile break through her tears, Mike touched his mouth to hers again and this time felt her lips part beneath his as he kissed her deep and long. When they finally broke apart, they simply looked at each other in amazement, before Mike said, a little breathlessly, "Oh Charlie, if only you knew how long I've ached to do that."

All she said was, "Mike," but her voice was a sigh.

"Now come on, my sweetheart," Mike said a moment later, "we must get cracking. We've got to get over to Ireland as soon as possible. So the first thing is to ring the airport and find out the flight times. Cork is it?" Charlie nodded and he brushed her lips again, and then gently disentangling his hands, moved to the phone. Within minutes, he was on the line to the airport, and to Charlie's amazement, he booked two seats on the late flight into Cork, cheerfully reserving them with his credit card.

"But Mike," she looked confused, "why two tickets?"

"You don't think I'm going to let you go and face this on your own, do you?" he demanded, before turning back to dial another number to order a rental car to be waiting for them at the other end.

"But Mike," she protested when he had finished that call, "you don't have to … I mean, thank you for getting me the ticket, but you don't have to …"

"Yes," he said simply, "I do." He sat down beside her again, and took both her hands in his. "Listen to me," he said. "I've loved you from the first moment I saw you at old Madge's barbecue back in September."

"But…"

Mike laid a finger on her lips. "Just listen to me," he repeated. "I love you, Charlie, and that's the truth. I've never said anything, because…well for lots of reasons, but mainly because I was afraid to. I'm much older than you, I wanted you to get to know me first as a friend, I didn't want to scare you away." He smiled ruefully at her. "I may have done so now, but holding you in my arms like that, well I couldn't help myself. If you don't want me to come to Ireland with you, of course I won't, but if you'd like the moral support, I'd like to be there to give it to you." His eyes held hers for a moment. "You only have to say, and I'll cancel the second ticket."

"But you don't know anything about me, about my past, about Kirsty."

"She's your daughter and you love her."

"Yes, of course."

"That's all I need to know," Mike said firmly.

"But what about her father?"

"What about him? If he was any sort of father to her he'd be going with you, not me…" He paused then, uncertain, "…unless of course he's waiting for you in Ireland?"

"He's not," Charlie said steadily. "But Mike…"

"Charlie, you know now how I feel, and for the time being that's enough. I'm not asking you to feel the same. I'm not asking anything of you, I just want to be here when you need me. If in time things change in any particular way, well we'll deal with that as it happens. OK?"

Charlie nodded, not knowing what to say.

"Right then," Mike said briskly. "We have a flight to catch. You go and pack a bag, we leave for the airport in half an hour." He got to his feet and pulled Charlie to hers. For a moment, he rested his hands on her shoulders and then having kissed her cheek he said, "And, I know it's a stupid thing to say, but try not to worry. Ring your parents and tell them you're on your way. Tell them we've got a car booked, so we'll be with them at the hospital as soon as we can. All right?"

Charlie nodded again and then whispered, "Thank you, Mike, I'll never forget this."

"Hush, no problem. Go and pack your bag."

When she had gone, Mike returned to the telephone and dialled Caroline's number. There was no reply and the answer-phone clicked in. Guiltily relieved at not actually having to explain what was happening to Caroline, Mike spoke to the machine.

"Caroline, it's me. I'm sorry, but something important's come up, and I have to go away for the weekend, so I can't have the children as arranged…" That sounded awful even to his own ears, so he added awkwardly, "It's a friend, been taken danger-ously ill." God, that was worse, it sounded like one of those SOS messages on the radio, so he simply finished lamely, "I'm sorry, I've got to go. Give my love to the children and say that I'll make it up to them soon. OK? Bye now."

Replacing the receiver he switched on his own answer machine and dashed upstairs to pack a bag for himself. For a moment, he glanced out of the window across the road to the lighted window of Charlie's room.

I don't believe this, he thought wildly, but the memory of Charlie's lips parting under his own flooded through him and he had to bring himself sharply back to the job in hand. As he came back down through the living room the phone rang. He paused but didn't pick up, waiting for the answer machine to accept the call. It was Caroline, and she was steaming mad.

"Mike you bastard! Are you there? Pick up the bloody phone. I know you're there because you only called me five minutes ago." Mike did not pick up the receiver. "Mike! How can you do this to them, and me? I had arrangements made for this weekend, and now it'll all have to be changed! And the kids were so looking forward to seeing you. You really are a selfish bastard. I don't believe a word about a sick friend...who is it? Why didn't you say who was ill? You're just off for a dirty weekend, that's all, putting some floozy before your promise to your own children. Well, stuff you, Mike Callow, don't ask to see them again in a hurry, because they won't want to come. They're tired of you mucking them about, and so am I. So, you just bugger off and play, and I'll see my solicitor!" The message ended with a violent slam of the receiver.

Mike pressed the erase button, reset the machine and hurried downstairs to the garage. As he backed the car out, he nearly ran over Oliver Hooper, standing outside the house. He wound down the window.

"Oliver! What are you doing there?" he demanded. "What do you want?"

Oliver peered in through the window. "Just coming over to ask you if Pete's about this weekend," he said.

"No," Mike answered, and then feeling he'd been a bit abrupt he said, "No, I'm afraid not. I'm away this weekend, so the children won't be coming. Maybe next weekend. OK?"

"Yeah, thanks." Oliver loafed off down the cut beside the Smarts' house, and Mike backed the car across to Charlie's house. "Though judging from Caroline's phone call, I doubt if they'll be here then either," he thought ruefully. Then he resolutely put that out of his mind. The important thing now was that Charlie needed him and he wasn't about to let her down. He got out of the car and was just approaching the front door of the Madhouse, when it opened and Charlie appeared carrying a large sports bag. Pulling the door to behind her, she looked up at a lighted window in number four where Annabel Haven was looking out, and waved, before handing Mike her bag and climbing into his car. Annabel waved back, and gave the thumbs-up signal. No one else saw them leave. There was no one at home in the Madhouse, Charlie had simply left them a note, saying her sister was desperately ill and she'd gone home for a few days. She would phone some time soon.

The flight was on time and the hire car was waiting, so that they arrived at the hospital in Cork with the minimum of delay. All the way over on the short flight, Mike had sat holding Charlie's hand, and she had let him, reassured by his nearness and his strength. When they reached the hospital Mike stopped at the main entrance and said, "You go straight in, I'll park the car and then come and find you, OK?"

"Yeah, OK." Charlie got out of the car and headed in through the door. At reception, they told her where to find Kirsty, and within moments she was outside the intensive care unit where her parents were waiting. She ran into her mother's arms, crying, "How is she? Mam, is she all right?"

Her mother hugged her tightly and said quietly, "So far, pet. So far she's holding her own." Her father put his arms round both of them. "She'll make it, she's a game little thing."

"Can I see her? Can we go in?" Charlie peered in through the glass panel of the door to where a cot stood, and the tiny form of her daughter was hooked up to drips and monitors.

"Not at the moment," replied her mother. "We have to watch her from here." Charlie stood with her nose pressed against the glass, trying to see Kirsty's face, but it was hidden by the cot sides.

"You got here very fast," Sean Murphy said. "No trouble getting a flight? And you hired a car? Wasn't that very expensive?"

"No, I mean, there was no trouble with the flight…a friend has come with me…he lent me the money. Mam, Dad, I had no money for a fare, I couldn't have come without him helping. He's parking the car."

"But who is he, Charlie?" asked her mother anxiously. She didn't like the sound of some man not only lending Charlie the money to come home, but of coming himself as well, and she liked it even less when Charlie turned to answer and said, "Here he comes now." Kath Murphy looked over her daughter's shoulder and saw a man approaching, not a young man, a student as she had imagined, but an older man, at least thirty-five. His slightly lopsided face had a certain raffish attractiveness and for a split second she wondered if he were the dreaded Duncan, Kirsty's real father, but Charlie was saying, "Mam, Dad, this is Mike Callow, who lives in the Circle. Remember I told you I babysit for him sometimes? He's brought me to see Kirsty. Mike, these are my parents."

They shook hands, but Mike was very aware of Mrs Murphy's scrutiny, and could well understand it, even though he knew nothing of Duncan, or the fact that Kirsty's father had been an older man as well.

"It's very good of you to bring Charlotte over," Mrs Murphy said.

Mike smiled at her. "I didn't think she should come on her own," he replied quietly. "She was very worried." He glanced at the door to the little ward and asked, "How is Kirsty?"

"Holding her own," Sean told him. At that moment a doctor came up, and after a brief word with them allowed Charlie to go into the room. Her parents and Mike waited outside.

"I don't want to be a nuisance…or to be in the way," Mike said diffidently. "Maybe I should wait in the car."

"Certainly not," Sean said straightaway. "There's a little waiting room just here where we can get a cup of coffee, we'll wait for Charlie in there."

They adjourned to the waiting room where there was indeed

a coffee machine, and having fed this with coins, they sat down with polystyrene cups of hot brown liquid to wait for news. Mike looked at the middle-aged couple who were Charlie's parents. Mrs Murphy was small, much shorter than her daughter. She had the same-coloured hair as Charlie, though fading to grey, and the same blue eyes, which missed nothing, and there was an air of strength about her, as if she took life's troubles head on and dealt with them stoically. Sean Murphy was a big man, tall and dark-haired, with deep-set brown eyes, but at present he seemed content to stay in the background, sitting nursing his coffee, his eyes fixed in the middle distance somewhere.

"You live in the same street as Charlotte?" Kath asked at last. Her use of the name Charlotte, instead of the familiar Charlie, seemed to Mike to be trying to draw a line of some sort between them, to be making some sort of point. Clearly, she didn't want him to be there, she didn't approve of him.

"Yes, just across the road." Mike was determined to sound at ease. "Charlie babysits sometimes, and helps me with the children when they come to stay. Their mother and I are separated."

"I see." Silence fell round them again until Sean said awkwardly, "It was good of you to lend Charlie the money to come."

"It was the least I could do," Mike said. "She's been a great help to me." He looked across at the couple sitting side by side on an ageing sofa and came to a sudden decision. "I love your daughter," he said simply, "and, if she'll have me, I intend to marry her."

The Murphys looked stunned at this sudden announcement. "Aren't you already married?" demanded Kath fiercely. "What are you doing to be talking about marrying our Charlie?"

"My wife is divorcing me," Mike replied levelly. "Nothing to do with Charlie, we'd split up before I even laid eyes on her."

"And does Charlie know?" Kath went on grimly. "Have you asked her to marry you...even before you're free?"

Mike refused to allow himself to be intimidated by Charlie's mother. "No," he said evenly, "for the first time this evening

I told Charlie that I love her, it has gone no further than that...nor will it, yet. I just thought that you should know. I don't know anything about her past, I only heard about Kirsty today, but it makes no difference. I love Charlie and I'll love Kirsty too. I wouldn't do anything to hurt either of them."

"That's all very well and good..." began Kath, but her husband stopped her, placing his hand on hers. "This isn't the time or the place to discuss this, Kath," he said gently. "We'll talk with Mr Callow about it another time." He gave Mike a level look, which brooked no argument, and Mike nodded. "Of course," he replied, "I just wanted you to know how things stood."

An awkward silence fell for a few moments, and then Charlie came in. "She's still holding her own," she told them. "They say I can sit with her...you too if you want to, Mam, though only one at a time. So I'm going to stay. Daddy, will you take Mike home with you? He can sleep in my room for tonight. I won't be coming home till the morning at least."

Kath was about to say something, but her husband forestalled her and said, "I will of course," and he directed a smile at Mike. "Will you stay with Charlie, Kath, or come with us?"

"I'll come with you," Kath decided, "and come back in the morning so that Charlie can get some sleep then." She turned to Charlie. "I think that's best, pet," she said. "I can see the children off to school and then come back to the hospital." She put her arms round her daughter. "But of course ring us any time if there's any change and we'll come back at once."

Charlie clung to her mother for a moment and then turned to the two men. "Thanks, Dad," she said and then, "You'll be OK, Mike? If you go home with Mam and Dad?"

Mike smiled at her reassuringly. "Of course I will. I'll see you in the morning."

"I'll just have one more peep at Kirsty," Kath told Sean, "and then I'll see you in the car."

Taking this as their dismissal, the two men went out to the car park while Kath and Charlie returned to the ward. After a moment, gazing at the tiny form of her granddaughter, Kath turned away and left Charlie to keep vigil with Kirsty. As she went out to the car park where Sean and the strange man Charlie had brought with her were waiting, Kath's cheeks were wet with tears. Her grief seemed double, she was Kirsty's mother and grandmother all rolled into one, Kirsty was as dear to her as any of her own children, and at the same time she grieved for Charlie.

*December*

## Chapter Nineteen

It was Madeleine Richmond's birthday, a bright, shining Saturday at the beginning of December. The air was sharp, and the sun struck fire into the last of the leaves on the row of beech trees that lined one side of the university rugby ground. Autumn had finally given way to winter and there was a distinct chill in the air. Madeleine, standing on the touchline waiting for the Belchers to emerge on to the pitch for their last game of the term against Loughborough Colleges, swung her arms and blew on her fingers to keep warm. She knew she wouldn't be able to feel her feet by the end of the match, but she was used to watching Dan play rugby in far colder weather than today, and she was looking forward to the game. It was always a hard fixture and Belcaster liked to have very loud vocal support from the touchline while they played. Students were drifting across the playing fields to the pitch, and Mad saw several of the regular supporters, including girlfriends of other members of the team. Then she saw Ben's ex-girlfriend, Angie, coming over and looked away, half-hoping Angie wouldn't see her. Since the night when Ben and Angie's relationship had ended, Mad hadn't talked to Angie, but she knew very well that Angie resented her and the others Ben lived with, thinking that they all took his side.

Even though there isn't a side to take, thought Mad, ruefully. It just ended.

She remembered, all too well, the night not long after the beginning of term when Ben and Angie had broken up. Ben had come home from the Flying Dutchman quite late, and was last in to the house. He had locked up and just come up to the kitchen, where he was chatting to Mad as he made a cup of tea, when there was a thunderous banging on the front door.

"Christ! Who the hell's that?" he exclaimed. He put down the kettle and went down to see. The knocking continued and before he could reach the front door, Mad heard Angie shouting at him through the letter box.

"Ben! Ben! Are you in there, you bastard? Let me in. Can you hear me? Ben! Can you hear me?"

"I imagine the whole Circle can hear you," Ben told her as he opened the door. "What on earth's the matter with you?"

Angie pushed past him violently and stormed straight along the passage towards his bedroom.

"You know bloody well what's the matter with me, you bastard!" she shrieked. "I won't be dumped just like that, at least you owe me an explanation." Her words were stumbling and slurred, and without seeing her, Mad could tell she'd been drinking.

"Ange…" Ben spoke with weary patience, "we've been through all this, I'm sorry but…" His words were cut off by the closing of his bedroom door and though Mad could hear Angie's voice still raised in anger, she couldn't hear what was being said.

Poor Angie, she thought, clearly they've had some sort of showdown this evening, and Angie is majorly upset. I'm not surprised, but surely she must have seen it coming. We all could. Ben's been pretty offhand with her all this term. He must have found someone else.

Madeleine made the tea and, pouring a mug for herself, she carried it through to the living room. She wondered if Ben did have a new girlfriend, and if so who it was. She hadn't seen him with anyone, but that didn't mean anything, their paths seldom crossed in college, though he certainly hadn't produced a new woman at the Dutch. Perhaps there wasn't anyone; after all,

Ben had to work pretty hard to pay his way through uni, he had his job at the Dutch and he was doing some odd jobbing at the Hammonds' as well. Perhaps he was just too busy. Perhaps he'd realised that there was no future with Angie and finally called it off.

Mad sat nursing her mug of tea and wondering what to do. Should she go to bed, or should she wait up until Angie left, assuming of course that she did leave, that they didn't kiss and make up. Would Ben want to be on his own or would he want someone to talk to? There was no music coming from Dean's room, so he must be asleep already, and she knew Cirelle and Charlie were both upstairs, probably in bed too. There was only her. She was just deciding he probably wouldn't want her and that she'd go to bed herself, when she heard the bedroom door downstairs slam open against the wall and angry footsteps head for the front door; only the door didn't open, the footsteps came thudding up the stairs and Angie appeared in the living room. Her eyes were red from crying and her mouth was pinched and angry.

Seeing Mad sitting there, she paused for a second and then said belligerently, "I've come to get my videos." She crossed the room to where the videos lay in an untidy heap on the floor and went through them tossing aside those that didn't interest her. It was clear she was still fighting back the tears, and even as she picked out her tapes, muffled sobs escaped.

"Angie," Mad spoke gently, "are you all right? Will you be…?"  ·

"Of course I'm bloody all right," Angie snapped, gathering up the pile she had collected. "He's only a man for Christ's sake!" She turned towards Mad, and her face crumpled again. "The sod!" she wailed. "He won't even tell me why! He just says it's no good, it's over and he doesn't want to see me any more. He's got someone else, hasn't he? He must have. Who is it Mad? You must know. Which cow's got her hooks into him?"

"Angie, I don't know. I promise you I don't. I haven't seen him with anyone, honestly."

"Is it that little tart Chantal, from over the road? She's always hanging round these days. Perhaps it's her."

Mad shook her head. "I don't know. I shouldn't think so. She's very young you know, like, much younger than we thought at first? I don't think Ben would be interested in her, really I don't. She's just a kid."

"Just a kid is she?" Angie sneered. "Well, it might pay you to watch your Dan around her, that's all I can say. I suppose you're used to him playing around, but you just watch him. *He* doesn't treat her like a kid."

Mad looked at her standing there, clutching her videos, and fought back an angry reply. She said tightly, "Will you be OK getting home, Angie?"

Angie looked suddenly deflated. "'Spect so," she said dully. "I've got the car."

"Are you OK to drive?"

Angie shrugged. "I dunno, 'spect so. If not, it's his fault isn't it?"

Mad looked at her with mild irritation. It certainly wouldn't be Ben's fault if Angie were done for drink-driving, but there was no point in saying that now, so she said, "Do you want me to drive you home?"

"No." Angie stalked across to the stairs and then looked back at her. "No," she said fiercely, "I don't want anything to do with any of you, you're all on his side, the whole bloody lot of you. Screw the lot of you!" She started down the stairs and as she did so, banged her arm on the banister and dropped the pile of videos. "Oh shit!" she bellowed. "Fucking, fucking shit!" She scrabbled on the stairs retrieving the tapes and then dumped them into the carrier bag Mad silently handed her. She turned without a further word and stumped down to the front door, which she slammed behind her with a resounding crash. Mad went to the window and watched as she struggled with the car door and then clambered into the car, shoving the bag of videos in on to the passenger seat, slamming the door behind her. She started the engine, and revving it to a roar, accelerated away with a squeal of tyres.

Mad turned back from the window to find Ben standing in the kitchen doorway. "Sorry," he said lamely. "Sorry you had to take all that."

Mad made a dismissive gesture and said, "Doesn't matter, she was upset that's all." She looked across at Ben and smiled faintly. "I guess you aren't going out any more!"

Ben summoned up a rueful smile too. "I guess we aren't," he agreed. "I need a beer, do you want one?" he asked, heading for the fridge to get one for himself. "Or more tea?"

Mad didn't want either, but guessing that Ben wanted to talk for a while, she nodded and accepted another mug of tea.

"I guess I'm just tired of her," he sighed as he dropped down on to the sofa. "But that's not something you can say to someone, is it? I mean, just turn round and say you're boring and I don't want to be with you any more." He pulled the ring on his beer and gulped down half the can. "I've tried to cool it this past few weeks, Mad, but she didn't seem to get the message. And now she's screaming at me that I've dumped her for no reason."

"She thinks you've got someone else lined up," Mad said, and after an infinitesimal pause added, "she thought it might be Chantal Haven."

"Chantal!" Ben looked thunderstruck. "She's only a kid!"

"I know," Mad agreed, deciding not to mention the accusations she'd made about Chantal and Dan. "That's what I told her, but Angie seems to think I'm covering up for you."

"Well, she's wrong. There isn't anyone else." Ben took another swig of his beer. "No one." But he didn't look at Mad as he said it.

"Well," sighed Mad, "I suppose it's better to be honest with her. I mean, if you don't want a proper relationship it's better to end it now. Not let it drag on. Give her a chance to find someone else."

"That's what I said," Ben agreed gratefully, "that's what I told her, but she couldn't see it, or wouldn't accept it."

Mad finished her tea and got to her feet. "I expect she will eventually," she said. "Give her time. After all nobody likes being dumped, whatever the reason, do they? And when she doesn't see you going round with anybody else, at least she'll know it wasn't that."

"Well, she certainly won't see me with anybody else," Ben said firmly, and tossing his beer can in the direction of the rubbish bin got to his feet as well. "Thanks, Mad. See you in the morning."

Mad had gone to bed then, and lain awake for some time feeling sorry for Angie. She quite understood her outburst; she was hurting and hitting back. Thinking about it, Mad supposed in a way that Angie had been right. It wasn't that they were on Ben's side exactly, but they were Ben's friends rather than Angie's, and if she disappeared from the scene they'd none of them really miss her. She wondered if it was worse to be dumped for someone else or just, well, dumped. She rather suspected it was the latter. What she would not allow herself to dwell on were Angie's remarks about Dan. They, after all, were sheer spite, there'd been spite in her eyes as she'd made them, and though Dan had a wandering eye, he would never look at anyone as young as Chantal Haven.

Now Mad saw her approaching across the windswept field. Since the night of the break-up, she had only seen Angie in the distance, in the union or across the street, and if there was momentary eye contact, neither of them allowed it to develop into recognition or greeting. It wasn't that they avoided each other exactly, they just made no effort to meet.

As Mad watched her coming over, clearly heading straight for her, she wondered what Angie wanted.

"Hi, Angie," she said cheerfully as the girl came up beside her. "How are you?"

"OK." Angie stopped beside her, staring back towards the changing rooms. Silence slipped round them for a moment and then Angie asked, "Is he playing today?"

"Ben? Yes, it's a tough fixture. They need their strongest side."

"Dan too?"

"Yes, Dan too."

"How is he? Dan, I mean."

Mad thought back to the last time Angie had spoken of Dan and said shortly, "He's fine." She glanced at Angie, trying to read her expression, but Angie wasn't even looking at her, she was still watching the changing rooms, watching for the teams to emerge.

Suddenly she turned back and said, "God! I'd forgotten how cold it is on these touchlines." She blew on her fingers, and then went on, "Dan said the other day that it's your birthday today."

Mad laughed in surprise. "Did he now? Well it is, but I'm amazed he remembered by himself."

"Going out somewhere, are you?" Angie asked, innocently.

Madeleine knew at once that Dan must have said more. "We're all going down the Dutch this evening, yes." Mad looked into Angie's face and knew why she'd asked. "We're hoping to celebrate a win over Loughborough too! You can come if you want to." She added awkwardly, "Anyone can. Everyone's welcome."

"I might," Angie said casually, "I'm not sure what I'm doing." But Mad knew that this was the whole point of this meeting and conversation. Angie had heard about the party at the pub and wanted to be there.

"Where did you see Dan?" Madeleine asked, equally casually.

"In the Blue Bottle at Belston St Mary," replied Angie. "Last Thursday, I think it was."

You know very well when it was, thought Madeleine angrily, that's another reason you've come to find me today. You wanted to tell me you'd seen him out without me, maybe even with someone else. Well, bitch, I'm not going to give you the satisfaction of asking anything about it.

She forced a smile to her lips and looking over Angie's shoulder saw the Loughborough team emerging on to the pitch, followed immediately by the Belchers. A cheer went round the ground and she joined in the university chant…"Hey Belchers! Go! Go! Go! Hey Belchers! Blow! Blow! Blow!"

Angie watched the teams explode on to the pitch as well, and then, touching Mad's arm, said, "Might see you later then…oh and happy birthday." Then she wandered off through the spectators, completely ignoring the game.

The game was hard and fast, and the spectators surged up and down the touchline, shouting and encouraging. As she turned to follow the game, Mad cannoned into someone next to her, and found it was Chantal Haven.

"Hi Chantal, what are you doing here?"

"Just come to watch the Belchers," said Chantal. "It's fun now I know some of them. Ben and Dan and people."

The chant started again and both girls joined in, "Hey Belchers! Go! Go! Go!" They had to struggle to keep their places in the front so they could see.

At half-time the score was 7–7, and as the teams separated for the allotted five minutes, Chantal said, as if she'd just thought of it, "Happy Birthday!"

Madeleine smiled, surprised. "Thanks, Chantal, how did you know it was my birthday?"

"D-Dean told me, I saw him the other day, we walked back from town together. He said there's a party at the Dutch tonight."

"Not really a party," Mad said. "We're all just meeting up for a few drinks, that's all."

"Mmm, he said," agreed Chantal, "he said I can come too…?" She didn't ask if it was all right, but the question was in her voice.

"Anyone can come," Mad replied. "We're only meeting in a pub," but then added, "if you're allowed."

"Oh, Mum doesn't mind if I'm with you," Chantal said cheerfully, "as long as I'm not too late."

"Yeah, well whatever." Mad wasn't particularly enthusiastic. Chantal wasn't one of their crowd, she was far too young, but if Dean had suggested she came, well that was up to him.

"Look there's Mrs Hammond," cried Chantal, "with Sylvia

and Thomas. Think I'll watch from the end for a bit. Probably see you later, Mad." She sauntered off in the opposite direction and disappeared among the other supporters.

"Yeah, see you," Mad said to her retreating back, and then looked round and saw Jill Hammond wandering round the field with her children. Madeleine had met the children on several occasions and was fond of them. She waved, and Jill came across, the children running on ahead of her as they saw Mad.

"Hallo," Mad laughed as Sylvia ran into her and hugged her waist. "How are you guys?"

"We've come to watch Ben play rugby," Sylvia said importantly. "We saw him just now. He was in that fight thing."

For a moment Mad looked puzzled, and Jill arriving and overhearing what Sylvia said laughed and said, "She means the scrum!"

"You're right." Mad laughed too. "It is a fight thing!"

"I like Ben," Sylvia announced. "He comes to our house and does painting. He's painted my bedroom and put galloping horses all round the wall."

"Has he now? I bet that looks great."

Thomas tugged at her jeans. "Ben's put Thomas the tank engine by my bed."

Mad bent down to give him a hug too. "You are lucky," she said. "And now you've come to watch him play rugby."

"He's very muddy," Thomas remarked, looking across at the huddle of players in the middle of the pitch.

"You'd be muddy too if you'd been rolling around on this field," laughed Mad.

At that moment the whistle blew again and the second half began. Jill scooped Thomas up into her arms and said, "Well, you two, I think we'll go now. It's very cold out here, and we've seen Ben."

"But he hasn't seen us," wailed Sylvia. "I want to see him play again."

"He did see us," Jill told her. "He saw us when they stopped for half-time. He looked over and saw us. I promise you."

"Well he didn't say hallo," muttered Sylvia.

"No, he didn't, but that was because he was busy. He had to stay with his team. Come on, Sylvia, let's go home for tea. We could have those crumpets you bought." She smiled at Mad. "Anthony's away for the weekend, and it's Isabelle's afternoon off, so I thought a walk to watch the rugby might pass the time, but it is very cold and the crumpets are beckoning!"

The play on the pitch hurtled towards them, and as three or four players careered over the touchline the spectators lurched back out of their way. Mad snatched Sylvia out of harm's way, and held her close as the bodies scrabbled about in the mud at her feet. Sylvia clung to Mad's neck as she watched the lads untangle themselves into a line out, right in front of them. Ben was in the line and as the ball came in, he was hoisted into the air, snatching it and passing it on quickly.

"There's Ben," squealed Sylvia in delight. "Mummy! There's Ben, jumping!"

"Yes, yes I see him, Sylvia."

"I seed him too," called Thomas, still safely in his mother's arms. "I seed Ben too."

The game moved away from them again, pushing towards the Loughborough try line, and Mad put Sylvia down again.

"Well, that was very successful," laughed Jill. "We've seen Ben jumping. Now chaps, we really must go home for tea. Say good-bye to Mad."

They all said goodbye and as Jill was turning away, Mad called after her impulsively. "Jill, if you're on your own this evening, with Anthony away, why don't you come and join us in the pub? The Flying Dutchman, you know, where Ben works? It's my birthday and we're all getting together for a few drinks."

Jill hesitated. "Well," she said, "I don't know. Thanks for asking, but I probably won't. Wrong vintage, you know?"

"Stuff," scoffed Mad. "Of course you're not. It'll be great...oh but you said it was Isabelle's day off."

"Afternoon. She'll be back this evening."

"There you are then, come and join the piss-up!"

"Is that what it'll be?" grinned Jill.

"Not to begin with, but it may degenerate…you know. 'Specially if these guys stuff Loughborough this afternoon." She swivelled her eyes back to the field, in time to see Dan make a break and fling himself over the try line to score. Cheers and whistles and shrieks of delight exploded from the Belchers' supporters, and Mad joined in, clapping and shouting, chanting the Belcaster chant. When she turned back, Jill had gone and was a hundred yards away, heading for home.

Watching the rest of the game Mad gave herself over to cheering the team and forgot all about Angie, Chantal and Jill. It was an exciting finish with Loughborough kicking a penalty two minutes before the end, but the Belchers managed to hold on and so scrape a win by two points. As the players came off the pitch, most of the spectators streamed away, heading for the union bar where the teams would join them later.

"Hey, great try," Mad called to Dan, and he gave her a muddy grin, clearly delighted with himself, before heading into the changing rooms to shower. "Well played, Ben," she said as he came past, "your fan club was here!"

Ben stopped abruptly. "What? What do you mean? Who?"

Mad laughed. "Sylvia and Thomas. Jill brought them to watch you play. They were full of it."

A flicker of relief crossed Ben's face, and Mad realised he must have thought she'd meant Angie. "Oh, yeah, I saw them," he said. He grinned at her. "See you later, at the Dutch."

The Flying Dutchman was crammed to overflowing when Jill Hammond pushed in through the door later that evening. Mad's party was obviously well under way, and there was already one very rowdy group singing in a corner. Even as she edged her way through the crowd, she was wishing she'd not come. It was mad to go into a student pub by herself, to join a group she hardly knew, but it was a chance to see Ben, and there hadn't been many of those lately. Anthony had been working from home a lot, and the madness was still on her. She thought of it like that, her craving to be with Ben, even if it was in a crowd, when they could hardly even acknowledge each other. She knew he was working behind the bar that evening, but she couldn't see him, and would have turned and fled had not Madeleine caught sight of her and grabbed her by the arm.

"Jill!" she cried. "You came. Good for you! Here, let me get you a drink. My dad sent me some dosh to buy everyone a drink." She turned and bellowed at the bar, "Hey, Ben, my man, a pint for Jill. You do drink beer don't you?"

"Not really," laughed Jill. "Red wine please, Mad."

"Pint of red wine," Mad called across to Ben, pushing Jill towards the bar in front of her.

Jill saw Ben looking at her thunderstruck, and smiled steadily. "Just a glass will do, thanks, Ben."

"Yeah, right." Ben regained control of his features and poured the drink, adding it to Mad's tab. "Didn't know you were coming," he muttered.

"I'm on my own this weekend, so Mad suggested I come and join her party. Great win this afternoon I hear."

"Hey Jill." Mad grabbed her arm and drew her into her group. "You know these guys don't you? Dino, Cirelle, and this is Dan. You know Dan, don't you?"

It was clear that Mad had been celebrating her birthday for some time, and she was going well.

"Happy birthday, Mad," said a voice behind her.

Mad peered over her shoulder. "Angie, you came. Great! Have a drink, they're on me. Ben! A pint for Angie." Mad pushed her way to the bar again, leaving Jill with the others from the Madhouse.

"Mad seems to be well away," she said to Cirelle, who laughed and, raising her pint glass, said with a slight slur to her voice, "I think we all are."

At that moment, someone started the Belcaster chant, and soon the whole pub was ringing with "Hey Belchers! Go! Go!

Go! Hey Belchers! Blow! Blow! Blow!" Then someone started shouting, "Jamie! Jamie! Jamie!" The cry was taken up and the scorer of the first try was hoisted on to a chair and given a pint of lager which, to the accompaniment of "Down! Down! Down!" he sank in one go. Then it was Dan's turn. As he was hoisted on to the chair, Jill saw to her amazement that Chantal Haven was also in the group.

What on earth is that child doing here, she wondered? Does Angela know where she is?

She watched as Chantal joined in the shouting and cheering for Dan, watched her drain her glass, and wondered what on earth she was drinking. It looked like Coke, but you never knew these days.

"Down! Down! Down!" bellowed the crowd, and Dan emptied his pint straight down his throat to a roar of delight from his friends.

Feeling extremely old, Jill drank her wine and decided that it had indeed been a mistake to come. Ben certainly didn't look very pleased to see her. She'd just have one more glass and slip away. But she'd reckoned without Madeleine. As she swallowed the last mouthful of her wine, another was put into her hand, and by the time she'd drunk that, she felt she ought at least to buy the birthday girl a drink before she left. She struggled to the bar and bought more beer for Mad and the rest of the Madhouse, another glass of wine for herself and a pint for Ben.

"What the hell are you doing here?" Ben muttered as he handed her the wine.

Jill gave him a helpless grin and said, "Mad told me to come! Honestly! Why? Do you mind?"

Ben raised his eyebrows and said, "No, 'course not, but watch out. My ex-girlfriend is just behind you, in the red sweater, and she's poison. Don't know why she's here either." He passed across the other drinks. "Are you going to stay till closing?"

Jill felt a warmth spread through her as she saw the expression in his eyes. "No…yes, maybe. I don't know."

"Wait for me after?" His eyes were bright, and she didn't hesitate with her answer.

"I'll be in the car. It's in the car park."

"Move it round the corner, in Fish Street. I'll meet you there."

She laughed shakily. "OK. I'll see you then," and taking the first two glasses, fought her way back to the group, who were now ensconced round a table entirely covered with empty glasses. The girl in the red sweater was with them, and so was Chantal. She was crammed in between Mad's boyfriend, Dan, and Dean from the house. Jill smiled across at her, and was met with a slightly defiant look, which dared her to comment. Jill shook her head slightly, thinking to herself that neither of them should be there, and went back to the bar for the rest of the drinks. When she returned to the table with the glasses, they all squashed together even more closely to make room for her, and she was crushed in beside Mad, and a girl called Pepper, who appeared to be with Dean; his arm was draped round her anyway.

Immediately she found herself involved in a drinking game, when to lose meant paying a forfeit, downing another drink, and before long she lost count of how many glasses of wine she'd had. Nor did she care. She was going to see Ben afterwards.

By the time Joe called "Time!" the whole lot of them were decidedly drunk. When Jane came over to clear the table and encourage them to leave, she suddenly saw Chantal.

"Chantal Haven," she exploded. "What the hell are you doing here? You know you're under age. You'll lose me my licence. Out! Now! I told you before you wouldn't be served in here. Out!" Chantal staggered to her feet, and Jane turned on the rest of them. "We're good to you lot in here. Let you make as much noise and carry on as you like, but if I catch one of you buying that kid a drink in here again, you'll be banned. I mean it!" She glared round at them in rage. When her face lit on Jill, she hissed, "And you, Jill Hammond, you know better than to buy a child her age a drink. Look at her, she can hardly stand."

Jill looked and saw that it was true. "I didn't buy her a *drink*, Mrs Short, I bought her a Coke." She spoke carefully to be sure her words came out in the right order. "Just a Coca Cola."

"Well, someone's been feeding her with booze. God knows what her mother'll say. Now, out the lot of you. I've got to clear up." She stalked back to the bar, and the giggles that had been suppressed round the table burst forth as they all staggered to their feet.

Behind the bar, Jane banged glasses angrily into the sink. She didn't mind the ragging, the noise, the drinking games, provided they didn't get too out of hand, but she did mind them risking *her* licence, *her* livelihood with under-age drinking. She looked across at Chantal who was still standing inside the door, looking most unsteady. "Here, Ben," she said, "didn't you see that Chantal girl over there? You know she's under age."

"No, sorry," Ben lied. "There's such a crowd in tonight."

"Nor did I," Jane muttered angrily, "and now look at the state of her!" She sniffed and then said, "Look, Ben, Joe and I'll finish up here. You go now and make sure that child gets home. She lives next to you, don't she?" Ben nodded. "OK, well none of them others is going to look after her, they're all out of their minds. You go and take her home."

Ben was happy enough to knock off work early, but he didn't want to be responsible for Chantal. He'd seen her in the crowd, but he had turned a blind eye to the odd rum being added to her Coke; after all she wasn't his responsibility, and Jill was waiting for him in her car. He nodded to Jane.

"I'll see you tomorrow lunchtime then," he said, and disappeared out through the door before Jane could change her mind.

Outside there was a crowd of students milling about on the street, noisy and laughing, and as he emerged he heard Mad's voice calling, "Party at our place. Come on, everyone invited. Back to the Madhouse. The beer's on my dad!" There was a general cheer and people began to move off towards Dartmouth Circle, most of them the usual crowd, but some hangers-on as well. Jane was right; no one was taking any notice of Chantal. She was still holding on to the door post, but Ben was determined it wasn't going to be he who took her home, he had other fish to fry... in Fish Street!

Ben grabbed Dan by the arm as he emerged from the gents. "Hey, Danny," he said, "take that kid with you. Chantal?" He nodded back to the pub. "Jane in there is furious she's been drinking, and is afraid she won't make it home and the police'll find her."

"You take her," Dan said cheerfully. "I'm looking for Mad."

"Mad's gone on ahead," Ben told him, "to let everyone in. I can't take her, I've got to go back inside and finish clearing up. Come on, mate, it isn't much to ask, it's hardly out of your way is it? We don't want Joe to lose his licence for allowing under-age drinking, do we?"

"Oh, all right." Dan turned to Chantal. "Come on kid, let's get you home."

Ben watched for a moment as Dan took Chantal by the arm, pulling her along the road, and then hurried back round the corner where Jill was waiting patiently for him in the car. He slipped into the passenger seat beside her and gathered her into his arms. As always, her response was immediate, and their kisses were passionate and demanding.

"God, I've missed you," Ben said when they finally broke apart. "I haven't seen you for over a week."

"Yes you have," teased Jill, "you saw me this afternoon."

"Yeah, across the pitch. Big deal! What were you doing there anyway?"

"Looking for you, of course. I haven't seen you for a week either." Jill laughed. "So I brought the children to see you play rugby. You looked quite hunky even among all the other hunks."

"Oh, I did, did I? Come here, woman."

Jill strained against him, her body beginning to quiver at his touch.

"You taste of wine," Ben said at last.

Jill giggled. "Not surprised," she said, "I've had one or three. Feel a bit squiffy." She twined her arms around him again and put her lips to his ear. "Ben," she whispered, "it's not very comfortable in here, and rather public, if anyone chose to look in. Let's go somewhere else. Somewhere warmer. Anthony's not at home tonight."

"Well, we aren't going to *your* house," stated Ben firmly.

"No, no. I'm not suggesting that we do." Jill ran a hand along his thigh, to stroke the bulge in his jeans. "Just saying that I won't be missed if I stay out, that's all."

"You will be in the morning," Ben pointed out, trying to ignore her roving hand.

"I'm not shug…shuggesting that I stay all night—" Jill was having trouble with her words and she began to laugh again. "Just that we go somewhere more comfortable now. Let's go to *your* room."

"We can't," Ben replied, "everyone's gone back there."

Jill snuggled against him. "To your room?"

"No, stupid, to the house!"

"We could shneak in, we could shneak in and lock your door and nobody'd even know we were there." She continued to stroke him through his jeans, and the bulge under her hand told him that he wanted her as much as she did him. "And I wouldn't have far to go in the morning!" She touched the side of his face delicately with the tip of her tongue and he groaned.

"Come on then, but I'll drive, you're in no state. Come on, change places." He got out of the car, but Jill insisted on scrambling over from the driver's seat and ended up in a tangle round the gear lever. "I've had too much wine," she announced, as they disentangled her.

When at last they were ready to drive home, Ben drove very carefully. He had no wish to be stopped by the police; even though he hadn't drunk more than a pint all evening, he wanted no questions asked as to why they were together.

When they reached Dartmouth Circle, Jill said, "Better leave the car on the road."

"Don't you want to put it in the garage?"

"No, opening the garage door might wake Isabelle. Don't want her to know what time I got back, do we?"

Ben drew the car quietly to a standstill. Jill still felt very squiffy. "Don't bang the car doors," she instructed, and when she got out herself she shut the door with elaborate care.

They walked round the Circle, not touching, until they were outside the Madhouse. The front door stood open and light spilled out on to the path. There was no one there, but music was thudding from the open windows of the uncurtained living room above, and the noise of shouts and laughter echoed down the stairs and out into the Circle.

"Come on." Jill took Ben's hand, and, pulling him behind her she crept on tiptoe through the open door and scuttled down the passage to his room at the back. Once safely inside, Ben turned the key and even before he turned round, Jill was behind him, her arms round his waist, rubbing herself against him as she struggled to undo his belt. The music above them thudded its bass notes through the ceiling, but Ben and Jill hardly heard it as they struggled with clothes and shoes and the fact that Jill's legs kept folding up underneath her. At last they were on the bed, naked and entwined, and as Ben began to thrust and thrust again, the only sounds they heard were the sounds of their own coupling.

Chantal hadn't realised at first that the Coke tasted funny, and by the time she did, it didn't seem to matter any more. She didn't feel sick like she had at Mike's New Year's Eve party with the disgusting Oliver, she felt very jolly and bright, and a lot of what she said was witty and made the others laugh. Still by the end of the evening, she found she was a bit woozy. Her head wasn't spinning, but she found it a bit difficult to focus. There had been a dreadful moment when Mrs Hammond had turned up from somewhere, but luckily she hadn't said anything, so that was all right; and then another, when Mrs Short had seen her and blown her top. Still, that had been at the end of the evening and she hadn't actually done anything about Chantal being there. She knew she was much later than she was supposed to be, but she'd just have to hope Mum was asleep when she got in. Mum had been going out to the theatre with some people, but she hadn't expected to be late.

As they all poured out into the cold darkness, Chantal shivered, and waited by the pub door. She had hoped to walk home with Dean, but he seemed to have some bird with him this evening. She didn't particularly fancy Dean, he wasn't her idea of a hunk at all; she much preferred Dan, but she'd regarded Dean as an anchorman, the one who had suggested that she come with them in the first place, and she was pretty fed up that he no longer showed any interest in her, and was already wandering off down the street, his arm casually over Pepper's shoulders. Someone was shouting, "Party at Mad's house. Come on, everyone, party at Mad's," and Chantal realised that she was going to have to let go of the door post and walk if she wasn't going to be left behind. Then Ben turned up from inside and persuaded Dan to look after her, and the evening took a distinct turn for the better.

At first Dan had just said, "Come on then," but as she had stumbled behind him, he'd turned round and put his arm round her to give her some support. The whole crowd was streaming towards Dartmouth Circle, but Chantal and Dan were the last. She looked over her shoulder, but there was no sign of Ben; he must have gone back into the Dutch to finish clearing up.

As she was still a bit unsteady on her feet, they made fairly slow progress, but then Chantal realised that Dan was no longer towing her along as he had been at first. He still had his arm round her, giving her support, but his hand was very gently squeezing her breast. She could feel his fingers through the material of her coat, and the flat of his palm as his hand moved. It made her catch her breath, and for a moment she stopped walking. His grip on her tightened and he bent his head and kissed her forehead. Chantal didn't look up at him, but she didn't pull away either. Slowly they started to walk again, but all the time Chantal could feel his hand, moving, pressing, fondling, and she found herself wishing that his hand was inside her coat. As they passed a dark shop doorway, Dan paused and then drew her into its shelter.

Dan was surprised himself that he was taking advantage of the opportunity Ben had thrown at him. He fancied Chantal all right, and had from the first moment she had appeared at the Madhouse in her mini skirt and skimpy top, but he wouldn't have done anything about it, made no effort to accept the invitation she seemed to be offering, if she hadn't been handed to him, as it were, on a plate. Now he had his arm round her and could feel her pressing against him, kissing her was just too much of a temptation to resist.

In the sheltering darkness of the doorway, he turned her to face him and murmured, "You are a very beautiful woman, Chantal. Did you know that? And very sexy!"

"Am I?" To her own ears Chantal's voice sounded rather squeaky, but Dan didn't seem to notice. He undid her coat and slipped his hands inside, running them down over both her breasts, which seemed to thrust themselves towards him of their own accord.

"Mmm," he murmured into her hair, "beautiful." One hand slid round her back and pulled her towards him, while the other cradled the back of her head, as he began to kiss her.

Chantal felt herself go limp against him. She had never been kissed like this in her life; she wasn't sure what to do, but when his tongue probed her mouth she obediently opened her lips and tasted his tongue with her own. She could feel him moving his hips against her now, and it was the most exciting feeling. Then his hand moved again, sliding down from her breast, over her waist and hips to caress her thigh. All the while, his mouth was roaming hers, so that she could hardly breathe, but she could feel his hand on her thigh, tickling and stroking. And she felt her skin quiver and contract under his touch. He felt it too and laughed even as he was kissing her. With practised dexterity he slid his hand up under her mini skirt and cupped her between the legs, one finger probing and stroking. Chantal tensed, but the teasing finger continued to move deliciously, lazily, until with a smooth flick it was inside her tights, inside her panties and moving against her burning skin. She tried to pull away, to catch her breath, but Dan held her firmly against him for another moment of exciting touching. Then he released her and she sagged away from him, gasping.

"There you are my beautiful baby," he whispered. "That's how it'll feel, only better, much better." He threw his arm round her again as they had been before and pulling her out of the doorway said, "Come on, let's go."

Chantal stumbled along beside him, as they headed on to Dartmouth Circle. She felt completely light-headed. She'd been shocked by what Dan had done, but she hadn't wanted it to stop. She felt slippery between her legs as she walked, and wasn't sure she liked it. His hand was back in its position over her breast, still holding her, still smoothing and squeezing, so that her body was still completely aware of him. When they finally reached Dartmouth Circle, they could hear the music thudding out from the Madhouse. As they approached, Dan saw two people get out of a car parked a little way along the road. Dan paused and pulling Chantal into his arms again, kissed her, but watched what was happening over her head.

It's Ben, he thought, with that woman from over the road. Dirty bugger!

Dan watched as the couple slipped into the student house, and then released Chantal, and taking her arm led her across to the party. Chantal held back for a moment, glancing at her own house. It was in darkness, but the garage door stood open and the garage was empty. Mum wasn't home yet, and Annabel must be in bed.

"Well, are you coming or not?" demanded Dan harshly.

Chantal looked up at him, and pulled free. "I don't know," she said.

"Suit yourself." Dan moved towards the Madhouse.

"Dan, wait!"

He stopped but didn't turn round. Chantal went up behind him and said, "What about Mad?"

"What about Mad?"

"Well, I mean..." Chantal hesitated, remembering his kisses and the delicious thrill of his hands on her body.

Dan shrugged. "Come to the party or not as you like, it's up to you."

"I'll come."

Dan made no comment, but walked in at the front door and Chantal followed him. They went upstairs to the living room where the music was blasting and apart from a few energetic types, most people were crashed out on the chairs with cans of beer in their hands. The air was thick with smoke, and Dan soon detected the sweet smell of pot. He didn't smoke much, but enjoyed the odd spliff.

He grabbed a can of beer from the kitchen and then moseyed over to Gig Tarbuck, a guy on his course, who was draped over an armchair with his girlfriend draped over him. Gig was always good for a smoke or two, and, dealing quickly now, Dan soon had two spliffs in his pocket. He looked round for Mad. She was on the sofa, a can of beer in her hand and her eyes shut. She wasn't asleep, her feet were tapping to the thud of the music, but she certainly wasn't taking any notice of Dan. He watched her for a moment as she drank from the can, still with her eyes shut. Downing his own beer, he took another. He saw Dean slide into his bedroom, propelling Pepper in before him, both of them laughing.

Shit! he thought, everyone's getting it but me. He wandered over to Mad. "Hey!" he said.

"Mmmm?" Mad didn't open her eyes.

"What are you doing?"

"I'm giving a party." Mad spoke carefully. "I need another beer, find me a beer, Danny."

Dan went to get her one, but by the time he came back with it, Mad had fallen asleep.

Chantal was standing in the kitchen wishing she hadn't come. She couldn't see any of the students she knew, except Cirelle, who was dancing in the arms of a huge black guy with Rastafarian locks, and Mad who appeared to be asleep. Charlie hadn't been there all evening, and there was no sign of Dean or Ben. There were others she'd seen in the pub, of course, the girl in the red sweater, Angie, and several others who appeared to be paired off, snogging on the floor, or dancing. There had been several cases of beer in the kitchen, but the cans inside them had disappeared rapidly. Chantal hadn't wanted beer, and feeling brave she opened the fridge and found one can of Diet Coke inside, so she'd helped herself. She looked at her watch. It was pretty late, perhaps she'd just slip away. But then Dan appeared at her side, holding a lighted cigarette in his hand. He offered her a drag and she took the cigarette and gave a tentative puff. She knew to be really cool she ought to inhale, but she was afraid it would make her cough. Dan didn't seem to notice her hesitancy, he simply pulled another cigarette from his pocket and lit it for himself.

"Got a drink?" he asked.

She raised her can of Coke. He looked out into the living room again, and while he did so, she risked a drag on the cigarette. The smoke filled her lungs and her head, making her feel woozy, but she managed not to cough, and let the smoke trickle out through her nose. Not too bad. She drew again, and this time it was easier, because she knew what to expect, in fact she felt rather good. Then Dan took the cigarette from her and pinching it out, put it back in his pocket.

"Come and dance," he said and pulled her into the living room. She followed willingly, half wishing she could have finished the cigarette. He edged her into a space and putting his arms round her, began to move his hips against her, and his hands down over her back. He felt her response as before, and with a quick glance over her shoulder at Mad, still spark out on the sofa, he moved towards the stairs. One hand slid down over Chantal's bottom, squeezing as it went, hitching her mini skirt up so that his fingers stroked the curve of her bum. He felt the buttock clench.

She may be only a kid, he thought, excited himself, but she's ready for me all right. Bloody asking for it, she is.

He remembered Charlie was away. Perfect, he thought, a private room. "Hey babe," he said, but Chantal pulled away, beginning to be afraid.

"I have to go to the bathroom," she said.

Dan nodded. "It's upstairs."

Chantal turned away and walked a little unsteadily up the stairs. Dan took a quick glance round the room, one last look at Mad blissfully asleep on the sofa, and followed her.

While Chantal was in the bathroom she decided it was time she went home, she didn't want Dan to go any further, but when she came out, he was waiting for her on the landing, two lighted cigarettes in his hand. He gave one to her and as he was blocking the way back downstairs, she took it and drew on it deeply as she had done before.

"It's very noisy down there," Dan said. "I thought we'd have a quiet smoke up here." He slid his arm round her again, and pushing open the door to Charlie's bedroom, he edged her inside. Once the door was closed he took the cigarette away from Chantal again, and crushing it out in a plant pot, pulled her into his arms again. This time he didn't waste time, his hands were up under her sweater and pulling at her bra.

Chantal made no move to stop him, she was hazy and lethargic from the hash, and her body quivered at the touch of his hands, even though that touch was far less gentle than before. She leaned against him as he began to kiss her and when his hands reached round under her skirt, pulling at her tights, she stood on tiptoe, rubbing herself against him.

Suddenly he let her go and she sat down on the bed with a bump, watching as he stripped off his shirt and jeans. She could see a huge bulge between his legs that leapt towards her as his boxers followed his jeans on to the floor.

"You're going to love this, babe," he grunted as he pulled at her skirt and tights. "You've been begging for this ever since I first saw you. You've been waiting for this." And he pushed her back on to the pillow.

## Chapter Twenty

Sheila and Gerald Colby had gone to bed early, well before the student party had left the pub, and she was fast asleep, when a loud thudding began to penetrate her dreams. For a few moments it was part of her dream, and then she was wide awake. She sat up with a jolt. The whole of her bedroom seemed to be vibrating with the sound, not only of heavy reggae music, but of voices and loud shouts of laughter.

"Gerald! Gerald!" She shook her still-sleeping husband awake. "Can't you hear that din?"

Gerald grunted that he could.

"It's worse than we thought," hissed Sheila. "Whatever time is it?" She peered at the alarm clock and then answered her own question. "Past midnight! Listen to them!"

"I can hear them," said Gerald, "and I agree it is a bit loud."

"A bit loud!" snapped Sheila, "it's deafening! The whole Circle must be awake! We must do something."

"Like what?" asked Gerald wearily.

"Bang on the wall," Sheila said. "I'm going downstairs to bang on the wall." She got out of bed and struggled into her dressing gown. "I'll bang on the wall of the stairs," she said and disappeared.

Gerald sighed. He knew banging on the wall wouldn't be any good. He doubted if they would even hear it above the racket they were making, but he did agree that the noise *was* too much at this time of night. He decided he'd better get up too, if only to stop Sheila setting off round to the students' house on a one-woman crusade. When he got downstairs, he found Sheila standing on the lower flight banging on the wall with a broom handle.

"Sheila, love," he protested, "it's a waste of time. They'll never hear you above that din."

But he was wrong. Even as he spoke there was an answering knock from next door, but a rhythmical one, bang bang-bang-bang bang, bang bang. Sheila hammered angrily on the wall with her fists, but little sound came from them so she had another go with the broom handle. The answering knocks sounded again, and there was a gale of laughter.

"Oh this is ridiculous!" she exploded. "I always said this would happen with a house full of students next door. I'm going to ring the police."

"Now Sheila, steady on," Gerald said, stopping her reaching for the telephone. "They are being very noisy, but it may settle down in a little while, and be fair, it is the first time they've done it."

"The first and the last," stormed Sheila. "Well, I'm going to ring Anthony Hammond then. *He's* chairman of the Residents' Association. He can come over and deal with them."

"Why don't you ring the students themselves and ask them to turn the music down a bit?" suggested Gerald. "Let's face it, Anthony won't be too delighted to hear from you in the early hours of the morning either."

"I imagine he's awake already," Sheila snapped.

"Even so, let's give the students a ring first."

"I don't know their number," Sheila grumbled.

"It's in our book," Gerald replied calmly. "Remember, the girl, Madeleine, gave it to us when she first moved in and we wrote it in our book." As he spoke he reached for their telephone index and looked up the number. "Here we are," he said and passed it across to her.

Sheila sniffed, but she took the index and dialled the number.

The line was engaged. "Either someone else is ringing to complain, or they've taken it off the hook," she said.

"Probably the Redwoods," Gerald said soothingly. "Let's give it a minute and see if they turn down the noise. I'll make us a cup of tea while we're waiting."

He made the tea, but there was no sign of the noise next door diminishing, and further efforts to phone were all greeted with the engaged signal.

"That's it," Sheila said when she'd drunk her tea, "I'm going to phone Anthony and demand he does something." She consulted their phone index again and dialled the Hammonds' number.

It was answered at the first ring. "Hallo. Jill, is that you?"

Not really taking in what he had said, Sheila launched into her complaint. "Mr Hammond? Anthony? This is Sheila Colby."

"Mrs Colby?" Anthony sounded confused.

"Sheila Colby," she repeated, "from number six. I'm ringing up to ask what you are going to do about the dreadful noise that those students are making. It's nearly one in the morning, and our whole house is vibrating to that dreadful music. Can't you hear it?"

"Oh, Mrs Colby. Yes, yes I can hear something."

"Something!" retorted Sheila. "It's positively head-banging from here. We've tried knocking on the wall and they just knock back. The phone is engaged, off the hook I should think. It's up to you to go over there and tell them to turn it off."

"Up to me? Why? You live next door."

"Mr Hammond, the whole street is being deafened by this din. You are chairman of the Residents' Association, it's up to you. Otherwise I'll call the police."

Anthony sighed. He didn't want the police called if it wasn't necessary. "All right," he agreed reluctantly, "I'll see what I can do."

Sheila rang off. "He's going across," she told Gerald.

Anthony put the phone down with a groan. He was still up and dressed, wondering with increasing anxiety where on earth Jill was. She had obviously gone out for the evening somewhere;

Isabelle had only been able to say that she had gone to drinks with friends, but she didn't know who.

Anthony had come home unexpectedly because his Sunday meeting had been cancelled, and he, himself, hadn't got in until just after half past eleven. Jill wasn't at home, and as it got later he was becoming more and more worried. Perhaps her car had broken down and she was stranded somewhere. But if she were stranded, why didn't she ring? Of course she didn't think he was at home, so she might have stayed over with the friends if her car wouldn't start and would ring Isabelle in the morning. If only he knew where she'd been for the evening, he could have gone out to look for her, but it was far too late to ring round their various friends to see if Jill had been there. And now this stupid woman was insisting that he go over to the student house and get the music turned off.

He opened the front door and started across the grass towards the Madhouse, aptly named, he thought as he was treated to the full blast of the music from the open windows of number seven. Suddenly he stopped short. There, parked outside in the road, was Jill's car. He ran and peered in through the windows. There was no one in it. He tried the door, but the car was locked. He stood on the pavement, looking round him, but there was no sign of her, or anyone. He looked round the Circle. Could she have been having drinks with one of their neighbours? Several houses had their lights on now, but that was probably due to the party in number seven. He called her name, softly at first, and then loudly, shouting in case she was in the central garden for some reason, but there was no reply. At that moment Paul Forrester's door opened, and he emerged with a torch.

"Paul? Is that you?" Anthony called.

The torch flashed across the garden and Paul made his way over.

"Anthony?" He stopped by the car and looked across at the Madhouse. "We used to have parties like that once upon a time," he said reminiscently.

"Paul. Have you seen Jill?" Anthony asked urgently. "Is she with you?"

"Jill? No. Should she be?"

"No, I don't think so. It's just that she went to drinks with some friends, I don't know who, and she isn't home yet. I'm getting worried."

"Isn't this her car?" asked Paul. "She must be in the Circle or pretty close by if her car's here."

"That's what's so odd," explained Anthony. "It wasn't here when I got in...at least I'm pretty sure it wasn't. I mean, I must have seen it if it had been here when I got home, mustn't I?"

Paul shrugged. "I'd have thought so," he agreed.

"And now, Sheila Colby's on to me about the noise from the student house, demanding that I should do something about it..."

"And saying I told you so."

Anthony laughed ruefully. "And saying I told you so. Well, I'd better try I suppose."

"I'll come with you," Paul said, "that's what I really came out for, to see if I could get them to turn it down a bit. We did try ringing, but it's always engaged. Phone's probably off the hook. Anyway, they've woken the kids, which is a pain, and we'd all like a bit of sleep."

The two men walked over to number seven. Anthony looked up and saw Sheila and Gerald Colby watching from the window. There were lights on in the Redwoods' house too, though David and Shirley were not at their window.

They've got kids in the house too, Anthony thought, they must be loving this noise!

The front door of number seven was ajar, and after some futile knocking Anthony was about to go in when the whole frontage was lit up by headlights, and a police car pulled round the Circle. Anthony drew back from the door and turned to meet the police. A constable got out of the car and said, "Good evening, sir, PC Woodman. Mr Redwood, is it?"

"No, Anthony Hammond, from number three."

"You didn't phone us, sir?"

"No. If it was David Redwood, he's next door at number eight. I was just going to see if I could get them to turn down the music a bit. I'm chairman of the Residents' Association and I've had a complaint from the neighbours the other side, the Colbys."

At that moment he was aware of someone at his side and turned to find Sheila Colby, dressed in her dressing gown. She had rushed down into the road when she saw the police car. "Thank goodness you've come, officer," she said to the policeman. "This noise has got to be stopped, it's a public nuisance."

"We'll see what we can do, madam," he promised and then turning to Anthony again, said, "I'm not surprised someone complained, sir. It is very loud isn't it? Who owns this property, or is it rented?"

"A girl called Madeleine Richmond. She's a student herself and rents out the other rooms."

"Well, sir, we'll deal with this now," said Woodman, "if you'd all like to go back indoors." Nobody moved. At that moment David Redwood emerged from his house, also dressed in pyjamas and dressing gown. "Good, you're here," he said without preamble. "You can hear the problem yourself, and this racket has been going on for nearly an hour now. It's too loud and too late!"

"Mr Redwood? Don't worry, sir, we'll sort it now, if you'd just like to go back indoors."

David didn't go back indoors, but crossed over to join Sheila, Paul and Anthony as they stood aside and watched the police. A policewoman had joined Constable Woodman on the pavement, and together they went to the front door of number seven and pressed the bell. If it rang, no one heard it above the noise of the music. Woodman pushed open the door and they went in. He went straight upstairs and immediately smelt what Dan had when he had arrived.

"You stay at the top of the stairs," he said to WPC Ford, "someone's using drugs in here." Then he strode across the room to the stereo system and turned off the power. For a moment the silence was deafening, then there was a babble of complaints before everyone realised who had turned the music off. WPC Ford switched on the overhead lights and Woodman said, "Right, everyone stay where you are." He spoke to Ford. "Ask for back-up," he said, "and then search upstairs, let's have everyone in here. No one's to leave this room," he ordered. "Which of you is Miss Richmond, and who else lives here?"

Cirelle came forward, looking scared. "I live here," she said. "That's Mad there." She pointed to Madeleine, who was sprawled on the sofa, but beginning to surface, woken by the sudden silence.

"Miss Richmond?" Woodman said as she looked up at him blearily. "We've had a complaint about the noise, and I'm not surprised. However, I'm more concerned by the use of drugs in this house. I intend to search everyone here."

Madeleine was suddenly wide awake, and looking round the crowd in the room, shrugged helplessly. "If you must," was all she said.

Dean, realising that something untoward was happening, came out of his bedroom, and stood in the doorway. "What's going on?" he muttered.

No one answered him, so he closed his door gently behind him and waited.

Mad looked across at Cirelle and murmured, "Where's Dan?"

Cirelle raised her shoulders in ignorance, but she knew why Mad was asking. Dan occasionally smoked pot, and Mad didn't want him caught with it on him. However, Mad's question was soon answered. After calling for assistance, WPC Ford had gone upstairs and now reappeared, shoving Dan downstairs in front of her and pulling Chantal along behind her. Dan was wearing only his boxer shorts, carrying his shirt and jeans, and Chantal was wrapped up in Charlie's bedspread.

Mad saw them emerge into the room, and staggered to her feet, but it took her a moment to realise just what she was seeing. "Dan?" she whispered incredulously "Dan…you haven't…?" But she could see by his face that he had. "You bastard," she cried. "You shitty, fucking bastard." She launched herself at him, her arm swinging to hit him across the face, but WPC Ford caught her, held her firmly.

"No need for that, Miss Richmond!" she warned.

"Isn't there?" She gave Dan a look of pure pain and with the fight draining out of her, she turned away. Immediately Dean was beside her, and putting his arms round her, he held her close, as she fought to control her tears.

Chantal looked terrified, and Woodman said, "And just how old are you then?" Chantal didn't answer at once and at that moment Dean's bedroom door opened again, and Pepper peered out bleary-eyed, to see what was going on.

"And still they come crawling out," remarked Woodman. "Right, out of the house, the lot of you, the party's over."

At that moment the back-up arrived in the form of another police car, its blue light and headlamps flashing, with two more officers in it, one of them a sergeant. Woodman quickly brought him up to date.

"Right," said Sergeant Trump, "I smell cannabis in here. Search them all, Woodman. Dawes," he turned to the man who had arrived with him, "look round the rest of the house, and see if anyone else is here. Start downstairs." Dawes nodded and disappeared down the stairs, while Woodman and Trump moved to begin their searches.

Denroy was first, but he looked the policeman in the eye and said softly, "I don't think, so, man. I'm leaving," and quietly, he stalked from the room. Others followed him, and soon very few of the party remained.

In the meantime, WPC Ford, instructed by Trump, took Chantal back upstairs and told her to get dressed.

She asked her name, and then said, "How old are you?"

"Seventeen," lied Chantal.

"Hmm, and where do you live?"

"Across the road, at number four."

"I see. And does your mother know where you are?"

"She said I could go out," Chantal said defensively.

"With your boyfriend."

"Yes," Chantal was more defiant now. She felt braver with her clothes on.

"I don't think the girl downstairs thought he was your boyfriend," Ford remarked. She reached into the plant pot on the table and retrieved two cigarette ends.

"Smoking, were we?" she enquired.

"So?"

"So, it's an offence to smoke cannabis, you must know that."

"Cannabis?" Chantal's hard-won courage evaporated. "I didn't... I mean it was just a cigarette."

"Did he give it to you, your boyfriend?"

"Dan? Yes, I don't smoke really."

"I see." WPC Ford looked sceptical. "Well, now you're decent again, we'd better go back downstairs."

It was the sudden death of the music that alerted Ben. He and Jill were lying exhausted on his bed, about to drift off into sleep, when the silence descended and then there was the sound of strange voices in the hall. As Ben dragged himself out from under Jill, she giggled and made a catch at him.

"Sssh!" he said fiercely, "there's something going on." He pulled on his jeans, and eased the door open. Looking along the passage he saw that the front door was open, and in the light, which revolved lazily blue, he saw a small crowd gathered outside.

"Christ!" he exclaimed, closing the door hurriedly and turning the key, "it's the fuzz!"

"What—" asked Jill a little muzzily, "what did you say?"

"Police," Ben said tersely. "They're here! Someone must have called them because of the noise. Shit! What are we going to do?" He picked up Jill's bra and tossing it to her, said, "Quick. Get dressed. We've got to think of something."

Sobering up rapidly, Jill struggled back into the clothes she'd cast aside so excitedly earlier. "Who's here?" she whispered.

"There's a police car outside, the blue light's still flashing," replied Ben, "but that's not all, there are other people out there too, from the Circle I imagine, come to see the fun."

"How will I get out?" cried Jill in panic.

"I don't know," snapped Ben. "Think for a minute."

"I could go out of the garden door," Jill said, tugging on her trousers over her bare bottom. She couldn't find her panties in her hurry to get dressed.

"No point," Ben said briskly. "There's no way out of the garden, and you could never climb the fence at the back. You'd be trapped."

"Maybe they won't come in here," Jill said hopefully.

"Some chance."

At that moment there was a rap on his door, and a man's voice said, "Open up."

"Stay behind the door, and stay out of sight," hissed Ben. "I'll go out willingly and they may not even come in." It was a forlorn hope but worth a try.

"Who's there?" Ben called sleepily, as if newly awakened. "What do you want?"

"Police! Open the door."

Ben opened the door and peered at the man standing outside. "What's the matter?" he asked rubbing his eyes.

"Just like you to step outside for a moment, sir," the policeman said, "and the lady behind the door too, please."

Ben was about to protest that there was no one in the room with him, when he realised that Jill was in full view in the mirror on the wardrobe door. "Come on, Jill," he said and held out his hand.

Together they came out, and were led to the stairs. As they

turned to go up a voice from outside spoke in utter incredulity. "Jill?" and then louder, a shout, "Jill! What the hell…?"

Jill took one look out through the front door. Her eyes met those of a stupefied Anthony, and the amazed eyes of Paul Forrester and Sheila Colby, and then she turned away and with leaden feet, followed Ben and the policeman upstairs.

At last it was over and everyone was sent home. No one was charged with drugs offences. The cannabis resin and the few ready-rolled reefers that were retrieved from the floor had not actually been found in anyone's possession. The noise causing the nuisance had been stopped, and the threat of impounding the equipment hung over the house should such a disturbance be caused again. The party was over, but the recriminations were about to begin.

Dan had vanished into the night as soon as he had dragged on his clothes. The police had made no move to restrain him, and the students who were still there ignored him entirely. He had made no move to speak to Mad, no further look had been exchanged between them, he simply slipped away into the darkness, and disappeared.

Angie was still there when Ben had come upstairs with Jill. She stared at him. She hadn't realised he'd come home and gone to his room with someone else while she was waiting for him upstairs to come and join the party. She went white with fury and marching across the room spat out, "I knew there was someone, Ben Gardner, I didn't know it was your grandmother!"

"Goodbye, Angie," Ben said wearily.

"Yeah! Too right, you bastard," she snarled. "I'm well rid of a shit like you." She went downstairs and out of the front door, where the police were encouraging the neighbours, who had come out to see the fun, to return to their homes.

"It's all over, ladies and gentlemen," PC Woodman was saying. "There's no noise now, so you can all go back to bed and to sleep."

Chantal was taken home by WPC Ford. As they reached her

front door, it opened before she could put her key in the lock. Annabel was in a towering rage in the doorway.

"Where the hell have you been, Chantal?" she began, but her words died away as she saw who her sister was with.

"Is this your sister?" asked WPC Ford.

Annabel nodded. "What's happened? Chantal, oh my God, are you all right?"

"Yes, I'm OK." Chantal glared at her. "I was at the party, that's all."

"We thought it best that I should see your sister home," explained WPC Ford, her glance taking in the fact that Annabel was pregnant. "Are your parents at home?"

"No, Mum went out for the evening with friends. She…she phoned earlier to say that she'd been drinking, so she was going to stay over until the morning."

"I see, so you're on your own in the house?"

"Yes. So…?"

"So you were worried about your sister coming home so late." It was a statement not a question.

"I was a bit," admitted Annabel carefully. "I wouldn't have worried if I'd known you were at the party," she said to Chantal, "you should have warned me, that's all." She looked at the policewoman and added, "Mum knew she was going out, she said she could go. It's the weekend after all."

"Yes, I see. Well, she's home now."

Annabel stood aside and Chantal scuttled inside. "Thank you for bringing her," Annabel said and firmly shut the door.

WPC Ford stood outside for a moment longer. "Seventeen? Bullshit!" she murmured to the air and went back to where Woodman was waiting for her in the car. The crowd had now dispersed, and the second car had already left.

"Must've really shaken this place up when that load of England's future moved in," Woodman remarked, and driving slowly round the Circle headed out on to Dartmouth Road.

Madge Peters sat in her window and watched the police cars

drive away. She had heard the music of course, even from the other end of the Circle it had been intrusive, the bass notes thumping out into the air, but she'd still been awake when it started, and she had watched the goings-on with interest ever since.

Well, she thought wryly, Sheila will be delighted to have been proved right.

## Chapter Twenty-One

When the front door of the Madhouse closed behind the police, the students who were left looked round at each other in silence for a moment.

Cirelle flopped on to the sofa and, speaking for them all, said, "Shit, what a mess!"

Madeleine still stood within the circle of Dean's arm, trembling with shock, anger and pain, but as if released by the sound of Cirelle's voice, she pulled free and went to the window. She looked out at the taillights of the police car disappearing into the darkness of the Circle and cried, "Bastard! Bastard! Bastard!" Then turning back to face her friends, she said more quietly, "What a shithouse!" Fighting back more tears, she said, "I'm going to bed. I think I'll sleep in Charlie's room tonight. We'll sort this place out in the morning."

Cirelle made a move towards her. "I'll come up with you," she began, but Mad said quickly, "I'm OK, Cirelle, really. I just want to be on my own, you know?"

"Fine, OK," Cirelle agreed, "if you're sure," but her eyes were anxious.

Leaving the others to do as they chose, Mad went slowly up the stairs to Charlie's room. The door stood open and displayed the bedclothes tumbled to the floor in a heap. Mad stared at them for a moment before realising what this meant. She opened the door of her own room and found it exactly as she had left it, and realised with an overwhelming flood of relief, that it had not been violated as she'd thought. Dan had not taken Chantal there, in Madeleine's own bed; he had used Charlie's bedroom. She closed her door again and went back to the door of Charlie's room. She could smell the sweet smell of the hash, mixed with...whatever. From the smell and the drink, she felt suddenly sick and had to dash for the bathroom.

Later, she sponged her face and hands, cleaned her teeth, and feeling marginally better, determined to face Charlie's room again. After all, it couldn't be left as it was, and as there was no way she was going to sleep, she'd feel better doing something. Drawing a deep breath she went into the room and threw open the window to the cold darkness. The chill air rushed in and swept round the room, scouring it, scooping up the sickly smell left by Dan and Chantal and wafting it out into the night. Immediately, Mad set to work. She pulled all the remaining bed-clothes off the bed, stripping pillow cases from pillows, duvet cover from duvet and sheet from mattress, and hurled them into a heap on the landing. She punched the pillows and hung them out of the gaping window, she shook the duvet and draped that over the top of the pillows. She tipped the remains of the cigarettes into the bin, and with the bin in one hand and the dirty bedclothes tucked under the other arm, she set off downstairs to the washing machine in the garage. She piled the dirty linen inside and set the washer going. She emptied the bin into the dustbin outside the front door and then went back upstairs.

The living room was empty now. Cirelle had disappeared to her own room, and there was no sound from Dean's room, so he and Pepper must have gone to bed too. Ben had followed Jill downstairs, when she had left and hadn't reappeared. The peculiarity of Jill and Ben being together was yet another thing Mad put to one side in her brain. She didn't want to think about anything, she wasn't yet ready to consider any of the dreadful events of the evening or their consequences.

The room itself was a shambles, empty glasses and overflowing ashtrays on every available ledge and shelf. Empty cans and bottles littered the floor, and when she glanced into the kitchen, it was the same in there, and the whole place was pervaded by the sour smell of beer and smoke. Madeleine looked at it all, but felt too drained to cope with it. She didn't want to go back upstairs either, so she simply shook out some of the cushions and the throw that covered the sofa and made a place for herself to curl up.

For a moment she rested, and allowed her mind to relax. It was a mistake; her misery flooded back. Dan! How could he? How could he do that to me? At my own party! I know he was pissed, but that's no excuse. He seduced that bloody Chantal, a bloody schoolgirl, if not in my own bed, under my own roof. He's a shit! A bag of shit! She wanted to scream the words at him, fling them in his face.

The pain surged through her again in a wave, and the tears poured down her cheeks in hot streams. She knew that this time there would be no forgiving Dan, no taking him back. She could not do it. She felt utterly betrayed, and anger at that betrayal combined with the pain, chilled her to the bone and made her start shaking again.

This is no good, she told herself angrily. Pull yourself together! You're behaving like a wimp.

In an effort to get warm she pulled the woollen throw around her, huddling into its folds, and as her tears began to dry, surprisingly, drifted off into an uneasy doze.

When Mad awoke, day was breaking. A dull grey light had stolen through the window, and the room was freezing. Curled into an awkward ball, her legs drawn up under her on the sofa, she was stiff and cold. The throw was still clasped round her but afforded little warmth. She realised with a start that the window was still open, as must be the one in Charlie's room. She hadn't been back up there to close it, or to bring in the bedclothes she'd hung out to air. Stiffly Mad got to her feet and closed the window, then she went upstairs to do the same in Charlie's room. At the door, she surveyed the room again. There was no smell any more, just a roomful of cold December air. She dragged the bedclothes in and shut the window. Pillows and duvet were all damp now, but at least they didn't smell any more either. Mad draped them around the radiator to dry again and then went into her own room. It was warmer in there, but Madeleine was wide awake now and too restless to settle to anything. She decided to have a bath and get warm.

After her bath she dressed from the skin out in clean clothes and went back downstairs. There was still no sign of anyone else stirring, but Mad couldn't stay by herself, so she decided to go out for a walk. It was early Sunday morning, and there was no one else about. She stepped out into the sharp winter air and paused, looking at the Circle. The garden looked bleak and damp, with soggy leaves lying on the grass. How different from the September barbecue, thought Mad idly; that day had been sunny and warm with colours still glowing in the flowers and shrubs. It seemed a long time ago, but then everything before yesterday seemed a long time ago. She walked round the Circle and decided to head for town, perhaps she'd get them a Sunday paper. As she passed number one, she looked up and saw Madge Peters sitting in her window, looking out over the Circle. Madge waved and Madeleine lifted a hand in reply. Madge waved again and pantomimed drinking a cup of tea. Madeleine stopped and pointed in enquiry to herself. Madge nodded and mimed the tea again. Madeleine managed a smile and nodded.

Why not, she thought, I've nothing else to do. And turning, she went to the front door and pushed it open as Madge pressed the door release from upstairs.

"Come up," Madge called, and added as Madeleine climbed the stairs, "you're up early after a late night!" She was in the kitchen, filling the kettle and organising a teapot and mugs. "Would you rather have coffee?" she asked.

"I'm sorry," Mad said, "if we kept you awake." She stood at the kitchen door and Madge saw her face, grey and drawn, her eyes red and puffy.

"My dear child," she exclaimed, "what on earth's happened?" She moved towards her and held out her arms. Mad was enfolded and the sympathy she felt engulfing her broke her self-control and for a moment she wept again. Madge continued to hold her, making sympathetic noises until the worst was over and then said gently, "Let's get that tea, and then we'll sit down and you can tell me all about it…if you want to." She poured the water into the teapot and then Mad carried the tray into the sitting room and set it on the table in the window.

Madge poured the tea and then, when each had her mug, looked across at Madeleine and smiled. "Good party last night, was it?" she enquired lightly.

Cradling the warm mug in her hands, Mad managed a wan smile. "No," she replied, "it was bloody awful."

"Well, it was quite noisy," Madge said. "I saw the police arrive. I suppose someone sent for them."

Mad shrugged. "Yeah, I suppose," she agreed. "Probably old Ma Colby next door."

"Well, it must have been very loud for her," Madge said reasonably. "But that's not the problem, is it." This wasn't a question, but a statement. "What's really upset you? Or don't you want to talk about it?"

If Mad had been asked earlier if she wanted to talk about Dan and his betrayal, she'd have refused, feeling that if she hadn't faced up to it, it might, somehow, not have really happened. But now, faced with Madge's kindly common sense, she found that she did need to speak of it, to bring it out and accept the fact that Dan was in the past.

"It's Dan," she began. "I've always known he eyes up other girls, like, chatting up any bird who'd listen, but I've put up with it. He always came back to me, you know…" Gradually she told Madge the whole story, ending with last night in the pub and at the house.

"I don't even know why Chantal Haven was there, except that she's latched on to us since we arrived here. Makes her feel grown up I suppose. She's always giving blokes the eye, Dan included."

"She's a flighty little piece," observed Madge, drinking her tea. "Get herself into trouble like that sister of hers, I shouldn't be surprised."

"I can't see what a man Dan's age would see in her," Mad protested. "She's just a kid."

"Kid she may be, but she's got legs up to her armpits and a very neat little bum," Madge said.

Madeleine looked startled at that, and Madge laughed and said, "I wasn't always ninety, you know."

Spike wandered into the room and seeing Madeleine sitting in the armchair, sprung gracefully on to her lap and made himself comfortable.

"Spike really likes you," Madge said. "He ignores most people, and Sheila Colby he actively dislikes, he walks out very pointedly when she comes to call!" Madeleine smiled at this and Madge was pleased to see it.

"What you have to realise, Mad," she went on, "is that most men are ruled by what's between their legs. Not all to the same extent, of course, but they do do some very stupid things, and then expect us to sort them out." She looked across at Mad. "Do you love him?"

"I don't know," wailed Mad. "I thought I did. We seemed to have something, well, special. But now...after this. How can you love someone who does this to you, you know?"

"Will you take him back?" asked Madge gently.

"No." Mad's answer was emphatic. "Not this time. Even if I do still love him! But I don't think he'll try to come back this time."

"Maybe not," Madge agreed, "but it'd be as well to be prepared in your own mind, so you know for sure what your answer will be." She reached out and took Mad's hand. "You must set a high value on yourself, Mad. You are an extremely attractive woman, and though it doesn't seem like it now, you'll soon find someone else. Someone who wants to be with you because you're full of vitality and fun, because you're good company, not just for your body and because you're good in bed! Someone who sees you as a whole person and loves you as you are. Don't downgrade yourself to Dan's level, Mad, set a proper value on yourself, and others will do the same." She gave a wry smile. "I'm not saying forget him and get on with life, it's not as easy as that, because you're hurting inside. It'll take time, but the hurt will heal and then we both know you can do it." The old lady smiled again. "There now, lecture over. Just remember there are other fish in the sea...I know, I know, who wants a fish?!" This earned her a smile from Mad. "But it's true all the same!"

An easy silence fell over them, broken only by the purring of the cat on Mad's lap.

"And now, I think," Madge said shrewdly, "you should go for a long walk, you'll find the fresh air and exercise clear your head, and you'll come home with a new perspective on things. Then you should try to mend a few fences. I'm not telling you what to do..." She was of course, and they both knew it, but Madeleine found she didn't mind and Madge wanted Madeleine to have an agenda for the day. "It wouldn't hurt to go round to the Colbys and the Redwoods and apologise for disturbing their sleep. Take them a bunch of flowers or something. After all, you've got to go on living next door to them."

"You're right, I suppose," Mad said, getting to her feet and placing the still-purring Spike on to Madge's lap. "I'll go to that garden centre place near the cathedral and find them something." She went over to the old lady's chair and took her hand. "Thank you, Madge, for everything, lecture and all! It's been a great help just talking, like, you know, getting it all off my chest. You're very easy to talk to."

"Good." Madge squeezed the hand in hers. "Well, come and see us again soon, we'll be pleased to see you any time, won't we Spike?"

Madge had listened to Madeleine going down the stairs and

heard her call a last "goodbye" before the front door closed behind her. She saw her appear on the pavement and with a final wave, disappear out into the Dartmouth Road. The old lady sighed. Suddenly she felt very tired, and she closed her eyes and thought about everything Mad had told her.

What a bastard! she thought. A cad…that's what my father would have called him, a cad. Madeleine's certainly better off without him. Lucky escape… I remember someone like him, what was he called? Jack, Jack someone or other… Jack the Cad… Jack the Lad… Quietly Madge drifted off into memories of her own and so slid gradually into a deep, peaceful and unending sleep.

Clare and Nicholas Richmond drove into Dartmouth Circle on the morning after Madeleine's birthday to take her out for lunch. They'd known that she would want to be with her friends on the actual day and had arranged to come over on the Sunday. It was nearly twelve o'clock when they arrived, but there was no sign of life from the Madhouse. As they drew up outside, they saw David Redwood washing his car with the help of his young grandson. Nick gave a cheerful wave, and was treated to a curt nod, before David went back in through the front door.

Nick shrugged. "He doesn't look very happy today," he remarked as they got out of the car and rang the doorbell.

For some time there was no reply and so he pushed the bell again. At last, a sleepy voice came down the entry phone. "Yeah? Who's that?"

"Nick Richmond, Madeleine's dad. Is she there? Can you open the door?"

The door buzzed as the catch released and Nick pushed it open. Clare went in ahead of him and wrinkled her nose in distaste. "It stinks of beer and smoke," she murmured. They went up the stairs into the living room where the debris from the party greeted them. There were beer cans everywhere, on the bookshelves and table and lying on the floor. Dirty glasses balanced precariously on ledges and the edge of the fireplace, and ashtrays overflowed on to the floor. Dean was standing surveying the scene as if he'd only just noticed it himself. He was dressed only in a pair of boxer shorts, and his hair was tousled as if from sleep.

"Sorry if we woke you," Nick said with gentle irony. "Is Madeleine not up yet?"

"Doesn't look like it!" remarked Clare looking round at the devastation.

Dean belatedly realised that Mad's mother was there too, and said hastily, "Sorry, we had rather a late night, there was a party…"

"So I see," Nick said wryly.

"I'll get dressed," Dean said and diving for the safety of his bedroom, disappeared.

"Looks as if she celebrated in style," commented her mother. "The place is a tip and smells like a brewery." She looked into the kitchen. "It's no better in there." She put down her handbag and took off her coat.

"What are you going to do?" Nick asked.

"First I'm going to make us a cup of coffee, if I can find any, and then I'm going to see about clearing some of this mess."

"Oh, no," her husband said firmly. "The coffee's a great idea, but there's no way you're going to be the one to clear this lot up. That's down to them."

Clare went into the kitchen and found the kettle. There were no clean mugs, but while the kettle boiled she washed up a couple and found the coffee and some dregs of milk in a carton in the fridge. When she had made the coffee she carried a mug out to Nick and then prepared to take one upstairs to Madeleine's room.

"Is that a good idea?" Nick asked.

"What, taking Maddo a coffee?"

"Could prove embarrassing?" suggested Nick.

"Oh, I see. Well, I'll knock first." Clare continued on her way up the second flight of stairs. When she reached the landing, she saw two bedroom doors open, Charlie's and Mad's.

Charlie's room was tidy enough but the bed was stripped and the bedclothes were draped over the radiator. Obviously no one had slept in there last night. In Madeleine's room the bed was roughly made, duvet pulled up askew, the usual heap of clothes on the chair and the desk was piled high with books and papers. There were two dirty coffee mugs on the windowsill, one with a week's growth of mould in the bottom, and the stereo system glowed like the flight deck of an aeroplane, but there was no sign of Madeleine. Clare shrugged and sipped the cup of coffee herself. Either Maddo had got up early for some reason, or she'd not slept there, and presumably would be home soon.

Clare went back downstairs to find Dean had reappeared. He was emerging from the kitchen with a mug of coffee as well.

"She's not here," Clare informed them. "Maddo's not upstairs. Do you know where she is, Dean?"

"No, sorry. She was here when I went to bed last night."

"Well, she can't be far," said Clare. "She was expecting us after all. We're supposed to be taking her out for lunch."

"Looks like some party," Nick remarked to Dean. "Whatever time did you finish?"

"Not sure," mumbled Dean. "Quite late." The door behind him opened and a bleary-eyed Pepper appeared.

"Oh," she said, "hallo."

"Oh, you're awake, Pep," said Dean. He waved a hand at Nick and Clare. "This is Mad's parents, only she's not here."

At that moment they heard the front door open and Madeleine came up the stairs, carrying a pot plant under each arm.

"Mum, Dad, you're early," she said, putting the plants down on the floor with relief, and giving them each a hug.

"Happy birth-yesterday," said Clare returning the hug. Maddo looked awful, her face was very pale and her eyes stood out huge and dark against the drawn pallor of her skin, but Clare said nothing. Time enough for that later, anyway maybe it was just the effects of burning the candle at both ends.

"Can see you had a good party," Nick said cheerfully.

"Looks awful, doesn't it?" Mad said. "We'll have to have a grand clean-up today, Dino. Oh, hi Pep, didn't see you there. Any sign of Cirelle or Ben yet?" The words flowed out of her, as if she were afraid that something might be asked or said if there were a silence. "You've got a coffee? Great. Think I'll just make myself one, if you don't mind. It's bloody cold out there." She rubbed her hands together as if to prove her point and disappeared into the kitchen.

Reboiling the kettle she gave herself a huge mental shake. She'd entirely forgotten that her parents were coming today, hadn't given them a thought until she'd seen the car parked outside. Now she would have to keep being cheerful and normal all day, and the last thing she felt was cheerful and normal.

"Nice plants," remarked her mother when she went back into the living room. Dean had cleared space on the sofa and spread the blue woollen throw over it again so that Mr and Mrs Richmond had somewhere to sit. Mad perched on the arm, nursing her coffee mug.

"Yes, well, I got them for the neighbours," she admitted. "Like, a sort of peace offering."

"Oh Maddo! I hope you weren't too noisy," cried her mother.

"A bit. Look, Mum, I think I'll just take them round, OK? I shan't be long." Madeleine put down her mug and picking up the two plants disappeared downstairs.

Leaving one plant on her own front step, she went first to the Colbys' with the other.

"Yes?" Gerald Colby's disembodied voice came from the entry phone.

"Mr Colby? It's Madeleine Richmond from next door."

"Is it indeed? What do you want, young lady?" His voice was crisp, but not exactly angry. Mad didn't like being addressed as young lady, but she was on a bridge-building mission so she simply pulled a face at the closed door and said, "I've come to apologise about last night."

"I see, well you'd better come up." The door catch released

with a buzz, and she went in. Gerald was waiting for her in the living room, and as she topped the stairs, Sheila came down from the floor above.

Before either of them could speak Mad extended the plant and said quickly, "I've brought you this from all of us, to say we're very sorry if we disturbed you last night."

"Disturbed!" Sheila Colby almost screeched, "it was a bit more than that!"

"Now, Sheila," Gerald remonstrated gently, "Madeleine's come to apologise."

"Hmm," Sheila said and then went on more calmly, "well, you certainly made the most frightful noise. That music was head-banging!"

"I'm sorry," Mad said again, still holding out the plant. "It was a birthday party, like, a one-off, you know?"

Sheila moved nearer and took the plant, saying with as much grace as she could muster, "Well, thank you for coming to apologise, and for the azalea. I don't suppose you'll be having another party."

Mad made no comment at the last remark, but she hadn't quite finished. She was happy enough, she supposed, to apologise for the noise, but she felt that the Colbys had been over the top, calling the police. "I'm sorry you felt you had to call the police, though," she said. "You could have rung to ask us to turn it down."

"Rung?" exclaimed Sheila. "We did nothing *but* ring, but the phone must have been off the hook. It was always engaged. I was going to come round..."

"But I wouldn't let her," Gerald interrupted, "and then the police turned up. But we didn't call them."

"Oh, I see." Madeleine felt at a loss. "Sorry, I thought it was you. The policeman said it was our neighbours."

"You do have other neighbours," pointed out Gerald.

"It could have been anyone," said Sheila with asperity, "I should think you woke the whole Circle!"

Madeleine decided she'd said all there was to say, "Yeah, well, whatever. We'll try to keep the noise down from now."

Gerald walked down to the door with her. "Don't worry too much about Sheila," he said, "she was upset last night, but she's got over it…or she will have soon!"

Mad went back to her own doorstep and picked up the other azalea. Finding out that it wasn't the dreaded Sheil who had rung the police had rather taken the wind from her sails. It must have been Shirl! Oh well, better get on with it. She rang the bell of number eight. The door opened almost immediately and she was faced with Melanie.

"Oh, it's you," she said. "What do you want?"

"I came to apologise for keeping you awake last night," Madeleine began.

"And so you should," snapped Melanie. "What a bloody racket! You woke the kids, you woke me, you woke my parents and I imagine you woke the entire neighbourhood!"

"Yes, well I'm sorry," began Madeleine again, but Melanie cut her off.

"Well sorry's not good enough, see? None of us got a wink of sleep. Once the kids were awake that was it. It was me who called the police and I'll do it again. It's not so bad for me, I don't really live here, but my parents don't need that sort of bloody noise next door. OK?" Melanie thrust her face at Madeleine, who, stepping back, held out the plant.

"I brought this for your parents. Perhaps you'd give it to them." Melanie almost snatched the plant and then slammed the door, and Mad went home, wishing she'd been able to see one of the Redwoods. Perhaps it would have been better if she'd left it to Cirelle to make peace with them as she worked there, still it was too late now.

When she reached her own living room again, she found Dean and Pepper making some effort to clear the place up. Nick Richmond looked at his watch as she came in. "Look, I've booked a table for one o'clock at the Royal Oak at Belstone

St Andrew," he said. "It'll take us half an hour to get there, we ought to be leaving."

Mad looked round at the half-cleared room, but Pepper said, "Don't worry about this place, Mad, we'll sort it, OK? Ben and Cirelle'll be up soon, OK?"

"Thanks Pep," Mad said gratefully. "I'll just go up and change, Dad, I won't be a minute."

"Maddo," her mother called after her, "we said to ask Dan too, if you wanted to. Is he coming?"

For a moment the question hung in the air and then Madeleine, pausing on the stairs, called back over her shoulder, "No. No thanks, Mum, he isn't." Her footsteps sounded on the stairs, and Nick turned to Dean. "Has something happened?"

Dean looked uncomfortable and said awkwardly, "I don't think they're going out any more," and then he escaped into the kitchen to help Pepper wash up the glasses.

"She'll tell us if she wants to," Clare said softly, while thinking, that must explain why Maddo looks so grey today.

Within minutes Madeleine returned, clothes changed and ready to go out with her parents, and the three of them went downstairs and out to the car. As they were getting in, Shirley came running out of number eight.

"Mad," she called. "Madeleine, thank you so much for the lovely azalea you brought round this morning."

Mad looked awkward. "I'm sorry about the noise," she began, but Shirley interrupted her.

"And *I'm* sorry about the police," she said. "It was only a party after all, and you don't do it every day. It's just that Melanie… well you know how she's been lately. She's a bit highly strung and she over-reacted."

"The police!" echoed Clare faintly, and Shirley, realising she had put her foot in it, went on hurriedly, "So don't think about it any more, Mad. And thank you again for the plant, it's lovely, and David can put it in his garden once it's finished flowering in the house." She smiled at Clare and Nick, who had frozen in the act of getting into the car. "Have a nice day," she said, and bustled back into the house, knowing she'd said too much.

The Richmonds got into the car and drove out of the Circle in silence. As they drove along Dartmouth Road, Nick asked quietly, "What police, Maddo?" He glanced at his daughter's face in the rear-view mirror and said, "You can tell us about it at lunch." For a moment he had to pull in to the side of the road to let a speeding ambulance pass, and he turned round to look at her. "Cheer up, love," he said encouragingly. "Whatever it is, we'll get things sorted."

The Royal Oak was an eighteenth-century coaching inn, long and low with its old stables still at the back, and a garden where it served meals in the summer time. Today the fire was alight in the huge fireplace, and the bar was full of Sunday-lunchtime drinkers. The restaurant was at the far end of the long room and they had to push their way through the crowd to find their table by the window.

Once settled, with drinks ordered, Clare reached out and took Madeleine's hand. "Maddo, darling, you look so unhappy. Is there anything that Dad and I can do?"

Mad shook her head miserably. "No, Mum, thanks. Dan and I split up last night, that's all. I'll get over it once I've got used to it, you know?" Her mother nodded sympathetically. "Poor timing, on your birthday," she hazarded, hoping Mad might say more but not wanting to pry.

"Yeah, well, whatever," shrugged Mad, and it flashed in her mind how odd it was that she could talk so easily to Madge whom she hardly knew, and somehow couldn't to her parents whom she loved dearly.

"Maybe it'll all blow over, whatever it was," suggested Clare, "and you'll get back together again."

"No!" The vehemence of her reply startled both her parents, and they physically drew back and knew not to ask any more. For a moment or two they took refuge in the menu and when the waiter came gave their order.

"What was all this about the police?" Nick asked when the waiter had left them. "What was Shirley Redwood talking about?"

Madeleine gave a sigh. She realised that the question had had to come. "Last night, when we got home from the Dutch, everyone was a bit rowdy. Like, we'd been playing drinking games in the pub, OK? And everyone had had too much. Then we all came back to our place. I'd got in the beer you'd said to buy, you know, and some of the guys brought other stuff as well, and, like, well it got a bit out of hand. The music was very loud, and people were shouting and laughing and stuff, you know."

Nick and Clare could well imagine and were both glad that they hadn't been living next door. "Couldn't *you* have turned it down?" asked Clare. "It was your party after all."

Madeleine had the grace to blush and said, "I wasn't really with it, you know? I'd had a lot of beer. We'd been celebrating the Belchers' win over Loughborough, as well." She paused and took a sip of water. "Anyway, Shirl's daughter, the one who's a bit doolally, she rang the police and complained and they arrived in a car. The door was open and they just walked in. I was asleep on the sofa, and the first I knew was when they switched off the music. I woke up then, and there they were in the living room. They said they'd had a complaint and could they look around. Some of the guys had been smoking pot I think. Anyway, they went upstairs… "

"Who went upstairs?" interrupted Nick. "The police?"

"Yes, they said they smelt cannabis and wanted to look around."

"And you let them? You didn't have to, you know?"

"I didn't think, Dad," Mad said miserably. "Like, they were there, OK, and were, well just looking. Anyway, they went upstairs and found Dan with Chantal Haven, the kid that lives at number four."

"Kid! How old?"

"I don't know, Mum, but they'd been together in Charlie's room." Clare remembered the stripped bed and the open window and suddenly understood. "Did they arrest him?" she asked. "She must be under age."

Mad shook her head. "No, I don't think so, he just left. Lots of people did, like, just slid away, you know. The police didn't try and stop them, just the policewoman took Chantal home."

"And no one was arrested or anything?"

"No, they warned us, like, you know, that if we made any more noise, they'd take away the stereo equipment, but the party was over then and everyone went home."

"So you all went to bed."

"I didn't," Mad replied. "I was too upset, I couldn't sleep." She thought back to the moment when the police had gone.

"So what did you do?" prompted her mother.

Madeleine shrugged. "Went upstairs, cleared up Charlie's room. That's where they'd been, not my room."

"Where was Charlie?" asked Clare. "Wasn't she at the party?"

"No. She's had to go home for a few days. There's some sort of family panic, I'm not sure what. Anyway, I cleared up in there and then, well, I don't know...I dozed a bit on the sofa. When I woke up I had a bath and went out. Mrs Peters, at number one? She was awake and sitting in her window, like she does. She waved and called me in for a cup of tea. I stayed there a bit and then I went into town. I went up by the cathedral. There was a service on, and I went in the back and just, like, sat there."

Nick and Clare exchanged surprised glances. Madeleine wasn't known for going into cathedrals, as she'd often been heard to remark, "I don't *do* church!"

"The music was lovely," she went on, unaware of their glances. "When it was finished I got the plants from that garden shop round there and came home. I looked up to show Madge that I'd got the plants for next door, but she was asleep. Then I saw your car was here..."

"And remembered that we were coming to take you out for lunch!" smiled her mother.

Mad grinned ruefully. "Yeah, well, whatever. Sorry, Mum.

I am pleased to see you both, really I am. It's just that so much has happened. Do you think the police will come back?"

"I can't see why they should," Nick said reassuringly. "The party's over. They must get dozens of calls like that at a weekend, it was pretty routine for them. But," he looked across at his daughter, "if they do come again, and want to search the house for some reason, don't let them in without a warrant, give me a call and by the time they've got one, I'll be there."

"Thanks, Dad." Madeleine smiled at him. "You're the best."

When the food arrived Madeleine found herself surprisingly hungry, and realised that she hadn't really eaten since yesterday lunchtime, and with Nick and Clare being determinedly cheerful, they got through the meal and found that despite everything, they'd all quite enjoyed themselves.

As they went out into the car park, they heard a voice behind them in the bar. Mad spun round, and at her reaction her parents looked round as well. Dan was at the bar, a pint in his hand, with a small group of friends. For a moment his eyes met Mad's, and then slid away. Mad, her head held erect, turned away and, linking her arms through those of her parents, walked steadily out of the door to the car.

When they arrived back at the Madhouse, they found it had been completely cleared. There was no sign of the party, and not even the kitchen had its usual clutter of washing up and unwrapped food. Cirelle and Dean were drinking tea in the living room.

Madeleine offered her parents tea as well, but Nick shook his head. "I think we'll be making tracks," he said, now he was sure that Madeleine wasn't going to be in the house on her own, and he and Clare left her with her friends.

"Thanks for doing all the clearing up," Mad said, collecting herself a mug of tea from the kitchen and dropping down on to the sofa. "Sorry you got stuck with it all, but I'd forgotten all about my parents, you know?"

"Yeah, no probs," Cirelle said cheerfully. "Pepper helped as well."

"Where's Ben?" Mad asked.

"Working," Dean answered. "Had a lunchtime shift at the Dutch. Wasn't that really weird, him being with Mrs Hammond? Couldn't believe my eyes when they came upstairs. I mean, she's old!"

"Not really. About thirty, not that much older than Ben anyway," Cirelle pointed out.

Dean shrugged. "Whatever. Still seems weird to me."

At that moment the front door opened and they heard Ben coming in. He went into his own room first and then came up the stairs to the living room.

"Hi," he said laconically. "Any tea?" He went into the kitchen and reappeared with a steaming mug. He looked at the other three and said without preamble, "I'm afraid I'm going to be moving out."

This was greeted with amazement. "Moving out!" echoed Mad, "why?"

"Decided to take that room Joe's offered me at the pub," Ben replied. "You've had the rent for this term, Mad. I'm afraid you'll have to find someone else for next, OK?"

Mad shrugged. "I suppose so, if that's what you've decided. But why, Ben? Why have you suddenly changed your mind?"

Ben looked at her with mild exasperation. "Christ, Mad," he said. "Why do you think?"

"Because of last night," Mad said flatly.

"Yeah. You all saw Jill last night. We'd been seeing each other for some time, but that's all over now. He husband was outside last night and saw us together, so...well, it just seems easier if we aren't neighbours and don't keep bumping into each other, you know?"

"But surely..." began Mad.

"Sorry, Mad," Ben said firmly, "but I'm moving out. I talked to Joe today. It's all arranged. I'll move my stuff tomorrow."

Silence fell and then Mad said softly, "Not one of our more successful evenings, was it? Did you know it was Melanie

Whatsit from next door who called the police, not old Colby after all?"

Cirelle nodded. "Yeah," she said ruefully, "I went round to take Todd out as usual, and Melanie told me she didn't want me to help any more."

"But that's ridiculous!" cried Mad. "What has last night got to do with whether you help with the children or not? How *stupid*!"

Cirelle shrugged. "She said she was leaving anyway. Said she didn't want *my* help with *her* children, like I was contaminated in some way? Said I'd been trying to steal Todd away from her. Like, I'd been trying to make him love me more than her or some such shit?"

"Excuse me?" Mad interjected. "She said what?"

Cirelle shrugged. "Anyway, she's going back home and good riddance! Her husband's changed his job or something, so he won't be away from home so much. She told me to get lost. I told her to piss off!"

"Cirelle," Dean exploded with laughter, "that's not like you!"

"That's how I felt," she said laughing too. "I should think David'll be over the moon she's going, she's been a real pain and he hasn't found it at all easy with them all living there."

"Tell you something else," Dean said suddenly. "I think that old biddy, Madge Thingy, was taken into hospital today."

"What!" cried Mad. "Madge? When? I only saw her this morning. She was OK then. Are you sure?"

"Don't know anything for sure," admitted Dean, "but soon after you'd gone with your parents an ambulance arrived. The doctor from opposite was there and they all went inside the house and came out with a stretcher."

"But that's awful," Mad exclaimed. "I had a cup of tea with her this morning. She wasn't ill then. Who'll know where they've taken her?"

Dean shrugged. "The doctor I suppose. It was the woman."

"Dr Fran, that's what she's called," Cirelle said. "She comes in to see Melanie sometimes. Why don't you go over and ask her? She's sure to know."

"Yeah." Mad thought for a moment. "Yeah, I think I will."

She went at once and having glanced at the dark windows of Madge's house, she knocked on the doctor's front door. Fran answered and invited Mad inside.

"I'm sorry to trouble you, Doctor," Mad said, "but I heard Mrs Peters has been taken to hospital and I wondered which one. I'd like to go and visit her."

Fran led her into the study. "I'm sorry, but I'm afraid what you've heard isn't quite right." She smiled sadly at Madeleine. "I'm afraid Madge died this morning."

"She what?" whispered Mad. "Oh no. She can't have. I was with her this morning, she wasn't ill. She was fine."

"She passed away very peacefully," Fran said, and seeing the effect that her words were having on Mad, she put a sympathetic arm around her shoulders. "Just went to sleep in her chair and didn't wake up. The best possible way, you know." She paused, allowing Mad to take in the news, then she said, "I know you used to pop in and see her from time to time, she always enjoyed your visits you know." She thought for a moment. "I wonder if you could do me a big favour."

Mad looked at her blankly, still thinking of her visit to Madge's that morning. There had been no sign then that death was hovering in the background. Madge had been fine then, alert and sympathetic, full of sensible advice. Mad stared at the doctor, almost overcome by her sudden sense of loss.

"I just wondered," continued Dr Fran gently, "it's Spike you see, the cat? Andrew has asked me to look after him until he can find another home for him. I just wondered if you'd be prepared to take him in for a couple of days, just until something is sorted out for him."

Mad's eyes refocused and she said, "Spike! Poor Spike. He will miss her."

"So could you look after him for a few days? I know Andrew would be very grateful."

"He may not want to come to our house," pointed out Mad.

"No, well if he doesn't, I'll give you a key and perhaps you could go into his house and feed him there, but it's worth a try don't you think?"

Mad shrugged. "Suppose so," she said.

Together they went across to the dark, silent house opposite, and Fran let them in. As they went upstairs, Spike appeared on the landing, mewing piteously. He rubbed himself against Mad's legs and she picked him up. The miaows changed to purrs as he snuggled against her.

"He obviously likes you," Fran said. "Will you give it a go?"

"Yes," Mad agreed, "yes, of course, but I'll start off feeding him here. He can't get in or out of my house, there's no cat flap."

When she got home at last she told the others about Madge and the cat, and they told her that Charlie had phoned from Ireland. Cirelle said, "Charlie rang. She says she'll be back at the end of the week."

"How's her sister?"

"Out of danger, but still in hospital, so she's staying to be with her parents until Friday. She said not to worry about her, things are fine. She certainly sounded more cheerful than usual."

I wish things were fine here, thought Mad sadly, as she went upstairs reluctantly to do some long overdue work. At least concentrating on an essay might help take her mind off other things. But the events of the weekend hung round her like grey mist and she did no work at all.

## Chapter Twenty-Two

Angela Haven sat in her kitchen and stared at the police-woman who had come to see her.

"You see, Mrs Haven, if Chantal is only fifteen as you say, this man Dan has committed an offence. She's under age."

"Yes, I see," Angela said bleakly. She was shattered by the suggestions that the policewoman made, Chantal in bed with one of the students. How could she? And yet a tiny voice at the back of her brain told her that it was true. Chantal, in her mini skirts or tight jeans, was so immature in so many ways, trying to be streetwise. Aware of her growing sexuality, yet unable to deal with its manifestations, she might well have got herself into such a position. "Did you talk to Chantal about this when you...found them?" Angela asked.

"I asked her how old she was," said WPC Ford, "and she told me she was seventeen. I didn't really believe her, but I had no way of disproving it. The man concerned had made himself scarce, so he obviously knew she was a minor. They'd been smoking pot."

"Pot? Oh my God!"

"To be honest, Mrs Haven, I don't think Chantal realised it wasn't an ordinary cigarette," admitted WPC Ford. "The man, Dan, had given it to her. It may be one of the reasons she had sex with him."

Had sex with him. How bald those words sounded, no question of making love, no emotional involvement, just had sex.

"You mean it was this thing, date rape?"

"Not exactly, no, but I expect she was more relaxed about it that she otherwise might have been." The policewoman got to her feet.

"What will happen now?" Angela asked. "What will happen to Chantal?"

"Nothing for the moment," WPC Ford replied. "I shall report back and things will go from there. It's not Chantal who has broken the law."

When the policewoman had gone, Angela sat in the kitchen and tried to come to terms with what she'd heard. She felt angry and guilty at the same time. Angry with Chantal, how could she have behaved like that? Angry with Ian, if he hadn't walked out none of this would have happened, Chantal would have had both her parents to watch over her. But mostly guilty. She should have been there more for Chantal. She should have seen the signs. She should have kept a tighter control, been stricter about times of going out and being home. If she hadn't gone out last night, and then stayed over, she might have prevented it all. She would have known that Chantal was late and taken steps to find her. She shouldn't have left it to Annabel. She'd have gone round to the student house and fetched her home. Now she had two daughters who were in trouble and she knew it was all her fault. She should have been there for them and taken better care of them.

Another voice inside said that was ridiculous, that she'd done all she could, that she had to go out to work to keep the family going, that other young teenage girls wore outrageous clothes, short skirts, tight jeans and skimpy tops, without ending up in bed with young men who knew they were under age. She heard this voice, but it brought her no comfort, she knew she should have recognised the signs.

Then another thought hit her, suppose Chantal was pregnant too. The bubble of happiness to which she had awakened this morning had burst with a vengeance, and a grey cloud enveloped her. She felt suddenly exhausted, as if there was a great weight on her shoulders. What the hell would Ian say when he heard this latest? She'd have to tell him, once she'd faced Chantal with it.

Ian. For a moment she allowed him to drift to the forefront of her mind. Two months ago he had telephoned and asked her out for a drink.

"Just need to have a chat about a few things," he said casually, but Angela's heart sank. He was going to ask her for a divorce at last. What would she say? Yes, she supposed. After all, there was no going back, and she was beginning to get used to being without him. It still hurt, but she had to be realistic, even if she blocked the divorce now, he would get it in the long run, all he had to do was wait.

Dignity. That's what she needed, she decided. She would accept his suggestion that the separation became formalised with dignity, and not allow him to see how much he could still hurt her.

They arranged to meet in a quiet pub near the cathedral. Ian had offered to come and pick her up, but Angela had refused.

"No," she said. "I don't want the girls to see us going out together. It might send out the wrong signals. I want everything finally sorted before we have to bring them into it any more."

"Whatever you say," Ian agreed, but she had him worried. He had decided to tell her that Desirée had left. He knew there could be no instant reinstatement into his family, he had forfeited the right to be there through his own stupidity, and he had long ago realised his mistake. Now he wanted to discover if there was any way, some time in the future, that perhaps they might repair the damage he had caused, perhaps pick up the pieces and try again. Because Annabel had discovered that Desirée had left him, he would have to make a move, and sooner rather than later, for he knew it was unfair to expect her to keep his secret for too long. Now, however, Angela was talking of "finally sorting things out". It sounded as if she had made up her mind and was going to ask for a divorce at last. She sounded so calm and distant as they made the arrangement to meet. Maybe he shouldn't tell her about Desirée leaving after all, should just accept that his actions had brought about the end of their marriage and that it was already too late to pick up any pieces.

He was waiting in the bar when Angela arrived. She was late, because she had changed her clothes three times before she was satisfied with what she was wearing. Finally, she settled for a smart navy trouser suit. It was one of the few things that she had bought since he had left. It was well cut and she felt good in it. It would give her confidence. She had swept her hair back off her face, which emphasised the line of her cheek bones, applied make-up carefully and having surveyed herself in the mirror decided that she would do.

"Where are you off to?" Annabel asked as Angela looked in to say goodbye.

"Meeting," Angela said succinctly. "Shan't be late. Bye!"

Chantal took even less notice of her leaving, glued to her favourite soap on the television. Her eyes never left the screen, she simply waved a hand over the back of the sofa in farewell.

Ian got up as she joined him at the table. He didn't kiss her cheek, or even touch her hand in greeting, he simply smiled at her and said, "Hi." She settled herself opposite him and he went on, "What would you like to drink, the usual?"

"Yes please, scotch and ginger." That would surprise him, thought the part of her that was watching the whole scene from outside, she'd always drunk gin and tonic, because he did. Since his departure she had changed her preference to scotch and ginger... a small piece of juvenile defiance!

Ian got her a large one without comment, though he wondered what other little things had changed in his absence, and a usual, much-needed, gin for himself. Carrying them back to the table he considered how he should start their conversation. He had rehearsed several openings to himself at home, but seeing her sitting there, so cool, calm and confident, his own confidence deserted him. He put the drinks down on the table and then sat down himself. For a moment, they sat in silence, and Angela sipped her drink. She wasn't going to help him, she had decided. If he wanted a divorce, he was going to have to ask for it himself. She wouldn't make life difficult for him, but she sure as hell wasn't going to make it easy either. Dignity. Dignity would prevail.

"How are the girls?" he asked at last.

"Fine," Angela replied. "I know they would have sent their love if they'd known I was coming to meet you."

"Where do they think you are?" he enquired.

"At a meeting," she replied. "They didn't query it. They've got used to the fact that I have to go out or work late some evenings."

"Mmm, I suppose they have." Ian looked across at her. Silence fell again. They were getting nowhere. He must take the plunge. He took a deep breath and said, "Angela, we must talk."

"Yes, you said on the phone."

"Yes, well we must." He rubbed his cheek with his hand, as if massaging his face. Angela readily recognised this unconscious sign of uncertainty. "It's just, well I don't quite know how to put this."

"If you've something to say, you'd better get on and spit it out," Angela said coolly. She put down her glass and looked him in the eye across the table. "For God's sake, get on with it, Ian."

"Yes, I'm sorry. It isn't easy."

"Then I'd better say it for you," said Angela tersely. "You and Desirée have decided you want to get married, and so you want a divorce as soon as possible. Don't worry, I won't stand in your way..." Her voice trailed away as she saw him shaking his head as if in disbelief. "Well," she rejoined sharply, "isn't that what this is all about?"

"No," Ian said quietly, "it isn't."

Dignity! she thought, keep your dignity. So she said nothing and waited for him to explain exactly why they *were* there.

"Angela, I have something to tell you. Annabel knows already. I didn't tell her, she found out by chance, but now she knows it is only fair that you should know too." He smiled wryly. "I no longer live with Desirée. We've split up. She's moved on."

Angela stared at him in disbelief. "What are you saying?" she asked.

"I'm saying that there is no Desirée in my life any more, and that I wish there never had been."

"Why? I mean, why are you telling me this?"

"Because it concerns you the most. You are still my wife. The girls are still my children."

"Didn't suit you to remember that when you wanted Desirée, did it?" said Angela, bitterly.

"If you want me to say that I'm sorry, I will," began Ian.

"It's a bit late for that, don't you think?" Angela snapped.

For a moment, Ian didn't answer, then he said, "Did you come here tonight to ask me for a divorce? Is that what you meant when you said that things should be finally sorted out?"

The question threw her and she glowered at him. "No," she admitted at last, "but I assumed we had reached the stage when you wanted it and we were going to have to discuss divorce. After all we can't really go on as we are, can we?"

"So, what shall we do? Do you want a divorce?"

She looked at him for a long moment, as if considering. "No," she said finally, "not at the moment, but if you think you can come waltzing back into our lives simply because your mistress has deserted you, you've got another—"

"I don't," Ian interrupted. "I promise you I never thought that."

"So, what *did* you think?"

"I thought I would ask you if, one day, you might ever forgive me for what I did to you and the girls," he said simply.

Angela felt the tears pricking her eyes, and she blinked them away. "Oh Ian, I don't know. It's too late. Too late to go back to how we were. We're not even the same people any more."

"I know that," he agreed, "I'm not asking you to turn the clock back. I'm not asking for me to come back home, either. I'm just asking if I can see you sometimes, for a drink, or for dinner. Is that too much to ask?"

"I don't know," Angela repeated.

"Is there someone else?" he asked tentatively. "Someone else you're seeing?"

Angela sighed. "No," she said, "there's no one else." She stood up abruptly. "I'm sorry, Ian," she said distractedly, "I can't discuss this any more now. I have to go home."

He got to his feet as well. "Can I phone you?" he asked. "Please?" She looked at him for a long time and then said, "Call me at work. I don't want any speculation on the part of the girls." And she walked out of the pub into the night.

It was several days before he rang, and during those days she had thought of little but Ian, and what he had said. Could they possibly get back together again? They were certainly different people from the couple who had married all those years ago. After the hurt and the upheaval, could they really rebuild their marriage? It would be a risk and she didn't know if it would be worth taking it. She had held out against divorce in the hope that Ian might one day come to his senses, and now that he had, she wasn't certain if it was what she wanted after all. How would the girls feel? Would they welcome him back with open arms, or would they feel that his betrayal and desertion had been too great to forgive? She knew they still loved him, but would they be able to accept him back into the family again? One thing was for sure, if there were any moves in that direction they would be made very slowly.

When he did phone, it was to ask her out for a meal. Would she join him for dinner one night this week? She was free every night, but she wasn't going to tell him that. She hummed and ha-ed and then agreed to Thursday, and pleading another evening meeting to the girls, left the house feeling an inner turmoil, as if she were going to meet an illicit lover.

The evening had been a success. They had not discussed the things that lay between them, those were not on the agenda. They talked about a play they both wanted to see, about how Annabel was getting on at the college, Chantal at Chapmans, incidents at work, normal everyday things that any couple might discuss. They found they were laughing a good deal, just like they used to, and when the evening was over, they parted easily.

"When I come for the girls at the weekend as arranged," Ian said, "may I come in?"

"If you want to," Angela replied.

After their first date, they met often. They met as they used to in the old days, going for a walk by the river, meeting for a quick drink after work, or at lunchtime. They went to an organ recital in the cathedral, and once even went to the zoo. They grew more relaxed in each other's company, but Ian realised that nothing could be hurried. He knew that he was on trial, that he must woo his wife, as he had before, but he became more and more determined that they should try to start their married life again. She allowed him to kiss her cheek in greeting and at parting, but that was as near as she would let him come. Every time he saw her, he ached to take her in his arms, to beg her forgiveness and ask her to take him back, but he was terrified if he moved too quickly she would back off, and decide that she had learned to live without him.

Angela held on to her dignity and her pride, determined to keep him at arm's length until she knew how she really felt, but she was beginning to think there might be some future for them if Ian really wanted to try again. He came to her with the same freshness that he had when they had first met, he made her laugh, she could talk to him or be silent without awkwardness, but most of all, he still had the ability to stir her, so that her heart pounded when she caught sight of him, when he touched her hand, when his face was lit by his smile.

He had, with great difficulty, got tickets for the play they had both wanted to see, but they were for a Saturday evening. Normally they didn't meet on Saturdays because that was the day the girls often spent with their father. However, after a little persuasion, Angela gave in, and agreed to go.

"I'm going to the theatre with some friends from the office," she told her daughters. "I won't be very late I don't expect."

"Can I go out too?" Chantal had asked. "It's Mad's birthday on Saturday, and I've been asked over for a drink."

"I should think so," Angela agreed. "Just one glass of wine now, Chantal, OK? Are you going too, Annabel?"

Annabel shook her head. "Doubt it," she said. "I've got this essay to finish for Monday."

So Angela had left them to it, and had met Ian at the theatre door, filled with the same glow of happiness as she'd had when they were first engaged. She had made her decision in the past few days. If Ian wanted to come back, and the girls wanted him, then she would give it a try. She wasn't sure how she was going to tell him, he had never asked her outright to take him back, but she knew that was what he wanted, and she knew she wanted it too. She had never stopped loving him, and she was now able to admit the fact, to herself and to him.

All through the play she wondered how to approach him. Should she make him ask, or should she do the asking, and tell him she wanted him as much as he wanted her? What about the precious dignity she'd been so carefully preserving?

In the end, it was surprisingly easy. They had a drink in the interval, in the crowded theatre bar, and as he raised his glass to her, she held out her hand and said, "I want you to come home, Ian. Will you?"

For a moment, he stared at her and then a look of joy suffused his face, and taking her glass from her set down both the drinks and gathered her into his arms. He crushed her against him and murmured into her hair, "Oh my darling, I swear to you, you will never regret it."

There were some mildly surprised looks from other people in

the bar, but neither of them was aware of those. Very gently Ian kissed her, and then released her and said softly, "Do you want to see the second half?"

Angela smiled and shook her head. He took her hand and together they left the theatre, and once they were safely outside in the anonymous darkness of the street, he gathered her to him again and whispered huskily, "Oh, my darling, I want you so much!"

"Where shall we go?" Angela asked, her voice equally unsteady, "not your place or mine!"

"To a hotel, come on. We'll check in to the White Bear."

"But we've no luggage," Angela protested, laughing.

"I don't need luggage, I just need you."

They went to the hotel in the centre of town and Ian checked them in. Angela stood apart as he did so, feeling the eyes of the receptionist on her, and imagining her thinking, well I suppose Haven makes a change from Smith.

They were given their key and made their way to the room. Once inside with the door locked, they stood for a moment looking at each other and then Angela said softly, "Welcome home Ian."

Later, much later, they lay in each other's arms. "I ought to go," murmured Angela. "The girls will be wondering where I am."

"Don't go! Stay the night," Ian urged. "You can phone them, tell them you'll be back in the morning."

"I can't," laughed Angela. "Where on earth should I tell them I am? I'm supposed to be at the theatre, with friends!"

"Tell them you've had too much to drink to drive home," suggested Ian, beginning to massage her back. "Tell them you're staying with the friends and that you'll be back in the morning. Let's face it, if you leave now you'll only confirm the receptionist's worst fears!" He kissed her again, and as he felt her yielding he added softly, "After all, we're going to tell them tomorrow anyway, let's just have tonight for ourselves."

Angela gave in and made the call. "I'll be back first thing in the morning," she told Annabel. "See you then." She hadn't asked if Chantal was safely home, Chantal hadn't been on her mind.

It was a night of rediscovery, and when they finally left the White Bear the next morning, both of them knew that their marriage was being given a second chance.

"Come round this afternoon," Angela said, "and we'll tell the girls together."

"Is that the best way to do it?" Ian wasn't sure. "You don't think you ought to sound them out first, do you? Supposing they don't want me back?"

"They will, especially when they see that we both want it," Angela reassured him. "They never stopped loving you as their dad, you know. They may take a little while to get used to it, that's all."

So it was arranged, and Angela drove home in a haze of happiness. She let herself into the silent house, no sound or movement from upstairs, and she decided to let them have their lie-in, she would tell them the great news when they finally surfaced, in the meantime she hugged it to herself.

The ring on the doorbell, and the arrival of WPC Ford with her devastating news, had brought Angela down to earth with a bump, and now she had to face Chantal and find out exactly what had happened while she, Angela, had been in the arms of her husband.

Gone was any thought of allowing the girls to have their Sunday lie-in. Angela went upstairs into Chantal's bedroom and drew back the curtains, allowing sunlight to flood into the room. For a moment she looked at her daughter, asleep in bed, one arm round her favourite teddy bear, the other flung back over her head. She looked so young, so vulnerable, that Angela knew a moment's rage that anyone should have violated her innocence. Her fists were clenched so tightly in fury, that her nails dug into the palms of her hands, and if Dan Whoever-he-was had been there at that precise moment, she might well have punched him in the face.

Consciously she made herself relax, and then she reached out and shook her daughter awake. Chantal muttered and kept her eyes firmly closed, but Angela wasn't giving up. "Chantal!" she said loudly. "Chantal, wake up. Wake up and get up. I need to talk to you."

Chantal opened her eyes, and screwed them shut again against the bright light. "Mum," she muttered, "what time is it? It's Sunday."

"I know it's Sunday," Angela replied briskly, "but I need to talk to you. I'm going downstairs to make some coffee. Put your dressing gown on and come down straightaway."

There was something in the tone of her voice that brought Chantal wide awake, and as Angela left the room, Chantal had the sinking feeling that she knew what her mother wanted to talk about. But how could she? Annabel wouldn't have said anything. They'd agreed last night when that awful police-woman left that it was better that Mum knew nothing about it.

"After all," Chantal pointed out, "I'm all right. I had a bit much to drink, that's all, and I just let Dan go too far."

"How far?" demanded Annabel.

Chantal reddened. "All the way," she muttered. Then she looked up at her sister defiantly, and added, "And I liked it."

That wasn't exactly true. She'd enjoyed the kissing and cuddling, and Dan had awakened and introduced her body to all manner of delicious sensations, but when it had come to the actual sex bit, the pushing and pumping, and the mess between her legs afterwards, she hadn't really liked it at all. Still, it was done now, she thought philosophically, and it would probably be better next time. She'd get used to that bit even if there didn't seem to be much in it for her, but at the moment she felt in sudden need of a bath.

What worried her more was the arrival of the policewoman, and the recollection of the look on her face as she'd found them in an untidy heap on Charlie's bed. The way Dan had scrambled into his boxer shorts and grabbed at his jeans had made her feel cheap. She knew instinctively that he hadn't wanted to be caught with her, that she meant nothing to him and he wanted to escape.

"But I thought Dan was Mad's boyfriend," Annabel was saying.

"He was," Chantal agreed, and added with bravado, "now, he isn't, he's mine."

"I doubt it," Annabel said discouragingly. "It was probably just a one-night stand."

"You're a fine one to talk," snapped Chantal, and though Chantal was defensive, Annabel was honest enough to know that she had no right to comment on her sister's behaviour. She shrugged her shoulders and said, "So what happens now?"

"Nothing," Chantal said with more confidence than she felt. "If you don't tell Mum, there's no need for her to know. Then she won't be upset. And after all I never told about Scott Manders, did I?"

"No." Annabel had to agree that Chantal had kept her promise there. "OK, well I won't say anything, but for God's sake be careful, Chantal. It would finish Mum if you got pregnant too."

"I know," Chantal agreed. She gave Annabel a wan smile and said, "Right now I want a bath," and she knew in her heart that it wasn't only her body that felt dirty. She sat in the hot water and scrubbed herself all over, and then lay back in the warmth to relax before going to bed, but even so, somehow she still didn't feel quite clean.

Now she crawled out of bed and pulled on her clothes. The events of the evening came flooding back to her and she felt sick inside. She remembered again the face of the police-woman as she'd come into the bedroom and found her on the bed with Dan collapsed across her, and the feeling of bravado she had maintained last night with both the policewoman and Annabel, but now she slid into a trough of self-disgust. How had she let it all happen? She remembered that he'd been waiting for her outside the bathroom, but the rest seemed confused. Slowly she got out of bed, feeling as if a heavy weight rested on her shoulders, and now she had to face Mum, who seemed to know...what?

She went into the bathroom, and found that at least one of her fears had been extremely short-lived, for, as she sat on the loo she discovered that her period had started. The relief was overwhelming!

Feeling slightly better now that that particular fear had dissolved, she got ready to go downstairs. She felt, somehow, that she would be at a disadvantage if she faced Mum in her nightie, so she pulled on her clothes before she went down to find out how much her mother knew about what. Angela was sitting in the living room with the coffee pot and two mugs in front of her.

"Sit down, Chantal."

Chantal sat.

"Now I want you to tell me where you were last night, and who you were with."

This seemed to Chantal to be a dangerous opening, but she reached for her mug of coffee and said as lightly as possible, "I told you. It was Mad Richmond's birthday. I went round for a drink."

"Where?" demanded Angela. "Where did you go for this drink?"

Oh, shit, thought Chantal, she must have seen Mrs Hammond. "Just to the pub for a quick one." Her eyes slid away. "I drank Coke, that's all."

"Is it?" Angela said flatly. "Then what happened?"

Chantal wondered how much Angela knew about the events in Dartmouth Circle last night. It didn't really matter, she'd know the main part soon enough from everyone else. What she might not know was what Chantal herself had been doing. Not many people knew that, and none of those would be likely to discuss it with Mum. She decided on the edited version. "There was a party, at the Madhouse. It was a bit noisy, and someone, probably old Ma Colby, called the police."

"And?" prompted Angela.

"And they came. They turned off the music and so everyone went home. Mum," Chantal realised that she must find out, "what is all this about?"

"It's about a visit I've had from the police this morning," replied Angela. "It's about the fact that they found you in bed with some student called Dan. It's about the fact that you'd been smoking hash. It's about the fact that I trusted you to go round to friends and you…you…Chantal, how could you? How could you behave like that? You're only fifteen. Supposing you're pregnant as well!"

"I'm not," said Chantal flatly.

"What?"

"I'm not pregnant," Chantal said. "I came on this morning."

"Well thank God for that," Angela said in heartfelt tones. "But that doesn't make things much better. You're under age. This Dan, whoever he is, may well be prosecuted for what he did. You lied to the police, you're in big trouble. It may all come to court."

She had finally got through Chantal's defences. The girl went pale. "Court?" she echoed. "I told them I was seventeen. That woman believed me!"

"No, she didn't," sighed Angela. "That's why she came round here this morning, to check up with me."

"And you told her?" Chantal said incredulously.

"She asked me your age. I told her. Why should I lie? I didn't know *you* had, did I?"

"And I might have to go to court?"

"I don't know," admitted Angela. "Maybe." She looked across at her daughter. "Oh Chantal, what on earth happened? How did you get into such a situation?" She blinked hard, but the tears that had been threatening ever since the conversation had begun finally overflowed and ran down her face.

Chantal began to cry too. "I'm sorry, Mum. Really. I did have a drink, when we were at the pub. I had rum and Coke, I thought it was just Coke at first and then, well there was a crowd of us having a good time and it didn't seem to matter. I mean, like, even Mrs Hammond was there, it was just a laugh. Then we went back to Mad's for a party and, like, well it just sort of happened."

At that moment, Annabel came downstairs and found them both in tears.

"Mum? Chantal? What's happened?"

"The police came round," Chantal cried. And Annabel knew then that her mother knew everything. For a moment she felt helpless, she looked at them both sobbing and knew she couldn't cope on her own. With sudden resolution she crossed to the phone and dialled her father's number.

"Dad? It's Annabel."

"Hello, Polly. This is a nice surprise." Ian wondered if Angela had changed her mind and decided to tell the girls what was happening before he arrived.

"Dad, can you come round? Mum needs you."

"Polly? What's the matter? What's happened?"

"Dad, just come," Annabel said, and was relieved to hear him say, "I'm on my way," before the line went dead.

"Dad's coming," she said.

When Ian arrived in Dartmouth Circle, he found a very sub-dued family waiting for him. It was clear that the girls didn't know anything about him and Angela getting back together. He walked up into the living room, and Chantal flung herself into his arms crying, "Daddy, I'm sorry, I'm sorry!" He held her close and looked over her shoulder first to Angela and then to Annabel. Neither of them spoke. He gave his attention back to Chantal.

"Come on, love," he said soothingly as she continued to weep on his shoulder. "It can't be that bad, whatever it is. Let's sit down and you must tell me what all this is about, eh?" He led Chantal to the sofa and sat her down next to him, still holding her hand. "Now then," he said and looked expectantly at them all.

It was clear that Chantal wasn't going to explain, so as quietly and unemotionally as she could manage, Angela told him what had happened, finishing up by saying, "It's my fault. If I'd been at home myself it would never have happened. I'd have gone over to the party and fetched her home."

"No, Angela, it is not your fault," Ian said firmly. "Chantal lied to you about where she was going. She knows she shouldn't be drinking, and she certainly knows she shouldn't be going to bed with anyone. Any blame for what has happened is entirely hers."

Chantal turned on him. "That's not fair! You never said anything like that to Annabel, and she's pregnant!"

"You don't know what I said to Annabel," Ian replied briskly, "and it has nothing to do with you, or with the present situation." He glanced across at Angela. "And I am not letting your mother blame herself for something that is entirely your doing." He spoke to Angela before she could protest and said, "Even if you had been here, you wouldn't have known what Chantal was doing."

"I'd have realised she must be at the party, and I gather that could be heard all over the Circle."

"I doubt if you'd have gone and got her, even so. You'd have waited for her to come home and given her a rocket then. It was not your fault." He could see he hadn't really convinced her, so he went on, "All we can do now is wait and see what happens. We'll just have to hope that the police don't take any further action."

"And if they do?" asked Chantal tearfully.

"If they do, we'll deal with it when the time comes. In the meantime, we want a promise from you, young lady, that you will have nothing else to do with the students over the road, is that understood?" When Chantal merely nodded he repeated, "Is that understood, Chantal?"

"Yes, Daddy." But her look was mutinous.

"Good," he said, ignoring the look. "Now, your mum and I have something to tell you."

"Ian, I'm not sure now's the time," Angela began.

"I am," he said firmly. "It's definitely the time. The next few months aren't going to be easy, one way and another. We need to be a family again." He stood up and looked at each of his daughters. "Polly, Chantal. I have behaved very badly to you and to Mum. I know it and I'm very sorry. I want to ask you if you can forgive me, and if I can come home again." Both girls stared at him and then looked across at Angela.

"What does Mum say?" Annabel asked quietly.

Angela smiled. "Dad and I have done some serious talking. We've been seeing each other..."

"Seeing each other? Like on a date?" interrupted Chantal angrily. "Without telling us?"

"Yes," Angela admitted, "like on a date. We didn't tell you in case things didn't work out."

"And have they?" demanded Chantal. "Where's Desirée? What's happened to her then?"

"She's gone," Ian said.

"Well I wish she'd never come," Chantal said fiercely.

"So do I," her father said. "I wish I'd never set eyes on her."

"I suppose Mum was with you last night," Chantal muttered angrily.

"Yes, she was," Ian admitted. "It was when she finally agreed to let me come home."

"She stayed the night with you, didn't she?"

"Chantal..." began Angela.

"She did," Ian answered coolly. "It's when we started our life together again."

"So does this mean you're coming back to live with us here?" demanded Chantal.

"If you'll have me," he answered.

"Mum?" Annabel looked again to her mother.

Angela moved over to Ian and took his hand, then she turned to her daughters, her eyes shining. "I want it more than anything in the world," she said simply.

Annabel hugged both her parents. "I'm so glad," she kept saying, "I'm so glad."

Chantal stayed where she was on the sofa and shrugged. "I don't mind," she said, "as long as you don't push off again."

Ian took her hands in his and looking her straight in the eye said, "That is one thing I can promise you. I will never willingly leave any of you again."

"So, when are you coming home then?" Chantal still spoke belligerently.

"Next weekend? When I've packed up my things and sorted the flat? Would that be all right?" He and Angela had decided to give the girls a week to get used to the idea of his return, before he actually moved back into the house.

"I think you should come now," Annabel said. "Today. I'll come and help you pack some stuff this afternoon if you like. We can do the rest another day."

Ian looked at Angela and his heart turned over at the love he saw in her eyes. "Take Annabel and get your stuff," Angela told him. "Chantal and I will be waiting here when you get back."

He felt the tears pricking at his own eyes and he pulled Angela into his arms, holding her tightly for a minute before he let her go and said with a choke in his voice, "Come on, Polly! What are we waiting for?"

## Chapter Twenty-Three

Anthony Hammond stared in through the front door of the Madhouse, almost unable to believe his eyes. But there was no doubt it had been Jill whom the police were shepherding upstairs with the student, Ben, the one who'd been doing the gardening and the odd jobs around the house. He'd called her name and she'd looked out at him briefly before going on up the stairs. Paul had seen too and probably David Redwood, though neither of them said anything. Sheila Colby had certainly seen them.

Feeling sick, Anthony turned away. Jill had been in that boy's bedroom. Boy! He wasn't a boy of course...that man's bedroom. It was past one o'clock in the morning, and she had thought that he, Anthony, wouldn't be home tonight. Anthony Hammond had no doubts as to what his wife had been doing that evening, and he felt sick and angry and hurt as he turned away into the darkness to hide his confusion.

Paul put his hand on Anthony's shoulder. "I'd go home if I were you," he said gently. "There's nothing more for you to do here. I'll chivvy the rest of them home."

Anthony gave a bitter laugh. "It's too late now," he said. "They saw her as clearly as I did. It'll be all round the Circle by breakfast time."

"She'd probably only dropped in on them for a drink," Paul said, but even as he said it he realised just how stupid it sounded.

"I think I will go home," Anthony said as if Paul hadn't

spoken. "As you say, there's no more to be done here." He moved away from the group that still hung about outside the front door, and as he did so, he heard Paul saying to the others, "Well, the noise has stopped, we'd better be getting home. You'll catch your death of cold out here, Sheila, in that dressing gown."

Anthony let himself into the house, and went up to the sitting room to wait for Jill. Perhaps she wouldn't come. Perhaps she'd stay with him, Ben. He didn't know, so he sat down in the armchair to wait and see.

He lost track of the time, but at last he heard the front door open and close quietly, and then the sound of footsteps coming softly upstairs. Jill paused as she reached the top and looked across at him, sitting silently waiting for her.

"Where've you been?" he said at last.

"You know perfectly well where I've been," she replied shortly, coming into the room and leaning on the back of the other armchair. "At Mad Richmond's birthday party. You saw me."

"Yes, I saw you. I saw you coming out of that downstairs bedroom with Ben Gardner. What the hell were you doing in there?"

"What the hell do you think? I was fucking him!" Jill's guilt poured out of her in anger, in language she would never normally use. She knew Anthony had every right to be furious, but she was still angry with him for making her spell it out.

"For Christ's sake, Jill," he exploded, "what kind of talk is that?"

"The truth, Anthony. I was in bed with Ben when the police banged on the door."

"But why? Was it the first time?" He shook his head as if trying to clear it. "What the hell were you doing at a student party anyway? Christ!"

So many questions. Jill rubbed her face with her hands and then looked at her husband, sitting looking so bewildered in his chair. "I went to the pub because Mad Richmond asked me to, to help celebrate her birthday," she began slowly.

"But why? Why did she ask *you*?"

"I saw her at the rugby pitches this afternoon." Was it only this afternoon? Jill was amazed, so much seemed to have happened since she'd been walking with the children round the rugby ground just so that she could have a sight of Ben. "We were chatting. I mentioned you were away for the weekend and she said don't stay in on my own, come to join them in the pub for her birthday, so I did. We all had far too much to drink."

"And?" prompted Anthony when she seemed to have come to a halt.

"And, when the pub shut the party moved to Dartmouth Circle. Ben and I...well we didn't join the party."

"So you were drunk," Anthony said flatly. "Is that your excuse?"

He was offering her an explanation, a reason why she might have done what she did, but Jill knew there was no point in half-truths now.

"No," she said, "I'd had a lot to drink, but I knew what I was doing. It wasn't the first time."

"You knew what you were doing," repeated Anthony.

"I was..." Jill paused to choose her words, "I was in bed with Ben."

"Having sex."

"Yes."

"And it's happened before." It was a statement, not a question, and Jill simply nodded her head.

"How long has it been going on?" asked Anthony wearily.

Jill shrugged. "A few weeks," she said. "Since he came to work for us."

"In this house?"

"No."

Anthony's shoulders seemed to sag as he took in what Jill was telling him. "What happens now?" he said bleakly.

Jill shrugged again. "That's up to you, I suppose."

"Up to me! Don't be ridiculous, Jill!" he snapped, his anger rekindled. "There's more to this than you and me. What about the children, or had you forgotten about them? Does Nancy know?"

"No one knows," Jill said quietly.

"Well, they bloody well do now," retorted Anthony. "Half the Circle saw you come out with him, and as old Ma Colby was in the crowd, the whole world'll know tomorrow. Oh God, Jill, what a mess."

"I'm sorry, Anthony..."

He cut her off. "Are you? Are you really, or just sorry I found out? Oh Jill, how could you do this to me...to us? You know I love you... I thought you loved me."

"I did... I do. It was just that, I seemed to have lost you. You never seem to have time for me any more, and Ben...well Ben just got into my blood."

"Got into your blood!" repeated Anthony. "How very dramatic! Got into your blood." He stared at her for a minute and then asked, "Is it because I wouldn't let you get a job? Is that it? Is this your way of getting back at me?"

"No! Of course not," snapped Jill. "It was exciting, that's all! He excited me as you haven't done, haven't had time to do, for months."

"So it's all *my* fault," said Anthony. "Is that what you're saying?"

"No. Yes... I don't know. It just happened, right?"

"And is it over... now that I know... or are you leaving me for him?"

Jill was horrified. "No, of course I'm not. It was just an affair, that's all, and it's over now."

Just an affair! Anthony winced. How could she be so dismissive? "Does Ben know that?" he enquired.

Jill thought of Ben as she'd left him in the hallway of the students' house.

"Will you be all right?" he had asked. "Do you want me to come home with you?"

"No." Jill shook her head. "I'll be fine, really. I've got to face him some time, it may as well be now."

"And us? Will we... I mean shall I...?" Ben began.

"No," Jill said gently, "No, Ben, it's over. I was mad to get

369

involved, but..." Her voice trailed off, and reaching up she kissed him once more on the mouth. "Take care, I loved being with you," she whispered, "but don't worry about me, I'll be fine, I promise."

Ben's expression had been a mixture of pain, anger and relief. There was going to be no drama, no scene, it was just all over. He held her for a moment, and then she slipped from his arms and, without looking back, she had walked away.

"Yes," she said softly, "he knows."

Silence settled round them for a long moment, before Anthony said, "Well, we'd better get some sleep. I can't talk about this any more just now." He stood up. "If you'll find me a pillow and a blanket, I think I'll sleep down here for tonight."

"You don't have to—" began Jill, but he interrupted sharply. "Yes, I do!" he shouted. "Christ Jill! You've spent this evening in another man's bed, with another man's prick inside you, and I do not intend to take you hot from his bed into mine...right?" He turned away. "Chuck the pillow and blanket down the stairs, I'll talk to you in the morning." When he saw she was going to say something else, he spoke through his teeth. "Not now, Jill. In the morning."

He turned away abruptly from her and he went down the stairs to his study where he stayed until she had done as he asked, and had gone up to their room by herself. Then he lay down just as he was in his clothes, pulled the blanket over him and closed his eyes. But he couldn't sleep; how could he sleep with the picture of Jill in Ben Gardner's arms continually playing and replaying like a film in his mind? His wife, his beloved Jill, their life together, their marriage was ruined, and as he lay in the darkness the tears ran, unchecked, down his face.

Upstairs alone in their bed, Jill couldn't sleep either. She felt empty and wrung out. She had hurt Anthony, she had hurt Ben, the children could still be hurt, and she was hurting herself, hurting like hell. From now on, whatever happened, everything would be different, there could be no going back. She didn't want to leave Anthony, to break up the family and its home, but how could she stay now, always assuming Anthony wanted her to stay? He would worry about the children as well. What would be best for them?

He's right about one thing, she thought in anguish, it isn't private between us. They all saw me with Ben, they'll all know, or they'll guess, and what they don't know they'll make up. If only I'd put the car in the garage, I'd have seen Anthony's car. I'd have known he was home and I'd have come straight in.

But would she? She wasn't sure. Her affair with Ben was all over now, but it might not have been. If she had simply come home to find Anthony there, she'd have come in, as from the pub and she knew she wouldn't have ended it. But discovery had forced the end upon her.

She lay alone in the big bed and she wept too, for herself, for Anthony, for Ben. Whatever happened, she could never see him again. Finally, she fell into an uneasy sleep, but was awake again before the grey winter light began to filter between the curtains.

She heard Anthony come upstairs and use the bathroom. She heard the shower running and the familiar knocking in the hot-water pipes, and she wondered how it could all sound so normal, now that their world had changed for ever. She knew, of course, that it all had to appear normal for the sake of the children, to maintain the pretence for Isabelle, but she wondered how they would manage it.

When Anthony came softly into the bedroom to collect some clothes, Jill feigned sleep until he had gone out again, but it fooled neither of them, it just gave them a few more moments before they had to face each other and reality again.

When she had showered and dressed herself, she went down, and found the children already sitting at the breakfast table eating cereal. Isabelle was in the kitchen making coffee, and Anthony was sitting, hidden behind the Sunday paper. She glanced at him over the top of it, and saw how tired and haggard he looked. Obviously he hadn't slept either.

As she had been getting dressed, Jill had come to a decision.

She needed, they both needed, some time and space to come to terms with what had happened. She would go to her mother, she thought, and take the children with her. She could stay for a few days, and give them both the necessary breathing space, before they had to find some way to reassemble their lives. With this decision taken, before she came downstairs, she had phoned her mother and asked if she could bring the children to stay for a few days.

Nancy sounded surprised. "But isn't Sylvia still at school? They surely haven't broken up for Christmas this early, have they?"

"No, Mum, they haven't, but I need a break, and it won't hurt her to miss a few days at her age."

"But isn't she a shepherd or something in the nativity play? Won't she miss the rehearsals?" Nancy wondered.

"Mum," Jill almost shouted down the phone, "just answer me, can I come or not?!"

"Of course you can come," Nancy said at once. "When shall I expect you?"

"I'm not sure," Jill said. "Some time today. Just expect me when you see me, OK?"

Nancy could hear that Jill was almost at breaking point and so she simply said, "Fine, darling. You just come when you're ready." She didn't ask if Anthony would be coming too, she didn't need to. She knew that her daughter was running away from something, she just didn't know what.

"Anthony," Jill began, "I thought I'd take the children to visit Mum for a few days."

He lowered his paper and looked at her impassively. "Whatever you think," he said. "I shall be away all week."

"Oh, I didn't know." Jill was surprised.

"Conference," he said shortly. "I wasn't going to go as I'd been away so much, but it would be better if I did."

"Yes, all right." Jill didn't know what to say, but she did feel relief at their being apart for a while. "Well, I'll pack after breakfast and we'll get there in time for lunch."

"Does Nancy know you're coming?"

"Yes, I rang earlier to say I would. I didn't speak to her for long." Anthony got the message, Nancy didn't know yet.

At that moment, the phone rang and Jill went across to answer it.

It was Ben. "Are you all right?" he asked.

Instinctively Jill lowered her voice and turned away from the room. "Yes, I'm fine, really."

Anthony materialised at her side. "Is that Ben?" he asked. Jill nodded wordlessly, and he took the receiver from her hand.

"Ah Ben," he said smoothly. "I'm glad you called. First of all I'd like to reassure you that Jill is fine, no cuts or bruises." He spoke without pause, not allowing Ben the chance to speak. "And then about the work you've been doing for us, I'm afraid there isn't any more, and as for what we still owe you, I think we may say that you've been paid in kind, don't you? Don't phone again, Ben. Goodbye." Anthony cut the connection with his hand and gave the phone back to Jill. Colour had flooded through her face at his words, but it had drained away as quickly, leaving her white-faced beside him. "I imagine that's the last we shall hear of him," Anthony said, and picking up his paper, went down to his study.

Jill replaced the receiver and then turned round to the children who, happily unaware of the atmosphere around them, were just finishing their breakfast.

"We're going to see Granny today, and stay for a few days," she told them. "You can choose some toys to take with us while I pack the case." She called through to the kitchen, "Isabelle, please could you help the children pack some toys into a box?" She turned again to the children. "Run up and choose, Isabelle will be up in a minute, I just want a word with her first."

When they had disappeared upstairs, Jill said to Isabelle, "Mr Hammond is away all week at a conference, so I've decided to take the children to my mother's for a few days. You'll be here to look after the house while we're away of course, and at Mrs

Forrester's when she wants you, but otherwise your time will be your own. You can do what you like. I'll be back on Friday afternoon, so just be here then, OK?"

Isabelle was delighted, and went happily upstairs to help the children get ready to leave.

When the car was packed and the children were ready, Jill called Anthony out of the study to say goodbye. He hugged each of the children tightly and told them to have a lovely time at Granny's, and then he helped strap them into the car as he always did. When they were safely in and the doors were shut he turned to Jill.

"Drive carefully," he said, and taking her hand, brushed her cheek with his lips before he stepped away from her.

Jill got into the driver's seat and wound down the window. "I don't know where you'll be," she said, "in case of emergency."

"No," said Anthony. "I'll ring you tomorrow and tell you."

Jill said, "All right," and then as there seemed to be nothing more to say, she wound the window up again and started the engine.

"Daddy looks cross," remarked Sylvia, waving to him as they pulled away. "Is he cross, Mummy?"

"No, darling," Jill tried to sound reassuring, "I think he's just very tired. Let's hope he has a nice quiet time today."

Jill had rung her mother again to say they'd be there for lunch, and when they arrived, Nancy was at the door as they stopped outside. She ran out to meet them, gathering her grandchildren into her arms and greeting them as excitedly as they did her. Over their heads she looked at Jill. One glance at her drawn, white face was enough to tell her something was badly wrong, and she bustled them inside into the warm, where the smell of Sunday lunch wafted from the kitchen.

"We'll deal with the luggage after lunch," she said. "I've put Granny's toy box in the sitting room, you two. Why don't you go and see what's in it?"

Sylvia and Thomas needed no further bidding, they loved the box of toys that their grandmother kept at her house, and were soon pulling them all out and crying out in delight as they found their old favourites waiting for them.

Nancy poured Jill a glass of wine and picking up her own said, "Mummy and I will be in the kitchen, getting the lunch," and led the way. Jill followed her, but the lunch was well under control, and they sat down at the table and looked at each other.

"Are you all right?" Nancy asked.

Jill managed a rueful smile. "Sort of."

Nancy nodded. "Good. I'm not going to ask questions, but I'm here if you want to tell me."

"Yes, I know. Thanks, Mum."

They both sipped their wine and then Jill said, "I do want to talk, it's just...well I suppose I don't know where to begin." She glanced through the door into the living room. "And I don't want the children to know anything."

"No, of course not. You can tell me later when they're in bed."

Jill shook her head. "I must tell you a bit now," she said. "It's burning me up inside."

"Well, why don't you give me brief outline now, and then we'll talk properly tonight." Nancy smiled encouragingly. Despite her apparent indifference, she was anxious to know what on earth had happened to cause her daughter to look so pale and unhappy.

Jill took a deep breath and said, "Anthony and I...well, I'm not sure we can go on as we are...things, well, things have happened."

"Things," echoed Nancy, "what things? He's never having an affair, is he?"

"Anthony? No, no, he's not having an affair...it's me." Jill had been wondering how to tell her mother what had happened, but it had slipped out as easily as that.

Nancy stared at her, unable to believe, for a moment, what she was hearing, and then said softly, "I see. You're having an affair." She put her wine glass carefully on the table and then said, "And does Anthony know?"

Jill nodded miserably. "Since last night."

"And are you leaving him? Anthony I mean."

"I don't know, Mum," Jill buried her face in her hands, "I just don't know. I don't want to."

"Well, are you going on with it...this affair?"

"No. It's over. I won't see Ben again."

"Does Anthony want you to stay?"

"I don't know," replied Jill flatly. "I don't know anything."

Nancy sighed heavily. "Oh Jill," was all she said.

Sylvia appeared at the door. "Is it nearly lunchtime Granny? I'm hungry."

"It'll be ready in five minutes, darling," Nancy said, getting to her feet. "Mummy and I were just having a glass of wine first. I'm just going to make the gravy, you can lay the table if you like, you know where the things are, don't you? Where's Thomas?"

And so the day passed, time crawling for Jill as they went for a walk to feed the geese, played with the toys in the Granny toy box, and at last had tea and bath and story and bed.

Finally ensconced in front of the fire with a large gin, Jill said, "Oh Mum, I don't know what to do."

Nancy gave her an encouraging smile and taking a sip from her own drink, said, "Suppose you tell me everything from the beginning, and then we can think about what you might do."

So Jill told her about the students moving in, and meeting Ben at the barbecue. "He was very attractive, right from the first," she said. "I can't explain, it sounds too corny, but it was like electricity between us." She went on to explain how he'd come to work for them, and of the chemistry between them and how she had succumbed. She told of the snatched times in the motel room, and finally about last night at the pub and afterwards in Ben's room. "I don't love him, Mum, even though he's a lovely person. He *is*," she insisted when she saw her mother purse her lips at this, "but I wasn't in love with him."

"Just in lust with him," suggested Nancy.

Jill flinched. "If you say so. He was like a drug, I couldn't get enough of him, and yet all the time…well, each time I swore it would be the last but then…." Her voice trailed away. She looked across at her mother. "It was Anthony's fault in a way."

"No it wasn't," Nancy said gently but firmly. "It was yours."

"But he'd been so busy and distant…" began Jill.

"Darling, when you got married, you promised you wouldn't sleep with anyone but Anthony."

"Oh for God's sake, Mother," snapped Jill, "it isn't that simple…"

"Yes it is, to me anyway. I accept you may have been having difficulties," Nancy said, "complications, but in the end, that is what it comes back to. You promised and you broke your promise, and now Anthony and you and possibly this Ben too, are hurt. The thing is, darling, that if you want to try and put things right and give your marriage another try, the first thing you have to do is be honest with yourself. You chose to have this affair. There was a point when you could have walked away from it, but you chose not to, and once it had started you were too involved to break it off."

"Mum, I came to you for help," Jill said angrily, "if you're just going to moralise at me, I might as well go home."

"I'm not moralising," Nancy said, "at least that's not the point of what I am saying. What I'm saying is, that if you want things to work out for you and Anthony and the children now, then you have to face up to what you've done. I'm not saying it was all your fault that things were going wrong, I'm sure it wasn't, but you have to take the blame for having the affair." She looked across at her daughter, longing to take her in her arms and cradle her and comfort her as she had as a child, but Jill was sitting stony-faced, stiff as a ramrod in her chair, and Nancy knew she would be rebuffed.

There was a long silence and then Nancy asked quietly, "If Anthony will have you, do you want to go back and try again?"

Jill nodded wordlessly.

Her mother smiled. "Good," she said. "Then we must work towards that. Let's sleep on it and see what we think we should do in the morning."

Amazingly, Jill did sleep. Perhaps it was getting everything off her chest to her mother, but she felt more at peace now, less hopeless about the future, and more sure in her own mind as to what she wanted. As she drifted off to sleep, she was writing a letter to Anthony in her head, asking him if they could try again to make their marriage work.

Over the next few days she became more certain in her own mind that she wanted to save her marriage. When she thought about Ben – and he often entered her mind unbidden – the whole affair had a strange unreality about it, almost as if it had happened to someone else, but having faced up to it as her mother had said she must, she now felt deeply and desperately ashamed. She thought hard about what she could offer Anthony, about what he might want from her and what she wanted from him. If they were starting again, she felt the ground rules should be clear, though she was not at all sure she was the one who should be setting them.

Anthony had called on the Monday evening to tell her where he'd be staying in case of emergencies. In the course of their short conversation he told her that Madge Peters had been found dead in her chair on Sunday and that the funeral was on Friday, but apart from that and telling her that he'd see her on Friday when he got home, they had no other conversation, and his voice was cold and hard. Jill decided that it would be best to write him a letter, and send it to his hotel, so that he could read it before they met on Friday evening.

"It'll be easier to say everything I want to," she explained to Nancy, "I won't get side-tracked and I can choose my words carefully so I really say what I mean to say."

"It's up to you," Nancy said, "but keep it simple, don't make it too long and involved."

"I'll show it to you before I send it," suggested Jill.

"No," Nancy said, "I don't want to see it. It must be entirely private between you and Anthony."

So Jill wrote a simple letter, saying she was sorry for hurting him, and that she wanted to give their marriage another try, if he was willing to forgive her. *"I know you'll find it hard to believe,"* she wrote, *"but I never stopped loving you. I was stupid and selfish and allowed myself to get involved with Ben. I never loved him, but I'm not sure if that makes it better or worse. I shall be coming home in time for Madge's funeral on Friday afternoon. Please can we talk this weekend, properly?"* She didn't quite know how to sign off, so she simply settled for her name.

When the letter was sent she tried to put it out of her mind, and enjoy the time with her mother and the children. She did some school work with Sylvia every day, which they both enjoyed, and they all fed the geese and went to the leisure centre to swim and generally behaved as if it were the school holidays. There was no Isabelle to make the children's tea, or put them to bed, and Nancy left all that to Jill. She had always thought that part of Jill's problem was having too much time on her hands, and if she wasn't going to have a job, she could at least look after the two children more. Jill found that she did indeed enjoy looking after them herself, and wondered what Anthony would say if she suggested that they didn't need Isabelle. By the end of the week, they were all ready to go home, and Nancy was ready to see them go. She'd enjoyed having them, but she did find the children a bit tiring, and she felt there was nothing more she could say to help Jill, from now on it was up to her.

Sylvia and Thomas were ready for bed when Anthony came in on Friday evening. They flung themselves at him, telling him, both at once, about the geese and the swimming and helping Granny make chocolate cakes, their voices high and excited, as they told him their news. Jill waited in the background as the children greeted their father, watching their delight at having him home in time to read them their story, and his pleasure at being able to do it. Whatever happens, she thought, we must hang on to this.

She was dreading being left alone with him. He had hardly spoken to her when he'd come in, just asking casually, "Did you get back in time for Madge's funeral?" and when she said yes he simply nodded and went upstairs with Sylvia and Tom. What would he say when the children were tucked up in bed and how would she answer?

She had dressed with care, having a shower herself while the children splashed happily in the bath, and redone her face. The dinner was ready in the oven, and she'd opened a bottle of wine. Isabelle had been given another night off, so that they would not be interrupted and any time now she and Anthony would have to face each other.

When Anthony came down from reading the story, he had changed into jeans and a sweater, and looked much younger than in his business suit, but still tired and drawn. Jill had poured him a drink, and then escaped upstairs herself to kiss the children goodnight.

At last, there could be no further procrastination. Taking a deep breath, Jill went down to the living room where Anthony was reading the paper by the fire. He looked up when she came in, watching her as she picked up her own drink, but saying nothing.

"Did you have a successful week?" she asked at last.

"Yes, not bad," Anthony replied. "How was your mother?"

"She was fine. She was great with the children, and they love doing things with her."

"Good." His eyes dropped to his paper again, and silence fell round them again, an awkward silence that Jill felt she must break. It was time to take the plunge.

"Did you," her voice came out as a croak and she cleared her throat, "did you get my letter?"

Anthony looked up again. "Yes," he said, "I got it."

"And…?"

"And we'll talk things through over the weekend."

"Couldn't we begin now?" asked Jill.

Anthony set the paper aside. "If you want to," he said, and

then waited. His face was cold and bleak, and he gave her no hint of what he was thinking, no help in starting to say what she needed to say.

"Anthony," Jill began, "I don't know what to say. Can you forgive me for what I did?"

"I don't know," he said. "I can try, but I don't know."

Jill stared at him. "So what are we going to do?"

"I don't know that either, not in the long term." He sighed. "I suppose we'll just keep going as we are for now and see how things are."

"But if we're going to try again...?" began Jill.

"But are we? I'm not sure I can put things behind me as easily as you seem to be able to. We can't put the clock back, and things will never be the same."

"I know that," Jill agreed, "things will be different, but they may end up better. If you still love me..."

"If I still love you? I don't know that either. Maybe that's changed."

Jill looked at him helplessly. "So what are we going to do?" she asked again. "What about the children?"

"It's for them that we must keep going," he said, "and see what can be salvaged, but I can't see far into the future. I don't know if we have one together or not."

Jill's eyes were filled with tears, and on a sob she cried, "Anthony, I'm so sorry."

"Yes," he said, "so am I."

They had an almost silent dinner and then Anthony said he had some work to do and would be in his study. "I've taken the folding bed from underneath Isabelle's, and put it up down there," he said. "So I shan't trouble you upstairs."

"But Anthony..." Jill protested.

"I'm sorry, Jill, but I'm not ready to share a bed with you at present."

"And will you ever be?" Jill whispered.

Anthony's eyes were as sad as her own. "I don't know," he said.

## Chapter Twenty-Four

Oliver Hooper had a problem. Indeed, he had several, but the one that concerned him most was news he'd heard from his father. The Smarts were due home for Christmas, and this meant that he must clear out everything he'd been storing in their shed before they arrived. He had tried to find out the exact day when they would be returning, but Steve Hooper didn't know.

"A couple of weeks before Christmas, I think," he said. "Why?"

Oliver shrugged. "Just wondered," he replied casually. "They've been away a long time, haven't they?"

"They've been visiting their daughter in Australia," Steve said. "If you're going that far and can take the time, it makes sense to stay for a good while. Anyway, Mike Callow's heard from them to say they'll be back for Christmas."

Oliver warned Scott that they had to clear everything out at once. "You'll have to take all I've got," he said.

Scott agreed. "Pity," he remarked, "it was a good scam, right?"

"It's not going to end," Oliver assured him with more confidence than he felt. "I'll get another place sorted." He was determined not to let his source of extra income dry up and having given it some concentrated thought, he came up with a plan that he thought would work. There was, perhaps, more risk attached to it, but there was no reason why, with a little care, things shouldn't go on as before.

Oliver's bedroom was on the ground floor. His father, security conscious as always, had long ago decided not to make his home office in the room that had been designed as a study. Being on the ground floor, he thought, it was too easy for thieves to look through the windows and see what computers and other office hardware were on offer. With the house unoccupied during the day, it would be simple enough for them to remove everything of value. So he used one of the bedrooms at the top of the house to work in and had made the study into a bedroom for Oliver. This actually suited Oliver very well. Beside his bedroom was the door into the garden. He'd had a second key cut and could now come and go, unobserved, at will. Once he was in the back garden it was quite easy to swing up over the fence into the car park of the office block that backed on to the houses on that side of the Circle. At night the offices would be deserted, and the car park empty. Provided he could store the stuff in his room, it would be easy enough to pass it over the fence, under cover of darkness, to Scott waiting with his van in the car park. The risk was in the hiding of the stuff in his room. Although none of the items was large, there was nowhere much to hide it where Annie wouldn't find it.

When Oliver first moved into the house permanently, the ground rules had been laid down. He was to make his own bed and keep his room tidy, and Annie would make sure it was properly cleaned once a week. However, he seldom bothered to make his bed, or took any trouble to keep the place tidy, and recently Annie had been complaining about the state of the room and refusing to go into it until he tidied it up. This suited his plans very well, so he didn't touch the dirty clothes heaped on the floor, or pick up magazines and school work dumped on the desk. At last, she refused to clean the room and in this decision she was backed by his father.

"If you can't take a few moments to clear up your room, Oliver," he said in exasperation, "Annie's certainly not going to do it for you."

"I don't want her to," Oliver snapped back. "I don't want her poking her nose into my things! I like my room the way it is!"

"Well, if you want to live in a pig-sty…"

Oliver had his victory, but even so he didn't trust Annie not to go into his room when he wasn't there and poke around. Then he saw his big empty suitcase on the top of the wardrobe. She'd hardly be likely to look in there, he thought, and anyway it had a key, so he could keep it locked. Until he could find somewhere better to stash his stuff, he decided, that would have to do.

Scott arranged to come round and clear the shed on Saturday night. He normally took the stuff on a Friday or Saturday ready to offload at Sunday boot sales.

"Better be late," he said. "Too many people about early Saturday evenings. I'll come round after the pubs chuck out."

Oliver didn't care how late Scott came. As far as he was concerned, it was easier to go to bed and then go out through the garden door. That way there were no awkward questions as to where he was going.

At midnight, when the house was dark and settled for the night, he slipped out into the garden, carefully locking the door behind him. In a moment he was over the fence into the car park and round the road to the track behind the houses opposite. Scott's van wasn't there yet, so he climbed over the fence and made for the shed. He could hear music coming from somewhere and for an awful moment he thought there was someone in the house. Then he realised it was coming from much further away, from the front of the house, loud reggae music, and he guessed that the students must be having a party. That'll shake up old Ma Colby, he thought with a grin.

He crept into the shed and by the light of his torch began to pack the last of his stash into black bin bags. He wasn't worried that the torchlight would be seen, as he knew that Mike Callow wasn't at home. He'd met him a couple of days earlier and asked if Peter would be about this weekend.

"No, sorry, mate," Mike had replied. "Not this weekend, I'm away."

There was more than he thought, and he sorted it out as he packed. Should be worth at least another hundred to Scott, this lot, he thought. There were some good CDs this time, but it would be the last of those for a while. He'd been buying magazines in a newsagent in town that sold sealed and packaged CDs as well and he had managed to smuggle several of them out on different occasions before disaster struck.

It had been on a Saturday morning when the shop was quite busy. Oliver paid for his magazine and then wandered over to the CD rack. For a long time, there was no opportunity to slide a CD between the pages of his magazine, and he realised afterwards that had been his mistake, he'd been hanging round the rack for too long and alerting the suspicions of Noshir Patel who ran the shop. As he reached the pavement a hand fell on his arm and Mr Patel's quiet voice said, "Excuse me young man, but I think you have not paid for all you are taking away."

Oliver looked up sharply, and tried to jerk his arm away, but Mr Patel had a firmer grip on his arm than he had realised and Oliver couldn't break free. Protesting he didn't know what the shopkeeper was talking about, he was piloted back inside and taken to a tiny office at the back. There Patel removed the magazine from his grasp and revealed the CD wrapped inside it.

"What then is this?" he asked holding it up, and before Oliver could answer, Patel turned to his wife who was at the desk and said, "Ring the police!"

For a split second, as Oliver watched her dial the police station, he felt a wave of panic, but then he pulled himself together and decided how to play it.

"Oh, please don't call the police," he begged. "I've never done anything like this before...it's just, well it's my dad's birthday next week, and I couldn't afford to get him a present. He likes music, my dad." He looked appealingly up at Noshir Patel, allowing his eyes to fill with tears, a trick he had always been able to manage, but the shopkeeper seemed unimpressed.

"I always call the police," was all he said, and then they waited for them to arrive. Mrs Patel went out into the shop to help serve in her husband's place, shutting the office door firmly behind her. Oliver considered his chances of making a dash for it and getting out of the shop, safely away into the crowd of Saturday-morning shoppers, but he knew two of Mr Patel's sons were in the shop, and even if he did make a run for it out of the office, he'd never get to the street.

Oliver tried again. Looking at Mr Patel with eyes brimming with tears, he said, "I'm very sorry, Mr Patel, really I am. I didn't mean any harm. I'll never do anything so awful again. It's my dad's birthday, see?" The birthday had been an inspiration. Oliver's dad did indeed have a birthday in the coming week, and he hoped if he kept saying as much, they might believe it was a first and only offence, a dreadful mistake, made simply to get his dad a present.

"What is your name, boy?" Patel asked.

"Oliver Hooper," murmured Oliver. He looked across at the shopkeeper. "I really am sorry, Mr Patel, I don't know what came over me."

At that moment, the office door opened again and Mrs Patel led in a policeman and a policewoman.

"This is the boy," Mrs Patel said. "He took a CD and hid it in a magazine. I think he has done it before. Lots of our CDs have gone missing."

"Oh, no, I haven't," wailed Oliver. "This is the first time, honestly! I'm so sorry, Mr Patel. I've never done it before, honestly."

"I think there is nothing honest about you," retorted Mrs Patel, entirely unmoved by his outburst. "You are a thief!"

The policeman cleared his throat and said, "Yes, madam, well, we'll deal with this now. Will you be pressing charges?"

"Yes," replied Mrs Patel firmly.

"Maybe," answered her husband at the same time.

"I'm PC Davison," said the policeman, turning to Oliver. "What's your name, son, and where do you live?"

Oliver gave his name and address, and then Davison said, "Well, I think we'll go down to the station and get your parents to come in. We'll talk about things down there."

The two police officers took an arm each and Oliver was led

unceremoniously out of the shop and hustled into the waiting police car. As he climbed into the back of the car, the policewoman at his side, he saw there was an interested group gathered to watch the proceedings, and there, disaster upon disaster, was Chantal Haven. She stared at him as he was put in the car, saw that he was in trouble and a slow smile spread across her face, a smile of triumph and revenge. It was not a smile that Oliver was likely to forget in a long time.

When they reached the police station he sat in an interview room and waited for his parents to arrive, well his dad and Annie. They were soon there and greeted Oliver with shock when they heard what he'd done. Oliver manufactured the tears again and said on a sob, "I'm sorry, Dad, I'm sorry."

"When is your birthday, sir?" enquired PC Davison.

Steve looked at him in surprise. "My birthday? Wednesday," he said. "Why?"

"Your son says he took the CD to give you as a present."

"Oh, Ollie." Steve looked at him in exasperation. "What will you do next?"

Oliver said nothing, and Davison asked, "Has Oliver been in any trouble like this before, sir?"

"No! None!" cried Steve. "I can't think what's got into him."

There was more discussion and the sergeant was called in from the front desk. Finally, after more talks with Mr Patel, who had followed them to the police station, it was decided that Oliver should be cautioned, not charged with theft, and after yet more time and paperwork, he left the police station flanked by his father and stepmother, and was driven straight home.

There were more recriminations there of course, but Oliver let them wash over him. He'd escaped! He wasn't going to end up in court. He wasn't going to be sent to a Young Offender Centre. He'd heard enough from Scott to know that it was not a place he wanted to go.

He looked at the CDs in his hands, the ones he had removed successfully before, and was glad they'd been hidden here.

His father had been told that CDs had been going missing over a period of time, and Oliver was pretty certain that his room had been thoroughly searched while he was at school for any evidence of them. He didn't ask, but he knew. It was why leaving stuff there from now on would be risky, Annie might search again at any time when he was out; on the other hand, if she hadn't found anything the last time, and she hadn't, then she might not bother again.

Oliver hadn't told Scott of his run-in with the police. There was no need to worry him with what was over and done with; it wasn't going to happen again, and he didn't want Scott refusing to deal with him any more simply because he'd got careless once.

When all his packing was done he slid out of the shed again and went to look for Scott at the fence. There was no sign of him. Where the hell was he? Oliver didn't feel in any danger in the dark shelter of the trees at the bottom of the Smarts' garden, but it was getting cold, and he wanted to go home to bed. He looked at his watch. It was well past one o'clock. Something must have gone wrong. He'd have to find out from Jay on Monday morning, but they couldn't wait much longer or the Smarts would be home and looking in their garden shed.

Quietly he shut the shed door and made his way round the side of the house, intending to slip out of the side gate into the Circle, but as he approached the gate he saw a flashing blue light. Cautiously he peered over the gate and saw two police cars parked outside the house. He ducked down again at once.

"Fucking hell!" he whispered. "How the hell did they find out?" Had Scott been caught and talked? He hurried back to the bottom fence and swung himself over on to the track beyond. He listened. There was no sound. Then it struck him. There was no sound! The music blasting from the party at the student house had stopped. "That's why the filth are here," he murmured, and slipping along beside the fence and through the cut, he waited in the shadows between the fences to see what was going on.

There was a group of residents from various houses standing

outside the Madhouse, watching as students came out and wandered off round the Circle towards the town. Even as he watched, the residents began to melt away back to their own houses. Then a policewoman emerged from the student house, and with her, her wrist gripped firmly by the policewoman, was Chantal Haven. Oliver watched in delight as the girl was marched away to her own home, and wished Chantal had seen him, revelling in her discomfort as she had in his a few days earlier. He continued to watch as the Havens' front door opened, and he saw Annabel in the light from the porch. Oliver hadn't seen her for some time, but there was something strange about her, she looked different, and then as she turned sideways on to let her sister pass into the house, he realised. She was pregnant! Oliver was wondering idly who the father was when it struck him suddenly that of course he knew. It was Scott Manders! Of course it was! That's what that note had been all about. Oliver hugged himself in delight. Now he really did have something on Scott, and something on Annabel too, maybe.

He stayed in the shadows and watched as the policewoman returned and the police cars drove away. He was about to move on home himself when someone else came out of the house. Oliver stepped back into the shadows, not wanting to be seen anywhere near the Smarts' house, and recognised Jill Hammond, going slowly back to her house.

Mrs Hammond! Oliver almost whistled in his surprise. Now what in shit was she doing at the student party? He had seen Mr Hammond in the group by the front door, but he'd left several minutes earlier. Mrs Hammond walked to her house without looking back, but someone was standing at the door of the student house watching her. Oliver didn't know his name, but it was the student with the pony-tail, the one he'd seen working in the Hammonds' garden. Oliver smiled a secret smile. When he got home, he would keep a note of all he had seen this evening in what he called his information book. Information was power, and though he had no idea how or when he would use the information he had collected, he knew that to have it, to know things about people, might give him some hold over them. It was a feeling he hugged to himself in pleasure.

Now all he had to sort out was what had happened to Scott and to get the stash safely away in Scott's van. He hoped they wouldn't have to wait until next Saturday; Sunday was always a good day for Scott to move the stuff along, but maybe next Saturday would be too late.

Oliver had no way of contacting Scott except through Jay, so there was little he could do the next day, and he hung about at home. There was minor excitement in the Circle when an ambulance arrived and took Mrs Peters from the house next door, but otherwise the day was very boring.

"Died sitting in her chair," Annie said, having been out to see what had happened. "That's the way to go, I suppose, she was a good age."

On Monday morning, Oliver was collecting the dues from the juniors when Jay came hurrying in through the school gates. Oliver grabbed his arm.

"Want a word with you, mate," he said.

They moved out of earshot of the arriving pupils and Oliver said, "Where the hell's Scott? He was due to pick up stuff from me on Saturday night and he never showed."

Jay shrugged. "Dunno," he said. "Ain't seen 'im all weekend. Didn't come round our place."

"Well, you'd better find out," Oliver told him sharply, "or we could all be in the shit. Gotta get the stuff moved out fast, right? You tell him. Bring the van tonight, half ten."

Jay nodded. "OK mate," he said. "I'll try and find 'im this afternoon. I got a skive on anyway."

"Where you going?" asked Oliver.

Jay tapped the side of his nose. "Business," he said and grinned. "Come on, mate, there's kids out there waiting to pay their dues. Mustn't let them slip, eh?"

That night Oliver was in the Smarts' garden by half past ten, but Scott didn't come and after waiting nearly an hour, Oliver went back home to bed. In the morning, he collared Jay the moment he walked through the gates.

"Where the hell's your brother?" he muttered. "He didn't come last night, either."

"No," agreed Jay. "An' 'e won't be coming, neither. 'E got picked up, and 'e's in the nick."

"What?!" exclaimed Oliver, horrified.

"Yeah, picked up Saturday, 'e was. Loading some computer gear he 'ad stashed in a garage. Must've been watching the place. I ain't seen 'im, but somebody must've grassed 'im up."

"Who?"

Jay shrugged his usual shrug. "Dunno, but I wouldn't like to be them if Scott knows who it is."

"So, what happens next?"

"'E'll be up in court today and then out on bail…maybe. Depends on the beak."

"Hmm." Oliver thought for a moment. "Well, if he gets out, tell him we've got to talk. OK?"

"Yeah, OK. If I see 'im."

"Jay, you've got to see him, right? It's important. We've got stuff to shift."

"'E may not want it now," pointed out Jay. "I'll take it off yer, if yer like."

"Better wait for Scott to decide," Oliver replied, not wanting Jay as part of the deal if he didn't need him.

Jay agreed readily enough to wait and see what happened. He didn't relish invading Scott's territory without permission, and he was pretty sure Scott would get bail.

It was Thursday, however, before Oliver saw Scott waiting on the corner at the end of school. He crossed over quickly and said, "You got out then?"

"Yeah, for now." Scott walked swiftly down the road and Oliver followed him to the Roxy café. Scott collected two mugs of tea and they sat down at a corner table.

"Jay says like, you're pressuring me, mate," Scott said. "Don't like to be pressured." His voice was calm but cold, and it made Oliver uneasy.

"Not pressuring, Scott, no, course not. Just worried about our stuff, in case these people come back before we can shift it, that's all."

"Your stuff, mate," Scott said blandly.

"You want out?" asked Oliver, trying to sound casual.

"Maybe. Gotta be careful for a bit. The filth'll be watching me while I'm on bail. Gotta keep my nose clean, right?"

"OK," said Oliver. "I'll deal with it myself."

"Hang about!" Scott snapped, and Oliver, who'd risen to his feet, sat down again. "I didn't say we couldn't do nothing, just we'd got to be careful, right?"

"Right."

"Thought we'd use Jay," Scott explained. "'E'd 'ave to 'ave a cut though."

"Yeah? How'd we work it?"

"Like, you could bring the stuff to school in a school bag and pass it over to Jay, right?" Scott suggested.

"No way, mate," Oliver replied. "Far too risky. He can come round on the track and I'll pass it over in the usual way."

"No van," Scott said.

"Look, Scott, there's five bin bags of stuff, a couple of switch cards and a pension book. Must be worth a hundred to you. D'you want them or not?" Oliver sounded firm and business-like and it appeared to be the right approach, for Scott said, "Yeah, I want them, just a question of how, that's all."

"Easy," Oliver said, getting into his stride. "You borrow a car, you come round to the track and collect, OK? Or Jay? Getting a car isn't a problem. Is it?" He had no idea if Scott or Jay took cars, but he assumed they did. "I'll be there this evening at half ten, and if you don't come then, the same tomorrow, OK? After that I make my own arrangements." Again, Oliver was about to leave when Scott stopped him.

"You ever see that girl in number four?" he asked.

Oliver looked at him and played dumb. "You mean that Chantal?"

"No, the other one, Bel."

"Annabel?" Oliver was sure now, the shortened name had given the game away.

"Yeah, Annabel."

"Saw her Saturday night in the distance. She's pregnant." He eyed Scott across the table. "Yours is it?"

"Like fucking hell it is!"

Oliver knew he was lying, but all he said was, "What about her then?"

"Nothing. Somebody grassed me up, that's all."

"Annabel?" Oliver was incredulous. "What would she know?"

"Enough," growled Scott. "She's a tart."

"Like her sister," Oliver said.

He left Scott sitting in the café and made his way home. He had a lot to think about. There was some connection between Scott and Annabel Haven, he'd known that before, and from the violence of Scott's reaction he was sure that Scott was the father of Annabel's baby, but there was something else too. If Scott was right and it was Annabel who'd been to the police, why had she done it? How could she have known about Scott's garage, and the computer stash in it, unless Scott had told her? And why would he do that?

That night he was waiting in the Smarts' garden again. At about a quarter to eleven he heard a car on the track, and he looked over the fence. He could see the shape of a car and he heard the driver's door close softly.

"Scott? That you?" Oliver hissed.

"No, me," came Jay's voice. "Got the stuff?"

"Yeah, here in the shed. I'll pass it over. You got the cash?"

"Yeah. Seventy-five."

"We said a hundred," Oliver said angrily.

"This ain't the time to talk about it," muttered Jay. "'Ere's the seventy-five, now give us the bags."

Oliver knew it was no good arguing with Jay now. He pocketed the money and heaved the bags over the fence. Jay pushed them quickly into the car and then said, "Scott said two cards and a pension book."

Oliver smiled in the darkness. "On Monday," he said, "if you bring the rest of the cash to school, I'll give them to you. But tell him the price has gone up. It's another fifty, or I sell them elsewhere."

"Scott won't like that," Jay remarked.

"And I don't like being messed about," Oliver said sharply. "He should have paid what we agreed."

Jay grunted and got back into the car and with only sidelights on, drove off down the track. As Oliver watched him go, he wondered if it was Scott who'd changed the deal, or whether Jay had decided to help himself to the other twenty-five pounds, not thinking Oliver would dare to query it. It would be interesting to see what happened on Monday.

He went back for one last look round the Smarts' shed. It was completely empty. No sign that it had been used for anything unusual and no sign of any garden tools or implements, just an empty work bench. Oliver picked up a rag from the floor, and carefully wiped the door and both its handles. There were no other smooth surfaces to wipe, everything had gone.

Oliver went to the fence for the last time and scrambled over it on to the track and then walked back through the cut into the Circle. As he emerged from the footpath, he almost bumped into David Redwood, who was closing his garage door.

The old man turned sharply and seeing only a shadowy figure in the darkness, cried out, "Who's there?" He made a sort of grab at Oliver, but Oliver shoved him away and turning back into the cut, pelted to the track beyond. He didn't know if Mr Redwood had recognised him, but he knew he must get home before Mr Redwood had time to think about it and go across the Circle. He ran out and along the Dartmouth Road and into the office car park. Within moments, he was over the fence and unlocking the garden door. Diving into the safety of his room, he threw his clothes off and leapt under the duvet.

It was less than five minutes later that the doorbell rang, and Mr Redwood stood on the step. Oliver could hear his father's voice raised in surprise at being disturbed after eleven.

"Oliver? He's in bed. Has been for over an hour."

"Are you sure?" David Redwood was not put off. "I'm sure it was Oliver who pushed me over and ran off."

There were footsteps down the hall and Oliver's door opened quietly. Oliver lay still, trying to keep his breathing regular as if in sleep. His father listened for a moment and then closed the door again.

"Sorry, Mr Redwood," he said, "but you must have been mistaken. Oliver is in bed, and he's fast asleep. It must have been someone else who pushed you over."

David Redwood didn't sound convinced as he said, "I suppose it must, but it did look like your boy. Jeans and a dark bomber jacket."

Steve Hooper laughed. "They all wear those," he said. "It could have been anyone."

Oliver heard the front door close and then a long silence in the hall, before at last his dad went back upstairs to bed. Shit! he thought, that was close. He got out of bed and took the cash Jay had given him, and the cards and pension book from his jeans pocket. He put them into the suitcase and having locked it, returned it to the top of the wardrobe. He wondered if Jay would bring the extra money on Monday.

## Chapter Twenty-Five

Madge Peters's funeral was on Friday afternoon at St Joseph's Church, where she had been a worshipper for over fifty years and one of the founders of the St Joe's day centre. Frank Marsh, the vicar, had suggested to Andrew that it might be fitting to have the refreshments he planned to offer after the service in the day centre.

"Most of our regulars knew her from when she was still able to come in and help," he pointed out, "they'd like to feel included I'm sure, even if some of them can't make it to the service. Mavis has already offered to lay on a tea if you want her to."

Andrew, who had been thinking he would have to arrange something at one of the Belcaster hotels, grasped the offered opportunity and having discussed what he wanted with Mavis, thankfully left it all to her. He liked the idea of using the church hall and knew that Madge would have approved as well.

When he arrived at the church half an hour before the service was due to begin, he was amazed at the number of people who were gathering in the churchyard or already inside in the pews. He had supposed most of Madge's friends to be dead, and indeed all her real contemporaries were, but she had always had the knack of getting on with people of any age and so she still had many friends living. Several of them had come a fair distance; her three godchildren, now in their sixties themselves, were all present, and despite the solemnity of the occasion there was an eager buzz of conversation as old friends met up again after years apart.

The Circle was well represented, much as he had expected, but he was surprised to see two of the students from the student house were there. One of them was the pretty little black girl, who his mother had told him helped at the day centre when she was able, and the other was the girl, Madeleine, who owned the house and had, thanks to Fran, taken over Spike. Andrew had never much cared for Spike and though he wouldn't have wanted to have him put down, neither would he have wanted to take the cat himself, and he was delighted Spike had found himself a good home. Dr Fran was there of course. She hadn't just been Madge's doctor, but also a good friend who went a long way back. Sheila and Gerald were standing with Mary Jarvis. Sheila was wearing a black suit and a large black hat, Gerald suitably attired in white shirt and plain black tie and Mary in a navy suit, but no hat. Andrew went over to speak to them and was touched by their concern for him, as they asked if there was anything any of them could do to help.

"Even if it's only sorting clothes or something like that," Mary said.

"That's very kind of you," Andrew said. "I'm sure I'll need help with lots of things like that. Perhaps I can let you know."

He turned away to speak to one of the godchildren, but as he went he heard Sheila say, "Look, there're two of the students. I didn't expect to see any of them."

"Why ever not?" Mary said sharply. "Madeleine often used to visit Madge, and Cirelle works at St Joe's."

"I think it's lovely to see them here," Gerald said repressively, "don't you, Sheila? Madge would have been so pleased."

Yes, I agree, Andrew thought as he moved on to the next group.

Everyone began going into the church now. Although the day was sunny, it was extremely cold, and the wind was chilly.

Andrew waited in the porch for the hearse to arrive. He had

decided that he wanted to be at the church to greet it, not to travel with the coffin, and so he had a chance to greet many of the mourners even before the service. Alison and Paul Forrester walked in together, Alison having waited at the gate for Paul to arrive. Jill Hammond hurried in at the last moment on her own, dressed smartly as always. The Redwoods were already in the church, Shirley a little anxious about leaving Melanie entirely alone with the children. She had hoped that Cirelle would have been able to come round, but Melanie didn't want her and anyhow Cirelle had decided to keep Mad company and come to the funeral herself.

"Anyway, if Melanie is going home next week, she's got to get used to coping with the children on her own again," David pointed out.

Shirley wasn't at all happy with the idea of Melanie going home the following week, but this wasn't the place to get into such a discussion, so she simply nodded, and said no more.

Just before the coffin was carried in, Angela Haven slipped in to the back of the church. She moved into the same pew as Jill, and they exchanged brief smiles before the coffin was carried in past them, followed at last by Andrew.

It was not a long service, but neither was it a sad one.

"We are here to celebrate Madge's life," Frank Marsh told them firmly, and they sang Madge's favourite hymns, "Praise My Soul the King of Heaven", and "Thy Hand oh God Has Guided". At the end of the service, before they went out into the cold churchyard for Madge to be laid in the grave next to her husband, Frank announced, "Andrew has asked me to say that he hopes everyone will come back into St Joe's hall afterwards, for some refreshments. And I would like to add, if there is anyone who would like to go straight there and not stand out in the cold, all of us, I, Andrew and Madge herself, will quite understand."

Slowly the coffin was carried out to the churchyard, and though some of the older members of the congregation moved straight to the welcoming warmth of the hall, most people followed to the graveside.

As she watched the short burial ceremony, Mad's eyes filled with tears. "Goodbye Madge," she whispered. "Thanks for everything, I'll remember what you said... and I'll look after Spike for you." Cirelle, standing with her, reached out and they gripped hands tightly as the coffin was lowered into the ground.

The wind was cutting and it was with some relief that the gathered mourners moved into the warmth of the hall. Mavis had done Madge proud and there was a huge spread of sandwiches, cakes, biscuits and savouries. There was hot tea to warm everyone up and there was also stronger drink for those who wanted it.

When everyone was inside, Andrew asked for their attention for a moment.

"I just wanted to thank you all, on my mother's behalf, for coming today. She always said she wanted a good send-off, with a party. You know how much she enjoyed a good party, so that's what we want now. No long faces please, she'd have hated that. Just raise your glasses or teacups and we'll drink to the memory of my mother, your friend, Madge."

"Madge. To Madge." The voices echoed round the hall, then as that was clearly the end of the formalities, the buzz of conversation increased again as people chatted, talking about Madge and the memories they had of her, catching up on news or just gossiping happily.

Alison Forrester drifted over to where Jill Hammond was standing alone, a cup of tea in her hand. "Hi," she said. "Had a nice time at your mum's?" and added, as Jill looked surprised, "Isabelle said you were away."

Though Paul had told her about seeing Jill at the rowdy student party the previous Saturday night, and as intrigued as she had been at the time, Alison was not going to mention it. Now she had other things to occupy her mind in which Jill's partying did not feature.

Jill forced a smile. "Of course. Yes, thanks, we had a very pleasant quiet few days. Mum likes to have the children to stay from time to time." Silence fell between them, and Jill said, "And how are your two? Are you coping all right with working as well?"

"Yes, it's not too bad," Alison replied, and then said, "We've had some bad luck, actually. We heard yesterday that Paul will be redundant at the end of the year."

"Oh no!" Jill's eyes widened with sympathy. "Oh, Alison, I *am* sorry. What will you do? I mean, will he be able to find another job fairly easily?"

Alison shrugged. "Don't know. I doubt it somehow, but of course he's going to start looking today. If he doesn't find something pretty quickly we shall have to move. We shan't be able to afford to stay in the Circle. It's so unfair," she burst out. "When he was head-hunted from Freddie Jones he was promised the world...more money, a partnership in the near future, and then it's suddenly cuts, cuts, cuts! In September everyone in his office agreed to take a pay cut to avoid redundancies, and now Johnson, Fountain is being taken over by the Belcaster & Belshire Building Society, and they're all redundant anyway! That bastard James Fountain must have been negotiating with the Belcaster all the time, while everyone was tightening their belts to save the firm. He gets a bloody great pay-out, and what do we get? Nothing, and Paul's office is closed due to amalgamation." She suddenly realised that she was shaking and her hands were balled into fists of rage and she gave a bitter smile. "Sorry," she said, "it's just that I'm so angry about it, and I can't let go in front of Paul, because he's already on a major guilt trip. He thinks it's all his fault for leaving Freddie in the first place."

"Well that's just silly," Jill told her firmly. "At the time it would have been stupid to refuse such an offer. He wasn't to know there'd be a takeover, no one was. You won't really have to move, will you?"

Alison shrugged. "I really don't know. I hope not. No, it

probably won't come to that. He must be able to find something, to tide him over at least." She glanced up and saw Angela Haven coming over to join them and said softly, "Don't say anything in front of Angela, will you? We aren't saying anything to anybody much. I just told you because of Isabelle. I mean, I shan't be able to afford her any more."

Jill nodded her understanding, and as Angela came up beside them she turned and smiled.

"Hello, Angela. Haven't seen you for a while. How are things? How's Annabel?"

"Getting bigger," smiled Angela, "but fine actually. Fran is very pleased with her."

They fell into easy discussion of pregnancies, births and babies. No one mentioned Ian, and Angela didn't either. They would all see soon enough that he was back in the Circle and that things in the Haven household were pretty much back to normal.

"I see Jill Hammond's back," Sheila Colby remarked to Mary Jarvis as they sat together on the other side of the room.

"I didn't know she'd been away," Mary said, sipping her tea.

"Left after that dreadful party," Sheila said darkly. "You know she was there…at the party I mean?"

"Yes," Mary said dryly, "you did mention it."

"Without her husband too. He was outside complaining about the noise, and then suddenly there she was coming out of one of the students' bedrooms."

"Oh, come on now, Sheila, you don't know she was in a bedroom."

"Yes I do," stated Sheila firmly. "They've made the down-stairs study into a bedroom, I've seen it, and they were coming out of that."

"Perhaps she was just leaving her coat or something," suggested Mary without any real conviction.

Sheila looked at her pityingly. "If you believe that, Mary, you'll believe anything. You should have seen Anthony Hammond's face!" She leaned closer to speak more confidingly. "It was the student with the pony-tail, and I haven't seen him in the Circle since, either."

"Been keeping watch, have you?"

"No," snapped Sheila defensively, "certainly not, but I see them all about, same as you do. Anyway, I think he doesn't live there any more, and Jill Hammond's been away ever since too. She's supposed to have been at her mother's, at least that's what that French girl told me, but I was beginning to wonder if they'd gone off together."

"Sheila, you're impossible," cried Mary in exasperation. "You put two and two together and make about ninety-five! Jill often takes her children to stay with her mother."

"In the term-time?" asked Sheila with a knowing lift of her eyebrows.

At that moment, Gerald rejoined them with another plate of sandwiches. "Now then," he said cheerfully, "which reputations are you two shredding?"

"Gerald, how dare you say such a thing," Sheila protested, but he thought that Mary had the grace to look uncomfortable. To change the subject he said, "Well here's another piece of gossip for you. Shirley's just been telling me that Melanie is going back home next week. She's feeling so much better, now that they're sure she will be able to cope."

"Wasn't she having counselling?" asked Sheila, turning to Mary. "Didn't I hear that from somewhere?"

"I'm sure you did," Mary said crisply. "Look, I'm just going over to have a word with Vera. She hasn't been to St Joe's lately because she's had the flu." Mary set down her teacup and leaving Sheila and Gerald together she went across to where the old lady was sitting, watching everyone round her.

"Oh, hello dear," she greeted Mary cheerfully as she came over, "this is a sad day, innit? That old Madge was a game bird, eh? Ninety, 'er son was tellin' me. An' Frank says she was one of them what started this place. 'E weren't 'ere then of course, neither was I, but she done a good thing startin' it, eh?" Mary agreed she had. "That black girl, that Cirelle, she's an 'elp an' all," Vera went on as she watched Cirelle and Madeleine handing round plates for Mavis. "She 'elps Shirley an' 'er girl, don't she? 'Ere, Shirley," Vera called to where Shirley was collecting a second cup of tea. She came over carrying her cup.

"Hello, Vera." She smiled. "Want another cup?"

"No thanks, dear. I've 'ad two and I don't want to spend the rest of the day in the lav, do I?" She cackled her irrepressible laugh, making Cirelle turn round. She too came over to join them, bringing the sandwiches.

"Sandwich, Vera?" she offered.

"I might manage one more," Vera said, helping herself.

"Cirelle," Shirley said, "could we have a word?"

Cirelle smiled at her. "Yeah, of course." She set down the plate of sandwiches conveniently near Vera's elbow and they moved out of earshot.

"I'm sorry Melanie has been a bit difficult this week," Shirley began, but Cirelle cut her off.

"Look Shirley, no sweat, OK? It's not a problem." Cirelle stretched out her hands in a dismissive gesture. "Don't worry OK? It's the end of term and I'm busy anyway. Next term they'll have gone and I'll find another job." She glanced round the room and said, "I'd better get on with helping, I promised Mavis." With a quick grin, she walked away, over to the table, leaving Shirley feeling as if she'd been rebuffed.

"I hear Mel's decided to go home," said a voice, and Shirley turned to find Dr Fran beside her.

"Oh, hello Fran. Yes, though if I'm honest, I'm very worried about it. Since she's been seeing that counsellor, she's much more in control of things and seems to have developed a much better bond with the baby, but I'm not sure how she'll cope if all that is put under any pressure. Still, she's determined to go, and I'm afraid David is encouraging her. He finds it a great strain having them living in our house."

"And you don't?" asked Fran gently.

"Well, I do of course, probably more than David if the truth were known, because I'm the buffer between the two of *them*, but if she goes too soon, everything may get worse than it was before."

"But I thought Peter had changed his job, and would be at home more."

"He has, and I'm sure that will be a great help…if he does actually take some of the strain off Mel's shoulders."

"But at least she'll have someone to talk to in the evenings, to share her day with. She must have been awfully lonely before."

"Yes, I think she must have been," admitted Shirley. "Anyway she's off next week and then we're supposed to be going there for Christmas. We shall see then how she's getting on. To tell you the truth, I'm wondering if we might need to move to be nearer to them."

"Grief, what does David say to that?"

"I haven't even suggested it," murmured Shirley glancing anxiously over her shoulder to where David was talking to Andrew, "not yet. But it is in the back of my mind. If we were just closer we could pop in and out from time to time and not always have to go and stay…on a sort of state visit! You know what I mean?"

Fran nodded. "Yes, I do. But would you really want to do that? What about David's garden?"

Shirley smiled ruefully. "I don't know. He'd have to start another one. We could find a smaller house, ours is really too big…"

"Except when it's full of grandchildren," put in Fran helpfully.

"Except when it's full of grandchildren," agreed Shirley, "but if we lived near by they wouldn't have to come and stay with us either."

"That might sell it to David," Fran pointed out.

"It might." Shirley sighed. "Anyway I'm not going to even broach the subject until after Christmas, then, well we'll see."

Then changing the subject she said, "I gather Madge went very peacefully in the end. She really was amazing, wasn't she?"

"Yes. Just fell asleep in her chair and didn't wake up. That's the way to go," said Fran. "Look, Shirley, there's Madeleine from the student house, I just want a word with her."

As Fran crossed to speak to Madeleine, Annie Hooper wandered over to Shirley.

"Hope you enjoyed all the music on Saturday night," she said with a grin. "It sounded quite good from our house!"

Shirley smiled ruefully. "We were a little close to it I must admit."

"Was it Sheila Colby who sent for the police? That was a bit over the top, we thought."

Shirley's lips tightened. "No," she said. "That was Melanie. The noise had woken her little ones and they were driving her mad."

"Oh." Annie gave an embarrassed smile. "Sorry."

"How are you enjoying having Steve's children with you full-time?" Shirley asked. Her question was innocent enough. She had no knowledge of the family politics that governed the Hooper family's life; but Annie assumed that she was getting back at her for the remark about the police, and answered very coolly, "Fine, thank you. It's nice to be a real family."

Mary Jarvis came up with a plate of cakes, and holding it out, said, "Anyone want one of these? Home-made this morning."

"No thanks," Annie shook her head, "I must get back. I only took an hour off from work." And she edged towards the door.

"I'm glad you came over, Mary," sighed Shirley, "I think I'd upset her, but I'm not sure why. I just asked her how she was getting on with the children."

"Ah." Mary's tone was all understanding. "She isn't, I think is the answer. The girl isn't too bad, but the boy, Oliver, I believe is very difficult. Always off where he shouldn't be. Madge used to say that he'd be in some sort of trouble before too long."

"That's funny," Shirley said. "David swears he saw him out

late the other night. Oliver, if it was Oliver, was coming out of the cut, and bumped into David. David sort of grabbed at him and the boy nearly knocked him over, and then ran back into the cut. David was quite shaken, I can tell you. He went over to the Hoopers', but when he knocked on the door, Steve appeared from upstairs and said that they were all in bed, including Oliver."

"Did he check? Steve, I mean, that Oliver was really there."

"Apparently he went to look and said Oliver was in bed; said David must've been mistaken. David could hardly insist on looking for himself, but he's still quite sure it was Oliver."

"Poor Annie," Mary said. "When she married Steve, she only took him. The children were apparently happily with their mother. Which reminds me. Caroline Callow was round the other day, looking for Mike. Did you know he'd gone away?"

"Well I haven't seen him around for a while, but quite honestly I don't take much notice of him, so I wouldn't know." Shirley smiled wickedly. "Sheila would be the one to ask."

Mary grinned too. "That's actually what I told Caroline. I said I hadn't seen him, but Sheila would probably know more. She was worried because his phone was permanently on the answerphone and he hadn't returned any of her calls. He said something about visiting a sick friend."

"Then he's gone Bunburying," Shirley said. "He'll be back."


Annabel left college early that afternoon. Her final lecture had been cancelled, which suited her very well. She was very tired and longed to get home. It would be the first weekend with Dad there properly. He had been living back at home since last Sunday, and though things had seemed strange at first, and Chantal had been more than difficult to live with this week, for Annabel it had been wonderful to come home every evening and find him at the supper table. Her mother, too, had blossomed again, like a plant that had been allowed to dry out and then suddenly received a dousing of water. As she lay in bed and heard the faint murmur of her parents' voices in the next room, Annabel felt a sadness for her own baby, that it would never have a father to love as she loved hers. Not having a father, not living with a father, was a large chunk out of a person's life. It was something she wanted to talk through with Charlie when she got home.

She's due back today, Annabel thought as she set off to the library to collect a book that had been ordered for her. Charlie had rung her on Monday evening to say that Kirsty was going to be fine, and was already well on the road to recovery. She and Mike would be home on Friday afternoon.

Belcaster library was in Crosshills and so having collected her book she set off home, taking the back way along the allotment track towards the cut into Dartmouth Circle. She never came home this way in the dark, but today the faded winter light still filled the sky and it was much quicker than going all the way round by the Dartmouth Road. As she walked, she heard a car coming up behind her, so she stepped on to the verge to allow it to pass. To her surprise, it pulled up beside her. It was a dirty white van and as it stopped she realised with a lurch that Scott was driving. He flung open the driver's door so that it blocked her way, and he got out. Another man got out from the other side and came round behind the van, trapping her between them. She spun round and found herself facing a younger version of Scott, standing behind her, blocking her retreat.

"Bel." Scott spoke calmly. "I want a word with you, right?"

"What about?" Annabel said croakily, suddenly afraid.

"Get in the van."

"No way!" cried Annabel, and then gasped and dropped her bag, reeling as he hit her a backhander across her face.

"I said get in the van." Scott raised his arm again, and Annabel lurched away from him, straight into the waiting arms of his brother.

"Put 'er in the back, Bazzer," ordered Scott, and Annabel found herself dragged round to the back of the van and bundled inside. Scott got in after her and Bazzer closed the doors.

"Now then," Scott said. "You grassed me up."

The only light that came into the back of the van filtered through from the cab, and Annabel could just make out Scott's face as he glowered at her. She stared at him blankly.

"I don't like that, Bel," he said.

"What are you talking about?" Annabel cried, at last finding her voice. "I don't know what you mean."

"Oh, I think you do, Bel. You went to the filth and told 'em about the computer-shop job. You told 'em where my garage is, and now I'm likely to be banged up for over a year. More than a year, Bel, and it's down to you."

Annabel finally found her voice. "Christ, Scott, I didn't tell them. How can I go to the police? I was there too, remember?"

"Yeah, Bel, I remember. But only you and me knew where that garage was. Someone grassed me up, Bel, and they had that garage watched, OK? It 'as to be you. Maybe you told 'em anonymous like. So now I'm giving you a little warning. Don't mess with me, Bel, only stupid gits do that, right." Without any warning he punched her in the mouth, jerking back her head so that it banged on the side of the van. A second fist drove into her stomach and then another. She screamed, clutching her arms protectively round the bulge of the baby, cowering away from him, but with nowhere to go.

"You understand, Bel?" He hit her again backhanded across her cheek, gashing her flesh with the heavy ring he always wore, making the blood flow, so that she moaned with pain, clutching her belly.

"Most grasses wind up dead, Bel," he said, still without raising his voice. "Consider yourself lucky, right? And don't go talking to them about this, neither, or you'll be right there beside me for the computer job. Don't tell no one, Bel, or I'll be back for you, right? Even if it's when I get out again."

"I didn't tell the police," she croaked, "I didn't tell *anyone*."

"You're a lying bitch, Bel. Now get out." As he spoke, Scott opened the rear doors of the van and with a violent jolt, jerked her past him, tumbling her out on to the track where she collapsed into a heap, curled up to protect herself from further punishment. Scott got out and looked down at her for a moment, then he said, "OK, Baz, let's go."

Baz looked down at her too, and said, "Scott, you ever think it might be that Oliver bloke what grassed you up? Jay says 'e wants your patch, mate. She ain't nothink…'e's your problem, bruv."

"Get in the van," Scott snarled, and Annabel tensed herself up for a final blow or kick, but none came; then she heard the engine revving and the van lurched away along the bumpy track.

For what seemed an eternity Annabel lay where she was. She ached from his punches and blows and from the fall from the back of the van. She knew she had to get up and get some help. She knew she must make the effort. She was shaking and cold and her cut face was in the mud, and worst of all, there was a griping pain in her belly.

At last she got to her hands and knees and crawled on to the verge. After a moment more to gather her strength she got to her feet and staggered the hundred yards or so to the cut between the gardens into Dartmouth Circle. Holding on to the fence she struggled up the path and lurched into the Circle beyond. There was a dampness between her legs, but she pushed it from her mind. Only another fifty yards to home, fifty yards and she could lie down again. A wave of pain flooded through her and she had to stop for a moment until it had passed, then she edged forward once more. She was concentrating so hard on her own front door that she didn't see the car outside Mike Callow's house, nor see Charlie and Mike beside it.

But Charlie had seen her, and her glance had taken in the blood and the already emerging bruises on Annabel's face. "Annabel!" she cried, and as Annabel turned and they both saw the true extent of the damage, rushed over to her.

"Call an ambulance," Mike ordered, and as Charlie ran towards the student house to do his bidding, he picked up

Annabel and carried her to her own home. There was no answer when he leaned on the bell, so he placed her gently on the step and said, "Where's your key?"

"In my bag. Mike, I'm bleeding."

"Don't worry, Annabel, it's only cuts and bruises." Mike tried to sound reassuring. "The ambulance will be here in a minute. Where's your bag?"

"I'm bleeding." Annabel's voice was weak. "Underneath." She clutched at him as another wave of pain went through her, and he suddenly realised what she meant.

"Shit!" He looked round him wildly. Charlie came out of the Madhouse.

"They're on their way," she said. "Can't we get her inside?"

"No key," Mike said shortly, and added very softly. "Charlie, she's bleeding. I think she's losing the baby."

Annabel moaned.

"Here." Mike fished in his pocket and handed Charlie his keys. "Open my door, I'll carry her over."

The ambulance arrived five minutes later, but for Mike and Charlie it seemed far longer. Charlie sat with Annabel, lying on the sofa in Mike's downstairs study, while Mike waited out in the Circle for the ambulance.

"She seems to have been mugged or something," Mike told the paramedics when they arrived. "We don't know what happened, we found her outside trying to get home. She's pregnant and she's bleeding."

Within minutes, they had her safely in the ambulance.

"You go with her," Mike said to Charlie. "I'll try and get hold of her mother."

Easier said than done, he thought as the ambulance pulled away, I haven't a clue where she works. He thought for a moment and then headed across to number six. Sheila will know, he thought. But there was no answer to his ring. He tried Mary Jarvis, but she was out too. Perhaps Jill Hammond will know, he thought, and rang the bell of number three.

Isabelle, the au pair, opened the door.

"Mrs Hammond is not at home," she told him, "she has gone to the..." she hesitated, searching for the word, "to the death service of Mrs Peters."

Mike stared at her. "Death service? You mean the funeral? Is Mrs Peters dead?"

"She died on last Sunday," Isabelle told him. "The... funeral? Yes, the funeral is this afternoon at the big church by Dartmouth Road."

Mike thanked her and hurried back to his car. She must mean St Joe's. Perhaps Angela had gone to the funeral too, if not surely somebody there would know where she worked. Within two minutes, he was outside the church. The car park was full, so he double-parked and ran in. The church was empty, but on coming out again, he realised that the day centre in the church hall was buzzing, and so he tried there.

Angela Haven was in a corner, talking to Madeleine Richmond, and Mike shouldered his way through to her.

"Angela," he said urgently, "thank God you're here."

"Mike." Angela looked at him in surprise. "What's the matter?"

"It's Annabel, she's just been rushed to hospital."

The colour drained from Angela's face. "Annabel? Why? What's happened?"

"I don't really know. It looks as if she was mugged. Charlie's gone with her. My car's outside. Come on, I'll take you."

Angela set down her teacup with exaggerated care and looked at Madeleine. "Will you go home and wait for Chantal? She'll be home from school soon. Can you tell her what's happened, tell her I'll ring from the hospital as soon as I can. Tell her that I'll contact her dad if I can."

"Of course." Mad nodded, but Angela was already pushing her way to the door, closely followed by Mike. No mention had been made of the baby, thought Mad, so perhaps that wasn't in danger.

She edged her way to where Cirelle was talking to Vera. "Cirelle, I've got to go." Briefly she told Cirelle what had happened. Cirelle stared at her wide-eyed.

"But that's awful," she said. "Who could have done such a thing?"

Mad shook her head. "I don't know, but I've got to go and tell Chantal, so I'd better do it."

"How badly is she hurt?" Cirelle asked. "Will she lose the baby?"

Mad shrugged. "I don't know. Mike didn't mention the baby and Mrs Haven didn't ask. I'd better go. See you later."

Cirelle caught her hand. "Will you be OK?" she said anxiously. "Do you want me to come with you?"

"No, I'll be fine. You stay here and help as we promised, OK? I'll see you back at home."

Chantal still wasn't at home when Mad rang the bell, so she went home herself and watched for her to arrive from her sitting-room window. It was almost dark when she at last saw Chantal loafing round the Circle, her school bag dangling off one shoulder. Mad went down and met Chantal as she reached her front door.

"Chantal," she called.

Chantal, who had been searching for her key in her bag, looked up and seeing who it was, said defensively, "Oh, it's you. What do you want?"

"Your mum asked me to give you a message," began Mad.

"Mum asked you?" interrupted Chantal.

"Annabel's been attacked. Your mum's at the hospital with her now. She says she'll phone you as soon as she can."

Chantal stared at her. "What do you mean, attacked?"

"I don't know. I'm just delivering the message, that's all. Mike Callow came to Madge's funeral and told her, your mum I mean. He's taken her to the hospital. She says she'll ring as soon as she can. She says she'll tell your dad too."

Chantal felt the tears well up in her eyes and overflow down her cheeks. She could no more have stopped them than have flown to the moon. It was the final awful thing in a week full of awful things, and Chantal stood on the doorstep and howled. Since Saturday's drama, Mad had no time or sympathy for Chantal Haven, her own anger and resentment were seething just below the surface, and she was on the point of walking away, but the sound of the wailing stopped her. She sighed and took the keys that were still clutched in the girl's hand. Opening the front door, she gave Chantal a little push.

"Come on," she said roughly, "you can't stand wailing on the doorstep. Inside."

Chantal allowed herself to be taken inside and upstairs to the living room. Mad sat her down and then put on the kettle. She felt in need of tea herself. Chantal continued to cry and Mad brought a roll of paper towel with her out of the kitchen, dumping it in her lap.

At last, the tears subsided and Chantal looked across at Mad, perched on the arm of the sofa. "I'm sorry," she sniffed.

"Sorry?" Mad raised an eyebrow.

"Sorry about everything. Sorry about Dan…"

"I don't want to discuss him," snapped Mad. She could manage to look after Chantal, make her cups of tea, sit with her if she had to until the phone rang or her father came home, but she could not speak of Dan, or hear that Chantal was sorry, stupid bloody useless word, for what she'd done last Saturday.

Chantal recoiled as if Mad had slapped her, and tears slid down her cheeks again, but silently this time, without the heaving sobs. Mad pushed the mug of tea towards her, and said gruffly, "Here, drink this, you'll feel better." She had tried all week to keep thoughts of Dan and his betrayal from her mind; she fought against images of him and Chantal which leapt unbidden into her brain. She had driven her misery underground with the force of her anger, not allowing the hurt to surface, concentrating that anger on both Dan and Chantal, and now here she was having to push the anger aside in its turn, to offer grudging comfort to Chantal as she waited to hear from the hospital on the condition of her sister.

Chantal tried to drink the tea, but it was too hot and she pushed it away. She blew her nose loudly on a piece of the paper towel. Then two things happened: the front door opened and the phone rang.

Chantal leapt to her feet and rushed to the top of the stairs, and seeing it was her father who came up towards her, flung herself into his arms, crying, "Daddy, oh Daddy," and trying incoherently to explain what had happened.

In the meantime, Mad answered the phone. It was Angela.

"Is Chantal there?" Angela asked.

"Yes," replied Mad, "and your husband has just got home too."

"Put him on please."

Madeleine passed the receiver to Ian.

"Hi," he said, "what's going on?"

Angela spoke at some length, and as she spoke Ian's expression changed from easy openness to one of anxiety. He said, "OK, don't worry, I'll come straight over."

Angela spoke again, and he replied, "I'll bring her with me, she's in a hell of a state." He listened again and then said, "Right, I'm on my way," and replaced the receiver.

"How is she?" cried Chantal. "Is she going to die?"

"No, of course not." Ian was reassuring. He put his arms round her and gave her a hug. "She's going to be fine. You and I'll go to the hospital now, OK?" He turned to Mad. "You're Madeleine Richmond, aren't you? Thank you for looking after Chantal till I got here."

"How is Annabel?"

"A bit battered and bruised," he said with an attempt at a smile, "but she'll be OK." He turned for the stairs, saying, "Come on, Chantal."

Mad didn't ask him about the baby, there seemed little point. He hadn't mentioned it, which could be either a good or a bad sign; either way there was no need to remind Chantal about it, for she hadn't asked either. As she watched the taillights of Ian Haven's car disappear into the dusk, Spike came stalking across the grass and rubbed himself against Mad's legs. She bent down and picked him up, burying her face in his soft fur, and as she stood holding him in her arms, she could feel tears welling up in her own eyes. She thought of Annabel lying in the hospital, bruised and battered, with or without her baby, and her rage at what men could do to women boiled inside her. She turned back to the Madhouse. There were lights on now, so someone must be home. Still holding Spike's comforting warmth in her arms she went across and let herself in.

She found Dean in the living room watching television. When he saw her tear-streaked face, he pretended not to; he simply got up and said, "Hi."

Mad let Spike drop from her arms and gave Dean a watery smile.

"Is Cirelle back yet?" she asked.

"Yeah, she was. She's gone out to the gym. She said something about Annabel Haven being attacked. Do you know what happened?"

Mad told him what she knew, and needed to blow her nose again hard when she'd finished. "I'd better feed Spike," she said, to change the subject.

"Hey, talking of Spike," Dean grinned at her, "I've got a present for you." He dived into the chaos of his bedroom, returning moments later with a carrier bag. He handed it to Mad. She took it, looking intrigued.

"What is it?"

"Open it and see."

Mad put her hand cautiously into the bag and pulled out a square metal contraption. It was a cat flap.

"My mate Flintlock, you know the guy I play squash with? Well he's coming round in the morning, he'll fit it in the back door for you."

Mad looked at him and the tears welled in her eyes again. She put the cat flap back in its bag and laid it on the sofa.

"Oh, Dino," she said, smiling through her tears and giving him a bear-like hug, "I do love you."

Dean's arms tightened round her and for a moment he laid his cheek against the tumbled darkness of her hair. "Do you?" he said softly, and then in a teasing voice, "I should hope so too!" Reluctantly he let her go and said cheerfully, "Come on, let's go to the Dutch, I feel in need of a beer."

*January*

## Chapter Twenty-Six

Mad Richmond and her father drove into Dartmouth Circle in early January, at the beginning of the Lent term. It was a grey day with dull and overcast skies, and a dampness in the air that chilled and clung. As they drove round the Circle they stared in amazement at the number of for-sale boards which had sprouted like weeds in the front gardens, standing like wooden flags of varying colours. Johnson, Fountain with its intertwined J and F in red on a green background stood outside numbers nine and eleven. The red and black logo of Freddie Jones and Co. stood stiffly outside number one and number eight, and a Mark Harrison and Son "Sold By" board stood tipsily in front of number four.

"What on earth is going on here?" Nick Richmond said as he drew to a halt outside the Madhouse. "Everybody's leaving! It must have been one hell of a party you had, Maddo! You've frightened them all away!"

"Dad!" cried Madeleine in horror, "don't say that!"

Nick gave her a quick hug. "Silly girl," he grinned, "I wasn't serious!"

"Well I am!" Mad said standing beside the car and looking round. "Dad there are five houses for sale. That's half the Circle! There wasn't one before Christmas!"

"No, well, you guessed that old lady's son would sell," Nick pointed out.

"Yes, that's fair enough," agreed Mad, "but look, the Havens have sold already and what about the Redwoods? Why would they leave?" She looked aghast at her father. "You don't really think it was because of our party, do you?"

"No, silly girl, I don't," he replied firmly. "There could be any number of reasons for them to go." He pulled up outside the Madhouse. "Now don't you worry about it, Maddo, it's not your problem. What you have to do is get that downstairs bedroom ready for your new girl. What's she called?"

"Hattie. Hattie Silverstone. I told you, Dad, she's an education student. She was on teaching practice in London last term, and the landlord of the place where she lived before decided not to have students any more. Four of them are looking for new places, apart from Hattie."

"Are they indeed?" Nick Richmond looked thoughtful. "That's bad luck for them." He got out of the car and said, "Come on, let's get to grips with this room."

Mad picked up the cat basket containing a protesting Spike, and they went into the house, where there was a wonderful smell of bacon. "Anyone at home?" Madeleine called, and Dean appeared, tousle-haired at the top of the stairs, wearing boxer shorts and a T-shirt. He had obviously only just got up.

"Oh, hi Mad," he said. "I'm just having my breakfast. Hallo, Mr Richmond. There's coffee if you want it."

Madeleine let Spike out in the hall before following her father upstairs to the living room. It was the usual tip and Mad had to clear a heap of clothes and papers off the sofa so that they could sit down.

"Has Hattie seen the place looking like this?" Nick enquired, looking round at the untidy sitting room.

"Oh yes," Madeleine replied cheerfully. "She said it reminded her of home. Coffee, Dad?"

"Just a quick one," he said, "and then we must get on with this girl's room. I've got to be back for a meeting by half four."

They had cleaned Hattie's room, washing down the paintwork, shampooing the carpet and cleaning the window and then Nick touched up the paint where the desk had scraped the wall. By the time they'd finished it looked clean and welcoming.

"When's Hattie arriving?" Dean asked as he joined them for a quick cup of tea before Nick left.

"Not sure, tomorrow or the next day," Mad replied. "Charlie comes tomorrow, I think, and Cirelle comes on Wednesday."

"Then you'll be a full house again," Nick said setting down his cup and getting to his feet. "Well, I hope she fits in all right, this Hattie. I must be off now, Maddo. I've an appointment with Freddie Jones in half an hour. Give us a ring soon." He planted a kiss on his daughter's cheek and went down to his car.

"Give my love to Mum," Mad said as he wound down the window. "See you soon, Dad." Spike wound himself round her legs and Madeleine picked him up. "Oh Spike," she murmured into his fur, "so much has happened. Everything seems to be changing, and I'm not at all sure about Hattie. I wish Ben was still living here."

On the evening of Madge Peters's funeral, Dean and Mad had gone to the Dutch for a drink. Ben was behind the bar. He looked tired and drawn, but he greeted them cheerfully enough.

"Hi," he said, taking two glasses from the shelf. "The usual?" They perched themselves on bar stools and waited for their drinks.

"So, how's the world of Dartmouth Circle?" Ben asked.

"It was Madge Peters's funeral today," Mad said. "Cirelle and I went. Lots of people from the Circle were there. Like, I still can't believe she's died, you know?" Then she thought of Annabel. "And poor Annabel Haven's been attacked, this afternoon, on the allotment path, you know just behind the cut? Mike Callow came and got her mother from the funeral. He took her to the hospital, and I had to go and tell that tarty little sister of hers."

Ben raised an eyebrow. "Can't have been easy," he remarked.

Mad took a pull at her beer. "No it wasn't. When I got there, I didn't care if she was upset. I hoped she'd be miserable, but when she was, I ended up feeling sorry for her! Can you believe that?"

Ben smiled. "Yes, knowing you, I can," he said. "But who attacked Annabel? Does anyone know?"

"Not yet," Dean said. "Charlie went to the hospital in the ambulance with her, but she hasn't come home again yet."

"Charlie did?" Ben was amazed. "Was she there when it happened or what?"

"No, she and Mike Callow were just getting out of the car …you know Mike took Charlie to Ireland when her sister was taken so ill…that was very odd too, don't you think? Like, I mean, I know she babysits for him, but even so."

"Mad, get on with the story," implored Ben.

"What? Oh well, yes…well they were just getting home when Annabel appeared at the end of the cut, crying, and covered in blood and bruises. They called an ambulance and Charlie went in it with her, and Mike came to find Mrs Haven."

"So, have you heard how she is?"

"No, not yet. Her dad came home and took Chantal to the hospital with him. I expect we'll hear more when Charlie gets back."

"Any other news?" Ben didn't ask directly about Jill Hammond, but they all knew what he was really asking.

"She's been away all week, I think," Mad said as if the question had been asked. "But she was at the funeral today."

"Does she know I've moved out?"

"I don't know," Mad said. "I didn't talk to her. She may do. Some helpful soul like Sheila Colby is sure to have told her."

"She's a cow," Dean said conversationally, and downed the last of his beer. "Fill them up, Ben."

Ben had pulled two more pints, before disappearing to the other end of the bar to serve other customers.

"It's funny without him," Mad sighed. "I had hoped he might change his mind and come back if I asked him. Do you think he will?"

Dean shrugged. "Don't know," he said. "Doubt it, somehow."

"In which case," said Mad, "I have to find someone else to take his place, because I need the rent. I suppose you don't know of anyone needing a place?"

"No," Dean shook his head, "but I'll ask around."

None of their friends came into the Dutch that night, and Mad found she was quite pleased. It was very relaxing sitting with Dean and just chatting. She had to make no effort with Dean, they were completely easy together. With Dan she'd always felt the need to be witty, and bright and clever, to hold his attention on herself in the face of the opposition always present in any bar.

When they left the pub at closing time, Ben had watched them go. He was sorry he couldn't go home with them as he used to, his room at the Dutch was poky and small, and he missed the buzz of the Madhouse, but he knew it would be stupid. Jill Hammond had got to him in a way no other woman ever had, and until it was all over he hadn't even realised it. Now he found he missed her with an almost unbearable ache. He hadn't realised how much he'd looked forward to seeing her, even if it was only when he was doing the odd jobs she'd found for him. Just being near her had become important to him in a way that he would never have believed possible, and memories of the times they had been together, making love, gave him physical anguish. If, at the time of the affair, he'd been told that he would have anything more than passing regrets when it finished, he would have laughed. A short fling with an older woman, that was all, very flattering to the ego and a good lay into the bargain, but nothing lasting.

When she had walked away from him at the party, he had known that that was it, that they wouldn't meet again. Anthony seeing them together would bring an end, a very abrupt end, to the affair. It was the next morning and over the successive days he discovered what he'd lost and the pain of that loss began to grow. He had thought of trying to contact her, of phoning during the day when Anthony would be at work. He'd even got as far as dialling the number, but had put down the receiver before anyone had a chance to answer. He knew it was over, and there was no point in tormenting either of them, and there was certainly no point in going back to live in Dartmouth Circle where they might bump into each other at any time.

Ben sighed and started washing the glasses, so that he could go up to his room. At least he'd be finished here in the summer and then, he decided, he was off round the world.

When Mad and Dean got home, Mad found she had forgotten, for a short while, the misery of Dan and Chantal, and the horror of the attack on Annabel. Not for long however, as Charlie was now back and able to tell them how Annabel was getting on.

"She's lost the baby," she said. "She was already bleeding when Mike and I found her. God, I'd like to get my hands on the bastard that did this to her!" And they all felt the same.

Over the last few days of term Madeleine had looked round for someone else to take Ben's room in the house. When she had suggested he might come back, he was quite adamant that he wouldn't.

"Sorry Mad, but no way. I'm fine here, and I still see you guys in the bar."

Then Cirelle came up with Hattie. She was in her final year of a BEd, a large, cheerful girl, with short bouncy dark curls and huge brown eyes. She seemed to fill any room that she came into with her laughter and non-stop chatter. Mad liked her well enough, but wasn't sure how easy she would be to live with. Still, she needed the rent, and she had to have someone, and at least Hattie would be down on the ground floor.

"Hey, this is really great," she boomed when she came round to the house to have a look. "I love the room and the house, and I just love its name. The Madhouse, is that cool or what?" And she roared with laughter.

Mad told her the rent and the ground rules, though when

they went into the kitchen it was Dean's day for washing up, and they clearly hadn't been adhered to.

"Sorry, it's not usually this untidy," Mad apologised.

Like hell it isn't, thought Charlie who was sitting in the living room and had overheard the comment, and she groaned inwardly as she heard Hattie reply, "Don't worry about it, Mad. I don't mind. Feels like home."

Hattie was introduced to everyone and then asked, "Can I leave my stuff here for the Christmas holidays? I don't really want to have to pack it all up and take it home and then cart it all back again."

"Well, I suppose so," said Mad doubtfully. "I was going to give your room a spring clean over the holiday before you moved in next term."

"Hey that'd be great," Hattie agreed. "Like, I can just leave my stuff in the cupboard, OK?"

"She's a bit noisy," Dean complained, speaking loudly to make himself heard over the thudding of UB40. "Still, I suppose we'll get used to her, and it's only for two terms."

Charlie laughed. "Well if she gets too much to take, I'll just go and work upstairs anyway. I've a dissertation to finish."

"You won't mind being the only bloke, will you, Dino?" Mad asked Dean a little anxiously. She didn't want him to move out of the Madhouse. He'd been such a good mate, while she'd been coming to terms with Dan, and she hated the thought of him not being around.

"No, 'course not…with a load of women to wait on me hand and foot?"

Mad aimed a fist at him and they both laughed.

"When are you coming back after Christmas?" Mad asked him on the evening before they both went home to their families.

Dean shrugged. "Don't know. Why?"

"Just wondered," Mad said. "Do you want to do something for New Year?"

"Sure," Dean replied easily. "Like what?"

Mad gathered Spike up on to her lap. "I don't know, something. Like, there must be a party somewhere we can crash!"

Dean laughed. "Oh, a party's no problem, I've already been asked to one. Flintlock's family have got a holiday house in Cornwall, he's invited a crowd down there for a party, you know. We can go to that if you like." He kept his voice casual. "What do you think?"

"Brilliant," said Mad, and then as an afterthought, "What about Pepper?"

"Pepper's going skiing for New Year, with her family," said Dean.

Dean's mum lent them her car and they drove down to Cornwall on New Year's Eve, the car loaded with warm clothes and sleeping bags. When they got there they found that the house, Sea Breeze, was not at all the twee cottage that it sounded, but a large, square, stone house which seemed to grow out of the cliff top. It was reached by a winding stony track across the cliff and had a magnificent view out over the sea.

It was early evening as they drove up and the house looked like a beacon lit up in the gathering darkness. It was already bursting with people, most of whom they knew but a few that they didn't, and they were greeted with cries of delight as they carried in the food and drink that they'd brought as their contribution to the party.

"Sea Breeze isn't the name for this place," Mad laughed when she looked out of the window across the cliff to the sea. "There's nothing between here and America!"

"Flintlock says his dad wanted to change the name to Howling Gale," Dean told her, "but his mum wouldn't let him. It's been in her family for years and it's always been called Sea Breeze."

Howling Gale would certainly have been more appropriate that night, as a stiff south-westerly, increasing to storm force, swept across the open cliff top and wailed round the house. But nobody cared, nobody heard it as the party far outdid the wind, with the noise of thudding music and shrieks of laughter.

It was a great party, and when midnight came everybody shouted "Happy New Year!" and rushed about kissing everybody else. Dean and Mad went into the kitchen to get some more drink, then armed with full pints looked into the huge, now darkened living room, where the music still blared and people still danced. Dean took Mad's hand and led her past that door, past the dining room, where the remains of the food everyone had brought was strewn across the table and much of the floor and through another door into a sort of family room. A lamp was on and there were cushions on the floor, tipped from the sofa, but there was no one in there now. The music still blared in the background, but the room seemed very quiet and welcoming.

Dean took Mad's glass from her hand and put it on a table beside his own and then, saying softly, "Happy New Year, Mad," he pulled her into his arms and began to kiss her. For a moment Mad was shocked and stiff, her brain whirled, she didn't want this, not with Dino, not with anyone, and then all of a sudden she found she did want it. His arms felt so warm and safe round her, his lips, soft and gentle at first, became increasingly demanding, and the length of his body, pressed hard against hers, was strong and firm. Seemingly of their own volition, her arms slipped up round his neck, and her lips, at first closed and cool, opened with warmth to his kiss, as she responded to him in a way she would never have dreamed possible. When at last they broke apart, breathless, she looked into his face wonderingly and said softly, "Dino?"

He still held her in his arms, and he looked down at her with a huge grin. "Yeah?"

"Happy New Year," she murmured, and they slid down on the cushions so thoughtfully left by someone else, and began to kiss again.

As they lay on the cushions, holding each other close, Mad said, "Dino, what about Pepper?"

"What about Pepper? We had fun, Mad, but she always knew she didn't stand a chance against you."

"Against me?" Mad was puzzled. "What do you mean?"

Dean laughed a low throaty laugh. "You really don't know, do you? Anyone else could have told you."

"Told me what?"

"Oh Mad," he said, "I do love you."

Mad looked up into his face, and all of a sudden realised that it was true, and the colour flooded her cheeks. Dean put his forehead to hers and said quietly, "Mad, my little Maddy, I love you and I want to make love to you, but not here. Not where anyone can walk in. In a private place, a place of our own, somewhere special. OK?" And at a loss for words, she had nodded and kissed him and found herself wanting to cry.

The rest of the New Year party passed in a haze of drinking, and talking and laughing. As the dawn crept into the sky, they fetched their sleeping bags from the car and zipping them together for closeness and warmth, snuggled together in a corner of the family room, surrounded by other collapsed couples, and went blissfully to sleep in each other's arms.

The next morning most of the other partygoers drifted off, leaving the house looking as if a bomb had hit it. Flintlock stood looking at it ruefully, thinking what his parents would say if they could see it and wondering if he'd ever get it back into anything like the condition in which he'd found it.

"The parents will schiz if they see it like this," he groaned.

"Aaah, no problem," Dean said, "we'll help you get it sorted. Come on Mad." So the four of them, Flintlock and his girlfriend Sally, and Dean and Madeleine, set to work to restore Sea Breeze to some sort of order. There was much laughter and it took them all day. All the while the howling gale raged outside, bending the cliff-top grass horizontal and moaning round the house like a demented ghost.

When at last they'd finished Flintlock said, "Let's go to the pub for supper, then you guys can spend the night here with us. We're staying on for a couple of days, you can too if you like."

So that night, in a room of their own, with the thick curtains drawn against the wind and the rain, Dean and Madeleine, slowly and lingeringly, made love together for the first time. Later as they lay contentedly in each other's arms, Dean quietly asked the question which had been tormenting him since their first real kiss: "You weren't thinking of Dan, were you?"

Mad hoisted herself up on to her elbow and looked down into his face. "Is that what you think?"

"It's what I'm afraid of," he admitted.

She put her arms round him and pulled him tightly against her so that her breasts were crushed against him and their cheeks were close. "I don't think I've given him a thought since we left home, and certainly not since you slipped from being my best mate into being my lover."

"Your lover," repeated Dean, enjoying the words. "That's what I am. Your lover." He pulled away from her a little and squinted at her, "I suppose you couldn't prove that to me again, could you?"

Since their return from Cornwall, they had been inseparable, and Mad wondered how she had ever got through her days without him. Oh, he'd always been about, but the sense of him being with her was an entirely new one.

"The problem is," she said to him soon after they got back to the Madhouse, "that Dad said no boy- and girlfriends could move in to the house. So I shan't tell the parents about us just yet."

"Well, we didn't break the rule," Dean pointed out cheerfully. "We weren't boy- and girlfriend when we moved in."

"No, and there's nothing they can do about it anyway, but I don't want to upset them, that's all."

"OK," Dean agreed. "We'll each have our own room to work in, and we can decide where we sleep...though I must admit that the beds provided by this landlord are not exactly built for two."

"Oh really?" grinned Mad. "Tried them out, have you?"

"On the odd occasion in the past, maybe more often in the future, who knows?"

"Well, we're luckier than you know," Mad told him. "There's a folding bed underneath mine that springs up to the same height to make a double if required."

"Oh, I think it'll be required," Dean said, sliding his hand under her hair and stroking the back of her neck. "Let's test it out now."

Mad had had to go home for a few days before the beginning of the term, to spend some time with her parents and to collect Spike, but all the time she was away, she longed to be back at the Madhouse, living with Dean. When she thought of him, she wondered how she could have known him for so long without loving him. He was so different from Dan, and now that Dan had finally slid into the realms of non-importance, she realised that that was exactly why she loved Dean so much.

When her father offered to come and help her with Hattie's room, Mad knew that she would have to be very careful not to let him see how she and Dean felt about each other. However, they seemed to have managed it, and he drove away to his meeting with no suspicion that the minute he was gone, his daughter and her lover were upstairs on the resurrected double bed, making up for the few days she'd been at home.

Charlie arrived the next day, driven by Mike Callow. They carried her luggage into the house, and then Mike disappeared home.

"Hey, what's this?" Mad demanded laughing. "Mike Callow fetching you from the airport? What are you up to, Charlie Murphy?"

Charlie smiled. "Not a lot," she said enigmatically.

"Oh, come on!" cried Mad. "He goes with you to Ireland when your sister is ill, he meets your plane today, and I bet he took you to the airport when you went home too! Am I right or am I right?"

Charlie wrinkled her nose as if considering and then laughed. "You're right," she admitted. "Mike and I have started going out together…and he's a lovely feller!" Her eyes were shining and Mad knew just how she felt.

"Wow," she said, "that's great." Then another thought hit her. "You aren't going to move out, are you, like, I mean and go and live with him?"

"No, I'm not," said Charlie. "I'm taking things real slow. Look, I'd better tell you, it wasn't my sister that was ill before Christmas, it was my daughter, Kirsty."

"Your daughter!" exclaimed Mad.

"Yeah. I got involved with a married man in my second year. He was older than me, and so, well, when I found I was pregnant he didn't want to know."

"And that's why you had to come back and repeat your second year?"

"Yes. So, I like Mike very much, but he's much older than me as well. I'm not going to be caught again, that's all."

"And he doesn't mind?" Mad asked curiously.

"He says to take all the time I need. He says he'll wait. Like, he's talking about getting married."

"Wow," Mad said again. "And are you?" Despite her new-found and increasing love for Dean, marriage certainly wasn't on her agenda yet.

"Not at the moment," Charlie said. "I've a degree to take."

Mad thought about her and Dean, and wondered briefly if they would ever get as far as marriage, but knew they had another year of sharing the house before they finished their degrees, and then, well, then would be the time for decisions. However, she did admit to Charlie that she and Dean now had a different sort of relationship.

"And about time too," Charlie laughed, "poor Dino's been very patient!"

"Well, he had Pepper," Mad pointed out.

"Only because he couldn't have you, dumb-dumb!"

"Are you sure?" Mad still had moments of uncertainty.

"Yeah, of course I am, it was only you who couldn't see it." Charlie grinned across at her. "And does this mean that the dreaded Dan is truly a thing of the past?"

"Definitely," Mad asserted. "I can't believe I put up with him messing me about for so long."

"Well, thank God for that," Charlie said in heartfelt tones, and gave Mad a hug. "Aren't you the great girl? I'm delighted! What do your parents say about you and Dean living together?"

"They don't know," warned Mad, "and that's the way it's going to stay... for now anyway!"

Cirelle and Hattie arrived at the same time the next day and all of a sudden the Madhouse was living up to its name.

"Hey, what's with all the for-sale boards?" Cirelle asked when she'd carried everything upstairs.

Madeleine shrugged. "Don't know. Haven't seen anyone yet. But it looks like the Havens will be moving soon. Theirs is already sold."

# Chapter Twenty-Seven

Annabel Haven sat on one of the few chairs left in the living room and looked down at the removal van backed into the drive. They were moving all the furniture today, and the family was staying in a hotel for the night before trying to move themselves into their new house in a village on the other side of Belcaster. They were lucky, Annabel's parents said, that the house had sold quite quickly, because now there were so many on the market in the Circle, they might be less sought after and slower to move.

Annabel was glad they were moving. She couldn't wait to get out of the house and live somewhere where nobody knew her, where nobody treated her with the particular kindness reserved for those who were bereaved, or recovering from some dreadful illness. She was tired of being an object of pity in the Circle, she was tired of being cosseted, however well-meaningly, she simply wanted to be left alone to get on with her life, to come to terms with everything that had happened to her in her own way.

After the attack, she had been kept in the hospital for three days. On the day she was discharged, she lay in a side ward and stared out of the window. The grey December sky met the rooftops of the buildings opposite, a flurry of rain dashed itself against the window pane, and the world outside looked a most miserable and uninviting place. She was waiting for her mother to come and fetch her home, but she hadn't got ready. The nurses had told her she should have a shower and get dressed, but she couldn't seem to summon up the energy; she would wait until Mum arrived to help her. She still ached from her bruises, but these paled into insignificance compared with the pain she felt at the loss of her baby. The doctors had done all they could, but though he was born alive, he survived for only half an hour. They'd asked her to give him a name, and through the haze of her exhaustion she had murmured, "Christopher," and little Christopher Haven had been baptised by the doctor and now lay in his tiny coffin awaiting burial.

When she heard that he had died, Annabel felt numb, and that numbness had persisted. She was confined to a grey world where every thought, every movement was an effort. She did the bidding of others, allowing herself to be washed and fed, but had no will of her own.

The police had been called of course. They had asked her if she knew who had attacked her. Had she recognised him? Annabel shook her head wearily, blocking Scott Manders out of her mind. What did it matter now? If they found Scott and could prove he'd beaten her up, it wouldn't bring baby Christopher back.

Charlie had been to see her, had sat beside the bed and held her hand for hours in silent support and communication. She recognised Annabel's need for entirely undemanding company. The police questions had achieved little in the way of information, and it had been decided that any further questioning should wait until Annabel felt up to answering. But Charlie asked her again if she knew who it was, and was stunned into awful silence by the answer.

"It was Scott, Charlie. He thought I'd gone to the police and told them where his lock-up was, you know with all the computer stuff?"

"You mean the garage?"

Annabel nodded.

"And he attacked you for that?" The words were hardly more than a whisper.

Annabel shrugged wearily. "That's what he said. He said I'd grassed him up, and he'd probably go to prison because of me, and then he started to punch me."

Charlie sat in silence for a moment still holding Annabel's hand, as she took in what Annabel had told her, then she took a deep breath and said in a low voice, "Oh my God. It's all my fault."

Annabel was uncomprehending. "What do you mean, Charlie? How can it be your fault? It's nothing to do with you."

"I'm afraid it is," Charlie said quietly. "You see, I sent an anonymous note to the police, saying if they wanted to find the stuff from the robbery at Belcaster Computers, they should search the garages in the yard off Camborne Road. I was the one who put them on to him. It's all my fault..."

Annabel stared at her. "*You* told them? But why?"

Charlie buried her head in her hands. "Oh, I don't know. Because he'd been such a bastard to you, I suppose." She looked up again and added fiercely, "He made me so angry, why should he get away with it? Men like him are better locked up!" Her face crumpled and the tears streamed down her cheeks. "But I never thought...I mean, to think he'd attack you..." *And the baby*...but these last words were left unsaid, though they both knew they hung between them. "Oh, Annabel, I'm so sorry... I'm so sorry!"

"It doesn't matter," Annabel said listlessly. "You did it for the best." She really didn't care any more. She didn't blame Charlie, she might even have done the same in her place. It didn't matter now, it was all too late.

"But you must tell them it was Scott who attacked you," Charlie said. "You must get him put away after what he's done to you."

"It won't bring Christopher back," Annabel said dully, and Charlie felt another stab of anguish at what she'd done, but she was determined that Scott Manders shouldn't be allowed to get away with it.

"I know," she said gently. "I know that, but we have to stop him doing anything like this ever again. He's obviously a violent man, he'll do it again, you know?"

"I can't tell them," Annabel said wearily, "or I'll go to prison for the robbery too."

"No you won't," Charlie said stoutly. "I'm sure *that* won't happen. Look, can I tell Mike about all this? He'll know what to do."

"Mike? Mike Callow?"

"Yes." Charlie smiled in spite of herself. "I think, well, we've been very close lately, you know?"

Annabel stared at her, jerked for a moment from her lethargy. "You and Mike Callow? An item?"

"Yes, no, well maybe. He wants to be, I'm not quite sure. Look, I'll tell you all about that another time. The thing now is to find out what we do about Scott, and I'm sure Mike will know. Like, that way we can decide things before you have to tell your parents, or speak to the police again, OK?" She could see Annabel was far from convinced and she went on, "Look, Annabel, something has to be done. We can't have this robbery thing hanging over you for the rest of your life; it's got to be sorted, right? I know there must be a way, some way. Let me talk to Mike and see what he says, OK?"

Annabel was too tired to argue. "If you want to," she said.

So Charlie had spoken to Mike that same evening. He was amazed by what he heard, but he was adamant. "She must go to the police at once and tell them everything," he said. "She may be charged with being involved with the burglary, an accessory or something, but even so she must tell them everything. Her parents will stand by her, won't they?"

"I should think so," Charlie said. "They did over the baby, and they'll certainly want to see Scott Manders put away for what he did to her."

"Tell her if it does go to court, they'll probably be lenient with her in the circumstances, but whatever happens she must tell them everything." He looked grim. "Thugs like that Manders guy should be put away for a long time," he said.

Charlie went over to see Annabel as soon as she got home from the hospital the next day.

"Mike says you must tell the police everything," she said firmly. "He says tell your parents and then go to the police. In the circumstances he doesn't think you'll be in too much trouble."

"That doesn't matter now anyway," Annabel said, "that's what I've decided. I'll tell Mum and Dad first, and see what they say, OK?"

"Yeah." Charlie gave her a hug. "Go for it."

So Annabel had gone for it. When her father came home that evening, she sat her parents down and told them everything, right from the start. How Scott had rescued her from the Crosshills gang, about learning to drive his van, about the hours she'd spent with him and finally about the burglary of the computer shop, the getaway and having sex in the van afterwards. Her parents listened in silence, only the changing expressions on her mother's face showing her increasing disbelief and horror at what she heard.

Annabel told them that Scott had been Christopher's father. She told them of his reaction to the news that she was pregnant, and at last how he'd attacked her because he thought she'd given information about his lock-up to the police.

When at last she finished, she felt quite light-headed from the relief at having told them everything. There were no secrets now, from them, anyway. All they had to do now was decide what to do for the best.

Ian got straight down to practicalities. "We'll find a solicitor and then go to the police," he said. "You do realise that we have to tell them everything, don't you, Polly?"

"But what will happen to her?" worried Angela. "Will she have to go to court?"

"I don't know," admitted Ian. "That's why we need a solicitor, but what I do know is that we are going to get this young thug put away for a very long time. He's attacked my daughter in broad daylight and killed her baby, not to mention tricking her into criminal activity. He has to be stopped and he has to be punished, and we're going to do whatever it takes. Agreed?"

They all agreed and Ian rang up an old friend, John Belmont, who was a solicitor with a large partnership in Belcaster.

John came round and having heard Annabel's story, he agreed to go with them to the police station. When they got there they were taken into an interview room and Sergeant Trump, who had been to the hospital to see Annabel when it first happened, came in to talk to them.

"I'm glad to see you looking a little better, Miss Haven," he said as he sat down with them. "And I want to tell you that while you've been in the hospital, we have been pursuing our enquiries. We've found a witness, an old man called Robert Hogan, who was working on his allotment at the time of the attack. Mr Hogan saw a scruffy white van driving along the track. It was going fairly quickly, so we're assuming that, if it did have anything to do with the attack, it was leaving the scene."

"It was involved," Annabel began, but John Belmont interrupted.

"Just a moment, Annabel. Sergeant, Miss Haven has come to see you today to make a full statement with regard to the attack and the various circumstances which led up to it."

Annabel made her statement, and the sergeant tape-recorded it. When at last she had finished Sergeant Trump asked a few questions about the burglary, and where the computers had been hidden.

When they finally left the police station, Annabel had signed her statement and been warned that she might be charged with being an accessory to the burglary, but that decision was not yet taken. John Belmont told them that he would represent Annabel if it came to court, and that he thought he could plead a lot of mitigation in her defence.

"There are many things that can be said in her favour," John Belmont explained to them. "She has come to the police voluntarily and made a complete admission to being involved in the burglary. It was a daytime burglary of shop premises, not someone's home at night. She is only eighteen, and this is a first offence, into which she was led by someone with a criminal record." He smiled at Annabel reassuringly. "I will have the opportunity to explain all this to the magistrates, and it will all be taken into consideration when they decide how to deal with you. With luck, and a sympathetic bench, they may be lenient. That's what I shall be asking them anyway, and we'll hope that they listen to me."

It all sounded reasonably hopeful, but for Annabel it was yet another thing that weighed in on her when she awoke each morning and had to face another day.

The decision to move house had been taken quite suddenly. It was two days after Christopher's tiny coffin had been taken to the church. Annabel and her family and Frank Marsh, the vicar, were the only people at the short service, and as they stood outside in the raw December air and watched Christopher committed to the earth, Ian felt that today, surely, they had plumbed the depths. He stood with an arm around each of his daughters as tears ran down their cheeks, he saw Angela struggling to be strong for Annabel and he thought, surely we have hit rock bottom now, surely things must get better.

The family was sitting round the dinner table a few days later when Ian said, "I looked at a house in Stone Winton today. A lovely house, converted from an old barn. I wondered what you all might think about moving."

At first, they were all stunned. None of them had thought of moving, but as the idea sank in, they all, for different reasons, found the idea becoming more and more attractive. They were all full of questions, but Ian was ready for every one.

"Yes," he told Chantal, "you can still go to Chapmans. Yes, I can drive you into college most days," he promised Annabel.

"Yes, we can afford it, even if you go back to part-time working," he reassured Angela. He looked round the table, where they had all forgotten the food in front of them and said, "I think we all need a change, a fresh start, where no one knows anything about any of the problems we've have over the last few months. Tomorrow, if you like the idea, we'll all go and look at the barn, and see what you think. I think it's a lovely house, but if you don't like it, we can look at other houses."

They did like it; they'd all loved it. There was plenty of room, more than in their house in the Circle, and both the living room and the kitchen looked out across water meadows to the River Winton beyond. The four bedrooms were all of a reasonable size, and there was a large room built out above the garage that could become a sitting room for the girls.

Each of them was sold on a different aspect of the house, but all agreed they would love to move there, if they were able to buy it. Ian rang the estate agents, Mark Harrison and Son, straightaway. He was determined that they should buy the house and move in to it as soon as possible, so he wasted no time but offered the full asking price.

"I've got to sell my own house first," Ian warned Mr Harrison, "but I don't think that will be too difficult as it's in Dartmouth Circle."

Harrison agreed and said, "My firm will happily handle the sale of your house, Mr Haven. Indeed I think I have a client who might well be extremely interested."

Miraculously, it proved to be so, and contracts were exchanged on both houses just after Christmas, with the sales finally going through at the end of January.

Once the idea of moving had been suggested, and she'd seen the barn, Annabel couldn't wait to go. She lived through Christmas and its celebrations, so much better than last year had been without Dad; she saw in the New Year with Chantal and their parents – no nightmare party like last year – and all the time she was on tenterhooks, in case for some reason one of the sales fell through. She longed to get away from Dartmouth Circle to the anonymity of Stone Winton.

"I can't wait to be somewhere else," she confided to Charlie. They had met for a coffee at the patisserie in town on Charlie's return from Ireland after Christmas, and were treating themselves to sticky cream cakes and catching up on each other's news. "Dad was right, we do all need a fresh start. He wants to be where no one knows that he left Mum. Mum wants to be where she doesn't have to remember him leaving, and Chantal wants to be miles away from your student house and Oliver Hooper." She licked a smear of cream from her fingers. "Of course, I still have to go to the Tech, and people there know about the baby, but I haven't any close friends there, so not much has been said." She smiled across at Charlie. "You're my closest mate now," she said. "You know how I feel about, well like, everything."

Charlie was touched and she felt the colour rise in her cheeks. She felt they were very close, was both pleased and relieved that her interference in Annabel's affairs hadn't broken their friendship.

"Any news about Scott?" she asked tentatively.

"Yes, they arrested him for attacking me and he's been remanded in custody, so he's safely locked away at the moment."

"What about the robbery?" Charlie asked. "What's happened about that?"

"He'd already been charged with that," Annabel said. "That was the trouble! Anyway, the two things are being sorted at the same time."

"And what about you? What's happening about that?"

"That's over too," Annabel said. "After I was charged, I was what they call fast-tracked, and came to court the next day. I pleaded guilty and then John Belmont explained to the court exactly what had happened. Then I had to wait while they went out and talked about me. Like, it was scary, you know, the waiting, but I was lucky. The magistrates gave me a conditional discharge. They told me how lucky I was, as it is a most unusual sentence for burglary, but they said they'd taken on board what Mr Belmont had said. As long as I don't get into any more trouble in the next two years, I won't hear any more about it, thank God."

Charlie squeezed her friend's hand. "Thank God, indeed," she echoed. At least Annabel wouldn't be going to prison or anything because of her, she thought, but she still fervently regretted the impulse which had caused her to send her anonymous tip-off to the police about Scott.

Annabel was saying something about Chantal, and Charlie pulled her thoughts back to the conversation in hand.

" …and luckily we've heard no more from the police about Chantal being under age. We don't know if anything has happened to Dan."

Charlie had heard all about the infamous party on her arrival home from Ireland in December. She, like Dean, had never liked Dan very much and felt that it was good riddance, but she had little sympathy for Chantal, even if Dan had taken advantage of her. She still thought Chantal was a tarty little piece who'd got what she was asking for, even if she was only fifteen. She chose her words carefully.

"We heard on the grapevine that the police have been to see him and are still pursuing their enquiries," Charlie said. "Don't know if it's true, we don't see him now of course. Poor Mad is still pretty upset with Chantal, and I don't blame her." She glanced across at Annabel a little guiltily. "Sorry," she said, "I know Chantal was led on, but it doesn't make it any easier for Mad to accept what they did in her own house at her own party."

From that point of view, Charlie was glad that the Havens were moving away, it would be much easier for Mad to put Dan's betrayal out of her mind if she didn't keep bumping into Chantal in the road.

"I agree," Annabel said, "but I'm not really in any position to judge, am I?"

Charlie shook her head. "Me neither," she admitted, "but,

like, I'm still angry, on Mad's behalf, you know? Still she's got Dean now. They're going out, did you know?"

"No, I've kept away from everyone."

"Well, they started going out at New Year, and Dan is a thing of the past. Mad's a different person."

"You will come over and see us, won't you?" Annabel said. "You're the only visitor I want from here."

"Of course I will," Charlie promised. "I'm longing to see the new house."

They ordered more coffee and Annabel said, "Now tell me your news. What's this about you and Mike Callow?"

Charlie's eyes softened. "Mike? Well he was great when we went over to Cork to the hospital when Kirsty was so ill."

"Yeah, and…?" Annabel encouraged her.

"And…he told me he loves me."

"Wow!" Annabel was impressed. "And what about you? Do you love him?"

Charlie gave a self-conscious grin. "Sort of."

"Sort of!" Annabel gave a shout of laughter. "What kind of answer is that?"

"It's the one you're going to put up with until I tell you something else," Charlie teased. Then she relented. "We'll be seeing quite a lot of each other I suppose," she said primly.

"Seeing quite a lot of each other," repeated Annabel. "You mean because you'll have no clothes on?" Both girls dissolved into giggles at this, the first time that Annabel had really laughed spontaneously since Scott had driven up behind her on the allotment track.

"Annabel Haven, you're a disgrace," said Charlie, when she was able to say anything at all. "That's not what I meant, and you know it." Suddenly she was serious again. "We're not rushing anything, OK? I've played this game before, remember. Mike's a lot older than I am, and he's married, and he's already got children. You can imagine my parents aren't over the moon at any of it."

Charlie thought of how her mother had reacted when she had come home with Mike to see Kirsty, and Mike had told them out of the blue that he wanted to marry Charlie.

"Doesn't he have one wife already?" her mother had demanded later when they were alone in Charlie's bedroom. "What are you thinking of, Charlotte, getting involved with a married man again, and an older married man with a family, at that? Did you learn nothing from last time? You'll break your father's heart."

"But Mam, we're not involved," Charlie protested. "I didn't know how he felt about me until yesterday, I swear it. I just used to help him mind his kids, that's all, honestly."

Her mother looked sceptical, but she said, "If you say so."

"Mam, it's true."

"Then why is he telling us he wants to marry you?" Kath Murphy asked. "'If she'll have me, I intend to marry her,' were his very words. What makes him even begin to think that you'll have him?"

"Mam, when I went to him yesterday to borrow the money to come home, I went to him as a friend. He was the only one I knew well enough who might have actually had any money to lend me, right? I was crying. I was desperate about Kirsty, and he simply put his arms round me to comfort me and then, well, he kissed me, and I felt..." Charlie paused, searching for words that might convey to her mother exactly what she had felt. "I felt that I'd come home."

"Hmm, all very romantic," Kath said. "And where does his wife fit into this little idyll, may I ask?"

"She doesn't," Charlie said briskly. "I've never met her. She and Mike have lived apart for well over a year now."

"Not divorced though."

"No, Mam, not as far as I know."

"So, you're having an affair with a married man."

"No," Charlie said patiently, "no, I'm not. I'm not having an affair with anyone, right?"

Her mother tried another tack. "Oh Charlie, you're only

twenty-two, he must be thirty-five if he's a day. He's too old for you, pet, he's nearer my age than yours."

"Mam, there's nothing between us, right. He's kissed me once, for God's sakes, but if he does speak to me, like, ask me for a date or something, well, I'll probably go."

Mike had spoken to her, not asking for a date as such, but he had talked to her about their relationship. They had been sitting in his living room the evening she had come to discuss what Annabel should do about Scott. He poured them each a glass of wine and when they had finished talking about Annabel and Scott, Mike turned the conversation to themselves.

"Charlie, about us," he began.

"We aren't really an 'us'," Charlie pointed out. She felt suddenly nervous and shy of him.

"No," he agreed, "but I do want us to be." He took her hands and held them against his cheeks for a moment. "Charlie, what I said to you that evening we went to Ireland, I really meant it, you know. I've loved you ever since I first set eyes on you. I've never believed in love at first sight, and all that, but I do now, because it happened to me. Charlie, I know you don't feel the same way about me," his eyes twinkled at her, "but I'll be working on that, I promise you."

"Oh, Mike, I don't know…" She felt confused. She liked him very much and she had to admit that she did find him attractive. The memory of his kiss was one she had relived many times. Yet, while they were in Ireland, he hadn't touched her again, and she found that confusing too. She had wanted him to, and yet she was afraid that he would. Kirsty was her priority there of course, and she had found his quiet support very comforting. But Duncan still lurked in the backwoods of her mind, still scaring her away from any deep relationship, especially with an older, married man.

"You'll be under no pressure, I promise you that too," Mike reassured her. "I just want to be with you, to get to know you and for you to get to know me…properly."

"Like, just go out, you mean?"

"Just like that," he agreed. "I don't want to rush you into *anything*, I can wait as long as you like, my darling. You're worth waiting for."

"I haven't told you about Kirsty," Charlie said, pulling her hands away and getting to her feet. She turned to face him across the room. "About what happened."

"And you don't have to, that's up to you. She's your daughter, that's all that matters."

"What about your wife? What about Caroline?"

"She's set divorce proceedings in motion," Mike said. "Nothing to do with you, just decided that we'd been apart too long ever to have a reconciliation and so she wants her freedom." He thought for a moment about the vitriolic messages which had been awaiting him on the answer machine when he got back from Ireland, but they truly did have nothing to do with Charlie, so he simply said, "It will be uncontested and go through quite quickly, I think."

"And your kids?"

Mike sighed. "With as little disruption for them as possible," he said. "They're used to us living apart now. I'll see them as much as I always did, that shouldn't change. I love them dearly and want to be as good a father to them as I can be in the circumstances." He, too, got to his feet and reaching for her hands again drew her softly into his arms.

"Darling Charlie, I know you've been hurt once, but believe me I wouldn't do anything to hurt you. Just give me a chance to show you how much I love you, OK?"

Charlie felt tears in her eyes as she looked up at him and nodded. As a tear escaped and ran down her cheek, Mike gently wiped it away with his thumb, and then equally gently kissed her lips.

"So?" prompted Annabel as she saw her friend had gone deep into a reverie.

"So," answered Charlie, "we're not 'involved' as my mother would say, but it may not be very long before we are."

"Will you move in with him?" asked Annabel. "Seems silly to be living almost next door."

"No, I won't," Charlie said firmly. "If this is ever going to work, we both need our own space while we get used to the idea, and I've exams to pass. Anyway, I've promised my parents that I won't. It'd break their hearts if I actually moved in with him."

The two girls had met up several times for coffee in the weeks running up to the move, and Annabel had watched Charlie slipping slowly but irrevocably in love with Mike. Even more did she want to get away from Dartmouth Circle, so that watching the men load up the removal van at last, she knew that she would never come back to the Circle. She had a lecture in an hour, and after her tutorial this afternoon she would join the rest of the family in the White Bear, and then tomorrow they would all go and unpack themselves into their new home in Stone Winton. She picked up her duffel bag and went to find her mother, who was closing the last packing case down in the study.

"I'm off now, Mum," she said, "I'll see you at the White Bear later on." She jerked her head in the direction of the van. "Good luck with the rest of it."

## Chapter Twenty-Eight

Jill watched the last of the Havens' home being loaded into the removal van from her window. Though she hadn't seen much of them recently, she knew she would miss them being next door.

"I'm so glad you and Ian have got back together," she'd said to Angela when they'd met Christmas shopping in town and decided to have a coffee together to recover from the morning's scramble.

"So am I," Angela had said simply, but her eyes shone and Jill felt a stab of envy at her obvious happiness.

"Do you mind if I ask...?" Jill hesitated. "I mean, was it difficult to...? Sorry, it's none of my business."

Angela looked across at her sympathetically. "Taking Ian back?"

Jill nodded.

"I suppose," Angela said slowly, "I suppose I always wanted him back. I wanted us to be a family again and the girls to have a real dad, but I knew he really had to want it too. Not just come back because the other woman had gone." She smiled shyly. "I still loved him, you see, but he had to love me too, more than before. Does that make sense?"

"Yes, it does, of course it does."

Angela wasn't sure quite why Jill had asked the question. Just out of interest, or was there a deeper reason? Had she got the same problem? Or, rather, had Anthony? She had heard, of course, the Circle gossip about Jill and Ben at the student party, but she was sure it had been vastly over-exaggerated. She couldn't imagine someone as attractive and level-headed as Jill, someone with a lovely family and a happy home, allowing herself to get involved with a student. It seemed a ridiculous idea, but Annabel had told her that Ben no longer lived at the Madhouse, and that perhaps bore out some of the story. She looked across at Jill with concern. "Is everything all right with you?"

Jill felt tears pricking her eyes. "Yes, yes it is, thanks." She smiled brightly. "I see you're moving as well," she said. "Where are you off to?"

"Well, fingers crossed, to a lovely converted barn in Stone Winton." Angela began to tell her about the move. "It will do us all good to get away from here," she said, "especially Annabel."

"Yes, I can imagine," Jill said. "I – we – were so sorry to hear about her being mugged...and about the baby."

Angela sighed. "It was dreadful," she agreed, "and do you know the worst thing? Some people have actually said, 'Oh well, perhaps it was for the best'! How can they? How can it be for the best that a girl is attacked and a baby is killed!" Her tone rose as she spoke, fury bringing tears to her eyes. Jill took her hand across the table and wondered who had been crass enough actually to say what, probably, had crossed the minds of many people, herself included. She felt amazingly shabby at having had the thought.

"Sheila..." she began, well aware who had enjoyed spreading the rumours about her.

Angela shook her head. "No, surprisingly enough, it wasn't her, she's been very sympathetic. She came round to see Annabel soon after she came out of the hospital. I didn't think Annabel would want to see her, but she did, and they seemed to get on like a house on fire." She smiled across at Jill. "Annabel wouldn't say what they talked about, but the visit did her good."

They had finished their coffee and gone their separate ways. Since then Jill hadn't seen Angela except in the distance, but she'd thought about her a great deal over the next few weeks, of what she'd said about both partners really wanting to make a second go at their marriage work, and she wondered if Anthony would ever forgive her enough to have another try. She wondered if he even loved her any more.

Christmas had arrived without any decisions on their future being taken, and it had been very difficult for both of them. They were still living side by side in the house, but neither of them had been able to restore the easy intimacy of their marriage before Jill's affair with Ben.

In retrospect, Jill knew it had only been a few weeks of complete madness. She had risked all she had simply because she was bored and fed up; the unexpected excitement and the irresistibly strong attraction she had felt for Ben had simply made her throw all caution to the winds. Now it was all over and normality of a sort had reclaimed her, she couldn't believe she'd allowed it to happen. Since the dreadful night of the party at the Madhouse, she had not seen Ben. She heard from other helpful residents of the Circle that he had moved away, but apart from the phone call on the morning after the party, she had heard nothing from him again, and she was relieved. It helped her to block out what she now saw was a sordid, squalid affair, for which she had risked her marriage.

For the sake of the children Jill and Anthony celebrated Christmas in the usual way, and Nancy came to help celebrate with them.

"I'm not sure I should come this year," she said to Jill. "It might be better if you had a family Christmas on your own."

"Oh no, Mum." Jill was horrified. "You must come! I can't cope with us just being ourselves. Isabelle is going home for Christmas and New Year, and Anthony and I will have too much time alone."

"But time alone is what you need, darling," Nancy pointed out gently. "You have to rebuild your relationship, and that will take time and effort. I would only be in the way."

But Jill couldn't face the evenings of strained silences, or the emptiness when Anthony disappeared into his study and left her sitting upstairs alone, and in the end she had applied to him to press the invitation on Nancy. Anthony did so readily enough, he too was not looking forward to the long hours of the holiday period that he would have to spend at home. The shock and the hurt he had sustained when he had discovered Jill's affair seemed still as fresh as ever. Only when he was immersed in his work could he forget the pain and feel at all like his old self. As soon as he left the office he began to dread the evening ahead. Jill was doing her best to be normal, to be as she always had been, pleased to see him home, a drink poured and waiting, supper in the oven, but it was that very effort at normality that he found so hard to take. How could she put this dreadful thing that had come between them behind her so easily? How could she act as if nothing had happened, when the whole of his world had been shaken to its foundations? He tortured himself with visions of her in bed with that pony-tailed student, of his hands on her body, doing things to her that made her writhe and cry out with pleasure. Anthony knew it was complete stupidity to torture himself in this way, but he couldn't help it, the visions rose unbidden to his mind. He knew he would be unable to make love to her while these pictures played in his mind, and rather than risk the humiliation of failure, he preferred not to touch her at all. If she touched him, even casually as she brushed past, he felt himself withdraw from her...and so did she.

Much better, he decided, if Nancy were with them over Christmas, making it as normal as possible for the children and allowing him and Jill to maintain a façade by providing one for her.

So Nancy had come. There was only one problem with that; it meant Anthony had to move back into the marital bed, as Nancy had to sleep in Anthony's study, as she always did.

"I suppose she could sleep in Isabelle's room," Anthony suggested, tentatively.

"No she could not," Jill had said firmly. "At least, I'm not asking Isabelle to clear all her stuff away before she goes. You can if you like."

Anthony hadn't liked. He simply moved his clothes back up to their shared bedroom the morning before Christmas Eve, leaving the bed already installed in the study free to be made up for Nancy. Since then, even after Nancy had returned to her own home, Jill and Anthony had slept side by side, each conscious of the other, but neither crossing the divide...one because he could not and the other because she dare not.

Christmas Day had relentlessly occurred. There was the early start when the children found their stockings waiting on the ends of their beds, the presents round the tree, Christmas lunch and tea. Games to play and stories to read, and the final tears before bed at the end of an exciting day.

As she watched them each going through a private hell, Nancy longed to knock their heads together and make them see sense. It was while Anthony had taken the children to the park on Boxing Day that she had the chance to tackle Jill about it.

"I don't understand you," she said as they sat together with a cup of coffee. "Haven't you discussed anything...said anything?"

Jill shook her head. "I can't, Mum. It has to come from him. He has to want me here. He has to make the first move."

"Why?" Nancy wasn't being obstructive, she genuinely wanted to know. "Why can't you say something?"

"Because, if he can't forgive me...if he doesn't love me enough to forgive me, it's never going to work. He says he needs time to decide, so that's what I'm trying to give him, that's all."

"But you still love him?"

"Yes," Jill said. "I really do, and as it's all my fault I've got to be the one who waits. If I push him into a decision, it may be the wrong one. I have to give him the time he needs."

"Well, I hope he makes some sort of decision soon," said Nancy, "because all this is tearing you both apart." She longed to talk to Anthony herself, but she knew that it would probably do more harm than good if she interfered, so she managed to bite her tongue and say nothing. After New Year, she returned home, and still nothing had even begun to be resolved. Jill and Anthony continued to live on the surface of their lives, talking only superficially, but neither had found the courage to take their communication any deeper. Isabelle had come back from France, and life fell back into its routine groove.

Then, last night, as they sat over the supper table Anthony had suddenly said, "Something's come up. After supper we must talk properly." He looked across at her. "Where's Isabelle, did you say?"

"Babysitting for the Forresters. She won't be back for some time yet."

Jill cleared the table and left the dishes in the sink. Now was not the time to be washing dishes, and anyway she didn't want to spend even ten minutes wondering if Anthony was going to say that he didn't want to go on as they were. She made them coffee and carried it into the sitting room. For a moment or two, she fussed about with cups and a coffee table, and then she sat down in her armchair, setting her own coffee cup on the floor beside her.

Anthony took a mouthful of coffee and then put his cup down too. "I've been offered a job in the London office," he said without preamble. "I've decided to accept, and I shall have to live in London."

Jill stared at him. "Does that mean you're leaving me?" she asked in a low voice.

Anthony gave a slight shrug. "That's up to you," he said.

"What do you mean, 'up to me'?" demanded Jill.

"Just what I say," replied Anthony calmly. "I shall go and live in London. If you want to come too, you can."

"And the children…?"

"Them too, of course, but this isn't about the children," said Anthony.

"Oh for God's sake, Anthony, of course it is," cried Jill. "They are our prime concern."

"What I'm trying to say," Anthony said patiently, "is that obviously the children will be with you, wherever you are, whether you come to London or you stay here, and which you do is up to you."

"Do you want me to come?" asked Jill softly, and then looking at his tired face, she plucked up courage to ask the question that would make her decision for her. "Do you still love me, Anthony?"

"Love you? Of course I still love you," his voice was full of anguish, "that's the problem, don't you see? I never stopped loving you, but that's why it's so difficult. I loved you all the time you were loving him... all the time I thought you were loving me."

Jill ached to go to him, to put her arms round him and soothe away his hurt, but she was afraid to, afraid that he would repel her, as the cause of his pain. Tears slid silently down her cheeks, and she could only murmur, "I'm sorry, Anthony, so sorry. I'm so sorry."

Something inside her told her that now was the time she should be fighting for her marriage, but somehow the words wouldn't come.

"Well, that's the situation," Anthony said. "My new job starts in two weeks. Think about it, and let me know what you've decided." He got to his feet, his coffee left cooling beside his chair, and walked to the stairs. Jill jumped up too.

"Anthony," she cried, "we can't possibly leave it like this. Please, let's talk things through, right from the start." She caught at his hand and he paused, looking back at her.

Now, now was her chance, and she might not get another. She must speak to him, take charge of the conversation. Her grip tightened on his hand as if physically to hold him from going down to his study, and she drew a deep breath.

"Anthony, you may not believe this," she began quietly, "but I love you more than anyone else in the world." His face remained impassive, but she could see he was listening. "I made a fool of myself, disgraced myself, and hurt you so badly. I, well, I don't know what to say to you. Sorry is such a useless word, I could say it to the end of time and not really tell you how I feel. You say you love me and you always have, but do you love me enough to forgive me for the torment I put you through?" Her eyes searched his face. "You have to love me enough to forgive me completely, Anthony, or else we've got no future together. It won't be any good going to London together if we simply take our problems with us. I want us to give our marriage another try, Anthony, more than anything, but I know now that it won't work unless we can both put my affair with Ben behind us. It'll be no good going to London and then to live there as we have been here the past few weeks. If we come with you, the children and I, we have to come as a complete family unit, a proper family." Her gaze held his. "I want to be with you Anthony, as we always were. I want to share your life, and your love and your bed, but I can't do it if you can't forgive me. I'm willing to beg for that forgiveness, but if you can't give it we have no future together."

Anthony moved towards her, he did not release his hand from hers but neither did he take the other, nor draw her into his arms. He looked down at her, and she could see there were tears in his eyes too.

"It isn't that I can't forgive you," he said huskily, "it's that I can't forget. I keep thinking of you and him together... imagining things he did to you, with you..." He choked on a sob.

Jill dropped his hand and very gently put her arms round him. "Anthony, darling, you must stop torturing yourself like that," she pleaded. "With Ben I had sex, with you I make love. Remember on the hill in Ireland? That was us, you and me, making love. You being beside me when the children were born; the two of us sitting up with Sylvia when she was so ill as a baby. That was us. Ben was a fling, a moment's madness because I was bored, fed up and lonely, Ben is a thing of the past, the real thing now is us, you, me, Sylvia and Tom.

"So. I'm asking you, Anthony, please can you forgive me, so that I can come back to you?"

She still had her arms round him, but he stood stiff and straight. "Don't you want me?" she whispered.

His arms closed convulsively around her and he spoke into her hair. "Of course I want you," he groaned.

Still holding Jill's hand, Anthony had switched off the lights and led the way upstairs. In the bedroom he had taken her into his arms and kissed her, gently at first and then as he explored her mouth with mounting intensity. By the light of the bedside lamp, he had undressed her, kissing her body as it was slowly revealed, her neck, her breasts with their taut nipples, the smooth soft skin of her stomach, and she had returned his kisses, running her hands down the length of his back and round under his buttocks, stroking, smoothing, tickling with the tips of her fingers. He laid her on the bed and let his eyes rove over her body, quivering, expectant, waiting for him, as he pulled off his own clothes. Jill reached up to pull him down beside her. For a moment his body was against her, the length of their bodies burning together and then suddenly he rolled away and lay with his back to her, leaving her cold and exposed on her side of the bed. For a moment she did nothing, so abrupt was his departure, then she rolled over herself, so that her breasts brushed against his back and whispered softly, "Anthony?"

"I can't," came his bleak reply. "I'm sorry, I can't."

She raised herself up on her elbow and resting her chin on his shoulder, looked down at him and saw that indeed he couldn't. She slid her arm round his chest and nestled against his back, curving her body round his as they had always used to sleep.

"It doesn't matter," she murmured into his ear. "It doesn't matter one little bit." But it did, and they both knew it.

Neither of them had spoken again that night. Anthony had simply reached up and turned the light off. The movement had removed him from the circle of her arm. Jill didn't know if that was intentional or not, but when he lay back down he was no longer close against her, and the sudden chill round her body also crept into her mind.

In the morning, Anthony got up at the usual time. Jill had not slept well. For hours she had lain wide awake, her mind churning as she went over and over what had happened. She had finally gambled everything to bring Anthony back to her and she had lost. He had responded as best he could, he had told her he loved her and wanted her but when it came to the final moment, his own body had defied him, leaving them worse off than before.

She lay in the bed with her eyes shut and listened to him moving softly round the room, gathering his clothes and then going quietly into the bathroom. At some time, they had to face each other in the cold light of day, Jill decided, and she too got up. She followed him into the bathroom and had her shower while he shaved, as she always had done, then she went back to dress. He had not turned when she came in, but he had looked at her in the mirror and said, "Sorry, didn't mean to wake you. I've an early appointment this morning."

They'd had breakfast and then he'd gone, and Jill was left wondering where they went from there. Neither of them had mentioned the previous evening, perhaps because neither knew what to say. Impotence wasn't something you could discuss across the breakfast cereal, and it was a relief to both of them when he got up to leave. When he'd gone, Jill took her second cup of coffee into the window and looked out across the Circle. She could hear Isabelle getting the children dressed upstairs, and knew that very soon she was going to have to be the usual, smiling Mummy.

It made her think of Nancy, and she suddenly knew then what she was going to do. She would go to Nancy and tell her about moving to London. She would ask her to have Isabelle and the children so that she could go with Anthony and look for somewhere to live.

"I'll take the children to school this morning, Isabelle," she said when they came down. "I have to go and visit my mother, so I'll drive straight on. Perhaps you'd like the morning off and then pick Thomas up. I should be back in time to fetch Sylvia, but if not please collect her and give them their tea."

It was a clear January morning, with a stiff breeze sending the clouds scudding across a slate-grey sky, but shafts of sunlight struck an occasional clump of snowdrops in the more sheltered parts of the hedgerows, and she found her spirits lifting. By the time she reached Meadow Cottage, she discovered that the drive had been therapeutic and she could talk quite easily to Nancy.

"Anthony is going to work in the London office," she told Nancy later, "we're moving to London."

"Does that mean you've sorted things out?" Nancy asked.

Jill smiled. "I think so," she said fairly untruthfully. "We're certainly going to give it another go. What I wondered, Mum, was whether you'd come and have the children again for a little while, so I can go up to London house-hunting. You'd have Isabelle too, so it shouldn't be too much for you."

"Of course I will," Nancy said, only too willing to help out if it meant that Jill and Anthony could start afresh, but she was surprised at the hug her daughter gave her. Jill had ceased to be demonstrative as far as she was concerned a long time ago. This hug had a sort of desperation to it, and even as she returned it, Nancy felt uneasy.

"Are you all right, really?" she asked anxiously.

Jill longed to tell her the truth of the matter, the real problem that now lay between her and Anthony, but she knew she could never disclose Anthony's humiliation even to her mother, so she gave her a reassuring smile and said, "Yes, fine. You know, Mum, I'm sure this will be the best thing for us, a new start in a new place."

"I'm sure you're right too," Nancy agreed, and set aside her own worry that Jill was trying to escape her problems by moving away from them. However, she was glad that they were going to work at their marriage. She was fond of her son-in-law and thought that Jill had behaved very badly.

"I'll look forward to coming," she said as Jill got in the car to drive home. "Tell them that when I come I'll bring a chocolate cake."

As the children ate their tea, Jill watched the removal van finally drive away from next door. Strange both families should be leaving Dartmouth Close so soon after each other, she thought. She remembered her conversation with Angela over their coffee before Christmas. Ian and Angela had rescued their marriage and were setting off to start again in a new place, surely she and Anthony could do the same thing.

When he came in that evening, Anthony greeted her with a light kiss on the lips, something he hadn't done since before Ben. Jill found that recently she judged things as "before Ben" or "since Ben". Before Ben, Anthony would sit in the living room nursing his drink and telling her about his day; since Ben he had taken to carrying his drink upstairs while he changed out of his suit, and then sitting straight down to supper before disappearing into his study. What would he do tonight?

It turned out to be a mixture of both. He went upstairs to change and say goodnight to the children, and then he poured them each a drink and sat down in his own familiar chair and said, "They're very pleased that I'm taking the London job. If you want to come up and house-hunt, they'll put us in a company flat. What do you say?"

Jill smiled at him. "I say brilliant," she said. "I've already organised for Mum to come and look after the children with Isabelle for a couple of weeks, so I can come whenever you want me."

That night they slept comfortably side by side, their bodies touching in tiny patches of heat, but with no move from either towards intimacy. Both of them knew that there was too much at stake to hurry anything now. It would take time, but, with luck, time was the one thing of which they had plenty, patience and love might accomplish the rest.

*Chapter Twenty-Nine*

Oliver Hooper came home from school with his usual homework to do, but he had little intention of doing it. Tomorrow he would be in the youth court again, and not going to school, in which case slaving over a history essay he wouldn't be there to give in, seemed a complete waste of time.

As he slouched up the cut into the Circle, he glanced over the fence into the Smarts' garden. The shed was still there of course, swept clean and as empty as when he'd left it. The police hadn't discovered where he'd been keeping the stuff he sold before he'd had to risk putting it in his bedroom, and it made him furious that he'd had to clear the shed because of the Smarts coming home. Even more infuriating was that they didn't stay for long. They had come home to put the house on the market so that they could emigrate, and live near their daughter in Australia. They had stayed until after Christmas and then packed up their home and, as far as Oliver was concerned, disappeared.

Oliver had been relieved there had been little mention of the tools that had gone from the shed. He'd been afraid if the police were called they might have put two and two together and realised he had something to do with the missing tools, but he was lucky. Martin Smart had mentioned to Mike Callow that his shed had been broken into and all his garden tools stolen, but he hadn't bothered to contact the police.

"What's the point?" he said resignedly to Mike. "They could have been taken any time we were away, so we'll never find them now. Whoever it was simply took everything out of the shed and dumped it over the wall on to the allotment track, you can see where they trampled the ground behind the bushes at the bottom of the garden. They must have loaded it into a van or something there. You didn't see anyone about, I suppose?"

Mike shook his head. "No," he replied. "Once I did think someone might have been in, and I went round to have a look, but there was nothing to see. Maybe David saw someone."

Martin shrugged. "Well," he said, "it hardly matters now. I wouldn't have been taking any of that stuff from the shed anyway."

"When do you go back to Oz?" asked Mike.

"As soon as we sell the house," Martin said. "Doreen wants to spend some time with her cousin in Birmingham before we go, so we shall pack up most of our stuff and move out. The agent will sell whatever furniture we leave when the place is sold." They had left in early January.

Good riddance, thought Oliver, what did they have to come back at all for? He considered making use of the shed again, but eventually decided against it. The estate agent might bring prospective buyers round any time, and they'd be almost certain to look in the garden shed. The risk was too great, so he still had nowhere to stash his stuff.

There was also the problem of Jay Manders. Since Scott had beaten up that Annabel girl, he was now held on remand, and Jay had begun to be difficult. Oliver knew with a smouldering fury that it had to be Jay or Scott who had dropped him in it. After all, they were the only other two people who knew that he had several credit cards and a pension book in his possession, and he was sure the police had known what they were looking for. Unfortunately for Oliver, by the time the police, in the person of PCs Woodman and Carver, came round to talk to his dad just before Christmas, he also had a social security benefit book, three more cards and several hand tools that he'd taken from a DIY supermarket.

Dad had been great to start with, standing up to the police, adamant that his son wouldn't be involved in anything dishonest.

"I'm sure you've got this wrong, officer, Oliver wouldn't take anything that wasn't his."

"He already has one caution for theft," pointed out Woodman.

"Yes, but that was a one-off, when he wanted to get something for my birthday." Steve became more defensive. "Even the shopkeeper didn't want to press charges. It shouldn't mean you come straight round here every time something goes missing!"

"Well, I'm sorry, sir, but we've had a tip-off that he is in possession of several stolen items."

Shit! thought Oliver. Fucking Jay, getting his own back because I don't do the business with him any more.

They had almost come to blows when Oliver had said he would only deal with Scott, direct, not through Jay.

"What's the matter?" growled Jay. "Don't you trust me or somethink?"

"No, I don't," Oliver declared. "You tried to rip me off with those cards last week. Scott never told you to pay me only seventy-five, did he? Do you think I'm stupid or what? You did that for yourself, mate, to get your grubby little hands on the other twenty-five. I'm not going to deal with you again, not till I've talked to Scott himself. Right?"

"Scott's keeping 'is 'ead down just now," Jay said. "The filth have emptied his stash, an' 'e's on bail to the crown court."

"He should have been more careful who he told about his garage," Oliver said. "Sounds like he was bloody careless to me."

"'Ow did you know it was a garage?" demanded Jay suspiciously. "You been keeping tabs, or what?"

"Got better things to do," scoffed Oliver, though he had once seen Scott go into the yard off Camborne Road and, on impulse, followed him. The information about the garage had been recorded in his notebook for future use. "He told me about it himself," Oliver lied. "Said he could put some of the bigger stuff there if necessary. Sounds like he made a mistake!"

Jay bristled. "Scott knows what 'e's doing. 'E don't need a little toe-rag like you to tell 'im how to run 'is business."

"Or one like you, trying to rip him off when you're just the errand boy," snapped Oliver. "He won't be too pleased when I tell him you tried to sell us both short, will he?"

"You won't be doing no business with 'im again," sneered Jay.

"No, I won't," Oliver had agreed. "From now on I'm going to handle my own stuff. Cut out the middle man and make myself some real dosh. I've seen your brother, mate. I've sussed most of his contacts. Now he's going to be out of the way, I'll deal for myself." He glowered at Jay. "And don't you come fucking-well sniffing round either, 'cos you're a loser, and I don't deal with losers. You just keep collecting your protection money, mate, but you make sure I get my cut, otherwise the filth might find out about that little earner an' all!"

Since then he and Jay had moved round each other like a pair of stalking wild cats, but Oliver was perceived to be the more dangerous, for he still received his cut of the protection money.

Two days after the stand-off about the cards, Scott had been arrested for attacking Annabel Haven and remanded in custody. Oliver was on his own whether he liked it or not, so he had kept his thieving to a minimum, taking only small, easily hidden and easily negotiable stuff, like the pension books and cards that were so often lying on the tops of shopping bags just begging to be lifted. However, despite his boasts to Jay, he hadn't yet found anyone else to dispose of them, and they were sellotaped to the back of the large picture of the England cricket team that hung on his bedroom wall.

Now this guy Woodman was asking to search his room. Oliver thought fast. Surely Dad wouldn't stand for that!

"Have you got a search warrant?" Steve was demanding. Oliver spied a ray of hope. If they hadn't, and there'd been no sign of one yet, they'd have to go and get one and he'd have time to shift everything somewhere else.

"No sir, not yet. We just wanted to speak to Oliver and see

what he has to say about this. It could just be a bit of spite on someone's behalf."

That sounded more hopeful. Oliver did his wide-eyed innocent act.

"I don't know anything about any stolen stuff, Dad," he said, with a tremble in his voice. "Honest! I don't know why anyone should tell the police I do. It's awful lies!"

"You see, officer, Oliver doesn't know anything about any of this," Steve said. "My son doesn't need to steal. He has plenty of pocket money, and everything he wants from us. Whatever you've heard can't be true."

PC Woodman smiled. "I'm sure you're right, sir, but in that case you won't mind if we take a look in Oliver's bedroom."

Steve looked uncertain, and Oliver cried, "Dad! Why should he?"

Steve shrugged. "It wouldn't hurt, Ollie. Get them off your back once and for all, mate." Not seeing the flash of panic on his son's face, Steve turned back to the policeman. "That's all right, I'll take you down and show you his room, and then you can leave him alone. Right?"

Woodman, however, *had* seen Oliver's expression and their search was an extremely thorough one. In the suitcase on top of the wardrobe, he found the secateurs, three sets of screwdrivers, some drill bits and a claw hammer, all in their original packaging.

Steve stared at the tools in horror.

"Well, Oliver?" said Woodman, tipping the things out on to the bed. "What are all these?"

Oliver was ready for him. "I bought them for my dad for Christmas," he said. "Now you've spoiled it," he added bitterly, "they won't be a surprise any more."

"And have you got the receipts for them?"

"Probably, somewhere." Oliver shrugged carelessly. "I don't know. Might be in my drawer." He pulled open the drawer of his desk and said, "You can look if you like."

PC Carver did look, but if Oliver thought that by offering them the drawer easily they were not going to look in the less obvious places, he had mistaken his man. PC Woodman was far too experienced to miss quite ingenious hiding places, and Oliver's stash behind the England cricketers wasn't that ingenious and was soon discovered.

"And what about these, Oliver?" Woodman asked quietly. "How did these come to be stuck behind here?"

Oliver didn't bother to reply. There was nothing he could say, he just stared at the policeman with a blank expression, and kept his mouth firmly shut.

"Ollie!" Steve was horrified at what they'd found. "Oliver? What are all these things?"

Oliver turned a faintly pitying glance on his father, but he still said nothing. They stood in silence, side by side, while the police finished the search of the room, but they found nothing else.

Woodman proceeded to caution him and then said he'd like them all to come down to the police station.

"I strongly suggest that you find a solicitor to represent Oliver, Mr Hooper," Woodman said. "I'm afraid we won't be able to let him off with a caution this time."

He had been right, and Oliver had been charged with stealing the cards and pension books. He was given police bail and told when to appear in court. He'd seen a solicitor, and then come home to the inevitable recriminations. It was bad enough from his father, but when Annie joined in it was past everything and Oliver blew his stack.

"For Christ's sake," he bellowed, "it was only a couple of fucking credit cards and a pension book. Anyone would've thought I'd nicked the fucking crown jewels the way you two go on. Shit! I hope they do put me inside, anything'd be better than this bleeding house!" He flung himself out of the room.

Annie rounded on Steve. "That's it! I'm not having him here in this house if he goes on like this, you hear me, Steve. If you don't do something about him, it'll be him or me!"

"Annie," Steve tried to sound conciliatory, "he's only a kid."

"No he's not," Annie shrieked, "he's a manipulative monster, and I don't want him living here. Send him back to his mother. Let her sort him out! He's *her* son."

"He's my son too," Steve said quietly.

"Then the time is rapidly approaching," Annie said through her teeth, "when you'll have to choose between your son and your wife."

Faced with such an ultimatum, Steve had phoned Lynne. She too had been giving him a hard time over the past few weeks, about having the children for Christmas.

"I want them for the whole Christmas period," she said. "They can come up on Christmas Eve and stay until New Year's Day."

"Oh come on, Lynne, that's not fair," Steve had said. "Be reasonable. We want them with us for some of that time, it's a time for families to be together."

It was exactly the wrong thing to say. Lynne flared up at once.

"Just what I'm saying," she snapped. "We are their family too you know, and we hardly ever see them. They were promised that they could come and stay in the school holidays, and this will be in the school holidays."

"I know," Steve tried to retrieve the situation, "but Christmas is special for everyone, so they should spend some of the time with me and some with you. That sounds fair."

"I haven't seen Emma since half term," Lynne shouted, "and Oliver, not since the summer. It's my turn to have them with me, and if you don't agree, Oslo says we'll take you to court. So think about it Steve. That is *not* an idle threat!" She had slammed the phone down and left Steve fuming at the other end of a dead line.

This time when he called her, however, the situation had changed and he decided to call her bluff. He was charm itself. "I've been thinking about what you said, Lynne," he said, "and I've decided not to fight with you on the question of Christmas and New Year. The children will be on the train that gets in at two-thirty on Christmas Eve, and I'll pick them up in Belcaster on the second of January off whichever train you tell me is suitable."

Lynne was almost silenced. She had been preparing a generous climb-down about New Year, never really having wanted the children with her for that long. Oslo certainly thought that the three days over Christmas were enough, and had told her so in no uncertain manner, but she had been at her usual game of using her children as a stick to beat Steve, and now she was caught out.

"I've been thinking too, Steve," she began sweetly, "perhaps I *was* being unreasonable to expect..."

"Not at all," Steve interrupted. "You were right, you should see more of them, and they should have a chance to get to know Oslo properly. He is their stepfather after all. Don't worry, it's all arranged." And indeed it was, for he had already booked himself and Annie into a country hotel for the Christmas week, as a sort of second honeymoon. There was no way he was putting his second marriage at risk, and though he knew very well that Lynne didn't want the children for the whole holiday period, he had played her at her own game...and won.

The only people who were not consulted were Oliver and Emma, they were presented with a fait accompli and were simply sent to their mother for Christmas.

It had been a disaster. Oslo made no secret that he thought they were both very much in the way. He was horrified when heard about Oliver's coming court appearance and ostentatiously locked his study door. Besides which, on several occasions, he was heard to tell people that they had a juvenile delinquent living in the house. Both Emma and Oliver hated him, and even Dartmouth Circle seemed a better option to Oliver after almost a week in London. His mother made little effort to entertain them and they were left to their own devices almost every evening while she and Oslo went out to drinks or dinner parties, and when she finally put them on the train back to Belcaster, Oliver sank back into his seat and said, "I am never going near either of them again!"

"Nor am I!" Emma agreed, but then she'd always preferred living in Dartmouth Circle.

Annie and Steve had made good use of their week of luxury on their own, to discuss their problems and come to some agreement. Steve had promised to try and spend more time with the children and to keep a much stricter eye on Oliver, and Annie had promised to leave the management of the children to him. "I won't interfere," she agreed. "I'll do the usual running of the household, but it'll be up to you to keep them in line in the house."

Since then there had been a sort of armed truce between them all. The new school term had started and Oliver had made his first appearance in court, but there would be others. From what his solicitor said, it didn't sound as if he would be sent away, but he would be under strict supervision.

At least they hadn't found my cash, Oliver thought. That was safely stashed in a secret building society account, and he kept the pass book, along with his information notebook, locked in his locker at school. No way was he letting anyone get wind of his escape fund. Everything that had happened recently had made him increasingly determined to leave both home and school on his sixteenth birthday and disappear.

Once this supervision thing is over, he decided, I'll get myself back into business again. The notebook might be of less use than he thought, as most of the information he had recorded in it was now common knowledge, but you never knew. He was still certain that knowledge about other people led to power over them, and power was still his driving force.

As he swung round the Circle, he came face to face with Chantal Haven. She was wearing the Chapmans' school uniform. Oliver knew a familiar stab of jealous rage as he saw it, and he glared at her. He had forgotten she'd been moved there.

Why the hell should stuck-up Chantal go there when he was stuck at shitty Crosshills? But the moment of fury passed. Oliver had changed since he'd left Chapmans. Crosshills was a tough place, and Oliver, learning fast, was tough too. Always manipulative, he had developed this skill to a fine art. He could make people feel how he wanted them to feel, and he wanted Chantal to be afraid of him.

He flicked his eyes at the estate agent's board outside the house. "See you're moving then," he said, casually.

Chantal looked at him disdainfully. "Yeah. Couldn't stand to live in the same road as you any more." Then pushed by some inner devil, she said with a smirk, "Saw you being arrested from Patel's the other day. Nicking stuff, were you?"

Oliver glowered at her. "Yeah? Like I saw you being marched away from that student party by a butch policewoman," he sniped. "Heard afterwards you'd been shagging that rugby player. Dan is he called? Hear the poor sod's being charged with rape. Rape? I bet you were begging for it!"

"He's not! I wasn't!" Chantal said confusedly, not knowing if he was right about Dan or not.

"Christ, he must've been desperate," Oliver remarked contemptuously, looking her up and down.

Chantal felt suddenly afraid. "At least he was a man," she said shakily. "Just 'cos I wouldn't let you touch me at Mike's party."

Oliver gave a shout of laughter. "Me! Touch you! Don't flatter yourself, kid. You were pissed out of your mind." His eyes slid down to her stomach. "You up the spout like your sister, then? Look what happened to her," and he reached out as if to touch her.

Suddenly Chantal lost her nerve, and gave a piercing scream. "Don't touch me!" she shrieked. She pushed him violently away, and ran up the path to her own front door, with his jeering laughter echoing behind her. As she reached the door, it was opened by Angela, who had heard Chantal's scream. Angela looked out and saw Oliver standing in the road. She had no idea what was going on, but she did know that Chantal was afraid of Oliver for some reason.

"Time you went home, Oliver Hooper," she said in a measured tone.

Oliver grinned at her. "Just chatting to Chantal, Mrs Haven," he said cheerfully. "Cheers, Chantal, see you another day."

"What on earth was all that about?" Angela demanded when they were both safely upstairs in the living room.

"Nothing," Chantal said miserably. "I hate Oliver Hooper!"

"Yes, well I suggest you steer well clear of him from now on," said her mother. She gave Chantal a hug. "Won't be for long, then we'll be safely at Stone Winton and you'll never see him again."

Chantal nodded, but she was feeling suddenly sick inside. Were the police really going to accuse Dan of rape? Was the detestable Oliver right, had she been asking for it? She really didn't remember much about the party, just that Dan had been waiting on the landing and it had all seemed inevitable and afterwards she wished it hadn't happened. She longed to get away from Dartmouth Circle.

"Mum—" she began and then stopped.

"Yes?" Angela tried to sound encouraging.

"Mum, do you know…I mean, well Oliver said Dan is being charged with rape, you know, after the party? Mum, is he? Will they put him in prison?" Tears were filling her eyes, and Angela put her arms round her.

Damn Oliver Hooper! she thought fiercely. What did he have to open his mouth for? But then he always was a spiteful beast.

"I don't know," she admitted. "We haven't heard anything yet. The thing is that you are under the age of consent. Whether you let him or not, he's not legally allowed to have sex with you. It is a crime, and he may be prosecuted for it."

"Does he have to be?"

"I honestly don't know, darling. But until we hear anything you must try and put it all out of your mind."

"But it was all my fault," cried Chantal.

"Rubbish!" declared her mother firmly. "It was *not* your fault. He knew perfectly well what he was doing. He's a grown man, and he took advantage of you."

"Oliver Hooper says I led him on, he said..." Chantal choked on the words, "Oliver said I was begging for it."

"Oliver Hooper is a foul-mouthed, poisonous toad!" Angela snapped. "Take absolutely no notice of what Oliver Hooper has to say! It was not your fault, right?" She hugged her daughter to her, feeling again that she'd failed her. How could she have let her get into such a dreadful situation? The move to Stone Winton would help, she supposed. Of course they'd be taking their problems with them, there was no leaving those behind in the Circle with the house, but at least they would be able to deal with them in private, in a place where no one knew them or the troubles they had, and without comments from bloody Oliver Hooper.

Chantal pulled away at last and said, "Think I'll go up and get on with my homework. Will you test me on my vocab later?"

"Yes, of course." Angela forced a smile. "Come down when you've learned it."

## Chapter Thirty

Shirley Redwood put the last of the biscuits on to plates and carried them into the sitting room. Everything was set up for her coffee morning in aid of St Joe's, and in about ten minutes her door would be open, she hoped, for her first customers. She had sent invitations to all her friends in the hope they would come and support her final fund-raising venture before she moved, and as she said to David when she decided to have the coffee morning, "It'll give me a chance to say goodbye to everyone."

"We shan't be moving for a bit yet," David pointed out.

"No, I know," she agreed, "but we know we are moving, and after this we shall have to begin sorting the house out, I shan't have time for lots of goodbyes. Far better to say them all at once, then if I happened to see people after that, all well and good, but if not…"

"You won't want me at this do, will you?" David asked hopefully. "I'd just be in your way."

"Up to you," said his wife, knowing he wouldn't stay.

"Why don't you ask Cirelle to come and give you a hand?" suggested David, relieved. "She helps at St Joe's as well, doesn't she?"

"Yes, I might do that," said Shirley. "I think she was a bit upset by the way Melanie spoke to her before she left."

"Doubt it," said David. "She's a sensible girl. Anyway, I gather she told Mel where to get off."

Shirley had approached Cirelle, asking if she could help,

and Cirelle had agreed willingly enough. If she was still upset by the things Melanie had said to her, there was no sign of it now.

"Yeah, no probs, Shirley. I'll give you a hand," she said, "and I expect Mad will too, if you like." Shirley did like, and Cirelle asked Mad.

"A coffee morning!" cried Mad in mock dismay. "I don't *do* coffee mornings."

"Yeah, you do," Cirelle told her cheerfully. "It's for St Joe's. Come on, Mad, like, it's only for one morning?"

Grumbling, Mad allowed herself to be persuaded.

"Well, I'm not going to any coffee morning," Dean said firmly, "but when you guys have earned your brownie points, I'll meet you in the union bar, OK?"

The girls had arrived early and helped set out the bring-and-buy table and the coffee cups.

"I'll be on the door," Shirley said, "so I can greet people when they arrive. You two can serve at the bring-and-buy table and Mary has said she'll pour the coffees. She'll be here in a minute."

Mary had volunteered her services in the kitchen as soon as she received her invitation. She was always ready to help fund-raise for St Joe's, but she was very sorry to hear it was the Redwoods' farewell, too.

"Are you really going?" she asked. "I know you had it at the back of your mind, but I didn't think it would be so soon."

Shirley smiled ruefully. "Nor did I," she admitted, "but the opportunity to buy a house nearer to Melanie came up and it seemed stupid to miss it. You know I was worried about her when she went home. Well, we went for Christmas as you know, and stayed for ten days. Quite long enough for me and far too long for David! Still, she does seem to be coping better than she was, and is more relaxed, but she doesn't find the children easy."

"Didn't you tell me her husband had got a new job and wouldn't be away so much?" asked Mary.

"Yes he has, so he is at home in the evenings," replied Shirley. "Not that he does much with the children, but it does mean she has someone to talk to when they've gone to bed. And since Suzanne goes through the night now at least Melanie gets some unbroken sleep."

"Absolutely vital," Mary agreed with feeling. "You can cope with almost anything if you have your sleep!" She looked across at her friend. "But have you found somewhere to live? I'm surprised you could get David to leave his beloved garden."

"It was really very strange," Shirley explained. "Fate almost. We took Todd out for a walk on Boxing Day, and went to a playground that he particularly likes in the next village, Derringham; and there on the edge of the village green was a cottage with a for-sale board outside. David was pushing Todd on the swings so I wandered over and had a look at it. Mary, it was just lovely, just the sort of house I've always wanted. Not very big, much smaller than here, but with a beautiful garden, though that's rather overgrown at the moment; and it's right in the middle of the village. I could see it was already empty," she went on conspiratorially, "so I went and looked in through the windows. David came over to see what I was doing, and I said I was just having a look round the cottage. I peered in the downstairs windows while he wandered round the garden. Anyway, to cut a long story short, we contacted the agent after the weekend and arranged to go and see it properly, and we both loved it. So we made an offer and it's been accepted."

"Have you sold your own yet?" asked Mary.

"No, that's the problem," sighed Shirley. "Now we've decided to go, we want to get on with it. Luckily the owner of the cottage isn't in any particular hurry. It was left to her by an old aunt, and she said she was happy to wait, so let's hope she is."

"We shall miss you in the Circle," sighed Mary. "I shall miss you very much."

"We shall miss you too," said Shirley, "but you can come and stay with us. We've got two bedrooms in the cottage, but that's all." She laughed and added, "I think that is part of the attraction for David. The family won't be able to descend on us en masse because we shan't have room, but we'll be close enough for Melanie to drop in whenever she wants to, and we shall see lots more of the grandchildren."

The first person to arrive at the coffee morning was Sheila Colby, with Gerald in tow.

"He's just going to have a quick cup of coffee," Sheila told Shirley as she paid at the door, "and then he's off to play golf with Andrew Peters, but I told him he had to support your morning first."

"Nice to see both of you," Shirley replied, smiling. "Thank you for coming. Coffee and bring-and-buy are upstairs."

The Colbys went upstairs, and Shirley could hear Sheila explaining Gerald's presence to Mary. Poor Gerald, she thought, and yet he never seems to mind, he must be quite fond of the silly old bat!

Dr Fran arrived next, and gave Shirley a quick hug. "Shouldn't be here really," she said, "but I need a quick coffee, and I've brought you some things for your bring-and-buy. How's Mel? Did you all survive Christmas all right?"

"Yes, thanks. Mel's doing pretty well now I think," Shirley replied. "We really are very grateful for all you did for her, Fran. I think you and your counsellor got to her just in time."

"I'm glad," Fran said simply. "Now look, I'm sorry, this truly is just a dash in and out, but let's have a pub supper somewhere, the four of us before you go."

"That'd be lovely," Shirley agreed, adding as Alison Forrester came up the path, "I'll ring you!"

Dr Fran disappeared upstairs and Shirley turned to greet Alison. "Alison, lovely to see you," she cried. "I didn't know if you'd be able to get away. Are you meant to be working today?"

"Yes, and we are frantically busy," Alison agreed, "but I've managed to slip away for half an hour. I always like to support things going on in the Circle."

"No children with you?" Shirley was surprised, she thought at least Harriet would be with her if she came.

"Didn't think they'd be an asset at a coffee morning," Alison laughed, "Jon's at school, but as Isabelle had Harriet this morning anyway while I was at work, I decided to leave her there."

She headed up the stairs and was soon followed by Jill Hammond. It was Jill's first social appearance in the Circle, apart from the few moments at Madge's funeral, since the night of the Madhouse party. She greeted Shirley with a smile and went upstairs with a confidence she didn't feel, to join the group in the sitting room.

Other helpers from St Joe's turned up to support the event and to take the chance of wishing Shirley luck in her new home.

"We're going to miss you, Shirley," Mavis said, "and not just because you're leaving a gap in the rota! All our clients send you their love, and say you will go in to see them before you go, won't you?"

Shirley promised she would. "Anyway, I shall still be doing my turn for a while yet. We can't move until we've sold this place."

Several more people arrived and Mavis took a turn on the door so Shirley could go and see how things were going upstairs. There was a cheerful buzz of conversation in the room, Alison Forrester chatting with Jill Hammond in one corner, their heads together over the coffee cups, deep in private conversation. Shirley left them to it and went to see how the bring-and-buy was going.

"I see you've put your house on the market," Jill was saying. "So you've really decided that you've got to sell? Hasn't Paul managed to find anything to suit him yet?"

"Well, we've decided to move anyway," Alison said. "This is certainly not common knowledge yet," she went on softly, "but we're going to Belmouth, and Paul is going to set up on his own."

"Is he? As an estate agent? Well done him!" Jill exclaimed. "Can he do that? I mean, is there enough work there to make a living?"

"Paul thinks so," Alison said. "He's got all the right qualifications and things, so he's going to try. We've seen a house in a lane off Front Street which has a garage already converted into a workshop. We're going to reconvert it into an office. I can do the paperwork and answer the phone and things, and Paul will do the surveys, valuations, sales and stuff."

"It all sounds very exciting," Jill said, "but isn't it a bit of a gamble?"

"Yes it is," Alison agreed, "but it's better than sitting around doing nothing. We shall have the money from the sale of the house, and the pittance Johnson, Fountain have paid in redundancy money, but our overheads shouldn't be too much as we're in our own premises." She gave a wry laugh. "Sort of living over the shop."

"Well, I think you're both very brave," Jill said, "and I wish you every success."

"Freddie Jones has been very sympathetic," Alison confided. "He couldn't offer Paul his old job back of course, obviously he's got someone else, but he says he'll put any work that he can't cope with our way. That should help. He has a very good name in the business." She gave a small triumphant smile. "And Johnson, Fountain never thought of Paul opening up on his own account, so they didn't bother to put any restriction on where he can practise."

"Could they have done?" Jill was surprised. "If they made him redundant?"

Alison shrugged. "Probably not," she admitted, "but they won't be very pleased if any of their clients go with Paul, and some might. Some people would rather work with someone they know than with a big company where you speak to a different person every time you ring."

"When does all this start?" Jill asked. She would have liked to support Paul by giving him their house to sell, but she doubted that Anthony would want it with the fledgling business Paul's was going to be. He'd want it sold quickly.

"Not until we sell the house," said Alison. "Until then we haven't the money to buy the place in Belmouth."

Jill felt guiltily relieved to hear that. There was no way they could wait to put their own house on the market.

"But you won't lose the property in Belmouth in the meantime, will you?" she asked.

"Hope not," said Alison. "It's Freddie who's got it for sale, and he says at the moment there's no one else interested, so we've got to hope it stays that way until we've sold ours. I'm still working of course, which brings in something, and in the meantime Paul is quietly following up as many contacts as he can, ready for when we open." She looked suddenly anxious. "You won't tell anyone any of this will you," she said. "It's all a bit hush-hush still. We don't want anyone to know until it is all signed and sealed." She smiled a little guiltily. "I shouldn't have told you really," she admitted, "but you've been so good about sharing Isabelle..."

"Don't worry, I won't tell a soul," Jill promised, and then added casually, "We're on the move too, actually. Anthony's been offered a place in the London office."

"London!" Alison sounded envious. "How lovely! So you'll be moving up there. Lucky you! I've always wanted to live in London. When will you be going?"

"Same as you really," Jill replied. "Just as soon as we can sell this house and find one up there. I'm going up next week for a few days to have a look around. My mother's coming to be with the children and Isabelle," she added, "so I'm afraid you'll be without Isabelle then. Mum needs her nearly all the time."

"Don't worry about that," Alison said. "Cirelle says she'll help out when she can. We'll sort something. Is your move a secret as well?"

"Not really, we haven't told people, but they'll know soon enough when the for-sale board goes up on the house."

One person who did know already, was Ben Gardner. Jill had bumped into him in the High Street the previous day. She had seen him looking in a shop window and on impulse went over.

"Ben," she said softly, and he spun round.

"Jill!"

Now she'd approached him she didn't quite know what to say, and for a moment they looked at each other awkwardly.

"How've you been?"

"Are you all right?"

They had both spoken together, and it broke the tension between them, as they laughed awkwardly.

"I just caught sight of you," Jill explained, "and I wanted to tell you we're moving. Anthony's been offered a job in the London office. We're going to live in London."

"Is that what you want to do?" Ben asked.

Jill drew a deep breath. "Yes," she said. "I'm looking forward to it."

"And have you made things up?" he asked. "Are things all right between you?"

For a moment, Jill thought of Anthony and his continued failure to make love to her. "Yes, everything's fine," she lied. "Are you OK? I'm sorry you felt you had to move out of the Circle like that... but thank you for doing it."

"Not a problem," Ben lied. "We just had a bit of fun, didn't we? We knew there was nothing more to it, and when it was over, like, the best thing was for me to move on." He looked across at the pub opposite. "Do you want a drink?" he asked. "To say goodbye?"

Jill shook her head. "No, I don't think so, Ben. Thanks all the same. But I wish you all the luck in the future." Lightly she put a kiss on his cheek and then turned and hurried away down the street. At the corner she glanced quickly back, but he had gone, disappeared into the throng of shoppers. She was glad they were moving away, for even after all the unhappiness their affair had caused, even though she had no intention of ever putting such a strain on her marriage again, she felt a sudden tug of longing for Ben's strong, lean body.

Alison and Jill finished their coffee and went over to the bring-

and-buy table, where Cirelle and Mad were doing a brisk trade. Then Jill caught sight of Angela Haven, just arriving and being greeted by Shirley, and moved across to join them.

"Angela, how lovely to see you," Shirley was exclaiming. "I was afraid you'd be so busy settling in to your new house you wouldn't have time to come."

Angela smiled. "It's such a good cause," she said, "and it gave me an opportunity to come back and say goodbye properly to everyone. We were in such chaos last week, before we left, I didn't really get a chance to see everyone."

"How's the new house?" Sheila Colby asked, coming up beside her, carrying a tray of coffee. Gerald had long since gone and Sheila had started to help Mary with the coffees as more and more people turned up. As always she wanted to be at the centre of things, and was in her element passing round cups and plates of cakes and biscuits. "Here, have a cup of coffee," she said, "and tell me about the house."

"Well, we're in," laughed Angela as she took the coffee, "and we've managed to shut the front door, but there are packing cases all over the place, and things stacked everywhere, waiting to be found homes."

"And Annabel?" asked Sheila with sincere concern in her voice. "How's she?"

"She's doing very well," Angela answered. "She's still going to the Tech, but she looks far more relaxed than she was."

"Does she know if she'll have to go to court yet?" asked Sheila.

"No, not yet. But we don't think so. We've been told the man will be pleading guilty, and if he does they won't need her, thank God. I don't want her put through anything else, and that would inevitably bring everything back to her."

"No need to reopen the wounds," Sheila agreed sympathetically. "She's had a lot to cope with, hasn't she, losing her baby and…well, everything?"

Angela felt the tears prick her eyes and said, "Indeed she has," and not wanting to talk about Annabel's unhappiness any more she said brightly, "I'll tell her you were asking after her, shall I?"

"Yes, please do," Sheila said. "Give her my love and say that I'm thinking of her."

Another surprise guest was Mike Callow. Knowing that he worked from home, Shirley had put an invitation through his letter box, but she hadn't for one moment expected him to come.

Mike had decided to come to discover if there was Circle gossip about him and Charlie, and if there was, he was ready to nip it in the bud. The person he was most concerned about was Sheila Colby, watching the comings and goings of the Circle from behind her sitting-room curtains. He was determined there should be no unpleasant gossip about Charlie, and he had the feeling that if there were it would emanate from her. When he got upstairs she was talking to Angela Haven, but Alison Forrester was standing by herself, so he went over and joined her.

"Hi," he said, "how's tricks?"

"OK," Alison replied noncommittally. "What about you?"

"I'm fine," Mike said.

"I saw Caroline the other day," Alison said, and then paused as if uncertain whether she should go on. Caroline had actually called round, ostensibly for a cup of coffee, but actually on a fishing trip. She wanted to know what Mike was up to. Alison was quite glad she'd seen so little of Mike since Christmas that she was able to tell her quite truthfully that she hadn't a clue.

"And?" encouraged Mike.

"And she said you were finally getting a divorce."

"Yes," Mike agreed, "we are. We're never going to get back together, so there's no point in staying married."

"I suppose not. Caroline thinks you've found someone else. She said you'd been away for a dirty weekend somewhere instead of having the children. She says they were very disappointed."

"Does she indeed?" Mike said grimly. "Well the weekend in question was before Christmas, and was anything but a dirty weekend. I've seen the children several times since then and they know exactly where I went...and why."

"Oh don't worry, Mike," Alison said hastily, "I'm not asking you. It's just that Caroline didn't seem to know."

"Oh, she knows all right," Mike said calmly. "She knows I want my freedom now, as she wanted hers, but what I do with it when I've got it is entirely my own business."

"Of course," Alison agreed, wishing she'd never mentioned Caroline, and she was relieved that just then Sheila Colby came up with her tray and offered Mike a cup of coffee. He took one from her, and said pleasantly, "How are you today, Sheila?"

"Fine," she said. "How are your family these days? I haven't seen much of the children lately. Have they been over?"

"No, you haven't missed them," Mike said cheerfully. "I'm sure you'd have seen them if they'd come."

Sheila looked a bit flustered, and said, "I don't know what you mean."

Mike ignored her confusion. "They won't be coming to stay for a little while," he said easily, "I was just saying to Alison, Caroline and I have decided to get a divorce."

"Oh dear, I am sorry," cried Sheila, wondering if Mary and Shirley knew yet.

"Don't be," said Mike. "I'm not. It's the best thing all round."

"Well, I suppose if you say so." Sheila edged away to pass on this latest titbit.

"There we are." Mike grinned at Alison who was still standing beside him. "That should be round the Circle in no time flat now, and saves me from having to tell anyone else!"

Alison gave a shout of laughter. "Mike Callow, you are a disgrace!"

"Mmmm,' he agreed with a grin. "Now tell me about you guys. Any luck selling the house yet?"

Alison shook her head. "No, 'fraid not, but someone's coming over it tomorrow, so we're keeping our fingers crossed."

Angela watched Mike talking to Alison and Sheila, and

waited. She wanted to speak to him, but in confidence. At last, he seemed to be edging his way to the stairs and she crossed quickly to cut him off.

"Mike, sorry, but could I have a word?"

Mike looked surprised, but nodded. "Yes of course." He caught her glancing at a quiet place by the window and led her over to it.

"Now," he said encouragingly, "what's the problem?"

"It's a bit difficult." Angela looked confused.

"Come on, spit it out."

Angela took a deep breath. "Mike, you know Oliver Hooper quite well. I mean, he's a friend of your Peter's, isn't he?"

"Yes, he is," Mike said with a frown, "and I wish he wasn't. I'm certainly not encouraging that particular friendship. Anyway, what about him?"

"Well, Chantal seems scared of him, and I wondered...well, she won't say why, but I have seen him hanging about, and to be honest I really don't trust him."

"No," agreed Mike, "nor do I. And, I think, with good reason. I was talking to Annie Hooper the other day and she's at her wits' end. There's never been any love lost between her and Oliver, but it seems he's been in real trouble lately. He was caught shoplifting and found to have other stolen stuff, credit cards and pension books and stuff hidden in his bedroom. Of course he's been up in the youth court for it, and apparently he's been made the subject of a Supervision Order, or something."

"Supervision Order? What's that?"

"Sort of junior probation I think," Mike said. "Anyway, he has a sort of private social worker who's supposed to keep an eye on him and make sure he doesn't get into trouble again. Poor Annie, she says it's all a complete waste of time. He's a cunning little bugger, and even after all this, Steve can't see it. He's got Steve wound round his little finger."

"But what would that have to do with Chantal?" wondered Angela. "I mean, she's not involved with any of that. The thing is, I want to help her, but she won't tell me why she's afraid of him."

"Well, I might be able to help you there," Mike said. "Oliver is a bully. He likes to frighten people, and he likes to feel he has power over them, I think. Anyway, there was an incident at our New Year's Eve party last year." Mike proceeded to tell Angela what had happened.

"I'm sorry," he finished, "perhaps I should have told you at the time."

"Yes," agreed Angela coldly, "perhaps you should."

"Well, at the time it seemed to be just teenage stupidity. You know, they were at a party and had too much to drink. Nothing happened between them, indeed Chantal had the best of it really. Oliver was the one with vomit in his hair!"

Mike's effort at lightening the mood had little effect. Angela was still coming to terms with what he'd told her. Oliver Hooper had got Chantal drunk and tried to undress her, was what he seemed to be saying.

"And you didn't think it worth mentioning to me?" she demanded.

Mike shrugged. "It came to nothing. There was no real harm done, and I thought the less that was made of it, the quicker it would all be forgotten. I didn't realise he would keep holding it over her." He sighed. "The truth about Oliver Hooper is that he's damaged goods. He's been dragged, pushed and fought over by his parents since he was a little kid, and he's survived. Survivors are dangerous people, because they soon learn that to survive you need to be completely self-centred. Intelligent survivors learn to use everyone round them for their own aims. Annie is quite right, this Supervision Order thing isn't going to do one iota of good, because Oliver is intelligent enough to seem to play along while maintaining a secret agenda of his own."

"Wonderful! And meanwhile, he's out to torment Chantal!"

Mike shook his head. "I doubt it now that you've moved away. I'm sure it was only because she was on hand, you know?"

"Well, I hope you're right," Angela said. "I think I shall tell Chantal that you've told me, then she'll know it doesn't matter what Oliver says, as I know it all already. And if I see that Oliver Hooper anywhere round in Stone Winton, I shall know exactly what to say." She gave Mike a weak smile. "Thanks for the explanation, anyway. Thank God he doesn't go to Chapmans any more."

"That, I think, is part of his problem," Mike replied. "He was at least happy there. Anyway, try not to worry about him too much. Perhaps this supervision order thing will work, who knows?"

"Well thanks anyway, Mike," Angela said. "I must get back now. See you some time, I expect."

"Yes, I expect so. Enjoy your new house, Angela."

"Yes," she replied with a note of determination in her voice, "I will. We all will."

As the morning progressed people began to drift away and by half past twelve only Shirley, Mary and the two girls were left.

"How much did we make?" Cirelle asked Shirley when she'd counted the money.

"Quite good," Shirley said enthusiastically. "A hundred and ten pounds and twenty-seven pence, and with the fiver Annie Hooper brought over this morning on her way to work, that's over a hundred and fifteen pounds!"

"Hey, that is good," exclaimed Mad. "What will it be used for?"

"Towards the roof repairs I expect," sighed Shirley. "I'd love it to be spent on things for our people to do, but I suppose the roof must come first!"

Cirelle went round the room collecting up dirty cups, and as she passed the window she saw a man nailing a slanting board across the for-sale sign outside Madge Peters's house.

"Hey, you guys, look," she called out to the others, "Madge's house seems to have been sold."

Mad joined her at the window and looked across at the workman hammering, before amazing them all by saying, "Yeah, it has. My dad's bought it."

There was a chorus of surprise from the others. "Your dad! Has he? Why? What for?"

Mad laughed. She'd been in the secret since the weekend, but had been sworn to secrecy until the "sold by" board went up, so only Dean knew.

"He's going to rent it out to students," she said cheerfully, and laughed again at the stunned look on their faces. "He's got three friends of Hattie's lined up to move in next week, just until the summer. After that, he'll do it up properly, like he did ours. He's bought it from Andrew Peters, complete with the contents. He says it suits them both very well."

"I sure it does," remarked Mary dryly. She, Shirley and Sheila had helped Andrew with the removal of Madge's clothes and other personal items, but she had wondered at the time what on earth he was going to do with all the furniture and other household effects. He had given them no hint, and she hadn't asked. Now she knew, and realised it was the obvious solution as far as Andrew was concerned.

"It was all very quick, wasn't it?" Mary said, feeling that at least he might have warned them.

"Not really," Mad said. "Dad guessed Andrew would want to sell the place, and approached him some time before Christmas. They exchanged contracts last week."

Shirley looked across at Mary. Another student house in the Circle; and she knew a moment of silent relief that she and David were moving to the quiet peace of Derringham. Mary gave no sign of her thoughts at the news. Then another thought crossed Shirley's mind, one that made her smile guiltily and decide it was something to discuss with David the moment he got in for lunch. She said nothing of her idea now.

It didn't take very long for them to get cleared up. Shirley thanked them both for all their help and then the two girls went as planned to meet Dean at the students' union.

"Join us for a sandwich?" Shirley invited Mary. "David'll be in for lunch a minute."

"No, I won't, thanks all the same," Mary said. "I've got a couple of things to do at home and then I'm on at St Joe's this afternoon."

Quite relieved that Mary had turned down the offer of lunch, Shirley set about preparing some food as she waited for David to come home.

When at last he arrived, she told him quickly about Madge Peters's house. "He's obviously buying it as an investment," she said excitedly. "Perhaps he'd like to buy ours too! What do you think?"

"I think it's most unlikely," said David, his tone pouring cold water on her brilliant idea.

"But you could ring him and ask him?" suggested Shirley, undeterred. "We've got his number, I've just found the card he gave us when we first met him. Surely it's worth a try, David. He might be interested."

"Anything for some peace and quiet," David finally agreed. "I'll give him a call after lunch, but how you'll be able to face Sheila and the rest if you sell this house to Nick Richmond for a student house, I can't imagine."

"I shan't have to face them," Shirley said cheerfully, "I shall be living in Derringham."

Mary had gone home and made herself a sandwich and a mug of soup, which she carried to her favourite chair by the window. She hadn't anything to do until it was time to go to St Joe's, but she was tired and wanted half an hour of peace in the blissful silence of her own home. She picked up the newspaper and her pen and turned to the crossword. A movement below in the Circle caught her eye and she saw Sheila, rushing across the grass, her face bursting with concern and indignation. She was coming to Mary. For a moment Mary was puzzled. Now what was the matter? What on earth could have upset her like this? Then she remembered, Gerald had been going to play golf with Andrew Peters... Andrew must have told Gerald his news. Sheila had just heard there was going to be another student house in the Circle.